DARK
HORIZON

DARK HORIZON

BOOK 1: HORIZON'S GENESIS

—— ERIC J. KUMIK ——

DARK HORIZON
BOOK 1: HORIZON'S GENESIS

iUniverse books may be ordered through booksellers or by contacting:

iUniverse
1663 Liberty Drive
Bloomington, IN 47403
www.iuniverse.com
1-800-Authors (1-800-288-4677)

ISBN: 978-1-4917-9960-4 (sc)
ISBN: 978-1-4917-9961-1 (e)

Library of Congress Control Number: 2016909569

Print information available on the last page.

iUniverse rev. date: 7/19/2016

THIS BOOK IS DEDICATED TO MY LOVING FAMILY, MY PARENTS, JACK AND SALLIE, MY BROTHER, Jeff (the real Torque) and my wonderful fiancé Debbie. Without your support and endless patience this story would've remained a distant dream.

I dedicate it also to my friends who have stood by my side and helped make this book a success.

Thank you all for helping to make my wildest dreams come true.

THE PICTURE FROM THE PROBE DID LITTLE JUSTICE TO THE BEAUTY UNFOLDING BEFORE Lieutenant Gage'ik. The island was far more impressive in real life and was bigger than she had expected. Although no lifeforms had been found apart from minor biologics, she could see how this planet could very well become a tourist destination in the future. The lush, tropical forest stretched out for a good distance to the south, four miles or more judging from her scanner. The forest floor was streaked with different colored flowers of every conceivable size which seemed to change their hues as their petals danced in the gentle beach blown wind.

Gage'ik looked around and made sure she was alone. Seeing that her crew were still a good distance off, she allowed herself to close her eyes and take a deep breath of the warm, salty air. A small smile crept onto her face as she heard the waves rolling in and settling on the beach to the east. It was calming in a way that she had just recently become accustomed to after her last mission. This was only the second time she had ever visited a planet with such an overwhelming sense of serenity and she wished she had been given more time to explore it.

It really had been blind luck that the planet had even been found in the first place. The deep space probe found this planet not more than three days ago and it laid very close to the restricted outer territory. The probe had sent back all of the basic information about the planet, temperature, air quality and whether or not it was capable of supporting life. As soon as IEC cleared the planet for exploration, Team Alpha had been chosen to go. The planet's discovery came as little surprise to Gage'ik, much of the outer territory was still unexplored but the beauty of this place caught her completely off guard. If she was not on such a time crunch, there was a very real chance she would have snuck off alone to admire the scenery. She sighed deeply and realized her momentary break was over and she needed to return to cataloging her findings. Gage'ik was not one to allow herself to become so distracted but there was a part of her that was having a hard time concentrating. She turned around and saw some of her crew having the same problem.

When the Team saw the initial information from the probe, they instinctively knew what was to be done; catalog anything unusual, check for planetary anomalies, ensure safety, take samples and so on down the list. Most other teams would find this work tedious but Science

Teams were different than most. Soldiers who joined the same division she had did so for usually one reason, it wasn't that they liked the tedious assignments and data collection, it was their desire to learn. They wanted to uncover the secrets of the universe, to understand the "why" in everything. It was that special craving which drove a Science Officer in the IEC but a place like this could make one forget there was a job to do.

"One more hour, then let's wrap it up!" Gage'ik's usually commanding voice was almost a purr in the quiet calm of the camp. They still had days' worth of research to compile but it could wait. Right now she needed to allow both herself and her crew some early downtime. Team Alpha was the best Science Team the IEC had, they deserved a little fun after knock off. This planet was a new discovery and what was the use of being part of a galactic exploration group if you never got to explore the places you discovered? Gage'ik smiled sheepishly for trying to justify her reason to knock off early and take a stroll on the pink sanded beach.

Gage'ik looked again at her watch and knew she needed to make her initial report as Master Admiral Tall'ani was not known for her patience. As she turned back toward the shuttle she saw one of her crew members making his way towards her. She recognized Braxa immediately. Having gone through IEC training on her home planet of Omaria she was still getting adjusted to working with humans. Humans, she shook her head, such strange creatures. The funny tufts of hair on their otherwise furless bodies gave them a rather mangy look and how they could function from day to day without tails for balance or claws to defend themselves, Gage'ik didn't understand. Then there were those tiny ears, still, she was a scientist and she had seen stranger things. As he came closer, Gage'ik noticed a confused look on his face.

"What's wrong?" she asked.

Braxa shook his head, "Lieutenant, there's something you need to see."

"I'm a little pressed for time, Braxa, can it wait?"

"I'd rather you came and see this for yourself," he answered.

Gage'ik saw the look on his face and nodded. She followed him back to the shuttle and down to the main research laboratory. Braxa slid a small door closed behind them and motioned for Gage'ik to sit down at the computer terminal on which he had been working.

He rolled another chair opposite her and leaned forward with his elbows on his knees, "I didn't want to say anything in front of the others but I think I've found something."

"Could you be a little more specific?" asked Gage'ik.

Braxa sat upright and pulled something off one of the trays which was on the counter next to him. He held it up to show Gage'ik what it was, "It's probably nothing but I thought I should show it to you first."

Gage'ik took the object from Braxa and examined it. It was a small, curved piece of metal. It was no more than twelve inches in length and three inches across. She cocked her head to one side and brought the shard of metal closer to her face. Across the top were markings of some kind which had been worn down as if exposed to the elements for a good number of years.

She examined the shard without looking at Braxa, "Where did you find this?"

"On the west side of the island, ma'am," he answered.

Gage'ik shot a look at him, "You should know better than that, Ensign, we were supposed to go to the west tomorrow."

"I know, ma'am, but everyone was getting crowded together around here and I-"

"And you went alone? Ensign, how long have you been an Officer?"

Braza shifted in his chair, "Two months, ma'am."

Gage'ik turned her attention back to the shard, "That's long enough to know that no one, myself included, goes into unchecked coordinates by themselves, ever. Especially on an unknown planet."

Braxa nodded his understanding, "Sorry, ma'am, it won't happen again."

"I know how tempting it is, Braxa, but I'm in charge down here and if you got hurt then we'd have to cut this short, right?"

Braxa nodded again.

Gage'ik gave him a comforting smile, "So what did you find out about this?"

"I scanned it but there's no information on the IEC database about any of the alloys that it's made from."

"And that's what got you all worked up?" she asked.

Braxa shook his head, "No," and he pointed her attention to the computer terminal behind her, "that was."

Gage'ik looked at the screen for a moment and then turned back, wide eyed, "You're kidding me?"

Braxa shook his head again, "No, ma'am. I carbon dated it and checked the results three times. I know, it seems impossible but that thing is over two and a half thousand years old."

Gage'ik whistled in disbelief. She studied the monitor and the shard for a moment before turning back to Braxa, "We know there's no life here aside from biologics but I wouldn't be surprised if someone out there has been here before. Maybe this is just something that fell off their ship."

"Twenty-five hundred years' ma'am. That predates Omarian space travel by a thousand years and Akoni by five hundred. And then there's this," Braxa got out of his chair and turned the shard of metal over so Gage'ik could see what he wanted her to. He pointed to a small black streak on the back of it and said, "carbon scoring."

"Carbon scoring?" asked Gage'ik, "You mean, as in blaster fire?"

Braxa nodded silently.

"What you're essentially saying is predated intergalactic war?" Gage'ik turned around to Braxa who merely threw up his hands up to say he was as clueless as she was at the moment.

"And those markings, nothing?" she asked.

Braxa drew in a deep breath and exhaled slowly, "I'm afraid that's the same answer ma'am. I ran those specs with everything in the database and drew a big, fat blank."

Gage'ik replied, "Right. I need to send what we have so far to Master Admiral Tall'ani. Go get Thomson and Mikela and go back to wherever you found this. Who knows, maybe you'll find something else."

Braxa nodded and left the shuttle. Gage'ik sat in silence for a moment and racked her brain for answers, anything definitive to put in her first report but nothing came to mind. Finally, she gave up and placed the call. Gage'ik was finishing her report transmission when the first tremor hit. It was as if a large tree had been felled close by. A small beaker which had been left by one of the microscopes, rattled as the liquid inside it sloshed around. She reached over and pushed the beaker back on the table so that it would not fall but as she was getting out of her chair, another tremor threw her to the ground. Outside she heard the muffled sound of shouting followed by something she could not place, a rapid hollow tapping sound that was at once both vague and familiar. As she got to the hall another tremor took the floor out from under her feet. The hair on the back of her neck began to bristle. Not trusting herself to stand Gage'ik crawled towards the shuttle entrance. The shouts were louder now, screams that echoed down the metal corridor. She knew now what that hollow tapping had been, gun shots. Fearing for her Team Gage'ik leapt to her feet and ran to the shuttle's ramp. Most of her crew were firing their side arms at something coming at them from the east. Those that were not firing were trying to help other Team members who looked to be badly hurt. Team Alpha was not a military unit and only had small, standard issue defensive weapons and whatever they were firing at was obviously not slowing down. Time froze for Gage'ik as she saw her officers, one after the other, being cast aside broken, limp and lifeless.

She ran down the ramp, drawing her sidearm free of its holster and tried to get a better look at what they were up against. The setting sun blurred her vision. Gage'ik tried to blink the sun away but it was no use. Something heavy slammed into her chest knocking the wind from her lungs as she landed flat on her back. Dazed and gasping for breath Gage'ik got to her knees. Her fur was wet and matted in the front by something warm and sticky. Something all too familiar coated her face. Wiping the blood from her eyes she stared down into the lifeless face of Braxa, his upper torso torn and twisted. A pool of dark blood and organs were all that remained below his exposed ribs. It was his face that haunted her the most, contorted in a look of terror and torture, rolling lifeless eyes over a mouth frozen wide in a silent scream.

Gage'ik recoiled and tried to scuttle away from the mangled remains but found herself blocked by the shuttle. All around her came the screams of her Team and the sounds of them being ripped to pieces. She pulled herself back up onto the shuttle's ramp and ran back inside praying that the metal structure might conceal her from whatever was outside.

She ran back to the computer terminal station. Her paws shook so badly that she was almost unable to get the computer back online to call for help. As the screen in front of her finally sprang to life, Gage'ik began the SOS message. As far out as this planet was, there was a twenty second delay before she would be able to get a response. Panicked and horrified she struggled to speak. As she sat gasping for words in front of the terminal, she felt the shuttle lift off the ground as if someone had triggered the engines. Gage'ik realized in terror that whatever was outside had picked the shuttle up off the ground. She screamed as the shuttle began to shake and rock back and forth. A loud cracking sound echoed all around her and daylight began to shine through the ceiling as small openings started to spider web their way across the hull. With a thunderous crash the shuttle was ripped to pieces and Gage'ik felt the floor beneath her break apart as she began to fall.

She closed her eyes as tightly as she could and braced for the fatal impact. Something massive snaked around her waist slowing her fall and tightened without mercy. Gage'ik pushed with all her might to get whatever was wrapped around her to let go. She could barely breathe but she felt her legs kicking for all they were worth. She flailed in vain to get away but there was no escape. She hung there, suspended in midair for a few moments before she felt the first rib crack. Gage'ik's breathing ceased as her lungs filled with fluid and her chest began to cave in. Her heartbeat thundered in her ears as the last of her adrenaline surged its way through her veins. The pain was overwhelming and she felt something in her chest burst apart. Her claws were bared and her ears were flattened back onto her head as Gage'ik beat down onto whatever was wrapped around her with all her might. With the last of her strength she buried her claws deep in her attacker's flesh. A sudden crunching noise filled her ears, drowning the feral screams of her compatriots as she vomited blood from her mouth. The hulking shadow of her killer was all Gage'ik saw before the darkness overtook her.

Master Admiral Tall'ani stormed into the Communications Center of her Omarian outpost. Tall, slender and sleek she was the picture of Omarian perfection and authority. Silently she crossed the room to where one of her crew was still seated, typing frantically at his terminal.

"What just happened?" Tall'ani growled from behind the young Communications Officer.

The young officer didn't turn around but continued working furiously, "Unknown, ma'am. One second they were there and the next, nothing."

"You had better come up with something more concrete, Lieutenant. One of my Teams does not just go missing."

The Communications Officer pressed down hard on his headset and punched command after command into the monitor but shook his head, "I'm sorry, ma'am, there's no response on any frequency. It's like they just disappeared."

A low growl built in Tall'ani's throat as she scanned the screen for information, her bright green eyes reflecting the monitors glow. She felt the Communications Officer flinch as one of her paws gripped the seat behind his head. Tall'ani's fur, jet black and shimmering with streaks of white, made her beautiful but the razor sharp claws that hid beneath made her equally deadly. None of her crewmen would dream of crossing her and that's the way she liked it.

Tall'ani scanned the screen but found nothing more. She stood back up and turned to the Duty Officer at the back of the room, "Do you have anything to add?"

The Duty Officer cleared his voice, "No ma'am."

"So we have nothing more to go on than this?" she waved her paw in disgust at the screen behind her.

"Yes, ma'am, I mean, not exactly. What we have is-"

"What you have, Commander," hissed Tall'ani, "is nothing. Team Alpha is the only Science Division I have out here and you've managed to lose them." Tall'ani turned back around to the Communications Officer and spun his chair around for him to face her. She bent down and stared into the Officer's face, her cold wet nose pressed close to his, "You, tell me again, exactly what happened."

"As near as I can figure out, ma'am, they were on the surface this morning and sent back some information about the planet. Lieutenant Gage'ik had sent some preliminary findings when we lost communications altogether. We've been trying to reestablish comms since we lost the feed but so far nothing. After five hours of radio silence, protocol dictates we-"

"I know what the grayed protocol is! Let me see the data stream," hissed Tall'ani.

The Communications Officer nodded and brought the video feed onto the monitor. The screen showed a young Omarian officer, a tawny mane framing her short muzzle and tufts of black fur tipping her ears. She was seated at their shuttles main research computer surrounded by various instruments. Gage'ik was showing photographs from the long range sensors, "Scans indicate the planet is predominately water. Apart from this small island there doesn't appear to be another landmass anywhere. As per instructions, we set down on the southeastern portion of the island and began sample collection and analysis. So far the readings sent back from the probe have proved accurate. Aside from plant life and a variety of microorganisms, this planet is uninhabited. We have a good deal of information so far from this portion of the island and will be exploring the western and northern parts tomorrow. Ensign Braxa made an unusual discovery this afternoon."

The data stream then showed some flashing images of a metal shard which Gage'ik now described, "As you can see, it is clearly a manufactured piece. Ensign Braxa ran a battery of tests and confirmed that this fragment is nearly three thousand years old, yet it looks almost new. Analysis of the metal revealed an alloy unlike anything I've ever seen. I'm no expert on metallurgy but I don't believe it's from this planet and there was nothing resembling it in the IEC database. The metal seems to have almost no weight at all but somehow has been able to survive both time and elements." A barrage of images flashed across the screen showing the information collected by Braxa. Towards the end of the data stream, Gage'ik came back on-screen and showed the markings untouched by time, "There are some markings on this side which also could not be found in the IEC database-"

Master Admiral Tall'ani saw the image on the screen and suddenly hissed at the Communications Officer, "Freeze it."

The Officer quickly paused the data stream. Tall'ani leaned in closer to the screen as her eyes traced the markings outline. The hairs on the back of her neck began to bristle as she scanned every inch on the monitor. Finally, she moved away from the screen unconsciously flattening the hairs down, "Continue."

The Communications Officer nodded and resumed the stream. A loud crash echoed somewhere off screen. They all watched as Gage'ik turned her head as if startled and then the screen went black.

Tall'ani had the Officer pull up the metal shard again. She studied the shard and the information Braxa had learned from it. The entire room had fallen silent around her as her eyes bounced back and forth making sure not to miss any possible clues.

Tall'ani leaned close to the monitor and spoke in a low tone to the Communications Officer, "And this was everything?"

He nodded, "Yes, ma'am. After this came in, I tried to hail Team Alpha but I didn't get any response from them or their scout shuttle's transponder."

Tall'ani nodded back, "Very well. Lieutenant, send everything we've just seen to my quarters. You are to continue your attempts to contact Team Alpha until I instruct you otherwise."

The Officer nodded his acknowledgement, "Understood, ma'am."

Tall'ani quickly spun around to the Duty Officer, "Commander, we have a very serious problem. As of right now, we are on alert level three."

The Duty Officer nodded his understanding as well, "Yes, ma'am. General quarters?"

"No." Tall'ani replied quickly and hushed her voice further, "Who do we have on standby?"

The Duty Officer shook his head, "No one, ma'am, all we have are medical vessels."

"No Hunter Class?"

"Negative. The Harbinger was sent to Akonis and the Sal-oc is out on patrol near Hydron."

Tall'ani hissed at the news. Both of her best Military Division ships were nowhere close enough to call back to Omarian space and that was a real problem.

Her ears slowly returned to an upright position and she gently placed her paw around the Duty Officer's shoulder and pulled him in close, "Until you receive direct orders from me, Commander, keep this under lock and key. Do everything in your power to reestablish communications with Team Alpha or their ship but do not, I repeat, do not signal anyone else until further notice." The Duty Officer acknowledged Tall'ani and turned to organize his crew with the business of finding Team Alpha.

Tall'ani left the communications center and quickly went to her personal quarters under orders of total privacy. She entered her quarters and locked the door behind her. She walked to her personal communications terminal and opened up a secure channel. Tall'ani typed the destination into her video screen and paced impatiently until her message was answered.

The voice on the other end sounded cheerful, "Oh, good morning, Tall'ani! I'm a little shocked to hear from you at this hour but what can I do for you?"

"Soren, we have a problem. I need backup as soon as you can get it to me."

"Problem?" asked Soren, "You're telling me there's something you can't handle?" he asked playfully.

"This isn't a joke, Soren, I need you to get your best Team out here and I need them NOW!" replied Tall'ani angrily.

Soren appeared in the view screen as his smile faded, "Okay Tall'ani, calm down. Do you wanna tell me what's going on?"

Tall'ani stopped pacing and moved close to her monitor, "One of my Science Teams is missing and-"

"And you need our help finding them?" interrupted Soren in shock.

Tall'ani lost her patience and slammed her paws onto the desk below causing the monitor to crackle. She hissed into the screen, her fangs bared, "Never interrupt me, old man! I have no time for you to spend guessing at my purpose!"

Soren's face took on a stern countenance, "My apologies, Tall'ani, please continue."

Tall'ani took a deep breath and collected her thoughts, "Apologies to you as well, Soren, my words were spoken in haste." Calmly she continued, "My Science Team has gone missing and must be located, this is true, however it's not the sole purpose of my call." She pulled up the file from the communications center and put the image on-screen, the markings clear as day, "I believe they found the Horizon."

Soren's eyes widened in disbelief. He was barely able to get the words out of his mouth, "Say again?"

"You heard me."

"Soren was close to speechless, "The Horizon? You're talking about the Horizon? Tall'ani, you know as well as I do that...how can you be sure about this?"

Tall'ani was on the verge of putting her massive paw through the screen, "You know these symbols as well as I do! It's the Horizon, it has to be!"

"Okay, I believe you, what do you need?"

Tall'ani released her grip on her desk and pulled her claws free from the wood, "Get your best Team out here and get them here quick. We can't afford to let someone else get their hands on this. Until we can reestablish communications with Team Alpha and prove it otherwise, consider this a very, very hostile situation."

Soren nodded his agreement and signed off without saying another word. Tall'ani switched off her monitor and stood upright again. Team Alpha was her responsibility and she didn't like having to ask for help but there was no time for personal pride. If it really was the Horizon, then the clock was already ticking.

OUTSIDERS

T HE SUN WAS JUST BEGINNING TO COME UP OVER THE MOUNTAINS SIGNALING THE BEGINNING OF a new day. The city in the valley between the mountains already appeared awake and alert though it rarely appeared otherwise. Early morning light reflected off the tallest buildings, casting deep shadows on the ground below. In a few hours the whole city would be bathed in shimmering light, a golden pond under the dawn.

The city of Odyssey was founded soon after the Gray War. Great monuments stood throughout the city to commemorate the fallen though little else of the war itself was known. The greatest monument, the pride of Odyssey and all the citizens of Earth, stood in the midst of the city. A spire rising far above the rest for all to see, the Interstellar Exploration Corps headquarters, a badge of honor handed to mankind by the High Council on the day of its inception.

Admiral John Kagen stopped to admire the buildings beautiful architecture. He had been there when the building was first erected but still it took his breath away. At last he had his fill and walked in through the wide arched entrance and over to the security. Though crime on Earth was now mostly confined to a few rough alleys, the safety and security of the IEC was still taken very seriously. Kagen was known throughout the base by name and face but still followed protocol, stopping at the booth and showing his identification to the guard. He smiled as he passed under a great arc that held the holographic image of a man which both welcomed visitors and directed them where to go. His smile faded, replaced by a twinge of sadness remembering his old friend, forever memorialized in the projected light.

The image came on automatically. A scientist wearing coke-bottle glasses, a bright yellow tie with a picture of a rocket ship and his clipboard forever in hand, "Good morning and welcome to the IEC communications center!" it started in a cheerful voice, "If this is your first time with us, there's a map located on the wall behind me. If you need any further help, I'm always available at the various holographic points highlighted on the map. We're glad you're here and hope you have a fantastic day!"

Kagen couldn't stare at the image for more than a moment before he dropped his head and walked right past it, "Good morning, Z. Good to see you, old buddy."

Kagen made his way into the building just as his wrist cuff sounded a small tone letting him know the others were already waiting. It was no surprise they had beaten him there. He wasn't a young man anymore. He had to use a cane on occasion to support a left leg which didn't work very well but he insisted on walking as much as possible. It was bad enough he had to sit behind a desk all day once he got there. When Kagen arrived at his commanding officer's ready room, he took a moment to look himself over in the mirror, his uniform was tight and strained the buttons around his midsection. Life behind a desk was taking its toll, more than he cared to admit. Kagen opened the door and saw the others seated in front of Master Admiral Soren's desk the way they always did for this kind of meeting.

The others nodded to him as he sat down, "Sorry to keep you all waiting."

Master Admiral Michael Soren, a human with a head of thick white hair which merged with his neatly trimmed beard raised an eyebrow and stared at Kagen with piercing green eyes, "Have a seat, Admiral," said Soren sternly, letting everyone know again that he was not the type that needed or wanted small talk. "I trust since you're all here that you each received my message," Soren began, "so let's get to it." Soren began to play the feed sent over from Tall'ani. "This is Science Team Alpha, with whom we've lost all communication just after this was sent. That was nearly twelve hours ago. Master Admiral Tall'ani has requested our assistance in retrieving her missing Team."

"Missing, sir?" Admiral Jaleer looked up from her briefing, her mesmerizing purple eyes gave strange life to her stone complexion, "How does one go missing on such a small island?"

"They may not be missing at all. The fact is that without the communication uplink we don't know what's going on down there."

"Blind, bloody fools!" growled Admiral David Kosos, a human with a short temper and even shorter mindset. "Did none of you see what was all over that girl's face? That was fear, plain and simple." Kosos froze the feed as Gage'ik turned toward the source of the noise, "Sir, you and I both know this was no simple loss of communication. Alpha's in trouble."

Soren leaned back in his chair, "For once, you and I might be in agreement, and for that reason we'll be treating this as a hostile engagement." He moved the transmission back to the technical data, "Do any of you know anything more about this planet?"

Kagen and the others shook their heads.

At the far end of the table Master Admiral Lokias sat staring at the screen before him, his black and white striped tail flicking back and forth in thought. Kagen broke the silence, "That shard she mentioned, the one Master Admiral Lokias is studying, could that have anything to do with the loss of communications?"

Soren shot a glaring look at Lokias who was too enthralled to notice. Kagen saw the dreaded look in Soren's eye from not having everyone's complete attention.

"That," Soren replied slowly, "is the other thing we need to discuss. This shard may very well represent an object of antiquity that is of special interest to the IEC. Whomever we send will be charged with not only the location and rescue of our wayward Science Team but also the recovery of this shard and any other remnants that may exist."

Kagen's throat went dry a Soren's words though he wasn't sure why, still he managed to speak, "But, sir, what is it?"

Soren's brow furrowed, "Some questions are better left unanswered. All you need to know is that the recovery of this item, or items as the case may be, must be accomplished at all costs. The retrieval of anything more to do with that shard must also stand now at priority one."

No one said anything for a moment while they let Soren's statement sink in. Kagen could feel the tension growing but he didn't dare press the issue further. He shifted in his chair and looked over to the picture which Lokias was still eyeing but the shard of metal held no answers for him. Kagen cleared his throat, "Sir, could the Hais be responsible for this? I know things have been quiet for a while now but that planet's extremely close to the border."

"It's a thought," replied Soren, "but the Dominion knows that planet's on our side of the fence. Still, all the more reason to proceed with caution."

"Not gonna be easy, sir," said Kosos, "that planet is way outside of bridging distance and if we've got no more information to go on than what we're staring at, I have no clue how much hardware to send out. If our people get into trouble out there, it'll be a week before we can get them reinforcements." He clasped his hands together in thought, "Take three, maybe four days before I can get a couple of Teams prepped."

Kagen watched as Soren's eyes met Kosos', "One day, Admiral. I want them airborne by dawn."

Kagen could see the wheels in Kosos' mind turning at a feverish pace, "Sir, that's not possible! We're running training missions as we speak and I couldn't even get some Teams back here before tomorrow."

"That's not all, Admiral. One Team goes. As Admiral Kagen pointed out, this planet is too close to the Hais Dominion and there are too many unknowns to risk another galactic incident. One ship we can explain away, any more than that and we may not get the chance to say anything at all."

Kosos was incensed, "One team? One team?! Sir, we don't know what they might be flying into, for all we know it could very well be the bloody Hais or something even worse! You can't send a single Team into a situation like that! Sir, it's suicide and unconscionable and I want no part of it. Besides, I told you, all our long range ships are running training exercises, won't be back till tomorrow at the earliest."

Soren turned to Kagen, "Admiral Kagen, you're in charge of our reserves, do we have any that are currently fit for duty?"

Kagen jumped at the mention of his name and began scrolling through his reserve lists. "Oh! Uh...none that I can see, sir. None that can be ready in that time frame. If I may, sir, Admiral Kosos may have been mistaken when he said all of our long range ships were out."

Kosos reeled on Kagen, "Are you saying I don't know my own fleet? All the ships are out. I gave the order myself."

Kagen took a breath to steady himself, he knew the storm that was coming. Master Admiral Lokias turned and gave him a knowing nod of encouragement. "The Widow Maker, sir," Kagen continued, "she's docked in high orbit and already outfitted with our latest tech. She could be ready to go by tonight if need be."

"Oh, no. No, no, no!" Kosos cut in, "You're not taking that band of idiots anywhere."

Jaleer turned to Kosos, "With all due respect, Admiral Kosos, Star Team Seven does have training for this type of operation. Seeing as how there is no one else available, I don't have to remind you that time is of the essence."

Kosos slammed his tablet down on Soren's desk so hard the screen cracked. He lurched forward in his chair and pointed directly at Kagen, "OH NO! NO WAY! There's no way on God's green Earth I'm gonna let that gray bunch of pirates out of my sight any time soon!"

Soren turned to Kosos, "I know you've had your differences with Captain Dorran but-"

"BUT NOTHING! I don't care if he was riding the last horse we have into the pit of Hades itself! Which he very well may be with the way this mission is shaping up! He, along with that stone pack of jackals he calls a crew, are grounded and that's that!"

Kagen spoke up, "Jaleer's right, Team Seven is the only Team available and they're more than capable of handling this. Captain Dorran may not be your first choice but he's the best we've got. We're all sorry for your loss but it wasn't Vincent's fault."

Kosos stuck a fat finger in Kagen's face, "Don't you DARE defend him to me! You and the stone-faced Akoni over there thinking he's up to the task doesn't change anything. The fact is that they're bound to this rock and that's where they'll stay!"

"ENOUGH!" Soren jumped to his feet backing Kosos down, "It's been long enough, Kosos, and you know damned well he didn't have any choice. That was then and this is now."

Kosos turned red with anger, "Am I or am I not in charge of flight operations, sir?"

"You are."

"Then Dorran stays put."

"In that case," said Soren directly, "from now on, Team Seven is no longer your concern." He turned and pointed to Kagen, "They're yours."

Kosos pressed his palms against the table. A large vein pulsed in his temple with the effort to control himself, "Is that an order, sir?" His words were barely heard over the sound of his grinding teeth.

"It is."

Kosos backed away from the table, "Then my presence here is no longer necessary." He turned to leave.

"Admiral Kosos, this meeting is not dismissed," said Soren.

Kosos paused as he reached the door and looked over his shoulder, "Bah, the Grays take the whole ASHEN lot of ya." The door slammed behind him leaving Kagen and the rest in silence once again.

Soren sat back down and shook his head, "God help me, I hope I never have to know what it feels like to be that man." He turned to Jaleer, "My apologies, Admiral Jaleer, for Admiral Kosos' behavior. As you're no doubt aware he's going through a difficult time right now."

Jaleer smiled at Soren, "Sir, I'm Earth born and as such am no stranger to the volatility of human emotion. The admiral's actions are unfortunate but so, I understand, are his present circumstances." With an arm of granite, she gestured toward the screens, "Please, may we continue?"

Kagen couldn't help but marvel at the Akoni, so large and imposing yet such gentle and understanding creatures. Jaleer may have been Earth born but she was Akoni through and through. Kagen was old enough to remember the world's first encounter with alien species. The Akoni came first, their broad intimidating shoulders with two sets of thick arms like four branches stemming from a mighty oak. Rock-like skin that despite its appearance was incredibly soft to the touch. Then came the Omarians, ferocious feline warriors without whom the Earth may very well have been lost during the struggle that became known as the Gray War. Some of the newcomers were less startling, though the Sageves had been unsettling for many, himself included. The Sageve people were masters of technology, humanoid but hairless with jet black, soulless eyes which never blinked. It was the last part that Kagen never got used to, like living dolls from a childhood nightmare. Kagen gave an involuntary shiver. So much had changed in his lifetime, the Earth he knew as a boy was difficult to imagine now.

"Admiral Kagen!" Soren's commanding voice startled Kagen from his daydreams.

"Uh...Yes, sir, sorry sir."

"As I was saying, Jaleer will be responsible for ensuring the Widow Maker is ready to go. She'll be catching a shuttle to the space station this afternoon and personally overseeing the preparations. I need you to make sure Team Seven is on that ship by morning. I know you and Nick go way back but Captain Dorran is nothing like his father. He's hardheaded, reckless and a general pain in the ass. The rest of the Team is no better, an unruly gang of miscreants but they'd follow Dorran to the devil's doorstep. Learn to control Dorran and the rest'll follow. I'll bring their personnel files to your office as soon as I can. Think you can handle it, Admiral?"

Kagen swallowed hard, "Aye, sir."

Soren turned his attention to Lokias, "Which just leaves you, old man. Since Omaria is the planet nearest our objective, if there's anything more that Kagen needs to know before his Team arrives it'll be your job to find it. Kagen wasn't wrong, this mission is incredibly dangerous and were it not for the critical nature of the assignment I would never push this kind of time frame. Find out everything you can about that sector. I want to shine as much light as we can on what they're flying into."

Lokias slowly nodded, a small pair of spectacles balanced on his massive snout. The once black markings that striped his snow white fur had begun to fade to a dingy gray in his old age but his mind was as sharp as the daggers nestled safely within his enormous paws, "I'll research the archives immediately, see what I can find."

"Well, it seems we have our work cut out for us. Are there any questions?"

"Sir," Kagen suddenly had a sinking revelation, "the Widow Maker is in dock, I know that much is true, but the Team? They've been grounded for a long time, certainly some of them have gone home by now, to their own planets, I mean. What if I can't get them together in time?"

"The one they call Blitz is an off-worlder but I have a feeling he hasn't strayed too far. His home world is near Sageve and the wounds there are still too fresh, I'm afraid. The Omarian, well, he's not very welcome back home and the other four are Earth born human. Besides, to go off-world they would have needed permission from Kosos and I don't see him doing them any favors. No, Admiral, they're here somewhere. Find them, Kagen, and do it quickly."

"Aye, sir."

"Dismissed."

Jaleer and Lokias stood and walked away but Kagen lingered.

"Something else on your mind, Admiral?" Soren asked.

"Well, sir, it's about that shard of metal. How will Team Seven know what they're after if I can't tell them what it is or what it looks like?"

"Believe me, John, if they find it they'll know."

By the time Kagen returned to his office the sun was already near midday. The meeting with Soren had gone much longer than he realized. He tossed his cane onto a small couch in the corner of the room and sat down at his desk. His head was still spinning from what had just happened. It wasn't uncommon for IEC teams to change commanding officers from time to time but not like that. Kosos was in the wrong without a doubt, but undermining his authority in front of his peers like that? Kagen shook his head, what was he supposed to do with a Star Team anyway? He was responsible for the reserves, making sure all their training was up to date before they rotated for active duty. He didn't direct active teams, maybe a Science Division from time to time but not Military Divisions. He hadn't been responsible for an actual military operation since the end of the Gray War. That was a somber thought in and of itself, such a long time ago, back when he was in his prime and useful. He slapped his hand down on his knee and managed a small smile, that had also been back when his body worked as a body should.

"They can fix that you know."

Kagen started at the sound of Soren's voice, "I didn't hear you come in."

Soren crossed the room and took the chair across from Kagen, "Bionics have come a long way since you and I were young. They could have that leg brand new again."

Kagen looked at Soren then down at his knee, "I'll keep it thanks, I've lost enough of my humanity for one lifetime."

"I suppose we all have at that," replied Soren. He reached in his pocket and removed a small golden disk, handing it to Kagen, "Here's the personnel files for Team Seven. Pay special attention to the neurovids, particularly Dorrans. The rest you can learn as you go."

"Sir, permission to speak freely?"

"Sir?" Soren interrupted, "John, I've known you for more years than I care to remember. There's no one here to impress so I think you can drop the formalities. After all, it doesn't seem that long ago I was answering to you."

Kagen paused before continuing, "I was just wondering, if Dorran and his crew are such wildcards why does the IEC allow them to continue serving? Why haven't they been disbanded, absorbed into other Teams that were more in line with the IEC standard or just discharge them completely? Why accept such a liability?"

Soren sighed and crossed his legs as he settled deep into the armchair, "Well now, that is the question. I suppose it's partly out of loyalty to Nick, mostly though it's out of guilt. What happened to Vincent was our fault, he was under the IEC's care and we let him down."

"Mike, what happened to him? What really happened to Vincent?"

"It's all in the file, John. Do yourself a favor and forget any rumors you may have heard. That boy went to hell and stared the devil in the eye."

"What about the rest of them?"

"What, you mean besides the fact that no other crew would have them?" Soren leaned close to Kagen, "I suppose that's because sometimes, John, when the chips are down, a wildcard is all you really need." Soren stood up smoothing out his uniform and headed for the door, "By the way, have you contacted them yet?"

"Not yet, I was just about to."

"Get to it. They're going to need all the time they can get and we don't have much to grace them with."

"Yes, sir."

Soren smiled, "Take care, John, and good luck." With that he turned and walked out the door.

"Yeah, you too, Mike," Kagen replied though the room was empty once again.

He turned to his vidphone. No use procrastinating. Soren was right, Team Seven needed all the time he could give them. He punched Dorran's identifier into the module and waited for a response but none came. After a few minutes Kagen ended the transmission. Not wearing your wrist cuff was a serious infraction but he doubted that mattered much to Captain Dorran. This was going to take a special approach. He punched in the identifier for one of his junior medical officers and was pleased when she answered promptly as he knew she would, "Commander Tivex, good afternoon."

Tivex jumped to attention, her flowing purple hair draped softly over her broad, craggy shoulders, "Sir, good afternoon, Admiral Kagen, sir." Two of her hands shot straight out in a traditional Akoni salute.

"At ease, Commander."

Tivex lowered her hands though her body remained as rigid as before. Kagen laughed to himself, this woman was uptight even by Akoni standards. She was perfect. "Commander, I was wondering if you might help me. I believe you're acquainted with Captain Vincent Dorran, isn't that right?"

"Affirmative, sir. Well, that is, when we were young. I have not had much contact with Vincent since his return."

"What about his brother? Are you still in contact with him?"

"Yes, sir. Torque... sorry, sir... Jeffrey, and I do still talk from time to time."

Kagen rubbed his chin, "New orders, Commander, you're being reassigned to Team Seven effective immediately as acting first officer."

"B-But, sir," Tivex stammered.

"I'm sending you the transfer orders now."

Tivex tried to regain her composure but it was no use, "Sir, may I ask why I am being reassigned? And to a Star Team no less? I am a medic, not a mercenary." Her bright golden eyes darted back and forth as her mind struggled to understand his reasoning.

"Be that as it may, Team Seven has been chosen for a special assignment, one that requires both skill and finesse. They possess the skill, their reputation speaks to that but, as I'm sure you know, they lack the subtlety that is often necessary in these situations. I'll be overseeing this operation and I need someone I can trust to tag along and help me keep Dorran in line. Are you up to it, Commander?"

"Sir, I understand your need to reel in Vincent but I do not think I am the right choice. We have barely spoken in the years since his return. I doubt seriously he will listen to me anymore than he listens to Admiral Kosos. I also must remind you that I have not had any further flight experience since the Sageve incident. To transfer me to first officer of a Star Team may not be the best course of action."

Kagen smiled at her, "I realize that, Commander, however your job is going to be mostly communications. And, it just so happens that Team Seven is without any medical personnel which makes you and your rank eligible for the post."

Kagen watched as Tivex's eyes widened as she tried to swallow, "Admiral, again, I must-"

"Commander," Kagen interrupted hotly, "did you or did you not have simulator training during basic?"

Tivex nodded.

Kagen asked, "And have you not at some point served in any other capacity other than medic which would have given you initial operating experience space time?"

She nodded again.

"Then you have as much experience as any others do. I'm not assigning this duty to you because I think Vincent will listen, I'm giving it to you because I need eyes and ears on that ship. If Dorran loses it out there I need to know so I can pull the plug on this operation before we have another intergalactic incident."

"But, sir, why me? There are a number of better candidates than I who could do that for you."

Kagen sighed, "Dorran isn't a very trusting individual. If I assign some random officer to his crew, he'll fight me on it the whole way and that's the last thing I need. I'm hoping your previous relationship will help soothe the fact that I'm placing a watchdog on his ship. Besides, I heard his first officer stepped down after the Dayna Kosos incident so there's a vacancy to be filled. You'll be the new first officer of the Hunter class ship SL19, codename Widow Maker. It'll be your duty to ensure that Dorran and his crew perform their duties within the confines of the IEC regulations. Any deviation from those regulations is to be reported to me immediately, is that clear?"

Tivex's eyes dropped to the floor, "Admiral Kagen, sir, I just do not think I am the right choice for this."

"I'm sorry, Commander, but I'm afraid we don't have another option. If it helps, you'll be looking out for the safety of Dorran and his crew as much as protecting the interests of the IEC. Your first action as first officer will be to round up your crew, I've already tried to contact Captain Dorran but his communicator seems to be down. Hopefully one of his crew knows how to find him. You have less than fifteen hours, Commander, I need your Team on the docks by oh five hundred tomorrow. You'll receive your briefing there. Am I understood?"

Tivex lifted her head, a new resolve in her golden eyes, "Aye, sir."

"Very good, Commander, I know you won't let me down."

Another quick salute and he ended the transmission.

Kagen reached for the small golden disk Soren had given him. He placed it into his vid module and brought up the personnel files. Bright red letters flashed across the screen, CLASSIFIED. Vincent's file was first on the list, he opened it and began reading. Halfway through, he stopped. Kagen was in utter shock, the pain, the loss, the horror of it all was too much for him to believe. He reached up with shaking hands and wiped a tear from his eye. That poor boy, Kagen thought, how could he ever have survived such a thing?

FAMILY REUNION

TIVEX TOOK A MOMENT TO COLLECT HER THOUGHTS AFTER KAGEN ENDED THE TRANSMISSION. Something was going on out in one of the IEC territories and it was bad enough to warrant Master Admiral Soren to release Team Seven from suspension. She closed her bright, golden eyes and drew in a deep breath. It was no surprise Hammer wasn't answering his wrist cuff communicator but it didn't lessen her concern over what he might be doing.

Torque was the logical place to start. Her friend since early childhood, the younger of the two Dorrans should be able to supply her with the information she needed. At the very least he was probably the only one that would be happy about their newest edition. A small smile crept across her face as she entered his identifier into her comm.

Torque's face dropped from the top of her screen, his shabby hair hanging off of his head like wild jungle vines. His beatific grin shining brightly amidst his grease smeared cheeks, "Hello, you gorgeous Akoni Commander, you!"

"Lieutenant! I expect in the future that I will be greeted in a way befitting a superior officer."

"Oh, so it's official business is it?" Torque groaned as he lowered himself off the scaffolding he dangled from and righted himself in her comm screen. Torque's hand came up in a quick salute, "Good morning, Commander Tivex, to what do I owe the distinguished honor of your presence?"

Tivex rolled her eyes, she could never tell if Torque's impropriety was good hearted levity or actual disdain for rules and procedures. A little of both she imagined, "Lieutenant, I take it from your appearance that you are still aboard the E1 station, is that correct?"

"Yes, ma'am. Testing out some new equipment in the antigrav today and making some real progress with it I might add."

"I will need you to discontinue what you are doing and prepare the Widow Maker for immediate departure."

Torque grinned widely into the screen, "Way ahead of you, sister, er, I mean, ma'am. I began diagnostic checks this morning and she'll be fueled and fired up by the time she gets here."

Tivex's face wrinkled in confusion, "By the time who gets there?"

"Admiral Jaleer of course, isn't that why you're calling? Her name was on a shuttle manifest to arrive this afternoon. It's not an inspection, I'm the only one up here and they wouldn't send an Admiral for any other reason unless it was one of those real urgent kinda days. So, I got to thinking, why not be prepared? I don't know why everything is always so cloak and dagger with them, it doesn't take a rocket scientist to figure out what they're doing." Torque started to laugh, "Well, actually I guess it does. Come to think of it, why are YOU calling? Is Kosos still not speaking to us?"

"Lieutenant, that is an Admiral you are speaking of and he will be shown the respect he is due. That being said, Admiral Kosos is no longer your CO. Team Seven has been transferred to Admiral Kagen and as your new commanding officer and he has appointed me your second in command." Torque's eyes lit up as she continued, "Team Seven is being recalled to active duty effective immediately. We will brief you further when we arrive tomorrow morning, until then finish prepping the ship. I may also suggest, for the love of the light, get yourself cleaned up. You look like slag." Tivex shot her friend a wink.

Torque's grin split his face from greasy ear to greasy ear, "Yes, ma'am."

"Oh, one last thing, Torque, do you know where I might find the others?"

The smile slid from his face, "Hammer and Dregs? Your guess is as good as mine. Blitz might know where to find them but good luck. He's been in a funk ever since, well, you know when and hasn't said much for a while now. Can't say I blame him, I'd be pretty messed up too."

"Do you know where he is?"

"Where he always is I suppose. After all, he barely leaves that place. A little action might be just what old bolts for brains needs," Torque added, his voice brightening a bit, "as for the twins, they're out testing a little something I dreamed up. Gotta love those two, they'd strap themselves to dynamite if you told 'em it could fly." His eyes darkened again, "Ah, slag, well, you know what I mean."

Tivex lowered her head in reverence, "Thank you, Lieutenant. Get back to work and we will see you in the morning."

"Right, yeah, see you tomorrow, Commander," Torque ended the transmission.

Tivex sighed. Team Seven wasn't ready to go back up, the wounds were still too fresh and none of them were far enough from them.

She left her quarters and started down the main corridor. If Torque was right then Blitz was only a few miles away and this was a message better delivered in person. As she exited the building the warm rays from the sun reflected off the texture of her skin, giving her body a subtle but beautiful shimmer as she walked. A cool breeze blew in off the mountains to balance out the midday heat. It was a beautiful day for going anywhere but where she was headed.

She cut through the park to save some time, its giant statutes a tribute to a battle that claimed the lives of so many. She walked amidst their shadows wondering, not for the first time, why so little about the Gray War was known. Both her own father and Vincent's fought to preserve all life on Earth during that awful time but since neither would elaborate, she eventually just stopped asking. It was a very, very dark chapter in Earth's history, one with more questions than answers. Tivex shook her head, now was not the time for childish curiosities. She passed the great fountain in the center of the park, still some time to her destination. There was a beautiful serenity in the park today, the gentle spray of the fountain and the wind through the trees being the only sounds. She hated to break the silence but there was still work to be done. She cast a look about to make sure she was alone and with a heavy sigh, opened a comm link to the twins.

Tivex knew the twins mostly by their reputations. She knew them enough to know they weren't actually twins, they weren't even brothers, but you never saw one without the other. Team Seven's pilot, Lieutenant Scott Wilcox, was well known throughout the IEC. His impressive reflexes and unmatched ability allowed him to slip smoothly out of many tight spots, earning him the nickname Silk. Silk was one half of the Team behind the Widow Maker's deadly reputation, the other was Kevin "Dusty" Sweardon. Dusty was called such because it was said that when the Team's weapons specialist was on the guns, dust was all he left behind. Between them the only thing to outpace the Widow Maker's fame was their legendary egos.

The comm link failed to connect to Silk, Tivex cursed under her breath as she ended the transmission. Pilots never kept their personnel comm's up during a flight, they had enough to concentrate on already. Impatiently she entered the number for Dusty, frustrated that she hadn't tried him first.

Soon a cheerful voice with a thick southern drawl came over the comm followed by the image of tall, bone thin man. His dazzling blue eyes glittered beneath the shadow of his wide brimmed hat, "Well, good afternoon there, ma'am! What can I do ya for?"

"Good afternoon, Lieutenant, I am Medical Field Commander Tivex. May I assume Lieutenant Wilcox is there with you as well?"

"Who is it?!" Silk yelled from somewhere off-screen.

"It's the ratchet man's pretty lil' Akoni friend!"

Tivex's face burned like hot coals. Didn't anyone in this outfit have respect for authority?

Dusty must have seen the anger on her face and he scrambled to recover, "Uh sorry, ma'am, uh, that's a big ten four! We just out cruisin' in this new hot rod Torque threw together. Gotta say, she's a lot faster than she looks," his cheeks grew redder by the word.

"You are both to return to the shuttle docks immediately."

Tivex heard Silk swear in the background as Dusty shifted violently on the screen. He pushed his Stetson hat further back on his head, "Ma'am, y'all know we're not in IEC hardware, right? We ain't breakin' no rules."

"I am not concerned with your current exploits, Lieutenant. Just get back to the space docks for your mission briefing."

"Our what?" yelled Silk "Ma'am, we're not supposed to be runnin' no maneuvers, remember? Admiral Kosos' orders. Anyway, we're too far out of range to be back much before tonight, ma'am. Hope whatever it isn't too urgent."

"Admiral Kosos is no longer in charge of Star Team Seven's affairs. You, or should I say, we, are now under the command of Admiral Kagen. To answer your question, Lieutenant, Team Seven has been recalled to active duty."

Dusty lurched forward in his seat and shot a look over at Silk. Tivex watched as Dusty raised his arm up towards Silk who slapped it hard back down. Dusty smiled sheepishly into the camera, "Well then, ma'am, uh, from the looks of things up here, I'd reckon we should be able ta git back to the docks in a few hours after all!"

Tivex nodded, "Just get back to the docks. And gentlemen, fly safe."

Dusty's grin widened and he pulled his hat brim down over his deep set eyes, "Aye, aye ma'am." He turned to look at Silk, "You heard the lady, drive it like y'all done stole it, son!" Dusty lurched to the side as Silk throttled the engines to full power and the transmission ended.

Three down, Tivex thought as she rounded the last corner to her destination. A large gate emerged from the trees ahead of her. She crossed the patch of wild flowers and gathered a small bouquet before walking through the iron archway. The ground here was littered with stone carvings, much smaller than those in the park but their meaning was the same. A small hill rose to the right, a dark obelisk protruding from the mound. A bright blinding light reflected off the hulking form beside it. As she reached the hill, Blitz turned to face her, his blue mechanical eye glowing brightly. Tivex placed her bouquet on the small plaque in front of the large marble carving. Her fingers brushed the engraving, a simple sentiment to last throughout time.

A PILLAR OF SHADOW FOR THE LIGHT WE HAVE LOST
IN LOVING MEMORY OF BOTH DAUGHTER AND FRIEND
DAYNA KOSOS

As she stood, she placed her hands on Blitz's shoulders. Even through the thick cotton of his loose fitting shirt, Tivex could feel plates of cold steel.

Tivex's eyes became misty at her memory of Dayna. The only daughter of Admiral David Kosos, she shared none of her father's boorish traits. It was Dayna who brought Vincent around after his return. She reached him when no one else could and how Tivex always envied her for that. Dayna taught him how to trust again, how to laugh, how to love.

Her ship, the Valiant, came under attack by the Hais. Vincent raced to save her but it was too late. They found her body bound and broken, next to a pile of high explosives and a detonator strapped to her chest. Blitz ordered the retreat but Vincent wouldn't leave her side. As Dayna drew her last shallow breath Blitz hauled Vincent up onto his broad shoulders and ran for the

Widow Maker. The explosion that followed tore the docking bridge to pieces. Blitz and Vincent were ejected into the vacuum of space and if not for Silk's deft maneuvering that would have been the end. Vincent was treated for injuries, most of them minor. The same could not be said for Blitz.

Tivex had been there when the Team arrived on Sageve. She remembered very well the state Blitz was in as they wheeled him into surgery. Ribbons of flesh hung where his legs and right arm had been. His back was flayed open from shoulder to shoulder exposing the once white bones of his spine. All over he was a mixture of raw flesh and char. The blackened hole that was once his right eye and cheek ended in a jaw that hung limp from the side of his mangled face. Even after being torn to shreds, somehow he remained alive. The Sageve surgeons and engineers worked in shifts for the next few weeks to save him. When they were done, his humanity had been almost as mechanized as the rest of him.

Less than a month later Vincent hunted the Hais ship deep into restricted space and sent a message to the Dominion which launched a two-year military conflict. Admiral Kosos blamed Vincent for his daughter's death. Blitz blamed himself. Time, it seemed, had severely wounded all heals.

"What brings you down here?" Blitz said finally, breaking Tivex from her thoughts.

"I am sorry, Commander, I do not wish to interrupt your time here, but Team Seven has been recalled. You are needed for a mission brief with Admiral Kagen tonight."

Blitz huffed, "Kagen, huh? Kosos finally found someone he could dump us on? It doesn't matter. And I'm not an officer anymore, Tivex."

"Yes, I am aware you have relinquished your position. You are, however, still the Team's operation specialist and as such your presence is required at the docks."

Blitz rose to meet her gaze. Tivex was small for an Akoni but she cut a handsome figure at a full six feet tall. Even still, she was eclipsed by the man before her, a mountain of straining muscle and machine. The aperture of his eye narrowed to a slit against the brightness of the sun. He looked her over for a moment, "So where do you come in to all this?" His gruff voice lost the sadness it held moments ago, replaced now with anger and distrust.

"I thought you would have guessed by now. I have been ordered to replace you as first officer."

"Fantastic," Blitz groaned as he turned toward the docks, "does Hammer know about this yet?"

"No, actually I have been having trouble locating the Captain. Would you happen to know where I might find him?"

Blitz rolled his head back to look up at the sky. He pulled a cigar out of his pocket and popped it unceremoniously into his mouth. The sunlight glared off of his metallic arm as he opened his hand. A small flicker of fire appeared in his palm and he puffed until the cigar was lit. Blitz closed his fist and let the smoke drool slowly out of the corner of his mouth, "You won't find him this early. He's probably still curled up in The Hole somewhere sleeping off last night's, um, indiscretions. He's been frequenting Fat Sam's down on the south side. That area's full of Helix dealers, junkies and thugs so don't let your guard down. Matter of fact, maybe I should go with you. You know, just in case."

"I believe I can look after myself, thank you," as she spoke her lower arms reached behind her back and unsheathed two long, deadly looking daggers, "I may be a medic but I am still an Akoni."

Blitz managed half a smile, "Maybe I should go to protect them from you."

Tivex replaced the daggers, feeling a bit sheepish that she was allowed to be goaded into such a display, "Admiral Kagen wants the briefing no later than twenty one hundred tonight. It will take at least that long for the twins to return. As you were, Commander."

Blitz took the cigar out of his mouth and nodded his thanks to Tivex. She turned to leave him in peace and followed the path back out to the main street. An uneasy feeling began to fill her as she thought about what Blitz had said. Fat Sam's was a bar nestled deep in one of the darker parts of Odyssey, a place locals called The Hole. The Hole was a labyrinth of alleyways as dark and dangerous as the people it harbored. That Vincent was somewhere inside this place was worrisome but what concerned her the most was the level of suffering that would lead a man there to begin with.

Sunset found Tivex wandering the filthy streets and darkening alleys of Odyssey's south side. Stinking piles of refuse gathered in every corner and a smell of rot and urine permeated the air. Large rats with long thick tails and bright beady eyes scurried nearby, undisturbed by her presence and growing all the bolder with the slowly failing light. Tivex hated rats but she knew the true vermin were yet to come.

Night fell almost without warning. The red glow of sunset blinked into darkness in the deep alleys. Slowly, the denizens of The Hole began to appear from the shadows. Two human women stepped into the golden glow of a street lamp. Fishnet stockings and low cropped tops displayed all they had to sell. A thin silver chain ran from the ankle of each, vanishing back into the blackness of a doorway behind them, puppets dancing on their master's strings. As Tivex approached they began to call out to her, soliciting services which would make an Omarian blush. Tivex unconsciously fingered the handle of her dagger. When it was clear she would not be enticed the women took to shouts of vile obscenities. Finally, a sharp tug on their silver leashes brought their insults to an end. As if she were never there, the women went back to work enticing another potential patron.

Tivex walked on, a sadness in her heart and a sickness in her gut for the way such people lived. Turn by turn she wound deeper into The Hole. With every alley the same as the last, it truly was a maze and Fat Sam's was at the center of it all. A man in a long trench coat stood against a nearby wall, vials of green elixir dangling from his dirty fingers. Helix, a venomous concoction of chemicals, it was the life blood of The Hole's economy. Originally a Sageve serum for DNA therapy, the street version maintained all of the hallucinogenic side effects with none of the drug's former benefits. Cheap production cost and a potent product made for an explosive market which never left the south side. Helix dealers and their soulless consumers seemed content with the dark, dank setting of The Hole for their insidious transactions.

A right turn took her down a long corridor, ink black with no end in sight. The night seemed to close in around her as she walked, the darkness consuming the path ahead as well as behind. She was beginning to regret not bringing Blitz along. Slowly she walked, one cautious step at a time. The light from the waning moon did little to aid her progress. A rustling in the darkness ahead made her skin begin to crawl. As if by magic two daggers appeared in her hands, their wicked blades poised at the ready.

"Well now, what do we have here?" A low voice echoed from the shadows up ahead, "A pretty, little Akoni is it?"

Tivex stopped, every muscle tensed against an attack. Her eyes strained to penetrate the oppressive darkness, to uncover the source of this new threat.

"The pretty lady has some fight in her I see," said a tall, thin figure as it stepped into the light. A dingy blue waistcoat several sizes too large hung from his scrawny frame like a sack. Strings of greasy brown hair hung down around his face and shoulders. The brim of a large top hat concealed his eyes. Many of his teeth were missing and the ones he had were long and yellowed but that wasn't what made his smile so unsettling. He ran a slimy tongue over his thin black lips, "I like a little fight," he pulled a thin silver chain from his pocket, "don't you boys like a little fight?"

Tivex spun as three large men appeared from shadows around her, one in front and two behind. The one in front carried a thick, intricately carved club, likely the leg of a large table. The two behind were armed as well, one with a heavy chain, the other with a long, thick knife. The man with the club stepped closer but Tivex lashed out with her dagger backing him down.

The thin man spoke again, "You see, my friends, they like you. I like you, too." His revolting smile gave his words a putrid stench, "A face like yours can bring big money. But, if you want to do things the hard way," the man with the knife made a menacing gesture in her direction, "I suppose we don't actually NEED a face."

The men took a step forward, closing their circle around her. Tivex slashed wildly with her daggers to create more space.

"Tsk, tsk, too bad, too bad. It was such a pretty face..." The thin man stepped back into the shadows, his wicked smile vanishing with his final words, "Boys, make her mine."

Tivex spun from man to man, her daggers extended to keep what little space she had from disappearing completely. One after the other the men tested her defenses, feinting in and out, waiting for their moment to attack. Then all at once it came. She ducked her head to the right just as a fat club came sailing towards her, a rush of wind filling her ear as it flew by. Instinctively she countered, her upper arms reaching out for her attacker. Her hands locked around the large man's neck, hugging him close while the daggers in her lower hands found their mark. The man bellowed in pain as she buried them to the hilt in his back. He shivered only slightly before he fell silent. She shoved the lifeless man away, letting his corpse fall to the ground between her and the other men. The odds were better now but watching their compatriot die did little to slow their advance.

Tivex backed against the alley wall, the man on her left swinging his heavy chain back and forth, to her right the glint of a hunting knife changing from hand to hand. She crouched, her daggers now in her upper hands, readying herself for the impending rush.

Together they came, closing the remaining distance in less than a heartbeat. She met the advancing knife with her own, bright sparks from the clashing steel illuminating the darkness. In that instant another shadow moved silently toward her then all was black again. She was locked in a battle of will, all four arms braced against the hands of the man with the knife as he struggled to overpower her.

Tivex felt the heavy chain tighten around her neck before she had time to react. With a quick heave she was pulled from her feet and slammed into the unforgiving brick of the alley wall. Her daggers clattered to the ground as she struggled to breathe. A pair of hands grabbed her right wrists pinning her to the wall, a second pair grabbed her left.

"Well now," the thin man's voice came echoing back from the darkness, "that was a good man you killed there. We can't let that go unpunished." He materialized from the darkness and picking up one of her fallen daggers, he slowly walked over to where the two men held her. He ran the tip of the dagger across her cheek, a droplet of blood forming on her ashen face, "You would have made a pretty pet." The dagger worked its way down her neck, "But I can't have you killing my men. So the real question is," the dagger moved down to her chest cutting off the buttons of her blouse one by one, "what...to do...with..."

A shadow suddenly leapt from the darkness knocking the thin man to the ground. The two men released Tivex to face their attacker but the shadow was already upon them. Its large hands grabbed the face of the one with the chain and smashed his skull into the brick. A sickening crunch and a squelching sound told her the man was not getting back up. In the split second it took her to realize who possessed the shadow, Tivex felt the raw power of the situation. It was the first time that she had seen what she had only heard about since his return. They didn't call Vincent "The Hammer" for nothing. The last thug let his knife fall to the floor and backed into the cover of darkness, the echo of his footsteps fading as he fled for his life.

Hammer walked over and picked Tivex up off the ground. A faint light reflected over his shoulder as the thin man thrust the dagger down toward Hammer's back. Tivex started to scream out a warning when a second shadow, seemed to separate from the very wall itself. Silently and with a speed and agility to surpass any human, the shadow flew towards the thin man. Claws as sharp as razors tore across his face leaving three gaping wounds from his temple to his cheek. The dagger fell as the thin man clutched his face in pain and horror. Blood quickly filling his cupped hands, he staggered away from this new danger, down the alleyway and back into The Hole that spawned him.

The dark figure rose, the fur on his neck still bristling. He wiped his bloody paw on one of the deceased and took his place at Hammer's side.

"Dregs," Tivex said, relief flooding through her body, "I should have known you would be here, too. You two are worse than the twins!" She managed a shaky laugh as the adrenalin coursing through her veins subsided slightly.

"What are you doing here, Tivex?" Hammer scolded as she collected her fallen daggers.

"I might ask you the same question," Tivex replied, attempting to regain her composure. "If it was not for you, I would not have to be in this light forsaken place."

"Funny, I don't remember inviting you," said Hammer as he turned and walked down the alley, Dregs close on his heels.

Tivex stared after them for a moment before running to catch up. The arrogance of the man was infuriating. At last the alley opened up into a large square. Fat Sam's sat in the middle, its dingy exterior illuminated by the red and blue of its many neon signs. A plethora of shady characters filled the square, many casting sideways looks at the odd trio as they passed but none of them advanced.

Hammer and Dregs pushed through the door of Sam's and took a seat at a corner booth. Tivex slid in beside them still a little shaken from their encounter. Hammer waved his hand at a serving girl and a bottle with three, mostly clean, glasses appeared on their table. Tivex picked up the bottle examining the label.

"Omarian Ale? Are you actively trying to kill yourself?" She regretted the words as soon as she said them.

Hammer snatched the bottle from her hands and sloshed a healthy helping into each of the glasses, "You still haven't told me what the slag you're doing here." He picked up his glass and drank down the liquor in one swallow before pouring himself another.

Tivex stared at her drink, dark brown and bubbling. It smelled like varnish, in fact she wouldn't be surprised if that's exactly what it was. She wrinkled her nose and pushed the drink away, "I am here because Team Seven has been recalled." She paused and waited for a reaction but none came, "We are to report to the docks tonight for a briefing with Admiral Kagen."

Hammer set his glass down, "Kagen, huh? What happened? Did that two-faced, back stabbing, piece of gray ash finally keel over?"

Tivex narrowed her eyes at Hammer, "Admiral Kagen is our new Commanding Officer and his orders are that we return to the dock immedia-"

Tivex stopped short as Hammer slammed his fist on the table, "What do you mean WE?"

Tivex swallowed hard remembering that this was not the man she once knew, "Admiral Kagen has ordered that I be transferred to Team Seven as your new first officer. Effective immediately."

Tivex watched her news sink in. Hammer swallowed another glass of ale and laid some credits down on the table. Then he stood and motioned toward the door, "I guess we should go and have us a little chat with Kagen then, yeah?"

Tivex nodded her approval and she and Dregs got out of the booth to leave.

A commotion outside stopped them just short of the door. Shouts of alarm sounded through the square. They hurried to a window just in time to see a dozen large men armed with pikes, daggers, clubs and chains pour into the square. Behind them, the tall thin man from earlier was screaming in rage, a blood soaked cloth pressed against the side of his face, pointed a bony finger in their direction.

"Well, that's not good," Hammer muttered mostly to himself. He turned towards Dregs, "any ideas?"

Dregs' eyes glowed in the low light of the bar. His gruff growl of a voice made Tivex's throat itch, "There's no back way out, my captain now."

Hammer grinned at his friend, "Hmph, I suppose we'll have to say hello then." Dregs smiled ferociously back and handed Hammer a pair of what looked like small silver manacles. Hammer slipped them over his fingers and closed his fists. The metal bands crackled to life, surging with electrical power. Hammer looked up at Tivex, "A little something Torque came up with. Packs quite a punch as long as the power holds out. Only get about two or three good uses out of a charge but it might be enough to punch a way outta here."

The men reached the steps of the bar. Tivex heard Dregs' almost purring sound as he watched with anticipation, "Stay on his heels till we're clear of the square. I'll lead you out from there."

The men reached the door. Tivex was a knot of nerves.

Hammer's fists sizzled with excitement, "Wait for it, wait for it..."

With a deafening crash the door of the bar exploded inward. Hammer's fists met the chest of the first man through the door. A loud bang echoed through the room as the large man was lifted off his feet and propelled back through the open door. The smell of singed flesh and burning hair lingered in his absence.

"NOW!" Hammer cried as he barreled through the entrance. Tivex ran behind, her daggers drawn, wishing for the second time that Blitz had come along.

The dazed men were recovering from the initial surprise of their friend's unexpected flight. They began to rally around the fleeing trio. Two men closed in on either side of Hammer, swinging fearsome pikes as they came. Hammer took the attack in stride. It was almost a dance as he swung his body to the left allowing the first lance to pass by harmlessly. His right arm extended, Hammer grasped the pike as it passed and flung its owner to the ground. Hammer fell to his knees, sliding underneath as the second spear was thrust towards chest. Gathering his feet under him he exploded up, burying his fist deep in the jaw of his attacker. Black smoke rose from the man's eyes as his body convulsed on the street.

Tivex watched this dance of death with equal amounts of amazement and disgust. They were halfway across the square with most of the men behind them. A hundred more feet and they'd be able to lose the crowd in the twists and shadows of The Hole.

A shrill cry from the thin man brought Tivex's head sharply around. He was charging right for her, his bony knuckles wrapped tightly around a long bladed knife and a look of madness in his eye. She had to reach the alley, she had to follow Dregs. She turned back just in time to see the club as it connected with her head.

Then the world went black.

She dreamt of floating, flying, high above the world, a world full of terrible monsters. Ferocious claws and teeth swatted and snapped at her from below. Loathsome apparitions that were both terrifying and frightfully familiar. The fog of her dream carried her on for what seemed an eternity. Finally, the fog began to lift.

As she opened her eyes the world was still black but there were voices now. Friendly voices, familiar voices. She tried to sit up but an ice cold hand held her down, "Just stay down there for a minute, you took quite a blow." The deep voice was so inviting. Slowly the world came into focus, it was still night and she was staring up at a starless sky. The lights of the docks, however, were bright enough to discern the faces of her new Team.

"W-what happened?" she managed, suddenly aware of an excruciating ache in her head.

"I told ya so, that's what happened," Blitz said as he took a seat beside her, "I knew I should have gone with you."

It all came back to her in a rush, Hammer, Dregs, the thin man, "How did I get out of there?"

"Hammer brought you out, him and Dregs. Carried you like a sack of flour all the way here."

A tall thin figure stepped out of the shadows and Tivex gasped. For a split second she believed the pimp from The Hole had followed her all the way back to the docks. She felt the tension lifted off her shoulders the moment she realized who this thin man was. He tipped his large western hat to her, "Evenin', miss. Sorry we missed all the fun."

"Yeah, we ain't had that kind of fun in a long time, but it won't be long now that we're back," said the lean cut, well-groomed black man standing beside Dusty. Silk slapped Dusty on the back, "Ain't that right, brotha?"

"Where are Hammer and Dregs now?" Tivex asked, finally sitting up to look around.

Blitz cast a glance toward a nearby hangar, "Hammer and Kagen have been at it in there for about an hour. The cat, well, he's not real social. He'll show up when we need him but not a minute sooner."

"What happened back there, how did we escape?"

"Yes, wouldn't we all like to know," Admiral Kagen asked as he limped over from the hangar followed by Hammer, "your new captain seems quite tight lipped on the subject. Perhaps you could illuminate the situation for us? Give us some details you can shed some light on."

Tivex hesitated, searching Hammer's face for a clue as to what to say. His only response was to lower his head and give a narrowed eyed expression which mentally told her to keep her mouth shut. "Uh, that is…no, sir. I am sorry, sir, but it is all very fuzzy still. All I know is that I went to find Captain Dorran, we were attacked and then I woke up here."

Kagen stared at her for a moment as if judging whether or not to believe what little she claimed to know. Apparently, appeased or just fed up, he moved on, "Very well, you're all lucky to be alive. I trust you'll use better discretion in the future." He looked directly at Tivex as if to drive the last point home, "Now then, to the reason you're all here. Please follow me." He waved his hand back to the hangar and for them all to follow him back.

Everyone took a seat as Kagan relayed the details of the missing Science Team, playing back the vid from Master Admiral Tall'ani in case he'd missed anything. When the brief was finished Kagen cleared his throat, "Ahem. So, are there any questions?"

"Where exactly is this place?" asked Silk.

"One hundred and seventy hours outside of Omarian territory."

Hammer leaned forward in his chair, "Are you saying it's going to take us a week after bridging out there to get to this planet, sir?"

Kagen nodded.

Blitz whistled, "Whew. Admiral, all due respect, but that's a fairly large distance to put between us and any kind of backup if we're going into a hostile situation. Who else is going?"

Kagen shook his head and pointed at Team Seven, "Just you."

Hammer nodded thoughtfully, "What kind of resistance are we talking about?"

"You've seen the vids, Captain, at this point you know what we know. You're authorized to make whatever preparations you deem necessary in order to find out what happened to them. My advice would be to prepare for the worst and hope for the best."

Dusty pushed his hat back on his head and leaned over to look at Hammer, "Sir, I can tell y'all right now, the best ain't all that good. Did you here that tapping in the background? That was gunfire sure as I'm standing. MK33 cluster fire to be exact, 'soul trains' I hear 'em called down on the range. No, sir, this ain't no accident, Alpha done got themselves in a whole mess of trouble."

Hammer turned back to Kagen, "How soon can we get out of here?"

"There's a shuttle standing by to get you to the space station as we speak. Admiral Jaleer flew up this morning to ensure the Widow Maker was prepped and ready for tomorrow morning's departure," answered Kagen, "and there's one last thing."

"Always is," sneered Blitz.

Kagen shot him a sideways glance, "Locating the Science Team is of secondary importance. Your main concern is retrieving that shard of metal and any other remnants you may find. Master Admiral Soren assures me that when you find it you'll understand, beyond that I'm afraid I don't know anything. Whatever you're after is classified well above my clearance level but know that it's of utmost importance to the IEC. Its retrieval must be accomplished at all costs."

"That's all?" Dregs hissed as he stepped out from the shadow of the hangar, "Sounds pretty flimsy to me."

Kagen nodded, "I agree, but it's all we have at the moment. Master Admiral Lokias is searching the archives as we speak for any information that might be useful to you. If I get more, I'll contact you immediately but I'm afraid there's no time to spare at the moment. Find whatever it is we're after, locate the Science Team and get out."

"One last thing, Admiral," Tivex said finally standing again, "Is there any Dominion threat that we should take into precaution? After all, that planet is dangerously close to the outer territories."

"We haven't ruled it out which means one more reason to exercise extreme caution. Isn't that right, Captain?" Kagen gave Hammer a long level look.

Hammer's fists clenched in white knuckled rage and the fur on the back of Dregs' neck bristled at the implication.

"Thank you, Admiral, I think that is all we need," Tivex said, stepping between Kagen and Hammer, "we will report back with our progress." With a quick salute, she turned, placing a hand on Hammer's arm and gently leading him away toward the shuttle. The rest of the Team followed, leaving Kagen sitting alone amidst the shadows of the empty hanger.

Elsewhere, nestled safely deeper in one of Odyssey's larger parks, Master Admiral Lokias sat, staring into the fountain deep in thought.

"I thought I might find you here," Soren said stepping off the path to take a seat next his old friend.

"It helps me when I'm feeling troubled," Lokias' voice rumbled in the empty park.

"Were you able to find anything in the archives?"

Lokias shook his head, "Nothing that helps. I'm afraid they're on their own."

A deep rumble sounded from the docks as a shuttle departed. Soren and Lokias sat in silence as they watched the light from the shuttle until it disappeared among the stars.

Lokias was the first to speak, "Do you think we should have told them?"

Soren inhaled deeply and leaned forward, resting his elbows on his knees. He rubbed his hands together and squinted at the fountain, "You know as well as I do we couldn't, old friend. Right now the fate of the entire universe is resting on the shoulders of Team Seven. The less they know about the Horizon, the better."

WHISPERS IN THE DARKNESS

(I'm so excited) (I wanna be a pilot when I grow up) (I can't believe we finally get to go) The children's laughing voices floated in an impenetrable curtain of darkness. (Hahaha) (Earth looks so small from here) (Hey, Vincent...) No faces, no names, just the ever present voices.

A flash of red colored the darkness and the screams of the innocent rose all around. (No! Please!) (No! Mommy! Daddy! Vincent, help me!) (Help us, Vincent!) (It hurts) (Don't let them find me!) The anguished voices of the children echoed in the darkness. M-Y-N-X. The bold letters hung suspended in the æther. Dark voices filled the night, twisted voices, evil voices. (Haess kaari taag velmetsa velmana!) (Monhaess velmana monkaari!) (Moncasa monhesh VELKASO!)

TIVEX WATCHED HAMMER THRASH IN HIS SLEEP, MUMBLING INCOHERENTLY. SHE SHOT A CONCERNED look at Dregs but the big cat just shrugged and turned back to the window, "You'll get used to it."

A moment later Hammer awoke. His shaky hand reached inside his coat removing a flask from which he drank hastily. Tivex tried not to stare, searching for someone, anyone else, to take her attention away from what she'd just witnessed but everyone else was still asleep. She turned to her own window, gazing past her stone reflection into the vastness of space.

It had been five hours since the shuttle departed. It was too turbulent a ride for Tivex to get any rest but for the rest of the Team it appeared to be no challenge at all. She counted the stars to pass the time, trying desperately not to think about Vincent.

Dregs' course voice landed on her ears like sandpaper, "Wake up, lads! We're here."

Tivex released her restraints and floated to a port hole near Dregs. Soon the rest of the Team was crowded around the windows as well. All were trying to catch a glimpse of the station, all except Hammer. He sat at his seat, staring intently ahead, an absent look on his face. Tivex turned her attention back to the window. As the shuttle turned, the station came slowly into view.

The El station was in high orbit above Earth, the primary hub for all the ships which were too large to be kept on the surface. The right side of the station held the Military Division. She knew by name or reputation many of the ships that docked there, the Onyx, the Crossfire, the

Dawn's Escape to name a few but today only one bay was occupied. The ship docked in the bay was lit from every conceivable angle by the station's lights. Gleaming from bow to stern in shining silver with deep hues of rich cobalt blue and ribbons of ebony black across her hull, the Widow Maker.

She was a stocky, sturdily built ship, with two sets of short, stubby wings mounted aft and stern. Heavy cannons were mounted to her wing tips and four large missile compartments hid where each wing fused with the fuselage. A light near the rear of the craft identified the control deck, its many glowing panels shining through the windows like a beacon guiding them home. Large bay doors at the front of the ship stood open while station crews loaded supplies. A short man with long uncontrolled hair that fell haphazardly around his shoulders stood among them pointing emphatically with every order he gave. Torque looked up at the approaching shuttle and waved.

Silk slapped Dusty on the back, "WOOHOO! WE'RE HOME, BOYS! WE'RE FINALLY HOME!!"

As the Team disembarked the shuttle, Tivex lagged behind. Hammer was still gathering his belongings when she approached, "Captain, is everything alright?"

Hammer's face contorted as he slung a heavy duffle over his shoulder, "Yeah, just fine." The tone in his voice said otherwise.

Tivex put a hand on his shoulder, "I know it has been a while but you are still my friend. If there is anything you need to talk about, I am always here for you."

Hammer jerked away from her touch pushing past her toward the door, "I don't need a shrink, I don't need a friend and the last thing I need is a first officer."

Tivex watched as Hammer stormed down the gang way. She wanted so badly to help him but she wasn't sure a man like that could be helped.

Torque's mop haired head popped through the door, "Let's go, sister, we don't have time for just sitting around. The real fun is about to begin!"

"Ahem?"

Torque rubbed his neck, "Sorry, ma'am."

Tivex rolled her eyes as she picked up her belongings and followed her friend onto the station.

The twisting corridors of the E1 station were bustling with maintenance staff finishing the last minute preparations on the Widow Maker. Torque eyed them all fiercely as he passed, he never liked other people working on his ship. One final corridor and they stepped out onto the Widow Maker's leading dock. Her bulky, iron plated frame rose high above their heads.

A loud crash sounded from somewhere near the thrusters, "Just my ashen luck," seethed Torque, "I gotta go handle whatever that was. I'll see you onboard," Torque called as he ran off in the direction of the calamitous sound.

Tivex stared at the ship. It was a large ship, certainly not the largest she'd ever seen, not even in the top ten, but still quite large. The open bay doors stretched wide enough to hold fifteen men shoulder to shoulder. As tall as it was wide, the gaping maw of the ship seemed to devour the workers as they carried their loads deep into the belly of the beast.

Just as Tivex began to climb the loading ramp into the ship's hull, a familiar voice stopped her short, "Commander Tivex, I presume?"

Tivex turned to face the other Akoni, her hands raised in salute, "Admiral Jaleer, good morning, ma'am."

"At ease, Commander," Jaleer replied calmly, "it's my understanding that you will be overseeing this expedition as an emissary for Admiral Kagen. Please let me know if there is anything I can do to assist you on your journey."

"Admiral Jaleer!" Hammer's voice echoed as he strode across the dock toward them, "My crew have work to do, if there's something to discuss you can take it up with me." He stepped between them, never taking his eyes off of Jaleer, "Commander Tivex," Hammer said in a more than direct tone, "report to the Widow Maker and assist with the launch preparations."

Tivex looked over his shoulder at Jaleer, searching her face for some indication that she was indeed dismissed but the woman was as stone as her complexion.

"That's an order, Commander."

"Yes, sir," answered Tivex as she turned and walked up the loading ramp. Probably better not to be present for this anyway she thought. Vincent's temper had been raging since they left Admiral Kagen and from the edge in his voice she imagined Jaleer was in for an earful. Tivex shook her head as she walked past the mountains of cargo being secured in the hold. She knew he had a problem with authority, especially IEC authority, but it was amazing to her that he was allowed to behave this way. Anyone else would have been court marshalled long ago.

Torque was talking with one of the maintenance workers when Tivex found him. His voice growing louder by the second, waving his hand at the engine compartments, "The next time you try uplinking the fuel cells to the main reactor, try reading the damned manual! Do you have any idea what that could have done to the stabilizer ballast?"

"What's the problem?" Tivex asked as she approached them.

"The problem? The problem is this wrench-head is fresh out of training and apparently knows better than me about orbital mechanics," raged Torque, "never mind the fact that this is my design! Who told you to touch the uplink anyway?"

Torque snatched the man's clipboard, scribbled on a piece of paper and shoved it back into his hands. The man stammered, "I'm sorry, sir! I was trying to-"

"Do me a favor, go work over there."

The worker looked down at the paper and then back to Torque, "Sir, that room is used for training."

Torque grinned, "Good, we understand each other. You come near my ship again and believe me, I'll have you back on Earth fixing vending machines." He spun around to Tivex, "If you need me, I'll be in the control deck making sure this numbnuts didn't do anything to take us out on pushback."

Tivex watched as Torque disappeared into the bowels of the Widow Maker, still muttering to himself. She moved past the sulking mechanic and followed Torque down the corridor, toward the lift.

"Do you think you may have overreacted?" Tivex asked as they stepped onto the lift.

Torque shrugged, "He'll get over it."

The lift came to a stop and the two stepped out into the control deck. Several dozen consoles lit the room with their soft blue light. Lighted keypads added their own splash of color. The room was littered with buttons and switches, all blinking in hypnotic sequence. Around the room ran a bank of windows offering a three-hundred-degree view of their surroundings, obscured only by the lift behind them.

Silk sat to the left, his mirrored glasses reflecting the preflight readout of his flight terminal. His dark curly hair was buzzed low and tight in typical IEC fashion. His normally dark skin was almost black in the halo of light that surrounded him. Behind him sat Dusty, his large Stetson hat perched atop his long blond locks. Bright blue eyes sparkling as he ran the diagnostics on his weapons systems. A less likely pair Tivex could not imagine.

Blitz sat to the right, an empty chair beside him. Wires from his bionics linked him to the ships navigational system, feeding him constant information on their whereabouts. Everything from universal guidance coordinates to immediate environmental changes was being fed into his central processing unit for strategic planning. Torque took the chair beside him and began punching number sequences into the large engineering mainframe.

Two chairs still sat unoccupied. One in the front nearest the communications terminal that she knew to be hers. The other one stood in the middle of the room, a great throne of welded iron.

"How are we looking, gentlemen?" Hammer asked as the doors of the lift slid shut behind him.

Torque looked up from his console, "She's good to go, Cap. Fuel cells one and two fully charged, backups three and four standing by. Automation systems are primed and ready, auxiliary systems are both green. Gravity and life support systems are one hundred percent."

"Weapons check, Dusty?"

"Locked and loaded, skipper."

Hammer nodded his approval and leaned over towards Tivex, "Commander, are we ready to cut loose?"

She crossed the control deck and took her seat. Tivex nodded as she pressed her earpiece, "Affirmative, Captain. Dock personnel report all clear."

"Silk?" asked Hammer.

"Main star drive controls reading five by five, Cap," and he turned back to Hammer with a wicked grin on his face, "she's hot."

Hammer took his seat in the large captain's chair, "Take her out."

Silk grabbed the controls and the Widow Maker shook as it released from the space station. A voice from the ground sounded in Tivex's ear. She raised her right thumbs to Silk "Separation confirmed."

Hammer eased back in his chair, noticeably more comfortable than he'd been on the surface, "Set a course for the Bridge and proceed at half power."

Silk pushed the throttle lever forward and the Widow Maker began to hum gently as she made her way towards the Bridge Gate. The Bridges were another Sageve creation, an intergalactic superhighway with the Gates acting as a series of secure off-ramps. Without the Bridge, a trip to Omaria would take several years instead of a matter of hours.

It took only ten minutes for the Bridge to come into view. A long piece of metal suspended in space, the Widow Maker could fit end to end four or five times along its length without reaching the edge of the Gate. Tivex pressed her ear piece, "E1, this is SL19 requesting Gate clearance."

The voice crackled back in her ear, "SL19, you are clear to the Bridge."

A row of lights came to life along the length of the Gate, blindingly bright in the darkness of space. Slowly it came to life, pivoting on unseen hinges to form the entrance to the Bridge. Two walls rising from the middle paralleled the two descending. When at last the walls reached their apex they had formed a luminous diamond, a star unlike any other in space. Slowly the walls began to turn, spinning from tip to tip so that soon it was impossible to tell which had been the top and which the bottom. As the walls gained speed, a touch of color illuminated the very center of the Gate. Hues of blue and green spreading outward toward the walls until they filled the Gate completely.

Hammer pulled his harness over his shoulders and the rest of the Team followed suit, "Lieutenant, take us in."

"Aye, sir," Silk replied as he throttled the ship into the welcoming light of the Bridge.

Tivex hated Bridging. The whole process put her stomach in knots. She was glad to be sitting up front so that no one could see the sickly look on her face. Silk increased the speed and as the nose of the ship touched the light they were at once through the Gate. Catapulted into the Bridge as if shot out of a cannon, and with much the same terrifying effect. Tivex felt as though she might be sick but a quick glance around showed she was the only one having difficulties.

As the ship gained stability, Blitz unbuckled his belt and swung his chair around to face

Hammer, "Alright, boss man, looks like we're on course to enter Omarian territory on schedule. After that, well, I guess we find out when we get there."

"After we check in with Tall'ani I want to review that disk again," said Hammer, "I want to make sure there's nothing we missed. We're gonna need every advantage we can get."

Torque also spun in his chair, "Not a problem, Cap, there's a whole lot of nothing between Omaria and that planet."

"That's what worries me," Dregs grumbled from the corner. Tivex jumped at the sound of his voice. She hadn't noticed him when she came aboard but now she couldn't help but see his looming silhouette pacing back and forth before the blue-green light flooding through the windows.

The crew nodded silently in agreement. Omaria was by far the closest to the Dominion Territory any of them wanted to get again. The Hais were notorious for being vengeful and fiercely territorial.

Hammer looked at Dregs, "What do you think the chance is of us getting in there undetected?"

"Zero would be highly optimistic" he growled, "I doubt they've forgotten you, me or this ship."

"Silk, Dusty, as soon as we clear Omarian space run her as quiet as possible."

"Aye, sir," they answered in unison.

Tivex felt the tension begin to mount. They were still a week from their objective and already she was nervous with anticipation. The next few hours passed with little conversation. Hammer left to review the vid disc, returning shortly before it was time to exit the Bridge, in a mood that told Tivex he had found nothing new.

Silk sat upright, "This is us, people."

Tivex fumbled trying to get her harness fastened, clicking it into place just as the Widow Maker slammed to a halt. Well, it felt like they were stopped, though the rapidly approaching Omarian space station told her otherwise. Silk eased the throttle back to half, a sluggish crawl compared to the speed of the Bridge.

A bright tone sounded in Tivex's earpiece, "Sir, the Omarian station is signaling for communication."

"Well, put them on then," Hammers irritated mood soured his words.

"Captain Dorran, can you hear me?" Tall'ani's voice crackled over the speakers moments before her panther-like face illuminated the vid screen.

"Master Admiral Tall'ani, we read you."

"Captain, is there anything you require from my station before you proceed?"

"No, ma'am, we're fully stocked and briefed, unless there's something else you'd like to add."

Hammer's unasked question lingered in the air until at last Tall'ani responded, "You know all that you need to know at this time, Captain. You are cleared through the Omarian sector. Good luck to you all. Oh, and Captain, I think I speak for the entire council when I say we do not want a repeat of your last performance."

Hammer's jaw clenched at her words.

"Thank you, ma'am, we hope to have news for you soon," Tivex interjected and quickly ended the transmission.

Hammer turned to Silk, "Set a course for our objective and proceed at full power."

Silk raised a questioning eyebrow, "Umm, sir, we're still in the space station proxy zone. Anything faster than this is a major violation."

Hammer snarled, "Like I care? Full power!"

"Aye, sir." Silk pushed the throttle forward and the ship bucked ahead, pushing Tivex back into her seat. It really was a fast ship, nothing compared to the Bridge but she was much faster than she looked at any rate.

Tivex's earpiece exploded with chatter as the Widow Maker rocketed past the Omarian docking bay, "Sir, they are not happy."

A self-gratified smile spread across Hammer's face as he rose and left the room.

The next few days passed without incident. Hammer had them running as few systems as possible to avoid detection. That meant, among other things, running with their shields down. It was a generally unpopular idea to have no defense in place, especially alone, so far from help and with so many unanswered questions but ultimately the desire for stealth won out. They took the controls in shifts, monitoring the scanners for any sign of trouble. For Tivex it was all just as well. Between Hammer's violent thrashing and Torque's wretched snoring it was impossible to get a full night's rest anyway.

It was day four of their journey. Tivex had just finished her daily report to Admiral Kagen when she arrived on the control deck to relieve Blitz. The scanners filled the room with white noise as they searched the empty heavens. Blitz stood and stretched, even his limbs weren't impervious to the rigors of endless vigilance. Tivex took his place in the chair, running her hands through her flowing purple hair as she prepared for the grueling shift ahead of her. Blitz turned to leave without saying a word when the lights began to flicker.

"Umm, what was that?" Tivex asked, a hint of trepidation in her voice.

"I'm not sure, she's never done that before. I'd better run a diagnostic check." Blitz pulled a thick cable from the console and plugged it into a hole on his arm, "Ahhh!" Blitz soured in pain as he ripped the cord from his arm. The console sizzled and popped. The lights and screens flickered and then all was dark. The Widow Maker slowed to a stop and the acrid smell of burning wires rose thick in the air.

"What happened? Are you alright?" Tivex asked as Blitz rubbed his neck where the flesh and metal fused.

"I'll be fine, it just singed me a bit. I don't know where that surge came from but it seems to have taken out all our systems."

A series of chirps sounded from Tivex's comm. The screen was dark but the voice was unmistakable, "Are you guys alright?" Torque asked, "What happened up there?"

Tivex looked at Blitz, the skin on his neck burned bright red but he seemed fine otherwise, "We are okay for now. We do not know what happened, some sort of electrical surge, but it has knocked out our whole operation."

"Yeah, we lost everything down here too. Hang on." There was a loud banging and a litany of curses from Torque's end before he finally found what he was looking for, "Aha!" A bright light lit up his face in her comm screen, casting long shadows that exaggerated every feature, "Okay, well the good news is not everything is down. We aren't floating away so the life support and gravity drive must still be operational. As for the rest of it, I'll see what I can do down here. Gotta get the lift working again before I can get you guys out so make yourselves comfortable."

"Great," Blitz moaned, "just so you know, the mainframe is toasted. You should be able to get the engines fired up but we'll be lucky to get the nav system back online."

Torque's ghostly visage grinned from ear to ear, "Worry not, my chrome compatriot, Torque the unequivocal is here! All shall marvel at my genius! The very world itself will bow before my-"

Tivex ended the transmission before Torque could finish, rolling her eyes at Blitz.

"Sounds like we're gonna be here for a while," Blitz sighed and slid down to the floor, resting his back against the still smoking mainframe.

The hours ticked by slowly. The myriad stars twinkling in the windows gave them just enough light to see by. Faint swirls of color in the distance revealed the location of other galaxies. Most, Tivex couldn't name but there was one, a swash of bright blue beyond the bank of windows on the far right of the control deck, that one she knew as the home of her people. It was not her home, she was Earth born, but it was a place of great history and she felt immense pride in being a part of it.

She took her attention from thoughts of Akonis and turned them instead to thoughts of Vincent, "Blitz? How long have you known Vincent?"

Blitz sniggered, "Who's Vincent?"

Tivex pursed her lips, "Fine, Hammer."

Blitz shifted to face her, "Oh, maybe about fifteen years or so, why?"

Tivex hesitated, not sure if she really wanted the answer to the question she was about to ask, "What happened to him?"

Blitz shook his head, "I don't know any more than anyone else does. He was 15 when he left on the IEC ship Galileo, back when they still had the young explorer program. His ship was attacked two weeks out of port by an unknown vessel, no survivors were reported. Then, almost a decade later, they find Hammer floating in a rescue pod with that fleabag Omarian. Only Hammer, Dregs and the IEC brass know the whole story."

Tivex sighed and slumped down next to Blitz, she knew all of that already, "So he has never talked about it?"

"Would you?" Blitz turned his hand back and forth as if scrutinizing the craftsmanship. He sighed and leaned his head back, "Some things aren't worth reliving."

Tivex reached out and took his hand in hers, "I am so very sorry. I did not mean to put the question in such a connotation."

He gave her hands a gentle squeeze, "I know. There's a lot of demons on this ship, it's hard not to stumble across one or two."

They sat in silence for a long time, staring out the windows into the vastness of space. Slowly the stars began to wink out of existence. One by one they disappeared, eclipsed by a shadow gliding by in the distance. Tivex's eyes grew wide as she watched. Blitz gave her hand another editing squeeze.

"What is that?" she asked.

"It's a ship, a big one too."

"Is it Hais?"

"I don't know, maybe I can…hang on a minute," Blitz stood and walked to the scanner. He reached down and ripped power cables from the floor.

"What are you doing?" Tivex whispered.

Blitz opened a panel on his chest, "I have an independent power source that runs all my biomechanics." He began stripping the wires and inserting them into his chest cavity, "If I can siphon off some of the power maybe we can get the scanner working and find out who they are." A bright spark flared from his chest as the last wire touched and the scanner came back to life. A blip on the screen showed a massive vessel, at least double the size of the Widow Maker, "Holy slag. It's too big to be Hais."

"Well, it is not one of ours."

Blitz pulled a second set of cords from the scanner, plugging them into his neck and the speakers in his voice box sparked to life.

"*Monhecate bushah.*"

"*Besamonkimet?*"

"*Monsut moncaan.*"

"*Il monkimet monkaari?*"

"Do you know what they are saying?" asked Tivex

Blitz shook his head, "No, my system would have translated it. Whatever they're speaking it isn't in the IEC database." Blitz raised a finger to his lips, "Shhh, we're being scanned."

Tivex froze, hoping that with all the systems down they may take them for a derelict vessel and continue on their way. Seconds seemed like hours as they waited for the mystery ship to complete its scan and move on. Finally, voices came from the speaker inside Blitz's throat once again.

"Kil Velkaso. Kil monkaari."

The large vessel turned heading away from the Widow Maker and her crew. Blitz and Tivex breathed a collective sigh of relief. The lights flickered.

"No, no, no, not now! They're too close!" Blitz screamed at the lights.

Tivex frantically punched Torque's identifier into her comm but it was too late. The engines roared back to life. Blitz stared unblinking at the scanner, watching the distance between them grow, hoping they hadn't noticed. A dark and vile voice sounded from deep inside his throat.

"Haess velmetsa moncasa monhesh Velkaso!"

Slowly the big ship began to turn.

The door of the lift slid open and the rest of the crew stepped in led by a beaming Torque. "Am I good or am I good?" He looked from Tivex to Blitz, "Man, what's with you guys? You look like slag."

The blip on the radar caught Hammer's eye, "Who is that?"

Blitz and Tivex just shrugged, "We do not know, sir."

"Do they know we're here?"

"They do now," Blitz replied.

Hammer wasted no time, "Silk get us out of here, NOW!"

"Aye, sir," Silk said as he sprang into his pilot's seat.

"Torque," Hammer yelled, "I need an update. What systems are functional?"

"Right now it's just the engines and ancillary power systems. We have no shields, no communications, no guidance system. It'll take me days to get this stuff back online."

"Well, we'll have to make do. Silk, evasive maneuvers."

"Aye, sir," Silk said as he throttled the Widow Maker up to full power.

Tivex and the rest of the crew scrambled to their seats. For a brief moment the sounds of harnesses fastening into place filled the room. Blitz still held the scanner. The large blip that was the behemoth spacecraft had already crossed half the distance between them. The Widow Maker was fast but somehow they were still losing ground.

Dusty pushed back his hat and fixed his bright blue eyes on the crosshairs in front of him. "Just give the word, Cap'n and I'll start the fireworks."

"Not yet, Dusty. We aren't gonna to be able to fight our way out of this one. Not without our shields."

The stars in the windows rose and fell, dancing left and right as Silk tried to evade their pursuer but the ship just kept coming, "Torque!" Silk yelled, "Is the overdrive operational?"

Torque jumped to his feet, "No, but it can be. Give me a minute." He ran to the lift. Tivex watched the scene unfold, it was controlled chaos. Every person had a part to play and they knew their parts well.

Silk called out again, "Blitz, what's my distance?"

Blitz checked the scanner, "Fifteen specs and closing."

"Dusty?"

"Already on it," Dusty said as he punched some numbers into his control pad.

"We only get one shot at this. Blitz, once he closes within ten specs I need you to count me down." Silk's eyes never left his screen as he shouted out commands.

Hammer opened a comm link to Torque, "How are we looking down there?"

"I just got here, give me a minute."

"We don't have a minute, Torque. Get the overdrive online now!"

Sweat began to bead on Silk's forehead, "How we doin, Blitz?"

"Inside thirteen specs."

"Torque?"

"I'm working on it!"

Dusty's fingers wrapped tightly around the spade grip of his artillery controls, his steady fingers resting lightly on the triggers. He swung his sights around searching for a target but they were still too far away.

Blitz looked up from the scanner, "Closing at ten specs now."

"Torque, you gotta gimme somethin'!"

"Almost there!"

"Nine specs."

Slowly the shadow began to form in Dusty's crosshairs, "I've got em in sight, Cap."

Hammer's voice was strong and steady, "Hold for my signal."

"Eight specs, closing in on seven," said Blitz.

"They're opening their weapon bays sir, their almost in range," said Dusty.

"Six."

"Hold, dammit, we can't do anything without that overdrive!" replied Hammer, his voice as focused as his eyes.

"Five."

"Torque?" yelled Silk.

"Cap, they're preparing to fire!" said Dusty, almost twitching in his seat.

"Four," said Blitz.

"TORQUE!" roared Hammer.

Torque's voice shouted over the comm, "We're online! Go, go, go!"

A small explosion on the port side rocked the ship. It wasn't a hit but it was too close for comfort.

"Light 'em up!" shouted Hammer to Dusty.

Dusty beamed, "Aye, sir!" Dusty let loose a barrage of missiles off the stern, "Missiles away, sir!"

Tivex finally found the nerve to speak, "Do you think that is enough to stop them?"

Dusty laughed, "Not even close."

"But then why…?"

Hammer raised his hand putting a finger to his lips he then pointed to Dusty. Tivex watched as the missiles on the scanner approached their target. At nearly three quarters of the way to their destination Dusty unleashed hell. His fingers squeezed the triggers of his heavy guns, lighting up space with molten metal. First one explosion and then another and another as Dusty detonated his own munitions. In less than a heartbeat a wall of explosions erupted between the two ships.

Silk yanked on the controls, "Hold on!" The ship pitched up rolling back and to the starboard so that soon they were flying directly into the immense wall of exploding debris. Dusty never missed a beat as he continued to build his barrier.

"Wait for it, wait for it…NOW!" Hammer shouted and Silk punched the overdrive. Faster than Tivex ever believed the ship capable, they burst through the minefield and over the top of their adversary.

Blitz watched the scanner as the distance grew. Seven specs, ten, fourteen, twenty, "No signs of pursuit, Cap."

"YEEHAW!" shouted Dusty. He looked over at Tivex, "Darlin', we call that little ditty the Flash and Dash." He stood up to take a bow.

Hammer's face was ghostly white, "Just keep it up as long as you can. I want to create as much distance as possible. Once we're out of range, change our heading, I don't want them stumbling back across us." He stood and left the control deck with Dregs close on his heels.

Dusty looked at Silk, "What? Was it somethin' I said?"

ECHOES

The world was milky gray, a soupy fog that stretched forever in all directions. A large ship materialized in the haze, a bulky wreck welded together with the scraps of its victims. The letters IEC in faded paint littered the cannibalistic hull. The voices returned, shrill and accusing. (Why, Vincent?) (Why did you let us die?) (Why didn't you save us, Vincent?) (It's your fault we're gone.) (It's all your fault!) (Why was your life spared?) (Come to us, Vincent.) (Join us.) From the depths of the fog stepped a man. No, not a man. A creature, a vile affront to nature herself. A writhing mass of bone and glistening muscle, he stood there in the gray. A crown of ivory daggers sat upon his head. His lips curled back in a rictus snarl revealing two rows of razor sharp teeth. A long clawed finger stretched before him, beckoning. "Come, boys, come home. Come kneel before me. Kneel before your king. Kneel before Velkaso."

HAMMER WOKE WITH A START, PULLING THE FLASK FROM HIS COAT AGAIN AND TAKING A LONG drink. Tivex watched intently, waiting for him to finish, "What is it you see when you close your eyes?" she asked when he was through.

He swung his legs over the side of his bunk and rubbed his eyes wearily. Hammer stood slowly and walked towards the door. As he approached the door, he slightly turned his head back to her and whispered darkly, "Ghosts."

Tivex followed him down the hall toward the galley. Hammer hadn't said much in the three days since the attack. He spent the first day locked in a room with Dregs, not coming out even to eat. When he finally emerged he was morose at best. Storming down the corridors one moment and sulking in his bunk the next. His nightmares seemed to be getting worse and Tivex wasn't the only one worried about it. Torque had his work cut out for him. Repairing the Widow Maker's main frame took every waking hour but when he wasn't soldering wires, she would catch him watching his brother from a distance.

Something about the attack had shaken him and she was determined to find out what, "Why won't you talk to me? We used to be close. Do you remember that?"

Hammer picked up an old dented coffee pot and poured its contents into a nearby cup. Slowly he sipped the thick brew, staring off into the distance, saying nothing.

"Well, I remember," she mumbled in frustration. Before she could say more, the galley began filling with bodies.

"So what about this Team Alpha, Cap?" asked Blitz, "You got any theories?"

Hammer set down his cup and took a deep breath, "Nothing on the disc has given us any further insight but there're a few things we can assume based on what we do know. First, we know the shuttle never would have been dispatched without a recon scan. So we can assume the creatures responsible either came along after or were shielded from the scans."

"Could it have been some kind of equipment malfunction? Perhaps it was no attack at all," said Tivex.

Dregs leaned forward, "Not likely."

"Why is that?" she asked.

"The only malfunction that woulda shaken the shuttle like that is an internal core combustion. If that was the case, they never woulda sent no SOS and there'd be nothin' more than a pile of ashes to sift through. Face it, we're gonna get our hands dirty on this one," Dregs replied.

Torque nodded his head, "He's right."

Hammer raised his eyebrows and looked back down at his cup. He sloshed the remaining contents around and thought for a moment. He turned to Torque, "What's our status?"

Torque beamed, "Ninety-eight percent of our systems are operational." His face darkened a bit, "Unfortunately, our communications are still shot. Most of the circuits have been repaired but without a new spacial transmitter, we won't be able to call for help."

"Did you figure out what went wrong?"

Torque's face turned beet red, "Oh, you bet your sweet paycheck I did. Let's just say there's a rookie mechanic who'll be spending the next few years sorting scrap metal. That is, of course, if I can ever make my report."

Hammer slammed his cup back down, "Slag that! Like we needed any help in the first place! But it still doesn't change the fact that it's time we quit wasting time worrying about what we don't have and get some kind of a plan together. I don't know about the rest of you space dogs but I don't want another repeat of what happened to Alpha." He stood up out of his chair and motioned for the others to follow him back to the control deck.

When they got there, Hammer straddled his seat and motioned for the others to get down to business. Tivex noticed that it was only when he was in that chair that Hammer seemed to reclaim any of his composure. She turned around to her console and heard the others beginning to type into theirs.

From behind her, Tivex heard Hammer, "Torque, bring up everything we have on that planet. I want terrain scans, topography maps, climate shifts and especially solar time down there. Blitz, we need plans for landing and evac, defense strategies, recon and cover. I want backup scenarios and backups for those. Plan for all contingencies, I don't want to have to think about it when we get there."

Torque nodded while typing something into his wrist cuff. He used the main viewing screen to project the data stream for everyone to see. They started with the first video from Gage'ik.

Hammer paused the stream where she was holding the scrap of metal and asked Dregs, "Got any ideas?"

Dregs shook his head and stretched, emitting a low yawning sound, "You got me, my captain now. It's not any writing I've ever seen before."

"Torque?"

"Sorry, boss man, whatever that thing's made out of doesn't even resemble anything we have."

Hammer leaned forward in his chair and ran a hand through his hair, "Wonderful." He didn't look up but asked Blitz, "What do you figure for ground ops?"

"Good question," answered Blitz, "these are the aerial photos of the planet taken before Alpha was dispatched. It's a relatively small island, roughly five miles in diameter." The pictures scrolled by and the island grew larger with each one. A large plateau rose in the center of the island. To the east were sheer cliffs which fell hundreds of feet to the crashing sea below. To the north, gentle slopes led down a sandy beach that stretched the width of the island. Both the west and south carried dense forests which sprang from the earth, lush, green and impenetrable from above.

"Alpha landed here," Blitz pointed to a point near the center of the plateau, "They had protection from the cliffs but they didn't keep enough distance between them and the tree line. I wouldn't recommend setting down in the same place for obvious reasons."

"Maybe closer to the beach, sir?" asked Dusty.

Blitz nodded, "That'd be my first choice. If Alpha was attacked by something coming out of the trees, we'd have the advantage of added distance between it and us. With our backs to the sea we should have only one side to defend if necessary. Once we get down there, I'll take Torque and Dusty with me and scout around the western perimeter where Braxa supposedly found that piece in case there's anything more."

Hammer nodded, "Agreed. Dregs and I will poke around Alpha's last location which leaves Silk and Tivex here with the ship." He turned to Silk, "Keep the engines hot, if we get in trouble we're gonna need to make a quick exit."

"Captain," Tivex began, "I would like to join you on this mission. It was Admiral Kagen's wish that I be involved in all facets of this operation."

"Stow it, 'Vex. You've never been on a mission like this and I don't want you out there if the situation starts to deteriorate."

"Captain, I do appreciate your chivalrous attention to my safety but I am fully trained in combat situations," said Tivex.

Hammer's eyes narrowed, "I'm not making this call for you, I'm making it for the safety of my Team. This is a battle seasoned unit. We survive because we can each trust the other to do their job. I'm not throwing in any more unknown variables than we already have. Besides, being in a simulator isn't the same as being out in the field and you know it. Or, do we need to discuss what happened in The Hole?"

Tivex's stone face glowed a faint red with embarrassment, "All the same, I would like the opportunity to do something other than babysit your ship."

"After we secure the area there's gonna be plenty for all of us to do."

Tivex started to protest but Hammer silenced her with a dismissive wave of his hand. His mind was made up and nothing she could say was going to change that.

They spent the remainder of the trip flushing out the details of their mission. Tivex hated not being included but she had to admit they knew what they were doing. Like Hammer said, they were a seasoned Team. The plan seemed simple enough, they were to land on the western side of the beach, away from the cliffs where an enemy might gain the advantage of higher ground. Once landed, Blitz, Torque and Dusty were to secure the western perimeter and search for Braxa's mysterious metal. It was up to Hammer and Dregs to reach the plateau and discover the fate of Team Alpha. Any sign of trouble warranted immediate retreat. They poured over the maps, memorizing the terrain, searching for hidden dangers, blind corners, dense thickets, anything that might hide an enemy. They were well versed in the island's topography by the time it came into view.

"There she is," Silk called out from the controls. He pointed out the window to a tiny blue dot, brighter than any star in the sky. As Tivex watched, the dot began to grow. A pin point at first, it was soon the size of a tack, then a small coin, then a large coin, a baseball and so on. Before long, the planet filled their window. Deep, blue tranquil seas wrapped its surface in every direction. Silk surveyed his console and turned back around. "From what I'm seeing, nothing's changed on the island from the photos but I can't seem to find Alpha's shuttle." He continued typing, "Blitz was right though, landin' anywhere other than the beach is going to leave us vulnerable on all sides."

Tivex spoke up, "There are faint readings of metal scattered in various places near where the shuttle was supposed to have landed."

Hammer looked over at Dregs, "Is there anything else out here worth knowing about?"

Dregs turned his head around from the main viewing screen and sneered back at Hammer, "You really wanna know how close we are to our Hais friends right now?"

Hammers face tightened, "Slag it, just take us down."

"Aye, sir," Silk replied. He moved the throttle lever back to the neutral position and entered in a quick series of commands into his console, "Star drive offline, switching to atmospheric. Vertical thrusters to manual, everyone strap in." The rest of the Team secured their harnesses and gave Silk the go ahead. He switched off the gravity generators and angled the Widow Maker for orbital insertion. He turned around to Hammer, "Sir?"

Hammer nodded, "Bring her in."

Silk nodded back, "Aye, sir." He double checked the shields and pushed the throttle lever to half power, "Thank you, lady and gentlemen, for flying Silk Air! Our flight today will be taking us over water. In the unlikely event of a water landing, please place your head firmly between your legs and kiss your ass goodbye. Be sure to see your flight attendant for your complimentary IEC travel brochure and welcome to the island of horrible, scary and very nasty death!"

Tivex shook her head, just when she thought they were finally taking things seriously.

Controlling the direction with his right hand and both speed and angle with his left, Silk brought the Widow Maker down and into the planet's atmosphere. The thickening air caused some minor red and yellow flashes across the windows but since they were not descending rapidly, the light show was over as quickly as it had begun.

As they dropped lower, Tivex was able to make out the island's various regions. It was a very small island compared to the vast oceans that surrounded it, an impossible speck of an oasis. It was amazing to her that this place was ever found in the first place. To the west and south was what appeared to be a jungle. It was not large, perhaps two miles deep but so dense she could not spot a hole in the canopy. The central plateau of the island where Team Alpha had been, was nothing more than a flat field covered in grass and sand.

Silk expertly piloted the Widow Maker down onto the beach on the island's north side and set her down with a gentle thud. He set the engines to standby and spun around to face the others with his hands raised in the air, "Touchdown and the crowd goes wild!"

Hammer unbuckled his harness and nodded, "Nice work. Alright boys, lock and load. Silk, stay on station, I want constant communication. Tivex, I want you on that scanner watching our six. If you see anything out of the ordinary, don't keep it to yourself."

"Aye, sir," answered Silk.

"I still say I should be out there with you," argued Tivex.

Hammer raised his eyebrow as he slid a magazine into his firearm, "This isn't open for discussion. We don't know for sure what we're dealing with out there and until we do you have your orders."

Tivex reluctantly nodded her understanding.

They marched down to the main boarding hatch and Silk opened the ground ramp. Tivex watched through the window as the others worked their way to their respective zones. Hammer's voice came over the comm, "The beach is secure, proceeding to target." Hunched over their weapons Hammer and Dregs ran up the plateau in short sprints, stopping often to check for any signs of danger. Blitz, Torque and Dusty reached the edge of the jungle and were quickly out of sight.

Tivex leaned back in her chair, "And now we wait."

Silk gave her a sideways look, "I know you wanna be out there but you have to trust Hammer, he knows what he's doin'."

"But I am not here just to be Admiral Kagen's messenger. I can help, I want to do something."

Silk pointed to the scanner, "We're watching their backs. That is doing something."

"I suppose you are right," Tivex said sighing deeply.

Time ticked by slowly after that. Hammer and Dregs reached their target first. Hammer's voice rang clear over the comm, "We've secured the plateau, there's no sign of Alpha but we did find this." The vid screen lit up with his live feed. Deep trenches cut into the earth and a trail of metal leading south into the forest. Hammer's voice came back, "Looks like something heavy was dragged outta here. We're going to follow this trail and see what we can find."

Blitz chimed in, "Cap, you want us to come give you a hand?"

"No, you keep up the search on your end, I don't want to be here any longer than necessary. Dregs and I can handle it, if we find trouble we'll keep to the plan."

"What? You mean run away?" Torque jibed.

"I mean we'll stick to the plan. Now get back to work."

The comm went silent.

Half an hour passed before Hammer and Dregs finally found the end of their trail. The vid screen showed destruction unlike anything Tivex had seen before. Twisted hunks of metal strewn across the forest floor and hanging from broken trees, "Torque, what am I looking at?" Hammer asked.

"Looks like the landing assembly just to your right. Off to the left, that's an exhaust manifold. The rest of it I'm not too sure, it could be anything, but that's definitely shuttle wreckage."

Tivex looked at Silk who merely shook his head, "Slag, I never seen anything like that before." She turned her attention back to her screen, not knowing what to say at what she was seeing.

"Hais?" asked Blitz over the speaker.

Dregs growled from off screen, "It's definitely their style but how'd they get it in here?"

Hammer dropped down to his knees and picked up a small piece of fabric. Tivex stared at the screen, it was covered in sand, ragged and torn with rust colored stains around the edges. Her heart sank as Hammer brushed the sand away revealing the letters IEC, "I guess we found out what happened to Alpha."

There was a moment of silence for their fallen compatriots and for however jaded and battle hardened Team Seven had become, Tivex could tell they all felt the loss. It was almost touching in a way.

Then, as quietly as the moment had come, it was back to business, "Blitz," Hammer began, "I'm gonna need your hardware over here. If any of Kagen's mystery metal is around this scrap your scanners should be able to pick it up. Torque, you had better come with him, maybe there's something here you can use to get our communications system up and running. Dusty, head back to the ship. If it was the Hais, I want you there in case those motherless pigs show back up."

"On our way, Cap," replied Blitz.

"Keep your eyes open, boys, we might not be alone down here."

Tivex stood and stretched, pacing the length of the control deck, "Do you really think it was the Hais?" she asked Silk as she reached one window and started back towards the other.

"I don't know, they like to destroy the evidence. You know, try to make it look as though they were never there. They're incredibly destructive creatures so that part fits but they're not too smart. Dragging that shuttle into the forest would have taken a level of engineering I'm not so sure they're capable of."

"Could they not have just use grav pads?"

Silk scratched his chin, "They could have done that but then we wouldn't have any tracks at all. Something about this just feels wrong."

As dusk began to settle on the island, four silhouettes appeared on the eastern slope heading down the ridge line toward the ship. Three large in frame and one thin with uncontrolled hair.

"Where's Dusty?" Hammer asked as they stepped into the room.

Silk looked puzzled and shrugged, "I don't know, he hasn't made it back." The worry began to grow in his voice. He jumped on the comm, "Hey, Dusty, are you there? Can you hear me?"

The comm was silent.

"Dusty, it's Silk, do you read me? Are you hurt?" Silk turned to Hammer, "Maybe he's just lost. I'll send up a flare."

He reached for his console but Hammer grabbed his arm, "Don't even think about it. We don't need to draw any more attention to ourselves."

"You think I'm afraid of the Hais? Cap, we can't just leave him out there," Silks voice was almost panicked.

"It's not the Hais," answered Hammer calmly, "it's something else, something big."

"What? What do you mean?"

Torque pulled some pictures up on the vid screen, "I found this among the wreckage." The photo was hard to make out, a pile of torn and twisted metal, "This is the shuttles landing gear skid. As you can see, it's been torn in two." Massive tears and scratch marks were evident along the length of the skid as well as some parts which looked to have been crushed, "No Hais is capable of tearing a ship apart like this. Damage like this is obviously physical, not weaponry. And then there's this," Torque pointed to the trees, "not a single char mark, and nothing broken above the twenty-foot mark. If this was an explosion we'd have damage clear through the top of the canopy."

"Well, what is it?" Silk asked.

"We don't know," said Hammer, "but I sure as ash don't want it coming back."

Silk looked hard at Hammer, "Sir, we can't just leave him out there. What if whatever did this is still out there?"

"We're not leaving him anywhere, Dregs and I will go look for him."

"I'm coming with you," said Silk defiantly.

"No, we still need you with the ship," said Hammer.

Silk stood nose to nose with Hammer, "Sir, all due respect, but that's my best friend out there, so," he slowly repeated his last comment with emphasis, "I'm...coming...with...you."

There was a firmness in his voice, an unwavering loyalty to Dusty that Tivex knew Hammer wasn't going to beat. Not wanting to miss her opportunity she spoke, "I am coming too." She watched as Hammer began to shake his head but she quickly countered, "If Dusty is hurt he will need medial attention," which lacked the conviction of Silk's words but she hoped it was enough.

Hammer sighed and threw his hand in the air, "Fine, we'll all go. Shut her down."

"Aye, sir," said Silk, never taking his eyes from Hammer's. Only after Hammer showed he was not about to flinch, Silk turned and powered down the engines.

Tivex followed the group down to the boarding hatch. Hammer handed her a large combat rifle. He pointed to a button on the side, "Alright, firefight one oh one. This your safety, press to fire, depress to lock. Keep it locked unless I say otherwise. You stay close to me, when I run you run, when I fight you run. Is that perfectly clear?"

Tivex took the rifle and nodded.

With that, Hammer stepped through the door and onto the moonlit beach. Tivex followed. The sand was deep and difficult to walk in. Tivex trudged along behind Hammer trying to mimic his movements as he pushed his way almost effortlessly across the sand. After a few hundred feet the ground beneath her became firm once more.

A cool, salty breeze blew in off the sea as they made their way to edge of the forest. One by one they slipped through the brambles that guarded the large trees and stepped into the shadows of the canopy. Hammer raised a finger to his lips and gestured to the others. Two by two they fanned out with Tivex and Hammer taking the middle. Hammer activated a small light on the top off his weapon and picked his way slowly across the forest floor. The trees were thick here, long vines hung from their branches like great chains binding an imprisoned giant. Hammer's light burned through the darkness, chasing the shadows in front of them. Their footsteps fell silently on the damp leaves that blanketed the forest floor. More than once Tivex stumbled on a root or fallen branch and had to be hauled to her feet. For two hours they searched, until finally another light appeared in the distance flashing a steady rhythm.

Hammer was off like a bullet with Tivex in tow. They hurdled a few fallen trees and found Torque and Blitz standing on the edge of a precipice in a small clearing. Soon Silk and Dregs emerged from the trees as well. Hammer motioned for a quick perimeter search and secured the area.

When it was all clear Hammer finally lowered his weapon, "Talk to me."

Blitz gestured toward the sinkhole, "My bioscan is picking up a signal down there. It's not moving but the signal is strong. If it's him, he's alive at least."

Hammer walked to the edge of the hole and shined his light inside, "Looks like about a fifty-foot drop. If he didn't break his neck, he's damn lucky." He aimed his torch at the far side of the chasm but it disappeared into darkness, "Whoa, how big is this thing?"

"A little over six hundred feet around, sir," answered Blitz.

Torque let out a low whistle.

Tivex saw Hammer's jaw clench, "Well, we're not gonna help him from up here. Who's got a rope?"

Torque grinned, lowered his pack and began rifling through his supplies, "Oh, I was hoping I'd get a chance to try this!" He pulled out a long thin cord, "It's my new design, I call it 'Spider Silk'. High tensile strength and extreme flexibility all in a lightweight package."

Tivex saw Silk raise both eyebrows in disbelief at Torque's decision to name one of his inventions after the only thing Silk hated, spiders. She assumed what he hated the most was the indignity of having his name attached to it.

Hammer examined the cord, rolling it between his fingers, "Are you sure this stuff is strong enough?"

Torque almost looked offended and snatched the line out of his hands, "This is an Omarian farnite alloy filament. I've tested its tensile strength at over five thousand pounds per strand. Yeah, I think it'll hold up."

Hammer put his hands up defensively, "Okay, okay, take it easy. Blitz, I need an anchor."

Blitz grabbed hold of the line wrapping it securely around his bionic arm. Hammer tied the end around his waist and backed up to edge. He eyed the cord one last time, "Five thousand pounds you said?"

Torque nodded, "Per strand."

"Groovy. Well, here goes," Hammer stepped back and dropped from sight. Blitz stood steady, not showing the least bit of strain at having an extra two hundred pounds dangling from his arm. Foot by foot he let out the line until suddenly it went slack.

Torque's communicator sparked to life, "Okay, I'm at the bottom." Tivex released the breath she hadn't known she was holding. "The ground in here is soft, almost spongy. It's all dead leaves and twigs. Probably the only reason he's not dead."

"Do you want a couple of us to come with you, Cap?" asked Blitz.

"No, stay up top. If I get into trouble down here at least you'll only have me to get out. Blitz, where was that signal?"

"About twenty degrees to your right, maybe a hundred and fifty feet ahead." The comm was silent for a long time as Hammer worked his way across the pit. Suddenly Blitz broke the silence, "He should be there, just to your left."

"I've got 'em. He's unconscious but he's breathing."

Silk grabbed the line, "I'm coming down."

"No! Stay up top. I'll bring him…wait, what gray slag is that?!"

"Cap, you okay? What's going on?" Blitz shouted into the comm.

Nothing but silence.

"Hammer, can you hear me?"

"Slag this," hissed Dregs, "I'm goin' in after him."

"Cool it, I'm here," Hammer's voice came back on the comm, "it's okay, but you guys need to get down here and see this."

Silk pushed the others out of the way and took the lead, looping the strand around his waist and stepping off the side. Slowly, Blitz lowered them one by one into the pit. Tivex was the last to go. She looped the line around her waist imitating the others as best she could. Blitz smiled at her and offered his hand, "May I?"

She smiled back sheepishly and placed the line in his hand.

"The secret is you have to wrap it low around your, uh, well you know." His fingers fumbled with the knot as he tried to tie her off, "When you step back just sit on the line and push off the wall with your feet." When he was done Tivex stepped to the edge eying the wire thin lifeline. "Just sit in the sling. You'll be fine," Blitz's words were less than encouraging.

With a deep breath she stepped back off the edge and fell. Dangling from her waist, she smacked repeatedly against the wall of the cliff, spinning and twisting like a fish on a hook. Blitz hauled her back up, "Maybe we should just go together, huh?" He tied the line off around several large trees taking the slack in his large metal hand. At a gesture from Blitz, Tivex wrapped her arms around his neck and waist and off he went. Blitz took the wall in long bounding leaps. Swinging down the line like a creature born of the jungle. In a matter of moments, they were at the bottom.

Tivex's feet gingerly settled on the spongy surface, "Blitz, could you not tell anyone about that?"

"About what?" Blitz said giving her a friendly wink. Tivex smiled and started toward the others. Sinking to his knees with every step, Blitz's lip curled into a snarl, "Oh, the slaggin' ash take it all! Tell them I'll be right there," he called after her as he trudged through the debris.

Tivex was about to turn back and help him before she saw the menacing look in his eyes. She knew that look all too well these days. She was also beginning to understand that you could offer all the help in the world to any of these men but unless they wanted it, you'd be wasting both your time and breath. She simply nodded back to him but slowed her own pace anyhow.

When they reached the others, Dusty lay on his side, his shoulders rising slightly with every shallow breath. Tivex rushed to his side, thankful there was finally something she could do and then immediately sorry for being thankful. She ran through his vital signs and checked for broken bones or swelling, "He definitely has a severe concussion, a couple broken ribs, possibly a punctured lung. I cannot be certain without my instruments." She looked up to find no one was listening, their attention drawn to something in the darkness behind her.

Slowly she turned around. Wide eyed she stared into the shadows. She caught her breath, "Is that...?" She couldn't finish her thought.

A hulking mass loomed in the shadows. Large holes perforated its sides and large portions were missing entirely but the shape was unmistakable.

Torque bounced his light off the frame. Bright metal untouched by time shone like liquid silver, with dark, familiar scripting etched along the hull. "Yeah," he replied, "it might be a really good idea to call Kagen now."

GRAVEYARD

"REST FOR A WHILE, LIEUTENANT, YOU TOOK A NASTY FALL," TIVEX SAID AS SHE TRIED to coach Dusty back into bed. His injuries were thankfully not as serious as she'd first feared. A concussion and a couple of broken ribs which she had wrapped but no greater internal injury. Minor scrapes and bruises decorated his fair skin but overall nothing serious, "You are lucky to be alive, you know."

Dusty was determined to rejoin the Team, "I'm fine, ain't no little spill gowon keep Dusty Swearden down. Now which way did they git to?"

"That was no little spill, you fell nearly fifty feet."

"Darlin', I'm right as rain," he patted his sides and his face contorted in pain.

"They went to scavenge communication parts from Alpha's shuttle. In your state you couldn't catch up to them before dark anyway, now lay down."

Dusty huffed and then begrudgingly acquiesced, wincing as he laid back on his bunk.

"Those ribs need time to mend. You will be back out again before long," Tivex said as she checked his bandages again.

It had been less than twenty-four hours since they found Dusty unconscious at the bottom of the large sinkhole. The rest of the Team had gone back out to salvage what they could from Alpha's wreck, but that was not the ship on Tivex's mind. She closed her eyes and saw the image from the night before shining in her mind.

Such a beautiful discovery. Long and graceful, it had none of the hard edges of a classic starship but nonetheless there was no mistaking what it was. Three exhaust ports clustered at the rear meant the propulsion system was at least familiar. Aside from the holes burned into its hull, there were no other openings. No windows, no port holes, no hatch, just a solid piece of shimmering metal with no recognizable origination. There was no question this was the item they had been sent to recover but why did the IEC want it so badly, and why was it such a secret?

Her thoughts were interrupted by the opening of the boarding hatch. Hammer, Dregs, Torque and Blitz stepped into the room.

"Well?" Dusty asked, pushing himself gently into a sitting position, "Did y'all find what we need?"

Torque stepped forward, smiling and presented a two-foot long metal prong.

"That's what you boys went to find? An oversized barbeque fork?"

"This barbeque fork is what makes intergalactic communication possible, cowboy," Torque chided, "and without it, our communications are limited to the range of your big flaggin' mouth."

"Why you stone lovin' little..." Dusty tried to push himself out of bed but fell back in pain.

Hammer stepped forward, "Alright, that's enough. Torque, go get that thing installed, I want Kagen on the line by dusk. Everyone else clear out, Dusty needs his rest."

Torque turned and led the others out of the room with Tivex bringing up the rear. As she shut the door a small silver flask appeared in Hammer's hand which he handed to Dusty. The door latched softly and she shook her head as she turned down the hall. The last thing a man in Dusty's condition needed was a drink.

She rode the lift to the control deck with Torque, "How soon can you have that thing up and running?" she asked.

Torque looked at the transmitter as if waiting for an answer, "It'll only take about twenty minutes to install the new spacial transmitter but the actual calibration could take a few hours." He stepped off the lift and crossed the room to the communications terminal. He exhaled dramatically, "Ah, the work of a genius is never done."

Tivex passed the next few hours staring out the window at the beautiful island. The forest looked completely different by day. Colorful flowers carpeted the interior as far back as she could see. Her thoughts turned back the unknown ship. It was a small ship, much smaller than the Widow Maker but even at a third their size it would have been impossible to get into that clearing through the dense vegetation, "Do you think it was there before the trees?"

"Do I think what was where?" Torque asked as he tuned the transmitter.

Tivex started, she hadn't realized she had asked the question aloud. She stepped back from the window and turned to face him, "The ship from last night. Gage'ik said the metal predated known star flight. They did not fly it into that jungle and there was no sign it was dragged there like Alpha's shuttle. Maybe the forest grew around it?"

"Who knows? I wouldn't mind getting a little more time with her though and see what makes her tick. Oh well, maybe next trip. Okay, there we go," Torque dusted of his hands as he stood up, "she should be all ready to go."

Tivex opened her comm, "Captain, we are back online."

Soon everyone but Dusty was gathered in the control deck. Hammer took a seat in his oversized chair, "Have you tested it yet?"

Torque patted the terminal, "Not yet but it'll work. It's not as complex as it may seem."

"Good, let's get Kagen on the line. After that, I want off of this rock."

Torque punched in the codes and soon a very surprised Admiral Kagen appeared on the viewer, "Captain Dorran, I'm pleased to hear from you. Is everyone alright? We've been trying to reach you for a week. I'm afraid we assumed the worst."

"We're fine, Admiral, we lost our communication systems for a while but we found the pieces we needed among the wreckage of Alpha's ship."

"Excellent! You've found them then?"

Hammer shook his head, "Unfortunately, no. Aside from the actual shuttle we haven't found anyone."

"What about their aggressor?"

Hammer shook his head, "Negative. We've found traces of whatever it was but nothing solid."

Kagen leaned back in his chair, "Any signs of life anywhere?"

"Judging from what little traces of them we did find, I think it's safe to say Team Alpha was killed in action."

Kagen's eyes lowered, "I see. That is extremely unfortunate news. We'll notify their families immediately. Have you had any luck locating the main objective?"

"I believe we have." Hammer uploaded the images from the night before, "Does this look familiar to you?"

Kagen's eyes darted back and forth as he studied the slender ship with its indecipherable markings. Finally, he shook his head, "No, nothing I've ever seen before. No doubt that's what all the fuss is about though. Can you carry it back?"

Hammer looked at Torque. Torque thought for a minute and frowned, "It's theoretically possible. It should fit in the hold without a problem but the takeoff weight might be too much. We may have to shed some gear if we want to reach escape velocity."

Kagen rubbed his chin thoughtfully, "Do what you have to do, strip your ship bare if that's what it takes. This mission is a top priority. I'll pass this on to Master Admiral's Soren and Tall'ani. They'll want to know what you've discovered. Good work Seven, collect that ship and come home."

Blitz cut in, "Sir, we did encounter some resistance on our way here. If we strip down of weapons how are we supposed to defend ourselves on our trip home?"

Kagen frowned, "Resistance, huh? Let me guess, the Hais?" and he raised a questioning eyebrow to Hammer.

"I don't believe so, sir," answered Blitz quickly, "It wasn't a ship I was familiar with. It was too big to be Hais but it was fast, sir, much faster than it should've been. It was covered in scrap metal, pieces of other ships just welded together. Maybe they were scavengers but they were extremely aggressive and heavily armed."

As Blitz described their attacker, Kagen locked eyes with Hammer. Tivex didn't know what that look said but she could feel the significance of the exchange. When Blitz finished Kagen spoke again, "Yes, well, I'm glad you are alright. I wouldn't worry about running into any more trouble. When we didn't hear from you for a couple of days, Soren had Admiral Kosos send two more Teams to assist with the recovery. They should reach you in the next day or two. Just load up the ship and wait for your escor....SSK!...Ca..SSK!..Dor.....ZZT!....there?"

Torque smacked the side of the terminal as Kagen's image flickered in and out. Soon he was gone and the connection turned to static. The static turned to silence and from the silence a voice echoed, *"Met ko besamonkimet monmet il. Met monsut moncaan. Moncasa monhesh Velkaso!" "ZZT!...ZZT!"* Tendrils of black smoke rose from the electronics housing and there was silence once again.

A low growl emanated from the corner of the room. Dregs' fur bristled from his neck, his muzzle peeled back to reveal the sharp canines below. Hammer's eyes grew wide and the color drained from his face. Tivex and the others sat in confused silence, wondering at the strange words which had solicited such a reaction.

Blitz was the first to speak, "Those words, the last part, I've heard those words before."

Tivex remembered as well, "That was what we heard from the ship that attacked us. Velkaso." Her eyes met Hammer's, "What does it mean?"

Hammer's face was taught, his jaw clenched and there was an overly hateful stare in his eyes.

"It means," Dregs growled out from the corner, "that some people don't know how to stay dead."

Hammer raised his hand to silence Dregs and stood. His voice was cold and commanding, "Strip the ship. I want us to minimum weight tonight."

"Who was that?" Torque asked.

"First thing tomorrow we load that ship and we're out of here."

"But, sir," Tivex objected, "Admiral Kagen instructed us to wait for our escort."

"We don't have that kind of time. We'll have to meet them on the run. Torque, can you get the comm up and running again?"

"Who was that?" Torque insisted again.

"Never mind that! Can you get it running or not?"

Torque reached back behind the terminal and pulled out the long blackened prong, "Not without another one of these." He tossed the burnt transmitter to the floor, "Without that, we can't tell our escort where to meet us. We'd be running with no defenses and no communications so we may as well wait here-"

"WE'RE NOT WAITING!" Hammer bellowed as he slammed his fists down on his chair. From across the room, Dregs shot a low look towards Hammer and growled lowly. Hammer dropped his head to his chest and took a deep breath. Steadying himself, he looked back to Torque, "There's no time."

Even though he had tried to calm himself down, a mindless hate still filled Hammer's eyes. Tivex could feel the waves of rage emitting from the very depths of him just as easily as she could see something else as well, panic, fear maybe.

Torque looked back at Hammer and tilted his head. Anger began to surge in Torque's voice, "Okay, enough of this slag! Maybe you should just tell us what's going on, huh? How come you and Dregs seem to be the only ones that understand what we just heard? Who or what exactly was on that ship that ship attacked us? And why are you so afraid of waiting for backup?"

Tivex jumped in her seat as Hammer leapt out of his chair faster than she knew him capable of, "What?! You think I'm afraid of him?!" In another blur of movement, Dregs dove towards Hammer and pushed him back down into his chair.

Tivex saw Dregs' lock eyes with Hammer, grab his face and push his muzzle closer to his as she heard him growl, "No, you flaggin' ingrate, he ain't sayin' nothin' like that!" Dregs leaned in even closer and was barely able to be heard, "None of them know who 'him' is so shut it!"

She noticed the way Dregs scanned Hammer as he tried to swallow the rest of his fury while at the same time fighting it the whole way, even though Dregs outweighed him by a good two hundred pounds. He seemed unable to speak at first before Dregs finally accepted the fleeting nods Hammer gave him.

Hammer, jaw still firmly clenched, turned back to his brother, "I don't have time to explain myself, Torque, I just need you to trust me."

Torque's face had become red with anger but slowly it subsided. He pointed to the discarded transmitter, "Well, anyway then, without that, we can't call for help, we can't send our coordinates, we can't even enter Omarian space. So unless you know another way to..." Torque went suddenly silent. His eyes went wide as they bounced from side to side. A vulpine look of giddy anticipation began to cross his face, "Oh, wait a minute, wait just one slaggin' minute. I wonder if maybe, yeah…if we, or rather I, took…" He ran his fingers through his untamed hair. "It might just work!"

Hammer was out of patience, "Spit it out!"

Torque flushed with frustration, "It's just that going into space without communications is a terrible idea."

"So you've said," seethed Dregs.

"Right, I mean it's such a terrible idea that no one would do it. I mean no one in the history of space travel would be stupid enough to do it. Nobody."

"TORQUE!" Hammer yelled.

"I'm getting there!" Torque roared back, "My point is if nobody in the history of space travel would go up without some form of communication then it's likely no one in predated history would've either."

Hammer's initial reaction was the same as what Tivex was feeling. What was that supposed to mean? What difference did it make what anyone in predated history thought or did?

The second she realized what she just figured out in her head was the same second she saw Hammer's eyebrow rise with his understanding.

Hammer patted Dregs on the arm and walked over to the window. He looked out in the direction of the forest clearing, "Do you think you could activate it?"

"I have no idea but we have to bring the whole gray mess back here anyway, right? Let me go down and take a look while you guys get the Widow Maker prepped."

"It's getting dark."

"Then I'll take a nightlight, mother. Listen, do you want off this rock or not?"

Hammer smirked and nodded, "Take some grav pads with you. Might as well get it prepped to move while you're there."

Tivex moved to stand with Torque, "I am going with him."

Hammer thought for a moment before shrugging his assent, "Fine, you'll be more help to him than here anyway."

Tivex prickled at that comment but she remained silent. It was enough just to be getting her way.

"Keep your guards up, just because we haven't encountered any danger doesn't mean it isn't out there. And don't wander off, we don't have time for another search party. As for the rest of you, let's strip this bird to her bones."

As the rest of the Team began dismantling the Widow Maker's nonessential systems, Tivex and Torque disappeared once again among the dense foliage of the jungle. Torque took one last look as they stepped out of sight and shook his head, "Probably better I'm not here for this anyway."

They walked among the gnarled trees in silence. The flowers Tivex noticed were not as thick nor did their carpet extend as far as it had seemed from the outside. The light was fading quickly but they were still able to pick their way easily through the fallen branches and exposed roots that now littered their path.

They were halfway to their destination before Tivex finally spoke, "You worry about him. I have seen how you watch him."

Torque's eyes never left the path ahead of him, "Well, even though he's a stone loving block head, I'm allowed to worry. He is my brother after all."

Tivex cast her eyes down over her own granite complexion, "I have never much cared for that term."

Torque stopped walking and blushed with embarrassment, "I'm sorry, you know I don't mean you."

"I know," Tivex said as she kept walking, "but it is still an awful phrase. So what do you think he is hiding? What could that voice have meant?"

Torque jogged a few steps to catch up, "Who knows? He and that cat have more secrets than the entire High Council combined. I'll tell you one thing though, I've never seen his feathers ruffled like this before. And what did Dregs mean about not staying dead? If they don't want to talk about what happened to him back then, that's fine, but if they know something about whatever danger were facing then we deserve to know about it."

"I am sure he will tell us when the time is right."

"Yeah, right about the time we're neck deep in trouble. What are you so worried about him for anyway?"

Now it was Tivex's turn to blush, "I care about him, too. I still remember the way he used to be. I knew he was different now but I had no idea the severity of his transformation. He is so angry, Torque, so volatile. Maybe if he did not drink so much he would be better able to cope."

"Drink so much? What're you talking about?"

"Do you think I have not noticed the silver flask he hides inside his coat? I am not blind. His hands shake with dependency."

"Oh, that?" Torque said as he kicked at a pile of decaying leaves, "Well you're half right. It is a dependency problem for sure but that's not liquor he keeps in his flask."

"Well then what is he sipping morning, noon and night?" she asked scornfully.

Torque shrugged and cocked a half smile, "Helix."

Tivex stumbled over a root in surprise catching herself on a nearby tree.

"Relax," Torque said, "It's the real stuff, not as dangerous as the cheap street knockoff. Aside from Dregs, none of us know what really happened to him out there but when he came back, believe me, it was with more than just bad dreams. The doctors said if he quit cold turkey his body would just shut down. He takes little sips throughout the day to keep himself regulated. Too much and he'll hallucinate, too little and well, let's just say it'd get really bad really quick."

"So he will die without it?" Tivex asked. She was having a hard time taking this all in.

"Well, not right away. First come the shakes, he usually gets those in the morning before he starts his routine. Within twenty-four hours the real withdrawals begin. Convulsions, cold sweat, vomiting, the works. After a few days the visions start. What he sees aren't your run of the mill hallucinations, these are real brain tweakers. This is the point where most people lose their minds but Hammer was a special case, he didn't lose it the way others would've. I guess you develop a pretty tough psyche when your life's been one trip after another through the worst parts of hell. That's how they found him you know, floating through space in a rescue pod, tied to a chair while experiencing what you doctor types call 'violent hallucinations'. Can't say I blame Dregs for tying him down, I bet Hammer was a real handful. After that they say his body would just shut down, one system at a time over a matter of weeks. Slowly, and most likely very painfully, he would eventually die."

Tivex's head swam with this new information. She felt sorry for Vincent and guilty for having judged him so harshly, "I am sorry, I had no idea."

Torque gave her a small smile, "Why would you? Only the IEC and my family knew at first. The Team knows now, from time to time he gives us a little nip if we get hurt. The regenerative properties of that stuff are astounding."

Suddenly it was all making sense, "So that's why he gave some to Dusty."

"Sounds about right. How do you think the tin man survived long enough to get his chrome plated facelift?" Torque stepped through the trees and out into the clearing, "Time to get to work, sister."

Securing the filament to a nearby tree Torque wrapped the line around his waist and stepped off into the darkness. Tivex took a deep breath and stepped to the edge. The sun was gone now and her flashlight did little to illuminate the great pit before her. She turned and looked at the strand around her waist just as Blitz had shown her. Tonight was not the time for injurious error. She backed her heels to the edge, took another deep breath and stepped back. She dropped down as if expecting a chair to have appeared in midair. Much to her surprise she found support from underneath. Her feet planted firmly on the wall she gave a gentle push and released a bit of the line. Slowly she descended, a few feet at a time until once again she stood upon level ground.

"Don't be in such a hurry!" Torque chided sarcastically.

They crossed the spongy floor of the pit and shone their lights on the flawless silver skin of the spacecraft, "Okay, this is it!" Torque announced as he walked up to ship, "Help me find the door," he said as he ran his fingers along the smooth finish.

Tivex shone her light on the aft of the ship, "Or we could just walk through that gaping hole in the side."

Torque frowned at her, "Sure, if you wanna take the fun out of it, sheesh." Torque's light shone through the breach in the hull as he searched for hidden dangers, "It looks clear but you better let me go first in case something goes wrong."

One leg at a time Torque climbed through the opening. Tivex listened as his footsteps faded down the hall. Soon she was all alone, alone in the darkness of the pit. She ran her light across the hull of the ship. Large, dark holes riddled the sides. Suddenly Tivex had a revelation. This ship predated the IEC histories and it obviously hadn't been alone. How many of these predated civilizations had mastered star flight? Obviously, the IEC knew what they were looking for so why was there no record of their existence? More importantly, where were they now?

Soft footsteps down the hall brought her back to the present long before she heard Torque's voice, "It looks clear, come on in."

The inside of the ship was as perfect as the outside. Every surface smooth and reflective with no discernible beginning or end. It was as if the whole ship had been born of a single mold. The now familiar scroll work lined the walls of the corridor. Torque started down the hallway and motioned for her to follow. Something about the ship felt wrong to her, a distant nagging feeling that she couldn't quite place. She ran her hands down the hallway, tracing the intricate etching with her fingertips. The metal felt cold beneath her hands, like a window on a frosty morning, crisp, cool and clean. Suddenly she realized what was bothering her. It was all *too* clean. There was hardly any dust at all. It seemed almost as though the ship had been there for only a few months rather than millennia.

Small rooms opened to the right and left but Torque walked by them without as much as a glance. The hallway ran thirty feet in all before ending in a large round room. The room was plain and empty. There were no chairs, no terminals, nothing but the long oval shaped wall that encircled them. There were no windows and the holes that decorated the rest of the craft seemed strangely absent here.

"Well, she sure doesn't look like much," Torque said under his breath, "I wonder what the IEC wants with her."

Tivex crossed the room from one end to the other several times studying the writings on the wall, "Do you have any idea what they say?"

Torque shook his head, "I'm an engineer not a cryptologist." Torque's eyes perked and a small, wicked grin appeared on his face, "But it just so happens I know someone who is." His comm flashed as he punched in the codes, "Hey, Ironsides, you got a minute?"

Blitz's voice was strained and his breathing heavy, "I'm a little busy right now, runt. Can it wait?"

"I'm afraid not. I need to pick your brain...uh...literally."

Blitz sighed and something heavy crashed in the background, "This better be good, Torque."

"It'll only take a second. You have a language translator built into your system, right?"

"Yeah, as long as it's in the IEC database, I can translate it."

"How about encryption?" Torque asked.

"I can decode any alphanumeric system based in the two hundred fifty-seven core galactic languages."

"What if it's not based on those? How many characters would it take for you to decipher an entirely new language?"

Blitz laughed, "Are you serious? The program isn't written to run that way. It's a logic based algorithm, it needs a known constant in order to operate. As long as the original language can act in that fashion, any variable of that base language can be deciphered."

Torque rolled his eyes at Tivex, "Wow! That's so...boring. Seriously though, I need your brain. I need to know what this says." He pointed his comm to the wall.

"I'm telling you it don't work that way."

"Yeah, yeah, I get it but I can't do it on my own so just jack in and let me take a crack at it."

A solemn look replaced the grin on Blitz's face, "Forget it, shorty. I'm not letting you hijack my head again. Not after what happened last time."

"Come on, we need this. Hammer wants us out of here as soon as possible and I can't get our communications back up until I know what I'm dealing with. Besides, you know that was just an accident. I'll be careful, honest."

The grimace never left Blitz's face. He seethed out an exasperated breath through his teeth, "Fine, but it's not gonna do any good anyway." He pulled a long cord from his arm plugging it into a port on the base of his skull, "Be quick about it."

Tivex curiosity was piqued, "What happened last time?"

Torque grinned widely and blushed, "I, *may* have mind you, inadvertently disabled his short term memory function. It took a week to get him operational again, mostly because he kept stopping me every twenty minutes to ask what I was doing. It didn't help matters that Dusty and Silk kept messing with him, believe me. They kept ordering him around, making him do all the grunt work and telling him they were Master Admirals. It's not something I care to repeat."

"Or me," Blitz's voice echoed.

Tivex smiled. She was beginning to see that this was more of a dysfunctional family than a Star Team and she was feeling more and more at ease every day. Torque pulled a thin plate of glass from his pack and wired it to his comm. The screen lit up instantly. Lines of digital coding scrolled by at mind numbing speed but Torque didn't seem bothered by the pace. His eyes scrolled right along with the text, whistling some unknown tune while bobbing his head along with the rhythm. When he found what he was looking for, Torque tapped the code he needed and the rest disappeared, "Here we go," he said as the program opened, "this should scan the symbols and construct a basic alphabet. Hopefully that will give us a starting point."

Torque began scanning the walls but as the laser from his tablet touched the wall, the scroll work began to glow. Tivex stepped back as the light grew brighter and brighter until she had to shield her eyes from the glare.

"AHHH!" Blitz screamed from the comm.

Torque yanked the cable free and the glare from the ship softened, "Are you okay? What happened?" Genuine concern filled Torque's voice.

"Whoa, that was a rush! Yeah, I'm okay. What did you do?" asked Blitz as he pressed his hands to his temples and tried to shake his head.

"I don't know," Torque stared at his tablet, "I truly don't know. I scanned the writing and it was like the ship fought back. Some kind of defense mechanism I guess. Are you sure you're okay?"

"Yeah. Yeah, I'm fine," Blitz rubbed his eye, "I don't think it was a defense though. It was uploading files. Massive files."

"Files on what?"

Blitz shook his head and blinked into the screen, "Star maps mostly but ones I've never seen before. I don't know exactly, it was cut off mid feed."

"Any luck on the language?"

Blitz shook his head again as if trying to clear out a fog only he could see, "No, not a clue. Maybe if you hook me back up I can find something."

"Slag that, I'm not gonna fry your circuits. We'll have to just see what we can do without you. At least it seems to be on. Hmph, what kind of machine has a few thousand-year-old power source that still runs? I gotta check this thing out. Why don't you get back to work and stop being such a slacker?"

Blitz made a vulgar gesture into the screen and closed the comm.

Tivex placed her hands over the glowing script, "It feels warm."

Torque shot a look at her, "Be careful, I don't need it zapping you too." Before the words were even out of his mouth the walls began to glow brightly once more. Tivex jerked her hands away but the light still grew brighter. Torque grabbed her by the arm and pulled her to the center of the room. Soon they were engulfed in the light and when the walls dimmed once again everything had changed. Where nothing had been mere moments ago, long control terminals now stood.

"How did you do that?" Torque whispered under his breath.

Tivex stood, gaping in awe, "I...I am not sure."

Torque stepped cautiously up to the machines, running his hand lightly over the complex array of buttons. Each button was marked with a symbol, some like the markings on the walls and many more Tivex did not recognize. Torque dropped his sack to the ground and ran his fingers through his hair, "This is going to take a while," he turned to Tivex, "look, nothing's blown up yet so I imagine we're safe." He pulled a large bundle of dinner plate sized disks from his bag and tossed them into her arms, "You might as well go strap on the grav pads, Hammer's gonna want us to move this thing ASAP."

"And how exactly do you plan to get it out of this hole?" Tivex asked crossing her arms over the grav pads.

Torque scratched his head in thought, "Honestly, I hadn't considered it." He turned from her back to the console, "One miracle at a time, if I can't get our communications running again nobody's going anywhere. Now, if you don't mind, I need to think." Torque made a shooing motion over his shoulder towards her.

Tivex gave a sarcastic bow to the back of his head and left the room. As she walked down the hall loud music began to echo through the ship. Loud, awful music. She laughed to herself as she climbed out through the hole, Torque claimed his music helped him think but she found it hard to believe anyone could function in that racket.

Outside, the terrible noise was muted and Tivex spent the night working in peace. Grav pads were not complicated devices themselves but installing them was a long and arduous process. She leaned her rifle against the fuselage and pulled the flashlight free, then she slung the bundle over her shoulder and set to work. Even with four hands to help her it was morning before she finished. The soft light of dawn filtered down through the hole in the canopy, chasing away the darkness of the pit. For the first time since they found it, Tivex was able to see the entirety of the hole. The ship sat a good two hundred feet from their point of entry and it was another fifty feet or so to the opposite wall but it wasn't the size of the pit that held her attention. At the base of the nearest wall sat a large cave. The opening ran a third of the way up the cliff face and it wasn't the only one. Even in the dim gray of an early dawn, Tivex could make out four other caverns of similar size scattered around the perimeter.

With a final turn she wrenched the last of the grav pads into place and slid back to the ground. Her body ached from the long night's work and she longed for sleep but the faint music escaping through the holes in the hull told her Torque was still hard at work. She turned from the ship and walked to the opening of the nearest cave. It was warm and moist with a pungent smell of decay hanging stagnant in the air. Tivex looked back toward the ship. Torque was already busy, there was no reason to bother him. She took a step inside, then another. With every step the air grew hotter and the smell grew stronger. She wrinkled her nose against the sweet stench but her curiosity urged her onward. The ground sloped down, deep into the belly of the island but the path was wide and easy to follow. The walls of the cave were the bright red of fresh clay and they were well worn, polished smooth like river rock. Within minutes the light of the entrance had vanished behind her but still she pressed on.

"Ti…w…you…" The walls of the cave were causing too much interference to hear Torque clearly but the intent of the message was clear enough, it was time to go.

Tivex turned to leave when something orange and yellow caught her attention. There was something strangely familiar about the object. Torque could wait, this would only take a second. A dozen feet below her the tunnel forked and it was at that juncture that she found it. A long orange sack stretched between the floor and the ceiling. It looked dry and tough like thick leather. In the midst of the orange leather hung a translucent orb colored yellow by the thinning of the membrane. Tivex gasped as her light made its way down the shaft. Dozens of similar structures lined the walls for as far back as she could see. She took a few steps closer, shining her light on the orb in front of her. There was something inside, something dark and opaque but difficult to make out.

The orb glowed brightly under the light like a small moon in a starless sky. Tivex placed her hand delicately on the surface, feeling the warmth of the life within. The creature inside began to stir in response, retreating to the far side of its enclosure. The liquid inside the egg swirled, clouding her view even more. Tivex leaned closer, willing her eyes to see through the haze, to make out what manner of creature was concealed within. Long silver tentacles reached cautiously toward her, exploring the wall between them until they were aligned with her hands. For a long moment she stood there, marveling at the life she had found. Then suddenly the creature appeared, slamming its body against the inside of the egg. Horrible gnashing teeth fought to reach her.

Tivex screamed and stumbled back, dropping her light as she fell onto a nearby pile of wet branches. She fumbled to regain her footing on the slippery cave floor. Reaching out blindly for something to hold onto her hand fell upon something soft. Cloth. She grabbed the cloth firmly testing its strength as she attempted to stand once more but the cloth gave way pulling something heavy and hairy along with it. Tivex screamed again as she scrambled to escape from her attacker. Coarse hair filled her mouth as she gasped for air, pushing and clawing her way to freedom when suddenly warm hands grabbed hold of her own and pulled her to safety. She was cold and wet and furious. Her daggers appeared in her hands as she squinted in the bright light of her rescuer.

"Whoa, easy 'Vex, it's me," Torque turned the light on himself for proof, a sickly grimace replacing his trademark grin. He turned his light back to Tivex, shining it down by her feet, "Oh, slag, poor Gage'ik."

A mass of tawny fur lay among a pile of broken bones beside her. Tivex could still taste the musk of Gage'ik's fur in her mouth. Using the toe of her boot, Tivex drew a line in the blood soaked cavern floor and watched it disappear as the fluid returned to its place. She brought her hands into the light. They were dark red and slick, with clumps of fur and clotted blood. As a medic she had seen a lot but the stench of death and decay that covered her was all too much. Hands on her knees she bent over, emptying the contents of her stomach onto the floor. She spat the last of it out, not daring to wipe her mouth.

Torque helped her up, handed her the light then stepped back to examine the egg, "What are they?" The creature was still flailing against the side, gnashing its teeth, trying desperately to escape.

"I have no earthly idea but they are truly awful creatures."

Torque brought his sidearm up to the egg sac wall, level with the creature's head, "Should we just exterminate them?" He asked cocking the hammer back.

He placed his finger on the trigger when a sharp sound from back up the corridor caught their attention. A hollow sound and far away but one utterly unmistakable to both of them.

Gunfire.

MAKE OR BREAK

AS FAST AS THEIR LEGS COULD CARRY THEM, THEY RAN BACK THROUGH THE CAVE BURSTING into the morning light of the pit. The sounds were louder now, clearer and becoming more frequent. They raced across the pit and up the rope, climbing hand over hand to the top. Tivex's muscles strained but the adrenalin coursing through her veins gave her the strength she needed. On through the forest they ran, deftly dodging the fallen branches and twisted trunks that attempted to block their way. It occurred to her that they may not make it in time to help, it might already be too late. She pushed those thoughts away. There had to be enough time, they had to be okay. At last they broke through the tree line and onto the beach.

Tivex was the first through the trees and the scene before her stopped her dead in her tracks. The beach was littered with crates and parts, anything that wasn't absolutely necessary for their trip home was scattered on the ground below, just adding to the overall chaos of the attack. A dozen silvery tentacles as thick as trees churned the sand below the creature. It stood nearly as tall as the Maker herself. Long, scissor-like claws protruded from a scaly, muscular body that shimmered like chain mail in the sun. A line of spiny fins ran down its back and two more fanned out on either side of its head behind a set of large glowing yellow eyes. Gill slits on its neck gave way to a great gaping maw of piranha-like teeth.

Silk and Blitz fired from atop the Widow Maker with only their side arms. On the beach, Dregs and Hammer danced around the creature's swinging tentacles, firing long guns from a nearby crate they had unloaded. Torque was already on the move kicking up a cloud of sand behind him as he ran. Tivex only hesitated for a moment before following his lead. She pulled the daggers from their sheaths as she ran, regretting quickly that her rifle was still back in the pit. As they got closer, the sheer size of the creature was overwhelming. It smashed against the side of the ship, raking its deadly claws across the hull and snapped its pincers at Blitz and Silk. Torque reached the fight first, but instead of firing he began searching containers.

Tivex ran to help, "What are you doing?" she asked, screaming to be heard above all the gunfire.

Torque didn't respond but just kept digging. Finally, he came up with two silver bands. Shouting, he tossed them quickly to Hammer.

The bands crackled to life as Hammer slipped them over his fingers, "Keep the gray thing away from the ship!" he thundered as he disappeared into the tangle of snaking tentacles.

A loud popping sounded from somewhere in the tangled mass and the creature reeled in pain. A screeching howl escaped its lipless mouth and it smashed against the side of the Widow Maker. The Maker rocked hard against the blow sending Silk and Blitz tumbling over the side and onto the soft sand below. Silk was still winded from the fall but Blitz was already on his feet running for the nearest crate of weaponry. He pulled two large caliber belt fed rifles from the crate, firing both at once he began to back the creature down. Another loud popping let her know that Hammer was still alive and delivering as much damage as he could. The creature writhed in pain against the two assailants. Backing away until its tentacles splashed against the tide, the creature reared as Hammer hit once more. The electricity coursed through its body, amplified by the salt water in which it now stood. Black smoke rose as the creature screeched one last time before collapsing on the beach.

One of the tentacles flung to the side and Hammer emerged, dusting the sand from his clothes. Tivex sighed in relief as he walked back toward the rest of the Team but as he moved the creature began to stir once again. Shifting its hulking body back and forth in an attempt to rise. Hammer sneered violently and appeared ready to finish the job as he turned to face the creature with no shred of regret. He squeezed the bands enveloping his knuckles which fizzled and faded with the last of their power. Hammer turned to retreat but the creature recovered and a silvery tentacle shot out to wrap around his waist. Hammer beat against the animal as its grip grew tighter.

Tivex watched in horror as Hammer struggled for his life. Something had to be done. Daggers in hand, she ran to his aid. The creature swiped with its massive claw but Tivex would not be deterred. Swipe after swipe missed their mark as she ran on dodging and weaving until she reached her target. Jumping up she grabbed hold of a thick spine and climbed swiftly up the creatures back to sink her daggers into the soft flesh of its gill slits. Orange slime oozed from the wounds on its neck. The creature thrashed violently, releasing Hammer and throwing Tivex to the ground. It turned toward Tivex, no longer interested in the ship, determined to destroy this new threat. With Hammer out of harm's way, Tivex raced for the safety of the ship. The creature was in close pursuit, its tentacles wriggling behind her like a nest of serpents. Her boots dug deep for traction, reaching for the protection of the ships walls with every step. Tivex spared a look for Hammer. His body still lay where it had fallen. She hoped desperately that he was alive, that she hadn't been too late and that this insanity had somehow all been worth it. A silver tentacle shot out swatting her leg as she ran. The toe of one boot caught the heel of the other and she tumbled face first to the ground in a cloud of sand. She scrambled to her feet, spitting the gritty substance from her mouth as she did so. She had barely stood when the creature was upon her, hammering its massive claw down on top of her. Too panicked to move, Tivex raised her arms in a futile defense of her life.

From behind her, something came from out of nowhere and knocked her out of the way just as the claw smashed into the ground. A pair of mirrored sunglasses flew through the air and landed on the beach in front of her, their lenses shattered by the impact. Tivex looked around trying to find her rescuer, trying to find any sign of Silk. As the monster raised its claw she found him, his broken body crushed and driven deep into the sand. The creature raised its claw again, determined to hit its mark. Tivex knew there was no escape. She lowered her head and awaited the final blow.

With a whirring sound from behind her, the Widow Maker's last heavy artillery gun came online. She lifted her eyes just in time to see the first round pierce the monsters thick hide. Then another and another, tearing through the creature at an incredible rate. From bottom to top the bullets sawed through the creature until at last its screams were silenced. The whirring sound returned as the gun spun down.

Tivex turned toward the ship. Through the windows of the control deck she could see Dusty, holding his side as he surveyed the scene from above. Even from that distance she could see the concern in his bright blue eyes.

Tivex turned back to the horrific sight of Silk. He'd sacrificed himself to save her. She felt guilty and honored and sad all at the same time. Blitz was already by his side, "He's still alive!" Blitz shouted, "But he's fading fast, massive internal injury. Hammer! Get your ass over here!"

Tivex seemed to be the only one surprised when Hammer lifted himself off the ground and began to jog in their direction. She stood, gaping, as he knelt next to Silk removing the flask from his pocket and emptying the bright green contents down Silk's throat. He cracked his neck and looked down as his fallen shipmate, "There, that'll keep him alive for now but we need to patch him up and get the hell out of here, that stuff isn't gonna last for long. Kagen's backup ship'll have to wait, we're leaving."

Torque interjected, "Bro, we still don't have a radio. We can't even get clearance to a system with medical facilities. Without some help either from IEC or that alien wreck we've got no chance."

"We'll discuss the particulars later, get him up and off this beach, people!"

Seeing that he was still breathing and the bleeding had slowed immensely, Tivex assisted the others in getting Silks broken body back aboard the Widow Maker. They carried him into an empty room which also served as the makeshift medical deck where Tivex was able to get him temporarily stabilized. For the second time, she found herself trying to save the life of one of Team Seven's members who had given their own life to save someone else's. She scanned his body and shook her head, without a miracle Silk wasn't going to make the trip home. Hammer had pulled Dregs and Torque aside to let her work and she could hear them talking behind her. Tivex pulled her stethoscope off and quickly tried to figure out what to say to Hammer when Blitz grabbed her arm first, his eyes scanning her for all they were worth.

She felt the cold steel through her shirt as she looked into his eyes and lowered her voice to him, "There is not much I can do for him."

Blitz's blue eye narrowed at her, "Don't give me that slag," he hissed, "I was twice as bad as he is and I'm still here."

Tivex was about to reply when Hammer's voice became louder behind them. She stood and turned towards them as he said, "So, you were able to get that things radio working?"

Torque lowered his eyes, "Well, no, not exactly. I, well, that is we," he gestured to Tivex, "we got a lot of stuff working, cool stuff. I'm just not sure what it all is. I'm working on decoding the language but it takes time. Give me a day and we're out of here."

Dregs stepped forward, "My captain now, Silky don't got a day and you know it. The lad needs medical attention, a hospital at the very least. The other bad news be we don't know how many of those bloody things are out there and need I remind you that Velkaso could be on his way. Staying here longer than another minute is madness."

Hammer looked at Tivex and she got the feeling he was seeing her clearly for the first time. He looked her up and down, "What happened to you?"

The now dry blood that coated her skin was caked with sand and a fresh layer of splatter from the monster's violent end. "It is not my blood," Tivex said sadly, "we found Team Alpha."

Tivex and Torque began filling him in on everything that had transpired, the glowing letters, the Blitz download, the eggs, Alpha, everything.

When they were finished Dregs let out a low growl and flattened his ears, "Perfect, so we're sitting on a nest of those things?" He turned to Hammer and hissed, "I'm telling you we need to get off this rock right now."

"I agree," Hammer said, "Blitz, have you learned anything from the files you downloaded?"

Blitz shook his head, "Nothin' yet, Cap. I didn't get it all and most of what I did get is still formatting. If I get anything useful I'll let you know."

Hammer looked at Silk, his breathing was labored and shallow. He rubbed his chin in thought and looked at Torque, "Fine. Get it loaded, you have four hours to get that ship into the cargo bay. You can figure out how it works on the ride home. Take Blitz and Dregs with you, they should be all the muscle you need."

"You want me to clear a forest, haul an alien ship out of a fifty-foot hole and drag it two miles back here in four hours? How exactly do you expect me to do that?" asked Torque.

"With these, genius," Hammer kicked the lid off of a crate at his feet revealing a pile of high explosives.

Torque's eyes grew wide and Tivex thought he might start to drool, "Yeah, that could work."

Torque and the other two raced off to secure the alien vessel with their new cache of explosives in hand. Without waiting for Tivex to say anything, Hammer cast a look at her and then to Silk. He looked as if he already knew the prognosis but was unable to get a word out.

Tivex took several deep breaths and tried to figure out what she was going to do about Silk. He wasn't dead but that was the only good news.

"How is he, Doc?" Dusty asked, limping into the room.

Tivex shook her head, "Not good, but at least he is alive. I do not have the equipment to deal with damage this severe. We need to get him to a real medical facility."

Concern filled Dusty's voice, "We're more'n a week away from the nearest help. How long can you keep him holdin' on?"

Tivex hung her head, "Two, maybe three days. Perhaps less."

Tears welled in Dusty's bright blue eyes as he held his friend's hand. Silk was still unconscious. His body was covered from head to toe in dark purple bruises. Thin lines of blood trickled from his nose and left ear. His eyes were swollen shut and a large gash ran the length of his cheek.

Tivex placed a comforting hand on Dusty's shoulder, "I am sorry, this is all my fault."

Hammer rose from the corner where he had been quietly contemplating, "It's not your fault, it's mine. We should never have let our guard down in the first place but nobody is dying today so suck it up, both of you."

Tivex glared at Hammer. How could he be so insensitive?

"No, not today," she replied, "but Omaria is the closest planet with the necessary equipment. It would take us five days to reach it if we left now and used the overdrive most of the way. If we overheat those fuel cells, then we are all no better off than he is." She didn't want to finish that thought out loud but the damage was already done. A look of hopeless despair washed over Dusty.

Hammer waved her off, "We aren't blowing the drive core and Silk isn't going to die. We're gonna put him in the ice box till we can reach Omaria. Do what you can to patch him up and then let's wheel him into the rescue pod. It worked for Blitz, it'll work again."

Dusty lifted his head, "Cap, that was just a few hours, this right here is a weeks' worth of travel."

"Regardless, it's all we have so it has to be enough. Meanwhile I need someone on those guns in case something else shows up. If we are on a nest, I can't imagine we'll be alone for long."

Dusty snapped a halfhearted salute and left the room, not a glimmer of hope shining through his mask of dread. When he was gone Tivex turned on Hammer, "The cryo unit is meant to slow down your bodies functions in order to conserve the rescue pods life support system. It is not a true cryogenic freezer. He will still continue to bleed. I cannot do anything about that without cutting him open-"

"Then do it."

Tivex was cut off mid-sentence, staring at Hammer, hoping she hadn't heard him correctly. He stood in front of her, his arms crossed firmly across his chest, "Whatever you have to do Tivex, I want you to do it."

Tivex pulled a shiny stainless steel gun from a nearby drawer. She pulled the trigger and orange foam rushed from the nozzle, "Do you know what this is?" she asked, wiping the foam on the countertop, "This is a clotting agent for sealing open wounds during combat. It is meant to keep you alive until you can get real medical treatment." She reached in another drawer and pulled out a long syringe, "This is an Akoni tranquilizer. This single vial could knock out this whole Team for the ride home but it will not do a thing to prolong your life. Everything in this room is for temporary patchwork or easing the suffering of the too far gone. This is not a hospital. You are not equipped for the level of surgery you're asking me to perform." Her eyes began to burn and she closed them tight against the frustrated tears that were building inside.

Hammer reached out, taking her hand and placed it gently over Silk's broken body, "I know we don't have everything you need. I know you're afraid but right now you're all he has and this is his only chance. We don't have the luxury of best case scenario, we never did. We do what we can, with what we have, wherever we are and we do a damn good job at it too. Team Seven didn't build our reputation on ideal circumstance, we took chances, rolled the dice, faced odds no one else would even consider. We always delivered because in this outfit, no one is allowed to give up. You're going to save this man, Tivex, not because you're a great doctor, not because you owe him your life but because this is the price of being Team Seven, victory in the face of certain defeat. If you want to be one of us, then it's time to start working miracles."

A loud explosion sounded somewhere in the distance, "Sounds like Torque isn't wasting any time. Good."

Hammer turned to leave when Tivex grabbed his arm, "Why are you not hurt? That creature out there was crushing you, I saw it happening, but you walk around as if it were nothing. Why are you not on this table as well?" Hammer pulled away and continued towards the door, "Is it the Helix?" she called after him.

Hammer's head whipped back around, eyes blazing. He looked her up and down as if trying to discern how much she knew.

She decided to save him the effort, "Torque told me. He said you came back with the addiction and that you cannot quit or you will die. Is that true?"

Hammer nodded slowly and pulled the flask from his coat, "I don't need much, just a few sips a day but without it there's a slow and painful death around the corner."

Tivex saw the opening and pushed on, trying to keep the momentum up, hoping she might finally get some answers, "That still does not explain how you are not dead, or at the very least gravely injured. How did you survive that? I know Helix can be used to speed cellular regeneration, but you just walked away. It should not be possible."

Hammer ran his hands over his torso, drumming his fingertips on his ribcage, "My situation does have its advantages, I suppose," he half grinned, "there's as much of that slagging stuff in my veins as there is blood. My bones are twice as dense as they should be and they're hard to break. Most of the wounds I get heal up pretty quickly too. It's saved my life more than a few times but it came with a hefty bar tab. Guess I'll be around for a while. You know, as long as the snake juice holds out that is."

"Torque said you give it to them sometimes when they are hurt. I saw you give some to Dusty and he seems to have made amazing progress. You gave some to Silk, will that save him too?"

Hammer opened the flask and turned it over. A bright green droplet formed on the rim before falling to the floor below, "What I gave him wasn't enough to correct that kind of damage. It bought us some time, that's all. Even if I'd had enough to help heal him completely, I wouldn't risk a dose that size."

Tivex stood frozen in place, entranced by the small green splatter mark at his feet. Hammer returned the flask to his coat pocket and held his shaking hand in front of him, "Looks like Silk isn't the only one racing the clock," he chuckled darkly, "better get to work, Doc, he's counting on you." With that he turned and walked out of the room.

Tivex searched the med deck for tools. There would be time to sort through this new information later, right now she had to perform a miracle. Finally, she had scraped together enough for a rudimentary surgery. It wasn't going to be pretty but it was the best she could do. She gave Silk a shot of the Akoni tranquilizer though she doubted he would have felt anything in his state anyway. She picked up a small knife she'd stolen from the mess hall and pressed it firmly into his abdomen. She pushed all thoughts of Hammer away as she made her first incision, "Stay with me, Silk," she prayed, "by the Light, please stay with me."

Torque wished Tivex had come along, he enjoyed his friend's company but he knew she needed to stay behind. Silk had saved her life and she was a medic after all. So he, Dregs and Blitz set out. With little time to accomplish their task, Dregs and Blitz began wiring the forest for demolition while he ran ahead to work on the problem of getting a three-hundred-foot ship out of a fifty-foot hole.

Soon he was again sliding down the Spider Silk into the sinkhole. Any fatigue he may have felt from the previous night's work was long forgotten as he set to solving this new problem. Thankfully, he'd had Tivex attach the grav pads already. They needed that kind of head start if they were going to hit their time window. He activated the grav pads and watched as the craft began to rise off the ground. It hovered much higher than he expected. While most objects its size would hover at only a few feet, this ship was floating nearly ten feet in the air like a large silver balloon. Suddenly, Torque remembered something from Gage'ik's report. She held that long piece of metal, remarking on how light it was, almost weightless she had said. It was all too clear now, if the whole ship were composed of this metal then it likely weighed very little. Torque rolled his eyes in frustration that they probably didn't need to strip the Maker after all. Oh well, he thought, too late to change it now.

Torque surveyed the pit, looking for a way out. His mind raced with scenarios. He imagined improvised crane systems and pulleys with timber for counterweight. He dreamed huge mechanical monstrosities that could be developed to serve his needs but ultimately simplicity won out. They needed a ramp. The cave they had explored earlier that day would do nicely. Torque shouldered his pack and headed toward the black mouth of the cave.

One by one he secured the explosives he carried to the cavern walls. Loud explosions from the forest above made the walls tremble and his heart jump. It took two hours to finish the job, fighting the urge to vomit as he worked his way back toward the stench of death and decay. When he was done he walked back out and gazed at the entrance, thinking to himself that this plan would serve two purposes, providing them with a way out and providing Team Alpha with a proper, albeit improvised, burial. An image flashed through his mind with that thought. An image of Gage'ik, standing before the camera after giving her report, and sliding a long piece of metal into her belt. Torque pressed his palm to his forehead, how could he have missed that. Back into the cave he ran, searching for the one piece which had started this whole mess.

The creatures in the eggs were more active now, slamming themselves against the sides in an effort to escape, as if they knew his plan. Torque slid to a stop on the blood soaked floor shining his light on Gage'ik's tawny mane. Her lifeless eyes bulged in their sockets. Her skin, so perfectly tan in her report, was now black and purple, giving way beneath his touch. Torque's stomach heaved as her flesh sloughed off her bones. He pulled her body up to a sitting position and saw the bright reflection of something metal glinting from her waist belt. He reached around and gave the piece a sturdy tug but it didn't budge. Gage'ik's body, bloated with decay, held it tight against her belt.

Torque's nostrils filled with the smell of rot as he struggled to free her belt. The crack of leather finally giving away echoed through the cavern but the belt still wouldn't budge. The sounds of trickling water splashing on the floor behind him caused Torque to turn around. Two silver tentacles wriggled through a tear in the egg sac. A steady stream of fluid poured from the side, mixing with the blood below in rancid pools. Another sharp crack came from further down the tunnel followed by another and another. Tentacles waving, struggling to escape, while large gnashing teeth attempted to chew their way to freedom. There was no time left but something told Torque not to leave without this piece. Desperately he struggled, pulling on the belt to release the clasp but the leather strap refused to give. The wet smack of bulbous bodies plopping on the ground erupted around him. He shined his light down the corridor, hundreds of tentacles slithered his way, topped by dozens upon dozens of snapping claws and teeth. The creature in the egg beside him plopped to the ground and lunged for his legs. Torque snatched up his rifle and cut the creature down in mid leap. He fired a few rounds down the corridor but he could tell from the rising cacophony of sharp cracks and wet slaps and plops that he was gravely outnumbered.

There was no more time to be nice about this, "Sorry, Gage'ik," Torque said as he threw her body to the ground. He placed his feet firmly on her torso grabbing her belt with both hands and stood up. Her body squished under his weight and vile fluid oozed from her nose and eyes but finally the belt gave way. Torque reached down and grabbed the shard just as the first creature reached him. It leapt from the darkness, knocking him onto his back. Strong tentacles wrapped around his throat, squeezing until he could no longer breathe.

He reached for his fallen rifle shoving it between himself and the sharp claws that threatened him. The tentacles squeezed tighter and his vision began to darken. With the last of his strength he pushed the creature back and swung his rifle violently at its fish-like head. There was a hollow, wet thud as the butt of his rifle connected. Immediately the tentacles released and the body of the creature fell silently to the floor. Torque shouldered his rifle and fired into the darkness. Pieces of the monsters flew through the air but still they came. Flashes from the gunfire showed their numbers were growing by the second. Snatching up the metal shard he turned and ran. Back through the tunnel he bolted as fast as his legs would carry him. Blitz and Dregs stood just inside the entrance, bewildered looks on their faces. Torque never broke his stride. Grabbing each by an arm he turned them toward the pit screaming for them to run.

Outside the cave Dregs and Torque sprinted for safety but Blitz sank into the spongy floor of the pit. His steps were determined but far too slow to get safely away in time. Moments later the creatures appeared, snapping and chomping, climbing over one another to reach them.

"Blow it!" Blitz yelled as he pulled one leg free only to have it sink down again with his next step, "Blow it now!"

Torque reached for his detonator and handed it to Dregs, "If they break my line, let 'er rip!"

He ran for the entrance as fire flew from the barrel of his rifle in short, violent bursts. One by one he cut them down. A pile of slimy wriggling bodies made a line across the cave and across that line no creature survived, but he couldn't stop the onslaught. For every one he killed it seemed two more took its place. When his rifle ammunition was exhausted he pulled free his sidearm. His wild untamed hair gave him a maniacal look as he stood firing his pistol into the tunnel. He never stepped back, never gave any ground. He stood in the caves entrance surrounded by explosives and emptied his weapon into the endless sea of enemies.

A furry hand grabbed his coat spinning him around, "Move it, short stack, he's clear. Time to haul out," Dregs raspy voice said but was barely audible above the ringing in Torque's ears.

Together they ran for safety. Dregs activated the detonator as soon as they too were clear. A large explosion rocked the basin. The frontline of creatures cleared the cave but those behind were engulfed in flame and buried under tons of rock and earth. Dregs and Blitz used their side arms to quickly dispatch the few that survived and soon it was quiet once again.

Torque's communicator broke the silence, "Y'all alright? We heard gunfire," came Dusty's voice as Torque fell to his knees and vomited violently.

"Yeah, yeah, Dusty, we're fine," Blitz said, patting Torque on the back, "just fine."

Tivex pulled the last stitch tight and knotted the end. For what seemed like the hundredth time that day she washed the blood from her hands. Silk was going to survive, she was sure of that now. Despite her lack of materials, the surgery had actually gone quite well. His internal damage had been significant but thankfully nothing beyond repair. She was proud of herself. Tivex patted Silk gently on the chest and said a silent prayer of thanks to the Light. She made sure Silk was stabilized and then took him to the escape pods cryo unit. Tivex laid Silk down and lowered the lid. Pressing a numbered sequence into the pad, the glass of the unit began to frost over with Silk inside. Tivex made sure everything was functioning properly and then returned to the lift to join the others.

She stepped off the lift and into the control deck. "How's our patient, Doc?" Hammer asked as she entered.

"Silk is good, Captain, great actually, I mean considering what he went through."

"Is he going to make it?"

Tivex nodded. "Yes, he should make a full recovery with time, though he still needs a proper hospital to monitor his progress."

Tivex watched as Hammer nodded his approval at her, "That's good," Hammer said as he pulled his flask from his coat and took a swig, "and you were worried."

Tivex was incensed, "I thought you said you did not have any more?"

Hammer smirked, "I thought you said you couldn't save him. So we both lied."

Tivex's face glowed red with anger.

"I don't know what you're so upset about. The way I see it it's the least you deserved for sticking your nose in my business."

Tivex was about to defend herself when Dusty cut in, "Cap, they're here."

Across the beach, a wide corridor of felled trees cut through the forest. Much of the lumber, charred and still smoking from the blast, had been pushed to one side or the other to make way for the trio marching triumphantly toward the beach. The alien ship floated behind them like three small children with an oversized balloon.

"Is Silk secure?" Hammer asked, turning to Tivex.

"Yes, he is in cryosleep and doing quite well."

Hammer crossed the room and stepped onto the lift, "Open the cargo bay, Dusty, I want to secure this package and get the hell off of this God forsaken rock. Tivex, your break's over let's get back to work."

Tivex felt her eyes narrow at Hammer as she snapped a sloppy, sarcastic salute and stepped onto the lift next to him. Hammer raised his hand and patted her roughly on the back. "Nice work today."

Despite her anger and frustration at the man, Tivex blushed at the compliment.

FAIL SAFE

I T WAS MIDAFTERNOON BY THE TIME THE OTHERS MADE IT BACK. THE SUN BEAT DOWN ON THE BEACH and a shimmer of heat rose from the burning sand. Torque wiped the sweat from his forehead, smearing orange slime across his face in the process.

"You guys okay?" Hammer asked as they reached the ship.

Torque gagged and spat the vile substance from his lips, "Yep," he managed before spitting again, "just great."

Tivex wrinkled her nose against the smell emanating from his clothes. It was a scent she knew all too well, she'd been doused in the substance all morning. Hammer's nose twitched and she knew he smelled it too. "You can tell me about it later. Get cleaned up and let's get out of here," he said.

Torque peeled the slimy shirt from his back and tossed the crumpled pile onto the sand, "Aye, aye." He sounded relieved, and more than a little tired.

Suddenly it occurred to Tivex how tired she was as well. Exhausted in fact. She put a hand to her mouth to cover a deep yawn. How long had they been awake? Nearly two days at least. Her bunk never sounded so good. She doubted if even Hammer's thrashing or Torque's snoring would be enough to keep her awake. The hot sun warmed her body and her eyelids sank under the weight of this epiphany but a sharp slap on the back brought her back to the moment.

"Don't get soft on me now, there's still work to do," Hammer said as he stepped off the loading bay onto the beach. Together the four of them hoisted the alien spacecraft into their cargo hold. It was surprisingly easier than Tivex would have guessed, due in large part to the craft's relatively light weight. Hammer tossed her the end of a large cargo net, "Let's get her tied down and get out of here."

Tivex began climbing the alien ship, cargo net in hand. Little by little she pulled the net over the top, dropping it unceremoniously down the other side. She was nearly through when a deep rumble began to build from deep within the ground. The rumble soon became a roar as the Widow Maker rocked in the wake of a violent tremor. The ship beneath her bucked hard and Tivex was thrown to the ground. Tangled in the netting, she hung from the side by her feet. All of their comms lit up with the sound of Dusty's voice, "We've got company!"

Hammer walked to the bay door and stood there staring. Blitz and Dregs joined him. Thanks for the help, Tivex thought as she struggled to free herself. Twisting her feet free of the rope she dropped safely to the floor and joined the others.

Outside, large and threatening waves crashed against the shoreline. On the far side of the beach, white foam sprayed high into the air as the massive waves pounded against the cliffs side. Another tremor rocked the ship and Tivex fell to her knees. The spray from the cliffs sparkled in the sunlight as it fell upon the shore, a pool of shimmering silver. The water receded but the shimmer remained and it seemed to be growing with every surge of the tide, growing and moving towards them. A sea of swarming tentacles rolled across the sand.

"I thought we buried those little grey buggers," Blitz said as he shouldered his rifle against the attack.

"Well, them tunnels had to lead somewheres," Dregs growled back.

The creatures were halfway across the beach and closing fast. Hammer put a hand on Blitz's rifle and pushed it away, "Forget it, there's too many. I hate to say it but that's not gonna do any good," as he opened his comm, "Dusty, light 'em up."

"Aye, Cap," Dusty's voice sounded almost cheerful.

Small bodies scattered and exploded as the heavy gun tore through their ranks but Tivex knew they didn't have time to watch. Hammer ran back into the cargo hold, barking orders as he went, "Get that net on the ship and lock it down! Close the bay doors! Move, move, move!"

Tivex scrambled to keep up, grabbing a discarded corner she began pulling the net towards the rear of the craft. The ground beneath them trembled again but this time she kept her footing. Inch by inch she pulled the netting over the smooth surface of the craft. She was only a few feet from finished when the net stopped moving. It happened so abruptly that she was nearly thrown off balance. A sharp barb of metal, bent up and towards the front like a hook, had snagged the line and refused to let go. Tivex tried to free the net from the ground but her efforts proved futile.

Hammer's voice rang out over the gunfire, "Why aren't those doors closed?!"

Blitz pressed the keypad repeatedly, "It's not working! The doors must have jammed when that thing hit us!"

Hammer screamed into his comm, "Torque, get down here now!"

The heavy gun continued to fire but the once constant barrage was now an intermittent burst. Dusty sounded worried, "I can't hold 'em off much longer, Cap! Ammo's gettin' real cheap, real quick!"

"Torque! Damn you!" Hammer was angry now, the veins in his neck were bright red and pulsing, "Slag it, Dusty, get us out of here now!"

"Aye, sir."

The gun ceased firing and the engines roared to life.

Hammer turned to Dregs and Tivex, "Is that thing secured!?"

Dregs looked up from where he was attaching the net to the floor brackets and shook his head.

Hammer followed Dregs' gaze to the snagged line, "Figure it out!" with that he ran to the terminal to help Blitz.

Dregs jumped up to give Tivex a hand. They pulled and flapped the netting against the sharp barb until it finally released. Together they moved it back over the engines just as the Widow Maker began to rise. Tivex risked a look out the open bay door. Thousands of writhing bodies poured into the space they had occupied only moments ago. Suddenly the Widow Maker pitched up violently. The alien craft slid backward knocking Tivex to the ground before the netting caught.

As the ship continued to climb, Tivex slid across the floor toward the gaping door and the army of monsters below. Her arms flailed, trying to find something to hold onto. An overturned toolbox slid past, emptying its contents over the side. She clawed in vain at the smooth metal floor but it was too late. Her toes slid over the edge and her body was quick to follow. Time seemed to slow as she fell. The Widow Maker became a shrinking silhouette against the glaring sun. She prayed to the Light to let it be the fall and not those horrible beasts that ended her life. Her heart dropped as the first tentacles appeared, blooming forth from the glare of the sun like a repulsive flower. The tentacles grew closer, dark and ominous, waving wildly as she fell. She screamed as they touched her face but there was something different about them, something familiar. Something about the way they felt and their smell. The smell of...of soap? Hands reached out and grabbed her, thin hands but strong. She stopped falling, swinging in midair far below the Widow Maker.

"You don't seem happy to see me!" Torque said smiling down from behind his mop of dark, tangled locks. His left eye was black and swollen and his chest was bare. A long cord led from the ship to his waist and a short white towel flapping in the wind. Tivex looked below, the mesa was gone. A smoking black hole was all that remained. Rivers of molten rock snaked across the island, setting the forest ablaze and chasing the creatures into the sea. Steam rose from the cliffs and a line of felled timber cut a path through the forest to a large pool of lava in the midst of trees. Lava tubes, Tivex almost said out loud. They must have used the heat from the volcano to incubate their young. She grimaced when she thought about how close they'd come to still being on that island when it blew.

A small white towel brushed her cheek as it flew by. Torque looked her in the eye and grinned sheepishly, "Well, ahem, this is awkward."

Torque was still pulling on his shirt when he stepped onto the control deck. Tivex couldn't help staring at the large bruise that covered his left eye and much of his cheek. Apparently he was just finished cleaning up when the first tremor hit. His face hit a sink on his way down and the next thing he knew they were airborne. He'd stumbled to the cargo bay just in time to see Tivex sliding toward the door. Grabbing a nearby lashing line, he threw an end to Hammer and dove out after her. She smiled gratefully at her friend. He might be a scrawny little bean pole but he was every ounce of him a hero.

"What's with the loading bay?" Torque asked sliding into his chair.

Hammer never looked up from his screen, "The doors jammed, we didn't have the luxury to land and fix it so we've sealed it off and we're just going to have to limp home."

Torque jumped to his feet again, "Sealed off?! I need to get in there. Without a radio we'll never make it home!"

Tivex watched as Hammer rolled his eyes, "Well, we didn't have much choice. So we're just gonna have to take our chances."

Torque fell back into his seat, "Yep, we're screwed." No one disagreed with him.

Dusty sat in Silk's pilot chair, his large Stetson hat pushed down on his head. He was a decent pilot but no substitute for Silk. It also meant they were down a gunner, though that mattered little since they had no guns to speak of.

The clouds swept by as they climbed through the planet's atmosphere, "Sorry 'bout tossin' ya out back there," Dusty said glancing briefly at Tivex, "when that old boy erupted we were damn near sittin' on top of it. My, uh, evasive maneuverin' ain't as good as ole Silky's."

Tivex smiled at Dusty, "We are alive, that is all that matters." She walked behind Torque and wrapped all four arms around him, squeezing him tight, "You, on the other hand, look a little rough."

Torque brushed his shoulder, "Ah, I look worse than it feels."

"You look like slag."

"Oh, then it's exactly how it feels!" Torque laughed, "Thanks for noticing."

"Seriously though, thank you. That is twice now I should have been dead. I owe you and Silk more than I could ever repay."

Torque patted her arm, "Don't sweat it, that's what we do around here. Besides, we need to keep you around. You're our lucky number seven."

The Widow Maker broke through the clouds and the blue sky faded to black. Tivex gasped, squeezing Torque even harder, "By the Light."

Torque stood slowly, "My God."

"Oh, you've gotta be kiddin' me," Blitz groaned.

Dregs' eyes locked onto the ship in front of them. Double their size and covered with the scraps of its conquests, it waited like a spider in a web, "What was that again about her being lucky?"

As the planet drifted away behind them, Team Seven scrambled for ideas. Dusty kept a white knuckled grip on the control sticks, "What's the plan, Cap? We didn't have the weapons enough last time but we sure as hell ain't got 'em now."

"We can't just sit here!" Torque pulled himself free of Tivex's grip, "If we can't fight then we run."

Dusty pushed the brim of his hat up, "In case you hadn't noticed, I'm just the interim pilot over here. You think you can outrun 'em your welcome to give 'er a shot but I saw what that thing is capable of and I know enough to know when I'm beat."

"So what, we just give up? After everything we just went through?"

"Cool it!" Hammer stood and crossed to the window, looking out at the new threat, "We can't fight and we won't run. Blitz, lower the shields."

"Are you serious? They'll annihilate us!"

"They could do that anyway, now do what I say."

"Aye, sir," Blitz said solemnly as he typed the codes into his terminal.

"Sir, they've armed their weapons," Dusty called out, "orders?"

"Kill the engines and activate the overdrive."

"WHAT?!" Dusty and Blitz screamed in unison.

Torque tried to make his way to his brother but Tivex held him back, "Are you insane?! You're going to get us all killed, you ashen idiot! Dusty, get us out of here. We'll take our chances on the run."

"STOW IT!" Hammer barked, "Another outburst like that and I'll have you confined to quarters for the duration of this mission."

"That's not gonna be very long if we all die here, you lunkhead!"

"Tivex, get him out of here! Dusty!" Hammer shouted again, "Kill the engines. That's an order." He looked around the room with daggers in his eyes, "The last time I checked I'm still Captain of this ship and we're doing this my way."

"Come on, Torque, apparently he knows what he is doing," Tivex said as she pulled the younger Dorran toward the lift.

A white light lit in the communications console, flashing a steady beat.

"Someone open that channel," Hammer ordered.

Tivex released Torque and ran to her station.

"Wait!" Dregs growled from the corner, "My Captain now, if Velkaso knows we're aboard he'll destroy us all."

"He'll probably do that anyway," replied Hammer without so much as a flinch, "Go ahead, Tivex."

A dark voice filled the air, *"Moncasa monhesh Velkaso!"*

Hammer's fingernails scratched at the arm of his chair, "Velkaso, this is IEC vessel SL1219 code name Widow Maker. I am Captain Dorran and you are threatening an unarmed ship."

"This voice...I know this voice. Did you think I dead, boys? Is no so easy kill Velkaso." Heavy, angry breaths filled the spaces between his words, *"Maybe I show you how kill better."*

"Tivex, bring him on-screen," Hammer managed through clenched teeth.

The viewer began to glow as the image of Velkaso took form. He was tall and slender. A crown of sharp bones sat upon his pointed head. His long face and toothy grin reminded Tivex of a large rat. His leathery skin stretched tight across his body, tearing in places to expose the bone and muscle underneath. Velkaso surveyed the room until his sickening gaze fell upon Tivex. She couldn't stop the shiver that ran up her spine.

"Maybe I start with you, girl. I go slow, show this boys how Velkaso kill. But first maybe we play." His long, slimy tongue traced a path across his taught lips, *"Then again,"* he said, placing a hand on the control panel beside him, *"Maybe I just kill you now."*

Hammer rose from his chair. There was a growing darkness in him that Tivex could sense just trying to make its way out of Hammer. When he spoke, Tivex noticed Hammer's voice seemed to drop down a few octaves, almost matching Velkaso's intensity, "I don't know how you survived but why don't you come over here and I'll see if I can finish the job."

Velkaso brought his hand to his face and lightly caressed the drum tight skin on his cheek, *"As you see, it has no been easy,"* his sharp fingernails pierced the skin and his bulbous eyeballs rolled back in his head as he peeled away a strip of flesh. A thin stream of blood ran down his cheek stopping almost as soon as it had begun. His eyes focused once again, *"but the pain is most good."*

"Well then, I'd be happy to give you all the pain you could want!" Dregs growled, stepping out of the shadows.

Hatred filled Velkaso's eyes and he gripped his pike menacingly, *"Filthy traitor! You I kill extra slow!"* From somewhere off-screen one of his crew began shouting in the strange language Tivex couldn't understand. Velkaso turned abruptly to the source of the sound and then calmly back toward the screen. *"I make you deal, boys. You has velbushah, give to me and I no kill you today."*

Hammer looked to Dregs who gave the slightest shake of his head, "Sorry, I don't know what you mean."

"The ship, stupid boys!" Velkaso hissed, *"We hear you transmissions, you not easy to find. I think you no know what you has but Velkaso knows. Yes, I know and I take velbushah one way or the other."*

"Come and get it!" Hammer's fist came down on the console ending the transmission. He walked over and patted Dregs on the back, "I think that did the trick."

Dregs merely grunted as his teeth bared.

"What in the hell was that?" Torque asked, blinking in disbelief.

"That, dear boy, was Velkaso," Dregs spat the name out, "an old acquaintance of me and your brother."

Hammer turned to Dusty, "Crank the overdrive to maximum."

Dusty's bright blue eyes were filled with worry, "Uh, Cap, you sure that's the best idea?"

"Oh, I'm positive of it," Hammer crossed to Dusty's station and cranked the knob himself, turning it until it broke off in his hand.

"Great," Torque said morbidly, "see ya later everybody, We're officially all flagging dead."

Hammer dropped the dial to the floor and ran a hand through his short cropped hair. By the time he addressed the crew again he was much more composed, "I don't like this anymore than you're going to but we're scuttling the Maker. It's the only way we get out of this. I figure we've got thirty minutes before those boosters overheat and vaporize everything in sight. That should be plenty of time to get the rescue pod a safe distance away. The IEC is just going to have to live without their cargo, it's better than letting someone like Velkaso get their hands on it."

"Fifteen minutes."

Hammer looked questioningly at Torque, "Huh?"

Torque cleared his throat, "When you turned the engines off you disabled the system that balances the power levels between the two boosters. It keeps either one from having run away power surges and causing a catastrophic event, like the one you just put us in. If the engines were on, thus leaching power from the boosters, and the systems were balanced, it would take an hour to reach critical levels. You thought shutting the engines down would prevent that power transfer and cut the time in half but now, instead of both boosters needing to reach capacity only one does. Fifteen minutes. Twenty if we're lucky. Ten if we're not. It was really nice knowing you guys."

"That's not enough time...," Hammer was visibly distraught, "not enough time. Bloody slag...we're dead."

"Not if you park that gray temper of yours and start listening to me!" Torque yelled, snapping Hammer back to reality, "There's still a way."

"Okay," Hammer said calmly, "make the call. What do we do?"

Torque smoothed his wild hair back, "Dig it, we can't turn the engines back on without risking a surge in the boosters but maybe we can siphon off some of the power if we hook the boosters to the shield generator. It won't be able to handle that level of power for long but it might buy us another half hour. There's just one problem, the shield generator isn't in the engine compartment, I'll have to run a line from the boosters to the generator's access panel."

"Which is where?" asked Tivex.

Torque grinned, "The cargo bay."

"How long will that take?" Hammer asked.

"I dunno, not long I don't think. Maybe more than we have but I don't see where we have a choice."

Hammer nodded and clapped Torque on the back, "Suit up. Tivex, you and Blitz get the spare power cable from the engine room and run it to the cargo hold then get to the rescue pod and wait there. Dusty, get the pod fired up and ready to launch. Dregs, Torque and I can handle the rest." Hammer grabbed Torque's shoulder and nodded at him, "Quick thinking on that."

"Yeah, yeah. Remember that the next time I tell you not to push the damn button."

It didn't take long for Tivex and Blitz to make their way to the engine compartment. Tivex began opening cabinets searching for the cable, "Where is this thing anyway?"

"You're standing on it," replied Blitz.

Tivex stepped off the large metal floor grate and Blitz muscled it open. The cable was enormous, at least as thick as Blitz's massive thigh. She reached down and hauled the end of the heavy cable out of the hole.

Blitz waved her toward the hall, "Take that and make your way to the cargo bay, I'll keep feeding you slack."

Tivex headed out the door. It was heavy lifting to be sure but thankfully Blitz was able to push the cable into and down the hall, leaving her the less difficult job of directing it where to go. When she got to the cargo door, Torque was waiting. Head to toe he was decked out in his zero suit. Hammer and Dregs stood behind him dressed to match, their long rifles at the ready.

Torque pulled off his helmet as she approached, "Once we open this door, the Maker's life support systems will be compromised. We won't be able to shut it again with this cable in the way," he smiled nervously at Tivex, "hey, in case we don't make it I-"

"Stow that talk, soldier," Tivex grabbed his helmet and pushed it back down over his head, "we are going to survive this. Besides, am I not your lucky number seven?"

A loud crash came from the other side of the door and the Widow Maker shook throwing all four of them into the wall. Torque picked himself up and looked at Tivex, "We probably need to stop saying that."

Hammer was already at the door, "Time's up, they're here. Tivex get to the rescue pod. If we're not there in five minutes, get the hell outta here."

Tears welled in her eyes at the thought of leaving them behind but she silently nodded her acquiescence. With that, Hammer swung open the door and disappeared through the opening. Torque screamed to stop him and before she could leave, Tivex's breath caught in her chest but nothing happened. The air was still breathable. They burst through the door behind Hammer. The open bay door was filled now with the hull of the Mynx. A small docking door stood in the middle hissing as the pressure between the two ships equalized.

Hammer and Dregs were ready, their weapons trained on the docking door, "Don't just stand there, get it done and get out of here!" Hammer yelled, "Someone, give him a hand!" The hissing stopped and the airlock latch began to turn. Tivex managed to throw a look towards Hammer who was sneering, "Come on, pretty boy, come get some!"

The door flew open and large, heavy bodied creatures poured through the opening wielding wicked pikes and angular swords meant for cleaving flesh from bone.

"Hais!" Dregs roared as he opened fire, "The gray lovin' fool has Hais!"

Tivex froze in her tracks. The Hais were a fearsome race. Large, muscular mercenaries they were not very intelligent but what they lacked in brains they more than made up for in unyielding aggression. With a large breast plate of bone covering their vital organs and naturally thick, dingy green skin covering everything else, they were incredibly difficult to kill. Oversized cone shaped teeth grew from their lower jaw like tusks and blood red eyes that seemed to burn with fire complimented their menacing, murderous reputation. Tivex had only heard stories and seen vids of the Hais. She had been in medical training during the Hais war and for the first time she was glad she had been. Fire flew from their rifles as Hammer and Dregs tried to slow their advance but the bullets only ricocheted harmlessly away.

"Check your fire, we're still pressurized!" Torque screamed over the din of their weapons, "If you breach the hull we're all space junk!"

"That ain't gonna matter much longer anyways!" Dregs growled back, "Just get it done, we can't hold 'em."

Torque snatched up the cable and began dragging it through the door. Tivex jumped in to help and within moments they were standing at the access panel. Torque scrambled to get the panel open, his thin, nimble fingers flying over the key pad as he entered the override codes. Red lights flashed overhead and a loud siren drowned out the sound of fighting.

"What is that?!" Tivex screamed cupping a couple of hands over her ears.

Torque continued the override sequence, "Slaggin' game's over! We're outta time! One of the boosters is about to blow!"

Tivex glanced over at Hammer. He and Dregs were plugging away at the Hais but making no headway. The force of the bullets only slightly slowed their progress. The Hais encircled the alien ship and stopped. From the entrance of the Mynx strange new creatures appeared. Much like Velkaso, they were tall and thinly muscular. They had long, rat-like faces with sharp evil teeth. Tufts of hair sprouted from their bodies in patches, giving them a look that was mangy and unkempt, yet wildly dangerous. They funneled into the cargo bay unhindered by the gunfire or wailing sirens.

"Got it!" Torque cried sliding the power cord into place. The alarms faded and the gunfire seemed almost quiet in their absence, "Time to beat feet, sister, time isn't our friend right now!"

Torque led the way through the door with Tivex close on his heels. Dregs and Hammer followed them through, laying down suppressive fire until they reached the doorway.

"You should have blown it, boys. You becoming monkaso?"

The voice stopped Hammer in his tracks.

"Where you going, boys?" Velkaso stepped through the door and into the cargo bay. He stood a head taller than the creatures around him as he strolled confidently into their midst, *"You no want to play, boy?"* He pointed a bony finger at Tivex, *"Maybe she want to play. Come here, girlie, I have something for you. Do you like my Hais? They what we say Kasochavet, it mean strong fighter. They give me victory, I give them plenty fighting and much fresh meat."* He pulled a long wicked dagger from his hip and drew it slowly across his neck.

Hammer took a step towards Velkaso but Dregs placed a halting paw on his chest, "Not here, my captain now, even jacked up you got no chance."

Velkaso shouted in his strange language and the sea of bodies around him parted. Tivex stared past Hammer and down the newly formed corridor of soldiers to where Velkaso stood.

"Come, boys, they no hurt you. Drop you guns, they no can help you. Come finish what you started. Just you and me."

Hammer took another step tossing his rifle to the ground.

Dregs wrapped his arms around Hammer, dragging him back toward the door, "Ya can't win it like this and you know it! Aside from our bloody ship 'bout to blow, he ain't in the kill zone. Time to fight another day."

Hammer shoved Dregs aside.

"Maybe you listen to you monkaso friend. Maybe the cat, he save you life again." Velkaso's yellow teeth smiled cruelly as he twirled the blade in front of him.

Hammer's fists balled as he moved toward the front line of Hais soldiers.

Dregs was on his feet again grabbing at Hammer, "Ya know, savin' your wretched hide is gettin' a little taxin' here!" Dregs jumped in front of Hammer and roared, "MOVE OUT!!"

Hammer shook his head and took another step, "This ends now."

Dregs winced and curled his upper lip, "You're gonna make me do this, ain't ya?"

Another step.

Dregs yelled out, "Anytime you're ready, shiny!!"

Hammer realized what Dregs meant and turned just as something large and metal hit him over the head, crumpling him to the floor. Blitz picked up his limp body and slung it over his shoulder and grabbed Tivex by the hand, "I'll apologize later, let's move!"

Velkaso cried out in rage and his soldiers' ranks collapsed as they raced towards Tivex and the others. Blitz led the way, an unconscious Hammer hanging over his shoulder like a sack. The thin, rat-like creatures poured into the hallway behind them, followed by the slower Hais. Dregs fired into the hall, his bullets ripping through flesh and bone. When they reached the rescue pod Dusty was already waiting. Dregs tried to shut the hatch but sharply clawed fingers grasped the door.

Blitz dropped Hammer to the ground and grabbed the door, crushing and severing fingers as he muscled it closed. Blood sprayed all over Tivex and Torque as Blitz yelled, "Dusty, get us out of here!" over the anguished screams coming from the other side of the hatch.

The engines fired up and the pod shook as it released from the ship and sailed out into space. To Tivex, it felt as though the pod was both a blessing and a curse as she felt defiled from the flight from Velkaso with no way to get the vile blood off of her. She shook her head in disbelief as what had just happened as she felt Hammer stirring beside her.

Hammer woke up rubbing his head, "Ugh, what happened?"

All eyes fell on Blitz, "Sorry, Cap, that headache is my fault. When the sirens started and you guys weren't back yet I came lookin' for you. When I found you, well, there wasn't much time for convincing."

"You should have left me in there," Hammer grumbled as he sat up.

Together they watched as Velkaso transferred the alien craft from the Widow Maker to his ship. Several thin creatures in zero suits guided the ship out of one cargo bay, floating gently through space to the other. It was a flawless transfer. Everyone moved together in perfect harmony. It was practiced, almost routine. Tivex realized that was most likely the way they gathered the salvage that became the welded skin of their beastly ship.

When the transfer was complete the ship turned away. As Velkaso and his ship shrank out of sight Hammer kicked the chair in front of him angrily, "Gah! Dammit, dammit, dammit! We had him! We should have blown that heaping slag up!" He sighed extremely heavily and let his head fall to his chest, "Velkaso was right, I got monkaso."

Tivex ventured a question, "What is monkaso?"

"It means weak, useless, me. I should have stayed behind. I should have killed him while I had the chance," Hammer kicked the chair again.

Dregs spoke up from the corner, "We already did that once, remember? Apparently it didn't take."

A bright blue light flashed in the distance as the overdrive ruptured and the Widow Maker was consumed by the explosion. The rescue pod rocked lightly in the shockwave that followed.

Tivex placed a comforting hand on Torque's shoulder, "I am sorry."

Torque didn't respond, he stared silently out the window at a cloud of debris that was once their ship and threw his favorite wrench down on the floor below.

Far from home with no way to call for help and drifting in high orbit above a hostile planet, Tivex looked around at the others. She began to feel the collective emotion resonating throughout the pod. Their mission objective stolen, their ship destroyed, each of them battered, broken and dreadfully tired and yet, somehow secure in the knowledge that they'd survived. There was nothing else to be done and she felt a merciful feeling begin to overtake her. It was an overwhelming power that seemed to grip the others, including Hammer, which seemed to be rapidly spreading. Alone and with nothing more to say, Team Seven collectively gave in to the strange power and finally slept.

NIGHTMARES

TIVEX SAT IN A LARGE MEETING ROOM ON THE OMARIAN SPACE STATION. IT WAS DAY THREE OF their debriefing and she was getting a little tired of telling the same story time and time again. They'd been on the station for almost a week, found after only a day in the rescue pod by the ships Admiral Kagen had sent to assist them. Since then, they'd been stuck between this room and their hospital beds. Everyone wanted answers, especially Admiral Kosos, who despite no longer being their commanding officer, seemed to have made it his personal goal to bring their tenure at the IEC to an end.

"Let me get this straight," Kosos hissed from across the table, "The way I see it, you've destroyed an IEC Hunter class ship, got two of your team injured, one of whom is just this side of death, and failed to discover anything that would further our understanding of this unknown planet or the ship you reported to find. The same ship you later claim to have surrendered during your escape. You turned over a piece of Top Secret hardware to an unknown hostile party? What kind of command decision is that?" He pointed his chubby finger at Kagen, "I thought your little Akoni was supposed to keep them on the straight and narrow, huh? Clean up their act? They're still as undisciplined, insubordinate, insufferable and completely unreliable as always! They've managed to completely screw up what were otherwise simple mission parameters!"

"It's good to see you again too, sir," Torque chided.

The veins pulsed in Kosos' neck, "You shut your mouth, boy!"

Master Admiral Lokias came to their aid, "In their defense, Admiral, we did send them completely unprepared into what turned out to be an incredibly hostile situation. I understand also that it was Admiral Kagen's decision they forfeit their weaponry in favor of the alien craft which left them vulnerable to attack. Given the circumstances we're just fortunate they survived."

"Bah!" Kosos spat, "Don't you be buyin' into their lies too. All we have is one short vid clip of a spacecraft and this half-baked story of an ambush. I've searched every database we have for this 'Velkaso', or the species they describe seeing and the only reference I can find is the neurovid we pulled from this maniac almost twenty years ago. There was nothing else, not even in the oldest Omarian files. I'm supposed to believe that there's an unknown race of aliens terrorizing the galaxy and the only one who's ever seen them is this animal here, and twice at that? No, sir, this Velkaso is nothing more than a Helix junkie's fever dream and somehow he's got the rest going along with it."

Hammer jumped to his feet, his face red with rage but it was Tivex who grabbed him and spoke first, "Admiral, with all due respect, I was reassigned to Team Seven for this excursion so that I could report on their activities to my superiors. If you are not going to believe my reports, then what was the point of sending me? Akoni do not lie, Admiral, you know that. The ship is real, Velkaso is real. Everything we have told you is the truth. By the Light, we almost died out there! The least you can do is hear us out!" She realized suddenly that she was standing, shouting at Kosos and every other piece of brass in the room. Hammer gave her a curious but approving look and took his seat. Tivex wanted desperately to sit as well but she didn't dare back down at this point.

Finally, Master Admiral Lokias spoke, shaking his short white mane as he addressed Master Admiral Soren, "It's time, my friend."

Soren nodded and gestured for Tivex to be seated, "Very well." He walked to the door and checked the lock before he continued, "What I'm about to tell you is highly classified. This information is kept deep within the IEC archives, accessible only by members of the High Council. Three of us sit before you today but there are many more not in attendance who would view what we are about to say as treason. For that reason, nothing you hear is to leave this room."

Tivex followed Soren's every move. Her mouth was dry with anticipation.

"It was during the Gray War," Soren continued, "long before most of you were born. The allied forces were gaining ground, driving deep into the Kuvvaa ranks. We'd routed the initial invasion but there were rumors the Kuvvaa had a weapon. A weapon so powerful it could turn the tide of the war."

"Bull and malarkey!" Kosos grumbled from his seat, "We searched every last vessel after the war. There was no sign of this weapon. It was just a story the infantry used to frighten new recruits."

Soren and Tall'ani exchanged a look that seemed to hold much more than words could ever express. Tall'ani stood and joined Soren at the end of the table. Her voice was a steady purr, "It was no rumor, Admiral, I've seen this weapon with my own eyes."

Lokias stood also, his large furry body swaying side to side as he hobbled to join them. His voice was low and resolved, "As have I."

Kosos looked awestruck as Soren began again, "There was a commander during the war, a man by the name of Gavin Harr. He was a brilliant tactician and military strategist who was tasked with discovering the whereabouts of this weapon and destroying it. If there was anyone capable of fulfilling those orders, it was Harr. He was brutal but extremely effective. Personally,

I thought he was a liability. He was too unpredictable, too trigger happy for my liking. Ten ships and five hundred soldiers were given to his command. Over the next few months we fought our way into the heart of the Kuvvaa territory. According to the intel we gathered the weapon was on the Kuvvaa home world awaiting transportation to the frontlines.

Tivex's mind was reeling as she watched Soren's eyes stare far off into the distance, cloudy with the memory. He continued, "The allies turned every ship they could toward this new target with our fleet leading the charge. We were cut down to almost half our force by the time we reached the planet's surface. In all, ten thousand soldiers touched down but it was my squadron that made the find. In the heart of the Temple of Kavi at the base of the Kuvvaa citadel we saw it. It was just as we'd heard it described, a tall cylinder topped by two concentric crescents rotating endlessly around a large glowing sphere. We tried to reach it but the Kuvvaa were everywhere. They swarmed around the weapon, outnumbering us ten to one. And then, slag it all, without warning it fired. A blinding light washed over the city, followed by a strange wave of energy that took my breath away. When I recovered from the initial shock I saw the true nature of the device. All around me people were transforming, mutating into hideous monsters. Humans seemed to be the only ones affected but out of every company, only a handful remained unchanged. The creatures were strong, and savage. They decimated the remaining allied regiment and everything in between. The Kuvvaa had not planned for this, they had no control over the beasts and soon they turned on their creators as well. Somehow in the frenzy, the weapon disappeared, vanished with no trace. In the end there were only four of us that made it off that rock alive, Tall'ani, Lokias, myself and Nicholas Doran."

Torque perked up, "Dad?"

Soren nodded, "Yes, your father was there. It was Nick who spotted the Kuvvaa vessel we borrowed for our escape. If it wasn't for him, there would be no one left who knows the truth about what happened."

Kosos shifted uncomfortably in his chair, "What do ya mean tellin' us this story? I out ranked both of you back then. As I recall, Nick found you wandering around aimlessly after the Main Base battle and took you under his wing. You were nothing more than militia that got folded into his company. After all this time, I've never heard the likes of any of that. The Kuvvaa nearly had us beat. We'd all be dead if it weren't for the plague that ravaged their home world."

"Admiral, the plague was the story. We couldn't very well tell everyone the truth, especially with the weapon still missing. The entire system would be in panic. We created the plague to cover up the truth. We needed something so devastating that no one would go near it. Something so terrible no one would ever learn what really transpired on Kuvvaa," replied Tall'ani.

Kosos opened his mouth to object but closed it silently instead.

Soren went on, "For the next several months we kept a close eye on Kuvvaa and its new inhabitants. They were a primal race, twisted muscle and sinew, nothing of their former humanity remained. They fought one another for dominance. It seemed as though they would kill themselves off and the newly formed IEC would be rid of this problem with no further involvement. Unfortunately, that wasn't the case. Among them there was one whose superior intelligence, strength and cunning set him apart from the rest. He quickly rose as a leader, brutally slaying anyone that opposed him until there were none left that challenged his authority. We knew him as Gavin Harr, Vincent and Dregs know him better as Velkaso."

Soren paused, alarmed at the sound of Hammer's teeth grinding in the background. Tivex wanted to check on Hammer but she was too drawn into the story.

"Shortly after his rise to power, the 'Spawn', as we took to calling them, just disappeared. They salvaged the allied ships and departed, living in the depths of space as pirates, ruthless vagabonds driven by hate and destruction. Without access to Bridge Gates they posed no real threat to us. That is until twenty-five years ago." Soren looked from Hammer to Dregs, "Would either of you like to fill in the rest?"

Neither moved.

"Very well. Twenty-five years ago the Spawn were responsible for the attack and subsequent destruction of the explorer ship Galileo. During which time, your illustrious captain here was taken hostage."

Hammer stood up and crossed the room. Unlocking the door, he stepped through shutting it forcefully behind him. Admiral Kagen pushed his chair back from the table, "I'll go talk to him."

"Good luck with that," Kosos sneered.

Soren cleared his throat to continue but Dregs interjected, "Uh, sir, if ya don't mind, I think I should tell 'em."

Soren looked caught somewhere between surprise and a rebuke but he took a seat. If the room had been quite while Soren spoke, now it was deathly silent.

"If you're gonna have to hear this, you may as well hear the whole thing," Dregs said. He looked right at Torque as he spoke, "When Velkaso attacked, your brother was only away from home a couple of weeks. He was a scrawny lil' joke, but he had a grown man's spirit and courage to match. While most of the kids were cryin' and helpless, your brother fought through his fear and took charge of the situation. Even when the Spawn overwhelmed the Galileo's armed defenders, your brother searched the dorms for the other kids, hiding 'em throughout the ship as he went. He never thought to hide or save himself. I found 'im in a provisions closet, hiding a girl a year or two younger than himself in a spice barrel."

"How would you know?" asked Torque.

Dregs exhaled a labored breath, "You're the genius, you tell me."

Tivex saw Torque's eyes bouncing back and forth. It took only a moment for Torque to reply, "Wait a minute, you two were found in that pod together …"

Dregs nodded.

"It was you?"

Dregs nodded again, "I hate to tell ya this, kid, but I turned those young two in to Velkaso, my master."

"You wanna run that by me again, furball? You worked for that psychopath?! You were the one that took my brother?! You son of a bitch!" Torque dove across the table before Blitz could grab him, "YOU'RE DEAD!"

Tall'ani stepped between them, her imposing form stopping Torque in his tracks, "As much as it would thrill me to see that happen, your brother trusts him and so must we. The fact of the matter is, despite his previous transgressions, if it weren't for Dregs your brother would be dead or worse. Now have a seat, Lieutenant."

Torque's nostrils flared with anger and his piercing eyes never left Dregs but he managed to sit once again.

Dregs dropped his eyes to the table in shame, "Look, I ain't sayin' I'm proud of what I done back then. I ain't sayin' it don't keep me up nights, but that was then, this is now. Ya see, Velkaso took a special interest in your brother. There was a strength in that boy, an undyin' defiance in his eyes which brought out the worst in Velkaso. He became obsessed with breaking 'im, crushin' his spirit, destroyin' mind, body and soul. Your brother's new hell began that night. He was forced to watch when Velkaso destroyed the Galileo, snubbin' out the life of every child Vincent had worked so hard to save."

Tears welled in Tivex's eyes as his story continued. Dregs held nothing back in his brutal recollection of events and in her mind she watched it all unfold.

It was cold and deathly quiet in his windowless cell. It smelled stale, as if the air hadn't been circulated in years. Vincent sat in the corner hugging his knees to his chest. It had been weeks since the destruction of the Galileo but still no one came for him. Twice a day food was delivered through a slot in the door. It was vile slop and for days he refused to eat at first. Now, he was just thankful for the darkness of his prison so he didn't have to look as he shoveled it into his mouth. The silence was maddening but mealtime was worse. Whenever the slot would open, for the brief moments it took to slide his tray through, his cell would fill with that sound. The anguished screams of the young girl. Helpless and scared Vincent prayed for the silence to return. Tears streamed down his face as he imagined the tortures that young girl was enduring, and the tortures that likely awaited him as well. The days passed, each one like the day before, until one day the screaming ceased. The food slot opened and yet the silence persisted.

Vincent staggered to his feet, having to remember after all this time how to stand. He was weak and bone thin. He stumbled to door of his cell, pounding his fists weakly against its unyielding iron. He tried to speak, to scream, he wanted to know what happened to the girl but his voice failed him. Giving up he slumped against the cold wall of his prison and sobbed silently into his hands. She was dead, he knew that, and soon he would be too. He wiped the tears from his eyes with the collar of his dirty shirt and felt better in his knowledge that at least the young girls torture was at an end.

Three more silent weeks passed and Vincent had given up on a rescue ever coming for him. His torture was to be forever confined in this cell without the satisfaction of even a whisper. Time held no meaning for him anymore, he slept when he was tired, which was often, and ate when he was hungry, which was becoming less and less frequent. Then one day his meals stopped coming. Vincent waited by the slot like an obedient dog but it never moved. Since meal delivery was his only way of tracking the days, he couldn't say for certain how long they starved him but when his captors finally came to get him he had not the strength to move.

Two large furry paws grabbed the back of his shirt, hauling him to his feet but he was unable to stand and collapsed to the floor. The large paws wrapped around him lifting him easily from the ground and tossed him roughly over a broad musty shoulder. Vincent's head spun as he was carried through the ships corridors. The light, though dim, assaulted his senses and blurred his vision. He bounced lightly on his captor's back, unable to orient himself in his new surroundings. He was carried through a series of doors and into a large room. He could hear voices but the language they spoke was unknown to him. The voices swirled around him as he was carried into their midst. Without warning he found himself being dropped unceremoniously to the ground. Bright lights came to life, blinding him with their brilliance. He brought a protective hand up to shade his eyes. Hazy shapes milled around in his peripherals, malformed and grotesque even through his blurred vision. From among them a large shadow emerged. Taller than the rest, he strode through their ranks until he stood towering over Vincent.

His twisted body writhed with anticipation at the sight of Vincent and his lips peeled back in toothy grin, *"Hello, boys,"* Velkaso hissed, poking at Vincent with a clawed toe, *"You think you brave boys? You think you strong?"*

Velkaso kicked Vincent hard in the ribs. A sharp crack and shooting pain told Vincent they were broken. He opened his mouth to scream but he still had no voice.

Velkaso tossed his head back in a wicked laugh, *"No, boys, you is no strong. You is no brave. You is no smart."*

Velkaso reached into a satchel held by one of his men and pulled out a glowing green vial. Clawed hands pulled Vincent to his feet, holding him effortlessly against his will. The strong paws that had carried him here pulled his head back and forced his mouth open.

"You is mine, boys!"

Velkaso poured the contents of the vile down Vincent's throat. The liquid felt warm, almost stinging, as it oozed its way to his stomach. There the warmth grew, filling him with a red hot fire. A piercing pain surged in his bones. His muscles convulsed and he felt as though something were trying to squeeze the very essence from his body like water from a sponge. Soon the pain subsided. He was weak now but not as weak as before, something had changed. His ribs still ached but his breathing was less labored. His eyes were adjusting faster to the light and he no longer felt the gnawing hunger that had been his only companion during his imprisonment. Vincent opened his mouth to speak but a sharp right cross from Velkaso caused him to fall back into silence.

Velkaso grabbed a fist full of Vincent's long, brown hair, pulling him closer until they were eye to repulsive eye, *"You no think I let you die so easy, boys? You no die, boy. You want for death but you no can has it. You beg for death but you no can has it. I make you suffer. I make you bow before Velkaso. I make you obey. Then I make you die."*

Velkaso gestured to his men and the crowd parted once again. A small girl walked through the crowd to where he stood. Vincent's heart began to race. She was alive, he had been wrong about her. As she approached his feelings of hope vanished. Her eyes never left the floor in front of her. Her shoulders sagged in permanent defeat. The dirt on her face was smeared by tears which no longer fell. When she reached Velkaso she stopped.

He smiled wickedly as he placed a clawed finger under her chin, *"Bow to you master, girls."* She dropped instantly to her knees, her face flat on the ground at his feet, *"You see, boys? Velkaso own her."* He picked the girl up off the ground and turned her to face Vincent. Her eyes remained locked on the ground in front of her. Velkaso stood behind her, bringing a hooked claw up to her neck he ran a slimy tongue across his pale malformed lips.

Vincent's eyes began to tear, "No, please, no. She's just a little girl. She's a child!" Vincent was screaming now, his voice revitalized by the strange elixir, "Let her go!" He struggled against the hands that held him but he was still too weak. His tone softened, "Please, don't do it. Please let her go. Please she's only-"

"She useless!" Velkaso snarled as he raked his claw across her throat. The girl gasped, her eyes finding Vincent's before collapsing to the ground in a pool of her own blood. Velkaso laughed as he watched the ruby river which poured from her tiny body.

"NOOOO!!!!!!" Vincent screamed. He struggled to reach her but the hands that held him dragged him away. Soon she was lost amidst a sea of disfigured bodies. The sounds of Velkaso's laughter followed him all the way back to his cell.

The meals came again and Vincent ate vigorously. His bones healed quickly and the elixir gave him a strength in his muscles he had not felt before. He spent the days replaying that moment in his head. Her bright green eyes, hopeless and frightened, floated in the aether of his mind. He had begged for her to be spared, pleaded for her life but the monster had claimed her anyway. It was then that he decided he would never beg again, ever. No matter the torture, no matter how long he must endure it, he would never give Velkaso that satisfaction. That was his power, that was still within his control, that was how he would exact his revenge.

It was a week before they came for him again but this time he walked out on his own. His guard was the very Omarian that found him on the Galileo. Dregs escorted him down a series of corridors, through several large doors and into the same large room he'd been brought to before. Again a crowd was gathered, though this time they seemed to be cheering as he approached. Hooked claws raised high in the air, they urged him forward. The lights burned brightly but his eyes adjusted without difficulty. As he reached the middle of the room, a red stain on the floor caught his eye. He fought back the tears, filling his heart with rage instead of sorrow. A sudden roar from the crowd announced the arrival of Velkaso.

With the swagger of a champion prize fighter he walked into the ring of bodies which formed around Vincent, *"Tonight, boys, I make you bow."*

Velkaso removed his cloak and flexed his long lean muscles. The crowd cheered as he made his way around the circle stalking Vincent like a ravenous wolf. Vincent's mind raced. He was feeling much better but he was no gladiator. Was he supposed to fight this creature hand to hand? He'd seen no weapons. He tried to back out of this makeshift arena but the fiendish onlookers merely kicked him back into play. Foot over foot, Velkaso traversed the circumference of the crowd, crouched low, every muscle tended to pounce. Vincent tried to maintain his distance, terrified of what this creature might do, hoping that in the face of actual torture he could be as strong as his prison cell convictions. Velkaso struck without warning. He closed the distance between them in two long strides landing a sharp blow to Vincent's jaw. Pain seared into his brain. The rich, iron taste of blood filled his mouth. Vincent staggered and fell to the cheers of the crowd. The world was a swirl of color and sound.

Velkaso laughed as he loomed over Vincent's fallen body, *"You no fighter, boys. Bow to Velkaso and die."*

Vincent pushed the pain from his mind, spit the blood from his mouth and pushed himself up off the ground. The fear was gone now. Pain and anger had replaced all other emotion. He might die tonight but he would never give this demon the satisfaction of breaking him. A loud crack announced the breaking of his ribs once again as Velkaso's fist found its mark. The air rushed from Vincent's lungs and he crumpled back to the floor clutching his sides.

"Give up, boys. You nothing, I Velkaso. You no can win, worthless, wretched boys!"

Vincent sucked air into his lungs despite the excruciating pain which came with it. He pushed himself slowly to his knees.

A wicked smile grew on Velkaso's twisted face, *"That's it, boys. Kneel!"*

Vincent placed a shaky hand on his knee fighting to stand, using his hate to shut out the pain. Fire raged in Velkaso's eyes as he snatched Vincent up into the air, dangling him by the throat. Vincent gasped for air in Velkaso's talon-like grip which threatened to crush the the very life from his body, *"This not over boy. I make you more suffer."*

Vincent screamed as Velkaso's free hand dug its claws into the soft flesh of his back. Velkaso threw Vincent to the ground but he was unconscious before he ever hit the floor.

When he awoke, Vincent was back in his cell. His back ached but further inspection showed no bleeding, in fact no wound to speak of. He found his breathing came easier as well. He ran his hands over his body, searching for injury but he seemed to be in one piece. He slumped in the corner, his head between his knees and sighed.

"That's the Helix workin' in your veins," a gruff voice spoke from the shadows.

Vincent started and scrambled backward, deeper into his cell before he could stop himself.

"It'll work its magic, keep you alive, make you strong, but it comes at a high price in the end."

Vincent gathered his courage, finding just enough to ask one question, "Who are you?"

There was the sharp metallic sound of a breaker switch and the acrid smell of old fuses. The dim lights of the cell sizzled under layers of dirt and grime. A tall, tawny Omarian stood by the open door. Vincent recognized him immediately. He was broad shouldered and heavily muscled but he was shabby and unkempt and unlike any Omarian Vincent had ever met. His bright yellow eyes seemed to glow in the low light, the feral shine of a caged animal which still recalls the thrill of the hunt. He snarled at Vincent, "The name's Dregs and I'm the one keepin' you alive. That's all you need to know. Can you walk?"

Vincent pushed himself off the cold floor and was surprised to find he rose with only slight discomfort.

Dregs looked Vincent up and down, "You're tougher than you look, runt, but if you're determined to be Velkaso's punchin' bag there are a few things you could stand to learn."

Vincent was confused. Wasn't this the Omarian who was responsible for his capture in the first place? Why did it sound like he was trying to help him now?

"Let's go," Dregs turned and walked out the door.

Vincent followed, confused and curious, "Where are we going?"

Dregs turned and brought his paw down sharply across Vincent's face, "Shut it! You talk when I says you talk!"

Vincent rubbed his cheek and nodded his understanding. There was something different about Dregs, he wasn't like the other creatures on this ship. Aside from being the only Omarian he was different somehow. He'd pulled that punch for one thing and that was the closest thing to a kindness Vincent had been shown since his arrival.

They stopped in front of a round metal hatch. Dregs released the catch and swung the door open. The smell was overwhelming and Vincent wretched, emptying what little was in his stomach onto the floor at Dregs' feet. Dregs sneered, "Get used to it, boy. That's your new home away from home. I convinced Velkaso to let me put ya to work." He handed Vincent a small trowel, "These waste lines get jammed up pretty good. It's your job to climb through all that slag and free up the worm.'

"My job? I'm a prisoner, I'm not helping you with anything."

Dregs slammed the hatch shut, "If that's what ya want, boy, then back to the cell with ya! Let Velkaso kick the slag out of you every night, it makes no difference to me."

"Are you saying he'll leave me alone if I help?" asked Vincent.

Dregs howled with laughter, "I wouldn't count on that, boy. My captain's gots a furious temper and what seems to be an intense hatred for you in particular. No, he ain't gonna stop as long as you live but I can't very well get work out of you if you're broken every day. So unless he plans to pump you full of Helix every night, he's gonna need to slow it down."

"Why are you helping me?"

Dregs laughed again as he reopened the hatch, "Helping you? Hahaha! Boy, I ain't helpin' you, I'm helpin' myself. This was my job before now." Before Vincent could react Dregs had grabbed him by the collar of his shirt and tossed him through the hole.

Vincent landed in a pool of biological waste, thick and warm. He breathed through his mouth in a futile attempt to keep out the stench. His stomach heaved but there was nothing left to throw up.

Dregs' voice bellowed through the hole, "Don't get any bright ideas. boy. There ain't no way off this ship. You'll have air enough to breathe as long as this hatch's open. The vapors in there might make you light headed now but if I close this thing you'll be dead inside ten minutes. So get it fixed and let's get going, I don't have all slaggin' day."

The thought of escape hadn't even occurred to Vincent. He realized that over the last few weeks he'd resigned himself to his new existence. Vincent crawled through the muck. A large metal corkscrew ran the length of the pipeline, caked over with all manner of unsightly things. Vincent took his trowel and began scraping the filth from the twisting metal of the worm. Slowly it started to slough off into the water below. When it was finally free of obstruction the worm once again began to turn, carrying the waste and all if it's smells down the line to wherever waste went on a ship like this. Vincent was not in the mood to contemplate such things.

Vincent climbed the ladder out of the hatch. As he poked his head out of the hole a blast of cold water hit his face. He nearly lost his grip and went tumbling back into sewer. Spitting and sputtering he continued to climb. The stream of water beat against his body, stinging his skin even beneath his clothes. When it finally stopped he saw Dregs, standing with a large hose in hand, water still dropping from the nozzle, "Well," Dregs said sounding almost apologetic, "couldn't very well have you walkin' around smellin' up my captain's ship." He tossed a fresh set of ragged clothes to Vincent, "Get changed, boy, we're not through yet."

The rest of the chores were mild by comparison, mostly lugging heavy supply containers from one part of the ship to another. By the end, Vincent was exhausted, his legs and back ached and he could hardly lift his arms. He thought he might feel worse now than after one of Velkaso's late night sessions. That thought washed the aches away. Velkaso still might send for him. Everything he did may not have saved him a single day. He eyed the door worriedly, waiting for what he hoped wasn't coming. True to Dregs' word, no one came for him that night, nor the next.

During the years that followed, Vincent's life became fairly routine. Every day Dregs would fetch him for chores and work him until he was bone tired and once or twice a week Velkaso would still send for him. Often he was beaten to the brink of death but the tiny green bottle was always there to bring him back. Over the years Dregs became almost personable. Vincent was able to speak freely now and the conversations they had were an adequate distraction if not altogether friendly. In the end Dregs was the closest thing Vincent had to a friend in this world and he no longer considered how sad that statement was. This was his life and he existed in it. Those were the hard truths. He had no room for hope, for thoughts of home or the life he once knew. The memories of what happened on the Galileo faded over time but one young girl with bright green eyes still haunted his dreams, fanning the fire of hate which kept him alive.

Seven years passed this way. He was taller now and broad, no longer the thin little boy who climbed aboard the Galileo so long ago. His steady regimen of Helix and long days of heavy lifting had turned a once scrawny kid into a formidable man. Dregs supplied him with oversized clothes, rags mostly but they managed to hide his physique well enough.

One night after cleaning the waste lines, while Vincent was changing, Dregs let out a low whistle, "Whew, boy. You get much bigger and one day you might not wake up."

"What are you talking about?" Vincent asked as he pulled a fresh shirt over his head.

"I'm talkin' about you, you overgrown ox. If Velkaso thinks for a minute you might actually be a threat he'll have you killed in your sleep. He's not gonna take a chance that one of these days you might fight back, or worse, win." Dregs glanced down the hall to make sure they were alone, "It's time, boy, follow me." Dregs led Vincent down a series of halls turning through doorways as he came to them.

"Where are we going?" Vincent asked when he thought it was safe to do so.

Dregs just kept walking deeper into the belly of the ship. At last they came to a door Vincent had never seen before. It was larger than any other door on the ship, stretching from floor to ceiling. It was heavy iron and covered in rust. Dregs stopped in front of it and placed his paws flat on the surface. After a few moments he seemed to have come to a decision, looking around cautiously before sliding the door open and stepping through. Vincent followed him through and the door slid shut behind them with surprising silence. Dregs stood in the middle of a large, relatively empty room. It was warm in this room, warmer than Vincent would be comfortable in but a steady flow of air blowing through a metal grate below their feet made it tolerable. Above his head a large tunnel seemed to rise forever. Several ladders lined its walls disappearing into the darkness above.

"What is this place?" Vincent asked a little awestruck.

"The engine access room," Dregs gestured to the ladders, "those lead up to the engine compartments." He stomped on the grate, "Down there is the cooling system. We're idle right now so it's safe to be here but if those engines fired up, we'll be cooked where we stand."

Vincent's face betrayed the worry he was feeling.

Dregs laughed and patted his massive shoulder, "Don't worry, boy, we'll get plenty of warnin' before that." Dregs walked over to a blinking panel on the wall, "Looks like we're clear, the engines are in working order so no one should be disturbing us here."

Vincent couldn't take it anymore, "Dregs what are we doing here?"

Dregs looked at him as though the answer were obvious, "Trainin' of course."

"Training? What training? What are you talking about?"

Dregs looked him over, sizing him up, "You got the body of a man, but not much goin' on upstairs. This is the trainin' you're going to need to beat Velkaso."

"Beat Velkaso?!" Vincent's head swam, "What do you mean beat Velkaso? Didn't you just tell me he'd have me killed if he thought I could win?"

Dregs nodded slowly, "I did, and he will. That's why it's important we keep this between you 'n' me. He'd ice me too if he knew I was helpin' ya."

"Why are you helping me anyway?"

Dregs sighed, "I got my reasons. Besides, I hate this place as much as you do and it's sorta my fault you're here. But mostly because I think you can win." He grabbed Vincent by the arms giving his biceps a light squeeze, "The Helix in your veins pumped you up, you're strong, way stronger than natural. Even your bones are stronger. I've seen it, the effort it takes for Velkaso to inflict the same damage he used to. You heal quicker now too, all side effects Velkaso hadn't planned on. It ain't gonna be long before he realizes you're too much for him and the moment he figures that out, you'll find yourself on the wrong side of an airlock. You have to strike before that moment. You need trainin' so that when the time is right you can put that monster down for good. Now then, let's see what ya got." Dregs crouched down, raising his large paws in front of him, "Come get some, runt! Attack me!"

Vincent came at Dregs slowly, testing the space between them. He circled, searching for an opening, a weakness in Dregs' defense. An alarm sounded from the panel on the wall and a flashing red light caught Vincent's eye. At once, Dregs was upon him, a wrecking ball of fur and muscle, hurling him to floor.

"Never lose your slagged focus!" Dregs hissed over the alarm, "It takes a fraction of a second to lose a fight. Drop your guard, look away, blink, even a moment of hesitation and it can all be over." Dregs stood up, helping Vincent to his feet, "But always know your surroundings. Let's get goin' before they're flushin' our ashes out the airlock."

As Dregs slid the door back into place Vincent could hear the engines, like slumbering dragons, waking with a deafening roar and erupting in furious fire.

As often as they were able, Dregs and Vincent would come to this room to train, far from the prying eyes of Velkaso and his men. Vincent was slow at first, and awkward in his movements but under Dregs' tutelage, he was soon holding his own. His weekly sessions with Velkaso became a different kind of challenge, learning how to take a beating now that he knew how to avoid it. Within a year he was more than a match for Dregs, dodging and lunging with nearly the stealth and swiftness of an Omarian.

"That's enough for today," Dregs sputtered, holding his side after a well-timed hit by Vincent. He limped over and slapped Vincent firmly on the back, "I don't think I can take much more of this abuse, kid. You hit like a fifty-pound hammer." He touched his side again gingerly, "When the time comes, Velkaso is gonna have his hands full."

Dregs jerked upright as the door to the compartment slid open. Velkaso and several of his crew stepped in. He didn't seem surprised to see them and eyed them both suspiciously while his men took positions on all sides, *"Why you down here, boys?"*

Dregs jumped in before Vincent could think of a response, "Just checkin' the exhaust ports, my captain, makin' sure everything is in workin' order."

"That is no your job, monkaso," Velkaso's searing eyes seemed to pierce through to Vincent's soul, searching for the truth.

"Yes, my captain, I just thought-"

"Silence!" Velkaso gestured to one of his men who disappeared up the nearest ladder. A few moments later he returned shaking his rat-like head. Velkaso held his gaze on Vincent, *"You getting big, boys, too big. I feeds you too much I think. No foods for you this week."*

"My captain, the boy needs to eat, he has his chores, he needs his strength to complete them," argued Dregs.

Velkaso turned to Dregs, *"Why you care for monkaso boys? What he mean to you?"*

"He means nothin' to me, my captain. He's marginally useful around the ship. I get much a lot more done with his help. I don't wanna fall behind on my duties because the boy is too weak from hunger."

Velkaso sneered and patted Dregs on the shoulder, dragging a long claw slowly down the side of his neck, *"Two weeks!"* He leaned in close to Dregs, grabbing a fist full of his collar, *"I is Velkaso, you no give orders to me."*

Dregs dropped his head, "Yes, my captain. I'm so sorry, my captain. It won't happen again."

Velkaso released him and turned toward the door, *"Back to work, boys, I no want your chores to suffer."*

It was a week and a half before Vincent found himself back in Velkaso's twisted arena along with the usual crowd gathered around him. It took two of Velkaso's men to carry him from his cell. His body dripped with sweat and his muscles ached and twitched uncontrollably. Ten days without food had left him weak but it was the Helix his body craved the most. Velkaso seemed especially hostile, his already prominent nostrils flared in rage. He must have missed these pummeling sessions Vincent thought grimly.

Velkaso snatched Vincent's wrist, twisting his arm to its limits with every ounce of his strength, *"You miss me, boys? You think I done with you? Pfft."* Velkaso spat on the ground, *"When I done with you, boys, I make you dead. You no forget."*

Vincent screamed as his arm snapped under the pressure of Velkaso's grip. Pieces of bone tore through his flesh, splintered and sharp.

"Hey! He's no good to me like that!" Dregs' deep voice rang out from somewhere behind Vincent.

Velkaso lashed out, the entirety of his rage seemed to funnel itself into one wicked slash of his claws. Vincent was going into shock. The pain in his arm pushed him to the very edge of consciousness but he watched as Velkaso's talon-like hand swept past, lunging into the sea of onlookers. A feral cry echoed off the walls of the cargo bay. When Velkaso's hand came back into view, ribbons of dark red flesh and tawny fur clung to his fingers, *"Take him away!"*

Vincent's head sagged as the pain overwhelmed him. Velkaso slapped his cheeks lightly, *"No, no, no, boys, you no sleep yet, Velkaso not done with you."* He grabbed Vincent's other arm twisting his wrist until Vincent squirmed in pain. He tried to turn, to see what had happened to Dregs, to see where they were taking him, *"What you looking for, boys? You think he your friend? He no your friend, boys. You has no friend. You has only pain. You has only Velkaso!"*

Vincent's arm gave way, the tendons tearing away from bone and muscle. The last thing he saw before darkness took hold was a small bottle of the green life giving liquid being brought to his lips.

Even with the Helix, it was several agonizing days before Vincent recovered from the wounds Velkaso had inflicted upon him. Dregs was alive, though without the Helix to aid him it was several weeks before he came to collect Vincent for any more chores. When he finally did come it wasn't the same. They rarely spoke and Vincent lost any hope he may have had for Dregs to be anything more than another of his captors.

The weeks and months began to blur together with no discernable beginning or end. He suffered through his endless chores in silence day in and day out. Every now and then Velkaso would call for him and he'd spend the next day or two healing. He began to look forward to them, to long for them. He yearned for the pain, he lived for it, his body ached for it. It ached for torture, it longed for Helix.

"Wake up, kid!" Dregs voice whispered harshly through the small slot in his cell door. "Damn you, wake up!"

"I'm up, I'm up," Vincent replied.

"Shhh…" Dregs cautioned, "Not another word. Follow me."

The door of Vincent's cell slid open without a sound. He pushed himself off of the cold metal floor and stepped out into the dim light of the corridor. There was an uneasiness hanging in the air. It was quiet, deathly quiet, and the halls which usually held scattered gatherings of Velkaso's men were abandoned completely.

"Where is everyone?" Vincent managed before Dregs silenced him with a large, tawny paw.

Dregs motioned down the hall and Vincent silently followed. Turn by turn Dregs led him back to the large engine room door. Dregs slid it open and motioned for Vincent to step inside.

When the door was shut behind them Vincent could hold his tongue no longer, "Okay, what the hell is going on? Why are we here? And why is there no one else on this ship?"

Dregs stepped passed him, no longer seeming to care about being heard. He leapt onto a ladder and climbed toward the lower engine compartment, "They're here, kid, no one's left." He called down as he climbed, "The bloody fools stumbled into a Lycete security patrol." He ripped the panel cover away and began working, still shouting with his head inside the manifold, "We were getting' low on supplies, usually we take a route that skirts what you know as the outer territory." His breathing became heavier as he worked, loud clanging noises drowned out much of what he was trying to say, "Velkaso got cocky…(clang)…(clang)…bloody idiot should have known…(clang)…tried to…(clang)…(clang)…(clang)…now we're in the middle of a…(clang)…(clang)…and there's nothing to do but…(clang)…" Dregs popped his head out of the manifold, "But I guess that works out well for us, don't it?"

Vincent stood gaping in bewilderment.

Dregs shimmied back down the ladder and grabbed Vincent by the shoulder, "We're gettin' out of here, kid, me and you."

Vincent didn't know what to say. How? Why now? What was going on? His mind fumbled over all of the questions, leaving his tongue frozen in his mouth.

Dregs turned toward the door, "That should do her in, let's go."

"What's going on?!" Vincent managed finally, much louder than he'd intended.

Dregs' eyes rolled in his head, "Slag it, kid, I just told you. Get the lead outta your ears. Velkaso crossed too close to the Lycete home world and they're worse than Hais. They've got security patrols sweepin' the area lookin' for us. He can't hope to fight them but he can't run yet either, he don't know where they are, ya see? Don't wanna run into them on accident. I figure you and I stow away in one of the rescue pods and wait for him to make a run for it. He'll be too busy runnin' for his life to worry about chasin' us."

Vincent frowned, "What if we get picked up by someone out here?"

"I imagine we're dead one way or the other, but I'd rather be stone dead than spend another day in this hell."

As sad as it was Vincent had to admit he was right, "So what were you just doing to the engine?"

Dregs' lips curled into a wicked smile, "I said I want him to run for his life, I never said I want him to make it."

Red lights suddenly lit up the room and a loud siren wailed in their ears.

"Damn!" Dregs cursed as they raced for the door, "They musta found us. We don't got time to lose, follow me." Through the door and around the corner they ran, twisting from one corridor to the next without slowing. A violent explosion rocked the ship sending them both to their knees. The ship grinded to a halt. "Damn!" yelled Dregs, "Of all the gray lovin' luck! It wasn't supposed to happen that fast."

"What happened?" Vincent asked staggering to his feet.

Dregs ran a large paw through his shaggy mane, "I weakened the shields on the main core. Once it got hot enough the whole side blew out. We're dead in the water now."

"Well, at least we know he won't be chasing us-" Vincent stopped as they turned the last corner.

Velkaso's men filled the hangar, pouring themselves into rescue pods, literal rats abandoning their ship. Their writhing pinkish bodies tearing at each other as they fought to escape.

New explosions rocked the ship, "Sounds like the Lycete aren't in the mood to negotiate," Vincent said wryly.

Dregs motioned to the far side of the hangar, a single rescue pod sat unoccupied and seemingly unnoticed, "Stay right behind me, don't stop for anythin'."

Dregs burst from the hallway at a full sprint. He lowered his shoulder charging into the fray. One by one he tore his way through the mass of bodies, his knife-like claws cutting a path to the other side. Velkaso's men seemed not to notice, fixated on their desire to escape. Vincent followed close behind stumbling over Dregs' fallen victims as he ran. They were almost there, only a few steps from freedom when from out of nowhere a large clawed hand landed with crushing force on the side of Dregs' head. He crumpled mid stride under the blow and fell to the floor, a motionless ball of fur.

"Where you going, boys? Velkaso no done with you yet." Velkaso stepped out of the crowd and his fleeing minions gave him a wide berth. He snatched Vincent up by the throat, his sharp claws digging into the soft flesh of Vincent's neck, *"This the last time, boys. This time I break you and leave you. You make worthless corpse too, filthy monkaso."*

Velkaso smacked his grotesque lips. His vice-like grip tightened, choking the life from Vincent's body. Vincent cast a desperate look at Dregs, still motionless on the hangar floor. They were so close to freedom, so close. Why had they even tried? Why did he continue to fight? Why couldn't he just die? For the first time in years of captivity Vincent lost all hope. He closed his eyes and let his body succumb to Velkaso's will. There was almost disappointment on Velkaso face as Vincent's body stopped struggling for breath and dropped, lifeless, to the ground.

In the ether of near death, a small girl materialized from the darkness. A face that had haunted him for nearly a decade. Her bright green eyes seemed to urge him onward. (Don't give up)...(Don't give up)...(Fight Vincent)...(Fight for me)...(Never stop fighting)

Vincent gasped and choked, sucking air back into his lungs. He wouldn't give up, he'd never stop fighting. "Velkaso!" He screamed pushing himself off the floor, "VELKASO! You're not done with me yet!"

Velkaso turned back, an amused smile on his rat-like face, *"Yes, boys, fight! No matter what you think, now is the time you die."*

Velkaso charged with blinding speed his clawed hand raking through the air towards Vincent's throat but he was not fast enough. Vincent deflected the blow, stepping deftly to one side, sending Velkaso harmlessly past with the skill of a well-trained matador. Velkaso spun to face him. His nostrils flared and a fiery hate filled his eyes. Again he charged but Dregs had trained Vincent well and again his attack fell harmlessly away. Then it was Vincent's turn. Balling up his iron fists he rained down his revenge upon Velkaso. Backing him into the wall Vincent allowed no room for retreat.

Velkaso's bones crunched and gave way under the violent fury of his attack. The anger in his eyes turned to confusion as the first few hits connected, followed quickly by surprise and pain. Vincent never let up, punishing Velkaso with his devastating punches. Every hit carried a face, a name, some child long forgotten on the Galileo, a small girl with bright green eyes. Vincent screamed as he brought his fists down time and time again on his now defenseless enemy. Blood covered his hands and spattered his clothes and as Velkaso's eyes closed he sank to the floor beside him. It was finally over.

"Time to go, kid," Dregs placed a comforting paw on his shoulder. Pressing a piece of cloth to the gash in his scalp he started toward the rescue pod, "He got what he deserved, now leave him be."

Vincent stood, wiping his face and hands on his oversized shirt. He closed the hatch and settled into his seat.

"Gah!" Dregs mumbled from the controls, "No wonder they weren't fightin' over this pod, the cryo units are fried. We won't be able to last more than a few weeks out there without 'em."

Vincent shook his head, "It's the only shot we've got so you might as well strap in."

Dregs nodded and took a seat. He lit up the controls and readied them for launch, "Looks like it's just you 'n' me from here on out, kid. What's your name anyways?"

The question took Vincent by surprise, no one has used his name in ages, "It's...Vincent...I

TROJAN HORSE

TIVEX AWOKE SUDDENLY FOR WHAT SEEMED LIKE THE HUNDREDTH TIME THAT NIGHT. DREGS' STORY from the previous day haunted her dreams. She had hoped being on a bed anywhere but the Widow Maker would be a relaxing and welcome experience, but her comfort couldn't keep out the images flashing inside her head. She checked the clock on her bedside table, finding it reading only oh five hundred. It was no use fighting it, she may as well start her day, perhaps an early morning run would clear her head.

A few short minutes later she was standing outside her quarters. She walked down to the mess hall feeling the crisp filtrated air filling her lungs. She breathed it in deeply, finding the air had a touch of flower scent to it. She knew the Omarians loved the smell of flowers. In fact, the entire planet below them was a massive jungle, teeming with amazing flora. Tivex managed a small smile at finding the irony of these massive feline warriors finding comfort in the most delicate creations in nature.

The space station was still for the most part asleep. Normally, full duties other than the posted watches wouldn't start for another hour. A few crewmen were in the mess hall, all of which gave her sideways glances when she walked in. Omarians considered the Akoni to be the antithesis of everything they stood for. Omarians focused on power and strength whereas Akoni used intellect and negotiation. Tivex heard their muffled talking and knew that whatever they were saying in hushed tones were undoubtedly insults of some kind

Tivex hadn't spent much time in space, other than for required training and the occasional medical emergency. When she had come through basic training, she had been assigned to communications before she was allowed to take the test for the Medical Division. Thankfully, her communications assignment had lasted a grand total of four months but was years ago. Tivex knew regular spaceflight was not on the top of her priority list, there was something about it that made her uneasy. The events over the last month had only proved her theory to be true. Her plan this morning was to get a simple breakfast and then go down to the recreation area. Even though she had been able to move around freely on the unknown planet, she found her muscles to be tight, although she had to admit most of it was from stress.

She finished her meal, returned the tray and left the mess hall as quickly as she could.

Tivex avoided contact with any other crew member she saw and made her way to the recreation area. When she arrived, she pushed through the doors and into the recreation area which was almost as large as a cargo bay. All around her lay various exercise machines, weights, grappling equipment, and true to Omarian heritage, excessive amounts of punching bags. Tivex stifled a small laugh as she walked over to a small running track.

She stretched as best she could and began to jog around the track. Her legs felt stiff, like two bars of iron trying to be made pliable. She forced herself to keep going feeling twinges of pain spike in her quadriceps. After the first lap, Tivex felt as if she had run a marathon already but her mind was beginning to clear ever so slightly. She continued to jog around the track, her pace picking up gradually. With every step she took, she felt as if she were somehow gaining more ground away from the last few weeks.

Tivex jogged until she knew her knees were about to give out. She crossed the final marker for the last time and literally collapsed on the floor. Her breathing was fast but not as fast as her heartbeat. She hadn't realized how much strain she had been through and it was catching up with her, making up for lost time. Tivex crawled back onto all fours, or in her case, all sixes and thrust her head down as best she could to try to get it between her legs.

"Is that how you feel today?" Master Admiral Soren spoke from behind her, "Upside down and unable to breathe?"

It startled her, partly because she had not known he was there, mostly though because he seemed to be reading her mind. She nodded slowly, finding it difficult to answer, "Yes, sir."

"That's not surprising," Soren remarked, taking a seat beside her on the floor, "You've been through the wringer the last few days."

"Sir?" she replied knowing the look on her face made the question unnecessary.

Soren shook his head, "It's an expression only people as old as me still use. It's not important. What is important is that it's over. We've decided we've heard everything you have to say. There's nothing more we can gain from pressing the matter."

"What about what Dregs told us? I mean, how did Vincent ever wind up an IEC officer after all that?"

Soren returned a half smile, "It was his choice. When he came back, he was way beyond any conventional help that we could've given him. It was either being locked up in a medical facility for what I'm sure would've been the better part of his life or enlist in IEC. Our training is meant to separate feelings from actions, you know that."

"What about Dregs?"

"Same choice. Normally I would've never considered it, but when he helped Vincent escape, it proved that there was some good in him. A severely small and mostly fractured piece, but good nonetheless. I made the call to offer them both the choice. I separated them on different planets for training but somehow they found their way back to one another. Did you know that's where Vincent met Peter Andrews?"

"Blitz?!" said Tivex in shock.

Soren nodded, "I had Vincent under a microscope from day one of his return. I had specially trained officers to deal with him in case he went rouge again. From what they told me, Vincent and Peter met in the mess hall on the first day of basic. They seemed to stick together and Peter had a way of getting Vincent to focus and open up about things our doctors couldn't. I suppose that's how Blitz was able to stay so calm about yesterday. I'm suppose he must've figured out something along the way even if Vincent never actually told him anything.

"If he did, I am surprised Blitz never said anything to the others," said Tivex.

Soren smirked, "He knew it wasn't his place to say anything at all. Why do you think Andrews was the original first officer? Why do you think Jeffrey is the engineer? Why do you think the twins never ask for promotion? But most of all, why do you think Dregs is attached to Vincent at the hip and has an unspoken language with him?"

"Because they are like family…" said Tivex as the stark realization hit her all at once.

Soren nodded, "For whatever else those gray jackals are, they stick together. They could be millions of miles apart and yet they always find their way back to each other. That's what makes them so special and that's why it was so imperative we keep them on the straight and narrow."

Tivex brightened a little but something still bashed at her brain. She flipped herself over and brushed the dust off her hands, "Sir, what does any of this have to do with that ship we found?"

Soren looked around cautiously but aside from them the recreation area was deserted. He turned to her, "The Sageve archives speak of a ship, a legend really, whose origins are as old as recorded history. It was a myth, a story told to inspire generations about a ship with limitless range. It could traverse the universe in moments without the aid of such crude technologies as Bridges. This ship was called the Horizon, designed by the creators of the universe themselves or so the story goes. Horizon sightings have been recorded in nearly every major event in Sageve history, but there's wasn't a scrap of hard evidence to prove it ever really existed. It became an icon, an omen for change. It reached its cultural peak a few thousand years ago. Then one day it disappeared from the records entirely. The legend of the Horizon became a ghost, no one has claimed to see it in over five hundred years."

"And you think that's what we found? A mystery alien ship from the beginning of the universe?"

Soren sighed, "I know how it sounds but when you're as old as I am you learn to have faith in the unbelievable. I've researched these accounts for many years, there's too much consistency in the accounts to be mere coincidence. The circumstances are too similar the descriptions too accurate to be lies."

Tivex's eyebrow raised in suspicion, "How do you know their descriptions were accurate?"

"I thought you'd have guessed by know," Soren said coyly, "Because I've seen it of course." He cleared his throat, "Not just me, Master Admirals Tall'ani and Lokias were there as well, and General Doran naturally. It was like no ship we'd ever seen, flawless and smooth, as if it had been formed of a single piece of metal. Beautiful, really. That ship was there, the weapon was there and then both were gone without a trace. If the others hadn't seen it as well, I would've chalked it up to a delusion of my senses. But, as it was, I couldn't let go of the idea the two things were connected. After the formation of the IEC, I spent months pouring over the archives searching for answers in case the weapon or the Horizon ever surfaced again. What I found was everything I've told you now. I believe the ship exists, and I believe the legends are true. I think the Kuvvaa knew it too. I think their plan was to load that weapon onto the Horizon and use it to bring the weapon here. The results would have been disastrous. That's why we can't risk the Horizon falling into the wrong hands, and that's why we're sending you after it."

"So you actually saw what, wait," Tivex's eyes widened, "what do you mean you are sending us after it?"

Soren nodded, "You heard me, Commander."

"Sir, I-"

"This isn't up for debate, Commander, we're sending Team Seven back out."

Tivex felt her rapidly beating heart seemingly skip a few beats as the news sunk in. Her arms felt as though they had become numb and her mouth went dry. She dropped her head to the floor as all of the stress she had try to run out of her returned and began knocking on the door of her sanity. To Soren's credit, he hadn't said anything more to upset her. A few silent moments passed before she lifted her head back up, "Have you told Vincent?"

Soren shook his head, "No, not yet. I'm telling you first because I have Kagen's recommendation that you've got the most level head we can count on now. Secondly, I know what you heard yesterday was hard and I know how it must've made you feel."

"Sir?"

Soren put his arms behind him and leaned back, "Call me old fashioned, Commander, but I saw the look in your eyes when Dregs came clean. I've seen that look before and I suggest you hide it from the others."

Tivex cocked her head, "What look was that?"

"You care for him, Commander."

"Of course I care for him! He is my friend! Or, at least he used to be..."

Soren raised an eyebrow at her, "Right. Like I said, I'd keep that stowed if I were you."

Tivex shook her head, "Sir, if there is any question about my motives, I-"

"Leave it alone for now, Commander." Soren grunted as he stood back up, "Go and wake the others and make sure they get something to eat before the briefing at oh eight hundred. Do not mention you and I've spoken."

Tivex nodded slowly, "Aye, sir."

Soren nodded back and took his leave.

Tivex watched him leave and then fell back onto the ground. She stared up at the ceiling and shook her head. She couldn't believe they were going back out. And how? They didn't have a ship anymore. She raised her upper set of arms up and covered her face, trying to block the frustrated scream erupting from her lips.

Tivex watched as the others gobbled down their breakfast with ravenous hunger. Everyone except for Hammer who merely stared down at his coffee and kept swishing it around the brim. Silk was still in the medical deck where he would remain behind for the mission. The mission she knew about and couldn't tell the others. The mission she knew they were about to find out about. While the others gorged themselves a few times over, Tivex tried to make it look as though she was enjoying her meal but found herself merely pushing the food back and forth on her plate.

Torque looked up at her, his cheeks jammed with food, "Hey, come on, shister! This stuphts way better than rationths!"

Tivex smiled at him, "Which I see is all over your shirt."

"Thavin' it for later," grinned Torque as he gulped down his forth glass of juice. He wiped his mouth on his sleeve, "What's with you anyway? You haven't said two words since wake up."

Tivex didn't look up at him, "I am just tired."

"Bull," heaved Dregs over his steak, "Your shirt's still wet, you went runnin' this mornin', didn't ya?"

"Not that it matters, but yes. A few moments of serenity away from you can work miracles."

"Hmph," huffed Dregs, "it wasn't like I was sleepin' real good last night either."

Torque glared at him, "Hmm, I wonder why that could be?"

Dregs emitted a low growl, "Like you're any better?"

Dusty leaned over the table at him, "At least he don't lie about stuff."

Hammer slammed his coffee cup down, "Stow it! He didn't lie about anything."

"No, but he did not tell us everything, did he?" asked Tivex. She set her fork back down and glared at Blitz, "And it would seem there is a lot of that going around lately, would you not agree?"

Blitz glared back at her. Tivex knew she had crossed the line but was beginning not to care. Blitz never took his eyes off her, "So I guess we should be heading back to the briefing room now?"

Tivex nodded, "I guess so." She stood up out of her chair so fast it fell over. She felt her upper lip curl into a snarl of her own, "We would not want to keep our superiors waiting, would we?"

Hammer kicked his own chair out from beneath him. He got between Blitz and Tivex. She could feel his blazing eyes trying to burn a hole right through her as he seethed, "Lead the way."

Tivex rolled her eyes and lead them back to the briefing room. Soren and Tall'ani were waiting for them. Judging from the looks on their faces, she knew they could tell things were delicate for Team Seven. The Master Admirals motioned for everyone to have a seat around the table. The only one who did not sit down was Dregs who preferred to stand alone in the shadows of the room, his arms crossed over his chest.

Soren spoke up, "Alright, down to business. In the interest of saving time, I'm just going to say that we have no further reason to doubt your report over the last few days."

"Finally," said Blitz.

Soren shot him a look, "Be that as it may, there's still concern over the whereabouts of the alien spacecraft. Concerns which are going to warrant another search and recover mission."

Dusty pushed his hat back onto his head, "Woo, boy, who didn' see that comin'?"

Tivex saw Soren draw in a deep breath to control his anger, "That's right. I'm assigning Team Seven to go after the ship that attacked you and retrieve that ship. Let me be clear about one thing, any means does not warrant you to go out of IEC protocols. You will conduct yourselves as the officers you are and I will stand for nothing less."

Tivex shuddered as she felt a wave a disregard pass from one person to the next. It was eerie.

"Now, with that being said, we're also authorizing your request, Lieutenant," said Tall'ani to Torque.

Tivex looked at Torque who was beaming from behind his wild locks. He rested his elbows on the table and grinned fiendishly at Blitz, "Hehehe, it's playtime!"

Blitz looked down his nose at Torque, "If you turn me into a toaster, I'm gonna kill you."

"Noted," giggled Torque.

"Excuse me," interrupted Tivex, "what exactly was the request?"

"Lieutenant Dorran requested a further inspection of the metal shard you recovered," answered Soren, "he believes that Lieutenant Commander Andrews may be able to decipher more about the alien craft from what was already downloaded."

Tivex wrenched her neck over at Torque, "And you were planning on telling me this, when?"

Torque shrugged, "You didn't ask."

Tivex rolled her eyes and turned back to Tall'ani, "Ma'am, I believe it was my duty to report any actions out of the ordinary?"

Tall'ani nodded.

Tivex threw her hands up, "Everything this Team does is out of the ordinary!" She waved her hands across the table, "Being that I am now the first officer, I believe it would have been prudent for me to have been at least notified about the request!"

"Why? So you coulda ratted us out?" growled Dregs from behind her.

Tivex spun around and glared, "No, you Omarian-"

"WATCH YOUR TONE!" thundered Tall'ani.

Tivex spun around again, not realizing she had let her emotions get the better of her. She slumped back into her chair and shook her head, "What is the point of having me on this Team if they do not trust me enough to let me in on their plans?"

"The point," said Soren trying to diffuse the situation, "is that I'm sure they are still feeling you out as you are them. Star Teams take years to come together and we've asked you to do it in a month, hardly enough time for any kind of bonds to be built. Regardless of how you all feel about each other right now, there are more pressing matters at hand. Before we allow you to check over the shard, I need to know what the probability is that you might find something?" he asked Torque.

Torque turned to Blitz. Blitz became silent for a moment before he shrugged back, "I can't see anything yet. Maybe after we check it out but there's a slag load of data to sort through."

Tall'ani twitched her nose, "That may very well be, Lieutenant Commander, but we need to find that ship and get it out of enemy hands as soon as possible."

Hammer stifled a laugh. Soren turned to him, "Something to add, Captain?"

Hammer couldn't stop from chuckling, "Sir, Velkaso'd be halfway across the galaxy with it by now. You'll never find him."

Soren leaned back in his chair, "You're exactly right, which is why we're sending you after him."

Hammer's eyes shot open, "Come again?"

"You heard me."

Hammer turned and looked at everyone around the table. He looked back at Dregs and then back to Soren, "Sir, we don't have a ship and even if we did, there's little to zero chance we'll find him. We don't even know which way he went."

Soren raised his brow and looked at Dregs and Hammer, "The two of you are our best bet. You know his mannerisms and his patterns."

"That very well may be true, sir," said Dregs as he stepped out from the shadows, "but that still leaves us with no ship and no way to find 'im. We'd have better luck tryin' to find Tall'ani here in a dark room at midnight while we was wearin' blindfolds!"

Tall'ani turned her head at Dregs, dropped her ears and hissed loudly, "Master Admiral to you, thief!"

Dregs heard the hiss and roared back at her, "Right back atcha, kitten!"

"ENOUGH!" yelled Soren, "Both of you, stow it!" Dregs and Tall'ani regained their composure but they both emitted low growls towards each other. Soren rolled his eyes and looked back to Hammer, "We have it on good authority that we may know of a good place to start looking."

"Where?" asked Tivex.

Soren turned to Tivex, "Dominion territory."

"Oh, you've gotta be kiddin' me, sir," said Dregs, "What are we supposeta to do? Just cruise on in there with IEC hardware and say hi?"

Soren answed, "After your last unauthorized entry into their space?" and Soren turned towards Hammer, "I think not. You're going to need a way to sneak in unseen and search without getting caught."

Tivex could almost feel Hammer's blood begin to boil at the mere thought of going into Dominion territory again. He merely gritted his teeth, "And how do you suggest we do that, sir?"

Soren folded his hands again and leaned back, "You're going to take a shuttle from here to the Ninth Circle."

"The prison planet?" said Torque.

Soren nodded, "Correct. A prisoner was recently caught and sent there which had a ship capable of doing what we need done. You are going to use that ship to enter the Dominion and find Velkaso."

"Just so we're clear on this, you want us, of all people, to take some criminal's ship to go into the worst possible place we could? Then you want us to go and bring back the most dangerous wreckage in history away from the thing that damned near killed Hammer?" asked Blitz.

Soren nodded.

"Oh, and you want us to do this our prime pilot out of commission?" Blitz added.

Soren nodded, "Correct."

Blitz whistled and kicked his feet up onto the table. He lit a cigar, "Slag it, sounds like fun."

Hammer looked back at Blitz and smirked wickedly. He turned around to face Soren and Tall'ani again, "Who's the prisoner?"

"That's classified," answered Tall'ani.

"Can I at least know where they came from so we know what kind of ship to expect?"

Soren said, "Relax, Captain, she's human."

"You sent a human to the Ninth Circle?" Hammer replied in amazement, "What did she do?"

Tall'ani bared her teeth, "Also classified."

Dregs sneered, "Hmph, can't wait to meet her."

"Oh, I guarantee the two of you are cut from the same cloth," hissed Tall'ani at Dregs as she turned to Soren, "are we done wasting time?"

Soren shot a brutal look towards Tall'ani and then leaned forward onto the table, "Captain, I realize what we're ordering you to do is unorthodox but it doesn't change the fact that we don't have any other options. Imagine if the Hais, Velkaso or even the Kuvvaas got their hands on the Horizon. There'd be no stopping them, even with an armada of Hunter classes and you know it."

Hammer nodded and looked around at the others. Each of them nodded back to him and he turned to Soren and Tall'ani, "We'll get it done."

Soren nodded back, "Good. There's a shuttle standing by, gather what you need from the armory and ship out on the double."

Everyone got up to leave and walked towards the door. Just as Tivex reached the door, Soren put his hand on her shoulder, "Commander, before you leave, a word?"

Tivex nodded and saw Hammer cast a quizzical, but extremely distrustful look in her direction. She felt a strange feeling creeping up in her, if he was going to keep things from her, maybe it wasn't a bad idea to let him think there was more to her as well.

As the shuttle approached the planet, Tivex stared out the window with a loss for words. She had never seen a place like this before and she couldn't image a worse fate than to permanently be sentenced. The Ninth Circle was a planet whose sole purpose was for the imprisonment and detainment of the absolute worst elements in the universe. If someone was sent to this awful place, it meant that there was no parole, no reprieve and no hope of ever leaving. Tivex heard the others talking quietly amongst themselves about how Dregs had almost wound up in a place like this and she had also seen him twitch his tail when they had entered the territory.

What she was staring at was beyond comparison to anything she had seen thus far in her limited travels. The Ninth Circle was a small planet which orbited a red giant star. The light which came from the star itself bathed the planet in an awful crimson causing it to look like the planet was bleeding from somewhere inside it. The closer the shuttle came to the Ninth Circle, Tivex could just make out various places where black, oily lines snaked across the surface. She assumed it was waste sent out from the numerous factories Torque had explained the prisoners worked in. Everywhere she looked, huge, billowing clouds of gray, black and orange decorated the sky, courtesy of the massive belching smoke towers below. Tivex wrinkled her nose as they dropped lower as the scent of sulfur, burnt metal and grime clung to her nose.

Tivex put one of her hands up to her face just as Torque walked up to her, "Yeah, this place does that to first timers."

"What is that odor?" she asked.

"Residue from the factories below," answered Torque. "That and say maybe twenty-five hundred prisoners who haven't seen a shower for years."

Tivex turned to Torque, "What kind of abominations could survive on such a place?"

Torque smirked, "Trust me, Commander, these are the worst of the worst. Killers and traitors mostly but there's also enemies of the state and a handful of galactic terrorists too."

Tivex swallowed hard but found her mouth was saturated with the bad taste in her mouth, "I trust we will not be here for long."

"We're in and out as fast as we can," answered Torque, "none of us wants to be here any longer than we have to. The air down there is barely above toxic and if you breathed it long enough, you'd be dead in three, maybe four years' tops. It can clog up rotor blades in a few hours too. That's why supply ships drop off the cargo at a certain elevation. No one ever goes to the actual surface unless they're, let's say, residents."

Tivex nodded. The shuttle continued to drop closer to one of the larger buildings and finally landed on a special dock. She heard Hammer say, "Alright, let's get this done and get out of here."

"Yeah, this slagged ash is messin' up my targeting," said Blitz.

Tivex noticed that Blitz had seemed a little off since they had left the Omarian space station. Well, she thought, more off than usual. He and Torque had disappeared into one of the research rooms while the others had gathered their gear. They had been absent for over an hour but when they came back, Blitz seemed to be shaking his head a lot, as if he were trying to shake off some massive headache. Tivex had attempted to ask how the shard inspection had gone but Torque had only shrugged and explained that when Blitz had touched the shard, he had gone catatonic for a good half hour before rebooting. When he had come back, Blitz said he was trying to sort out all the information and it was going to take some time. Torque also said that when Blitz held the shard, his mechanical blue eye began to glow more intensely, almost burning to a white color. Since then, Tivex chalked the whole inspection up to being yet another mystery in a puzzle which seemed to have more pieces all the time.

The shuttle hatch opened and Team Seven were ushered off the shuttle and into the massive complex. Tivex noticed as soon as she had stepped off the shuttle the temperature was far below what she had expected while the air was twice as thick. She was having a hard time catching her breath until they went inside. They walked down a dark corridor where a continual sound of something which sounded like it was grinding against the walls followed them the entire way. They reached what looked to be an office where the Sageve warden waved them in to sit down.

Tivex stared into the unblinking, black eyes of the warden as he introduced himself by shaking hands with Hammer, "Welcome to the Ninth Circle. I'm warden Seretak."

Hammer replied, "I wish I could say it's nice to be here."

Seretak smiled, "I understand, however, it's nice to see an IEC Team here. We haven't had a real Team in these parts for longer than I care to admit." Tivex watched as Dregs looked around him and shook himself a few times. Seretak picked up on his discomfort and looked at him, "It's alright, I know who you are but other than the business you came for; I assure you you're not staying."

Dregs huffed a small laugh, "Beggin' you pardon there, warden. Not my first pick for an assignment."

"Nor mine," answered Seretak, "however this place does produce the biggest Seralium ore in the universe and we need it for our technology. Unfortunately, that does require our race to have to rotate through here."

Dregs nodded, "Sorry ta hear that."

Seretak nodded and retuned his attention to Hammer, "I assume you're in a time constraint judging from Master Admiral Soren's orders?"

Hammer nodded, "They didn't tell us much in the mission brief other than you have a ship here that was confiscated from a prisoner."

Seretak nodded again, "That's right. It's docked four levels above us but it's been here for a while. As soon as I received the orders I had my technicians give it a good once over."

Hammer nodded back, "I appreciate that. Is there anything about the ship that we need to know?"

"Nothing imparticular," replied Seretak, "it's a standard issue Destroyer class."

"Destroyer class?" said Dusty suddenly, "As in Hais Destroyer class?"

Seretak nodded, "One in the same. The prisoner was not happy about us looking at it and she was most uncooperative with questioning."

"Yeah, I'll bet she was," said Dusty, "I'd be too if I'd got tagged in somethin' that illegal."

Tivex was beside herself with what she was hearing. When she was assigned to Team Seven, she knew there would be certain things she would have to get used to. Now, the list was about to include being thrown into a Destroyer whose previous owner was a human of all things. She shook her head, trying to be as nonchalant as possible and asked, "Is there a reason you are holding a human female on this planet?"

Seretak turned his lifeless gaze towards her, "I'm sorry, Commander, but that's classified."

Tivex looked at Hammer who shook his head, silently telling her not to press the matter. She pursed her lips together in frustration. They were about to take this condemned persons ship and for all they knew could be riddled with antipersonnel traps, if not worse. She looked back to Seretak who was again discussing some of the flight controls as well as the ship's capabilities but kept her eyes diverted from Hammer. She didn't appreciate being told to keep quiet and what made it worse was that she had seen a look in his eyes she didn't like. When Soren and Tall'ani had sent them on this mission, without actually saying it they had basically given Hammer carte blanche. She knew the order to stay within IEC protocol would be out the door the second he was out of earshot. Tivex knew all about Hammer's history with Velkaso and the looks exchanged by both Dregs and Hammer gave her pause. Something wasn't right and she could feel it.

She heard Seretak saying, "So, really, outside of the main drive being substantially more aggressive, your pilot shouldn't have any trouble."

Hammer nodded his head and replied, "Thanks very much, warden, we'll take that into consideration."

Seretak nodded, "If you'll just follow me." He got out of his chair and motioned for everyone to follow him. Team Seven was led down a dizzying amount of passages and hallways which wound through the complex. Tivex imagined the need for such a complicated setup was good for security as it was almost impossible to keep up with the twists and turns. Before heading down one of the passages, Seretak turned back and said, "I'm sorry, but the only way up is through here. Watch yourself, we're going through one of the cell blocks and as you know IEC security is responsible for putting most of the inmates in here. They should all be in lockdown now but keep a sharp eye out."

Seretak entered an extremely complicated code into a terminal with expert speed and a hatch opened up. They walked through the opening into a long passageway. As they made their way through, Tivex heard the jeering from the inmates on both sides. They catcalled, whistled, screamed and yelled every obscenity that Tivex knew among many she didn't. She noticed that they all used a great deal of profanity, most of which infuriated her.

Tivex tried to keep her calm as she heard one inmate yell out, "Hey! Yeah you! The big Gray Girl! What happened, baby? Got plowed by a couple Hais, huh? Yeah, why don't you come on over here and use all them arms on me!"

Another yelled, "Go slag yourself, you Akoni freak! Your race ain't nothin'!"

Yet another one screamed, "Oh, here come the big, bad Akoni! Whatcha gonna do, huh? Insult me to death? Yeah, I took some of your kind out before, bled them nice and slow! Didn't know your Gray asses bled blue, nice color for you freak!"

Tivex was nearly at the breaking point when Hammer turned around and walked back to her, "'Vex, keep your eyes down. They already think you're weak."

"I really could care less, Captain. Are we almost to our target?"

Hammer walked beside her, "Should be there in a minute. Just keep your eyes down and don't look at them."

"Thank you, Captain, I will keep that under advisement."

She could feel Hammer's eyes on her but she didn't look back at him. Finally, amidst the degrading calls, she heard him say, "I've never heard that one before."

"I believe he was referring to you," she seethed.

Hammer smirked and replied, "Wow, I dunno if it was a compliment but I'm flattered."

Tivex again said nothing. She felt her jaw clenching together and her hands had balled up into fists. Everything that had happened in the last few weeks was beginning to catch up with her and she felt herself on the proverbial breaking point as she knew it. She knew Hammer hadn't meant anything by the comment but yet, in some strange way, it infuriated her. They had reached the end of the cellblock and she knew he was about to say something else but they were stopped by another voice coming from their right.

The voice was feminine and shocked both Tivex and Hammer as it said, "Hello."

Tivex was all for moving along but Seretak was using another keypad and hadn't gotten the door open yet. They were standing far enough away from the cell where there was no immediate danger but there was nothing to do but wait. Tivex turned her eyes to look into the cell which must have belonged to the prisoner Seretak had referred to but she could see nothing but darkness.

Hammer looked down at his wrist cuff when the voice came again, "That won't work here either." Tivex watched as Hammer became irritated and tried to see if the door was open yet. There was a gentle giggling from the cell as the voice said, "You're in too much of a rush to say hello?"

Hammer seethed and turned to the cell, peering in. Seeing nothing he turned back and said, "I don't talk to shadows."

Tivex heard the giggling again, "Not anymore? Hmph, you're taking my ship, aren't you?"

"What do you care? It's not like you're going to need it anymore."

"Such a shame. First you won't talk to me, then you take something away from me. You're a big meanie, aren't you?" asked the voice.

Tivex watched Hammer become even more uncomfortable and then tighten his jaw as he always did when he was angry. Tivex knew he was playing right into the prisoner's little game and for the first time, she was going to let him do it without her advisement. She couldn't shake her anger with him for some reason.

Hammer cocked his head back towards the cell, "Is there something you want or are you just catty?"

More giggling, "Me? Catty? That's funny, especially since you still have that Omarian attached to your hip."

Tivex watched as Hammer's body followed his head by turning towards the cell. His eyes narrowed and he tried to see into the blackness, "Still? Do I know you?"

"Oh, I know you," giggled the voice.

Hammer had the unmistakable look of someone about to do something very stupid. Just as quickly, Tivex marshalled her good sense and got a hold of herself. She stopped him from getting any closer to the cell by grabbing him by the shoulders, "Not advisable, Captain."

The giggling continued, "And I see you have an Akoni bodyguard, too? My, my, my, you have come a long way, haven't you?"

"Who the hell are you?" demanded Hammer.

The giggling ceased almost eerily and was replaced by a much darker tone, "Later. Be careful with my ship, Dorran, I'll be coming to get it."

Almost as fast as lightning, something leapt from the shadows into the light. Tivex saw a human female, expertly built with honed reflexes. She was a palms span shorter than Hammer with electric green eyes which reflected the reddish light palely. Her hair, though shaved clean all around the base of her head, was black and thick on top, tied back in a ponytail with a scrap of fabric. Jet black tattoos covered her neck, extending to the top of her hairline and all the way down both arms. The most shocking thing Tivex noticed about her was the long scar which ran from one side of her neck to the other, close to the collarbone.

Tivex looked down at Hammer whose face shown absolutely no recognition of this person in his life. The prisoner stayed behind her bars grinning wickedly at Hammer who brushed off Tivex's hands and shrugged at the woman, "Lady, I have no idea who you are or how you know me but I hope you have a nice stay here. Oh, and thanks a bunch for the ship."

The prisoner simply grinned at Hammer and Tivex noted that she never blinked once during the whole interaction. Seretak called back for them to follow him down to the ship. Tivex looked at Hammer who looked bewildered, "I see your track record with women is as stellar as ever."

Hammer did a double take at her, "What the hell was all that about?"

Tivex smirked, "Obviously, she knows you somehow."

"Did she look familiar to you at all?"

Tivex shook her head, "No, but your reputation is known. Perhaps it was a fluke."

Hammer shook his head again and followed Seretak and the others down to the prisoner's ship. As Tivex walked behind him, a strange smile crossed her face. She felt inside a release that she had poked fun at Hammer for the first time without him even knowing it. The thing she didn't understand is why that seemed to feel so good.

CROSSOVER

TIVEX WATCHED AS HAMMER GLARED DARKLY AT THE SIGHT IN FRONT OF THEM. THE GUT WRENCHING feeling which was obviously twisting him up inside caused Tivex to wonder if he'd be able to contain his emotional rising storm. She knew they were about to step aboard a Hais ship and it sickened Hammer to no end. She looked at the Destroyer class ship sitting in front of them again and them back to Hammer who shook his head when he saw how it had been modified. Its presentation did little to ease her own hesitations about this mission. What had made the feeling escalate further was when she learned the ships name.

From what Tivex knew, a Destroyer class ship was outfitted in much the same way IEC Reaper class ships were. The one major difference was that the Hais were never shy about showing off their weaponry and did little to hide or mask it. Destroyers were appropriately named so due to their overuse of intimidation. Tivex knew also that once any vessel came in contact with a Destroyer, there were usually no survivors. The ship Team Seven was about to take was no different.

Having a triangular wing shape, the hull was dull gray and botched and scarred from numerous, and evidently extremely violent, battles. Sharp angles and rigid metal were everywhere showing the trademark Hais design. There were laser ports from every angle she could see and a massive canon below where he knew the control deck would be. The Hais were fearsome enough without this kind of weaponry and what made things worse was that they knew it.

As if on cue, Hammer spat on the ground and looked at the others, waking Tivex from her daze, "Alright, let's get this over with."

"Hey, it could be worse, Cap," said Blitz as he jabbed Hammer in the shoulder, "they coulda just sent us out there with nothin' more than our slaggin' blasters and a pat on the back for good luck."

Hammer sneered, "Trust me, if I'd known this is what we were gonna end up with, I'd taken them up on the offer."

Torque whistled, "Whew, wow...the 'Beautiful Nightmare', huh? Really?"

"Sounds just like your typical Hais hooker ta me," seethed Dregs, "the more I look at it the more this place don't seem so bad."

"Regardless, we have no other option left open to us," said Tivex.

Hammer looked at Tivex. His eyes seemed to be burning right through her and she could feel his anger from where she stood. He twisted his neck to one side and heard it crack loudly, "And thanks so much for remembering that."

"Dandy," said Dusty with far less enthusiasm than Tivex had ever heard, "just what I was hopin' for. Cap, promise me if I get wasted in this thang you'll ditch me out an airlock."

"Everyone quit gripin' and let's move out, it ain't like big V is gonna wait around forever," said Blitz forcefully, "personally, I'm glad."

"About what?" asked Torque.

Blitz smirked and lit a cigar, "Because, we got us an unmarked ship and we're goin' to the one place where we might get to do some major damage."

"Blitz," replied Tivex, "we are on a recovery mission. This is not some cavalier charge into the Dominion. I understand that under the circumstances-"

"Understand?" interrupted Blitz, "All due respect, Tivex, but you've never been out in the Dominion. If we don't go in reckless, we come back out in pieces."

Tivex narrowed her eyes at Blitz, "And too much aggression will give us away."

As soon as the words left her mouth, Tivex wished she could suck them back in. She knew she had overstepped her authority by implying any kind of strategy. In fact, the only time she had ever encountered a Hais was when they had stormed into the Widow Maker. The simple truth was that she had found herself at her limit with being pushed to the backseat of this Team. She was tired of their recklessness, over being treated like a cadet but most of all, she was sick of their constant barrage of thinking they were better than her. Though she never took her eyes from Blitz, she could feel the others turning their attention towards her.

Hammer asked, "And how exactly would you know about that?"

Tivex turned back to face him, "Captain, you know I am a medic. I know the difference between rational and irrational behavior. I know more about the situation we are about to enter into than you think."

"'Vex, simulations are one thing but real life is different, you know that now. We know how they fight, how they think and what to expect," said Torque.

She turned to Torque, "I doubt that sincerely. We have not even crossed the Dominion border yet and you all have the look of vipers getting ready to strike. Judging from the look on Hammer's face, I believe we have as low a chance as we can possibly have right now."

Dregs pushed Hammer out of the way and scowled at Tivex, "So what're ya sayin', lady?"

"I am saying that whether you want to admit it or not, all of you are in an emotional state that is going to get us killed," she could feel her temper rising with every word, "and if do not wish to live that is your business, however, I do."

She watched as Dregs was about to say something before Hammer pulled him back, "You think you're in a position to question our motives?" he said through clenched teeth.

Tivex merely turned her head to one side and glared back at Hammer, "I question nothing," she replied, "how will the Hais retaliate if they so much as know who we are? If they find out that you of all people are in command of one of their ships and are parading around as one of them, from what I saw they will slaughter us without hesitation."

Hammer narrowed his eyes back at Tivex, "And what, exactly, is that supposed to mean?"

"It means that instead of constantly treating me as if I am the last person in the universe you want on you Team, you should take into account I am trying to save your life! There was a time when you trusted me more than you did yourself but you have chosen to forget that. I cannot begin to comprehend what you went through with Velkaso but unless we work together he is always going to be out there somewhere. I had the ability to shut down this mission the second I heard what the objective was but I chose to stand by you!"

Hammer drew back at seeing Tivex in this state. He looked at the others who merely looked as shocked as he did, "I-"

Tivex wasn't about to let him gain any ground, "It appears to me that the only way to get anything done on this Team which does not involve some new horror is insubordination," she stared dead into Hammer's eyes, "fine, so be it. The Widow Maker is gone, deal with it! The man, or whatever the slag he is, who took her away from you is out there somewhere and he is going to use the Horizon for the Light knows what. If you and this gray bunch of henchmen you have do not go about this mission properly, you are no better than Velkaso is!"

The silence around her was almost deafening. Tivex had never lost control over her emotions like that before and she felt a good amount of weight lifted off her shoulders with every word that had come from her mouth. She had even stooped so low as to use the gray euphemism out loud. She felt her chest heaving, her hands shaking and her pulse echoed in her ears. It was the most elated feeling she had since she found out Hammer was still alive all those years ago. For the first time, she could see it in his face. She had somehow dented the wall that enveloped Hammer. His eyes were wide and his mouth was open. He was speechless. Finally, she thought.

Hammer drew back and shook his head, "This little conversation is far from over." He looked around at the others as he tried to make sense of what had just happened, "Load up." He looked at Tivex as if to say something more and then just pushed past her.

No one said anything further until they reached the control deck. Seretak's crew had done a stellar job at making sure the ship was ready. Hais technology was far different than IEC's so they had taken the liberty of outfitting most of the terminals with normal control consoles. These would function exactly as Team Seven was used to but the configuration of the control deck itself remained untouched. True to Hais form, the captain's station was now singled out in front of everyone else. Behind Hammer would be Dusty and Dregs followed by Tivex and Blitz with Torque at another singular terminal. During Seretak's briefing of the Beautiful Nightmare, he had said that the prisoner may have had a full crew at some point. However, when she had been captured, his workers had found some stolen technology that had allowed her to completely automate the ship. During questioning, she had not divulged how the technology worked and Seretak had ordered the ship to be stripped of the hardware until he was sure none of it was dangerous.

When the various readouts came back to say that the Beautiful Nightmare was in full working order, Hammer asked, "Torque, we good?"

"Umm, sure," answered Torque shakily.

"That's reassuring," hissed Dregs.

"Agreed," added Hammer, "Torque, are we set to leave or not?"

"Look, I'm trying to translate everything I know about Hais engineering here," said Torque, "from what I can tell, we're good to go but I have no idea what's going on with the main star drive."

Hammer turned around, "What's wrong with it?"

"As far as I can tell, it's about to overload. Maybe it's supposed to look like that but I've just never seen anything this aggressive before."

"So, what, we'll go faster?" asked Dusty.

"Yeah, either that or incinerate taking off. One way or the other, it should be kinda fun, huh?" joked Torque.

Hammer slapped his hand to his head and spun back around, "Forget it, we're leaving. Dusty, punch it." Without waiting for anything else to happen, Dusty engaged the vertical thrusters and the ship began to lift off the landing pad. At first, Hammer thought he was seeing things when he looked out the view screen and saw that they were rising much faster than he expected. He looked back at Dusty, "Whoa, easy there, cowboy."

"I am," replied Dusty, "the busted thang is on low!"

Tivex felt her eyes widen. She knew the Hais built their equipment for power but this was intense. The Beautiful Nightmare rose higher until it was far enough away from the prison for Dusty to angle it upward and engage the main thrusters for planetary breakaway. If the vertical lift was shocking, the main thrusters were like strapping them directly to someone's back and lighting them up. Tivex felt herself pushed hard against her chair as Dusty broke out of the atmosphere and into space.

Once free of gravity, Dusty tried some basic maneuvers to get a better feel for the ship, all of which felt like he'd had the ship at full power.

Hammer turned around to Dusty, "Are you done with the cheap moves yet?"

Dusty grinned, "Sorry, sir, just gettin' a feel for her is all."

"Yeah, feel her up on your own time," said Hammer, "just get us pointed in the right direction."

Dusty tipped his hat towards Hammer, "Aye, sir." He leveled out and lined the Beautiful Nightmare on the right coarse heading. Dusty checked his readouts and looked up at Hammer, "All clear, Cap."

Hammer turned around to his console so no one could see his jaw clenched tighter than it ever had and said through his teeth, "Give this thing everything it's got."

A fraction of a second later, Tivex felt the main star drive open up to full power and she was pushed hard back into her chair. Normally, they would reach the border in just over eighteen hours from where the Ninth Gate was. Judging from the power the ship had, Tivex doubted it would take nearly that long. Although the Beautiful Nightmare was Hais, the ship responded incredibly well to Dusty's piloting skills. The thrusters were as smooth as anything Tivex had felt and there was little to no residual vibrations.

The view coming from the screen in front of him showed the stars in front of them seemingly grow larger but Tivex knew it was just an optical illusion coming from the high speed forced perspective. She scanned for any communications even though she knew from this point forward there would be little to pick up on.

She watched as Hammer glared into the darkness of space, a hunter bent on finding his prey. He looked down at his console and then turned around to Dregs, "Am I reading this right?"

Dregs stifled a small grin, "From the looks of it, yeah."

"We're going to be there in five hours?"

Dregs nodded, "Seems to me after we pull this off, your brother should take this slaggin' thing back to Earth and see if he can't get our bloody ships to move this fast."

"I heard that," hissed Torque.

Tivex smiled. There was something comforting in the banter between them. She knew she was going to have to answer for what had happened on the landing pad but something inside her told her not to worry. She both understood and misunderstood at the same time what had led her to such an outburst. She knew it had come from caring about Vincent but it was more than that. Tivex knew she had no true understanding of what he had been through. The horror of it all was too much for any one person to handle on their own and she knew that when Dayna had come along, she had eased a good deal of his suffering. When she died, whatever part that was still Vincent had died with her. Now, only the Hammer remained and Tivex doubted that he would ever be the same man again. To him now, especially with the Widow Maker destroyed and hell bent on seeking out the very creature that corrupted him in the first place, there was no room for feelings. If they didn't somehow manage to pull off this mission, Tivex knew Hammer most likely would be lost again.

After a while, Hammer stood up and looked at Dusty, "Think you can handle this thing solo for a while?"

Dusty nodded, "Not a problem there, Cap. You goin' for a walk?"

Hammer nodded and looked around at the others, "Torque, take Tivex down to the engines and make sure she knows everything there is about what we're flying into."

"Aye…Cap," Torque replied questioningly.

"Dregs, Blitz, you're with me. I want to take a look around and see what we come up with." Hammer looked at Torque again, "Call it one hour. Once we're done, I want you to upload everything that Blitz has and see if you can make anything out of it. Once we find Velkaso we're not going to have the luxury of time to jumpstart the Horizon."

Hammer, Dregs and Blitz poked around some of the rooms and found them to be virtually empty. Most of the Beautiful Nightmare had been cleaned out thoroughly by Seretak and his crew and Hammer was disappointed to find there was nothing out of the ordinary.

While in the cargo bay, Blitz hopped up on one of the spare munitions crates and sat dangling his legs. He blinked a few times and yawned, "So, I noticed you kept your cool when Soren dropped this pile of slag in our laps."

Hammer stretched and leaned against the wall, "I have no idea what you're talking about."

Dregs propped himself up on his elbow behind Blitz and grinned ferociously, "Uh huh, like we don't know what ya was thinkin', my captain now," as he pointed to himself and Blitz.

Hammer raised an eyebrow, "We've had replacement ships before, boys. This isn't something new."

"It is when you consider what we're supposed to do with it," replied Blitz, "as in, I think we all know what you're planning."

Hammer smirked and dropped his head, "I'm reformed, remember?"

"Stone that," replied Dregs, "and I'm getting' a feelin' up my spine that says we're about to get real dirty on this run."

Hammer looked up to see Blitz staring right at him as he said, "Hammer, the three of us go ways back, yeah?"

Hammer nodded.

"So level with us."

"About what?"

"You bloody well know what, my captain now," said Dregs with bared fangs, "what's the plan?"

Hammer looked away from both of them and sniffed. He tried to wipe all the emotion or any tells from his face and shrugged, "We have orders."

"Uh huh, and that's why you sent Tivex off with Torque. Hammer, we know you better than you think we do. You wanted her distracted," said Blitz.

"Look," said Hammer snapping back at both of them, "what do you want me to say? You want me to lie and say I'm not planning on pointing everything we have at Velkaso and shoving it so far up his ass it'll come out his throat?"

"No," replied Dregs nonchalantly, "I just wanna know hows come you get to have all the fun?"

Hammer narrowed his eyes at Dregs and then turned to Blitz who smirked and looked at his reflection in his mechanical arm, "Look, boss man, all I'm after is a little payback from the Hais. I'd hate to miss the chance to tell them how I really feel about 'em."

"So, what you're both basically telling me is that we're all after the same thing?" asked Hammer.

"Let's just say, when they sent us of all people, out to the Dominion to search for Velkaso, it was like throwing a slagged shark into a blood bank and telling it not to sniff out anything," answered Blitz.

Dregs grinned wickedly, "And if we happen to ice out Velkaso in the process, I ain't gonna lose no sleep over it."

A feral smile crept over Hammer's face as he pulled the other two in closer, "Keep this quiet until we figure out what's going on with Tivex."

Dregs growled lowly, "She's been actin' weird since we left the Circle."

"Cap, I like her but I'm with Dregs on this one," added Blitz.

Hammer nodded and looked off to one side. He pursed his lips together and scratched his chin, "Well, we have time to deal with whatever's going on with her."

"Come again?" asked Dregs.

"You know how big the Dominion is, Dregs. Trying to find Velkaso in there is going to be next to impossible," answered Hammer.

Blitz grinned, "Oh, I wouldn't necessarily say that."

"Why not?"

Blitz tapped the metallic part of his skull, "Uploads, baby, wave of the future! Whatever got zapped into my head came with a little bonus."

"Such as?"

"Such as I can sort of 'see' the Horizon's ion trails."

Hammer blinked in disbelief, "And you're just telling me that now?"

Blitz nodded, "No way was I gonna let that out during the debriefing. I figured after IEC lied to Team Alpha and us at the same time, they didn't really need to know more than they told us."

"Spectacular," said Dregs, "and that'd come in mighty handy if Velkaso was drivin' the Horizon but last I knew, it wasn't even turned on."

Blitz turned to Dregs and nodded again, "Absolutely right. But whoever said anything about needing to turn it on to see the trail? I've got more dirt on that ashen thing than IEC ever did."

Hammer grabbed Blitz by the shoulders, "How far out can you see the trail?"

"I'd safely say I could get a fix on it as long as it's within a twenty four hour window, give or take," answered Blitz.

Hammer let go of Blitz and fell back against the wall, "Dammit. With the head start that bastard has on us we'd be lucky to find anything on it now."

Blitz shrugged, "So, we start lookin' and start kickin' over some stones."

Hammer looked back at Blitz, "And how long do you expect us to get away with cruising around the Dominion?"

"We just run silent," answered Blitz, "I'm the operations officer, boss man. I plan things like this out in my sleep."

"What happens when we gotta recharge the fuel cells?" asked Dregs, "Or do we just let 'em dry up and float around hitchhiking?"

Blitz shook his head, "Recharging is what we need to do and do it as much as we can. My first choice would be to completely drain them as soon as possible and only get 'em charged enough to get to the next station."

Hammer picked up on what Blitz was trying to say, "In order for us to stop at every station we can to find out information."

"Exactly," said Blitz.

"Yeah, but that still leaves us the problem of humans in the Dominion," said Dregs and pointed at Hammer, "especially him."

Blitz grinned and lit another cigar, "You know the Hais don't hate humans, they just hate everyone. But, they'd be hard-pressed to find a better class of scum to trade their black market gear with, you and I both know it. Ever since we went up against them after the, well, you know," said Blitz as Hammer scowled at him for bringing up Dayna. Blitz cocked his head and continued, "They never got their hands on Hammer, here. If we play it cool, like we've got him to trade for something big, then they might welcome us in with open arms."

"What about us in this ship?" asked Dregs.

Blitz smiled, "They could care less who's in it as long as it ain't IEC."

"We are IEC, genius," laughed Dregs.

"Slag it, they don't know that! All we gotta do is play make believe like we're black market traders from inside IEC space. They might even take it as a compliment that some really bad assed humans were tough enough to do something to get a Destroyer class," said Blitz in defense.

"And what happens if one or more of them recognize this ship?" asked Hammer.

Blitz brushed some nonexistent dust of his shoulder, "We lie and say we suckered that lovely young lady back in the Circle out of it."

Dregs turned to Hammer, "Yeah, about that, my captain now. How did she know your bloody name?"

Hammer shrugged, "No clue, but she knew you too."

"She did, huh? Where we know her from?"

"Like I said, no clue," answered Hammer.

Blitz looked to Dregs and then to Hammer, "Who cares? It was probably a fluke so let it go and come back to the problem at hand, huh? Are we doin' this or not?"

Hammer looked hard at Blitz, "Using me as bait? For the Hais? You'd better know what you're doing."

Blitz slapped Hammer on the shoulder, "Lighten up, sissy. It's a standard Kansas City shuffle."

"Look left and get cold cocked from the right?" asked Hammer.

Blitz nodded, "No one, ever, sees it comin'."

Hammer smirked and shook his head, "You've got balls, I'll give you that."

"Titanium, boss man, sheer slagged titanium."

Hammer looked at Dregs who nodded his approval of the plan unflinchingly. Hammer sneered at both of them and finally nodded the green light. While he loathed from the very bowels of his soul the mere thought of having to act subservient to any of the Hais, he did see the validity of what Blitz was going for. He also knew how otherworldly arrogant and twofaced the Hais could be and a plan like this might be the only thing that would work.

Hammer thought about it in his mind's eye. Trading the one human the Hais would be all too happy to put on public execution for nothing more than some information about another ship, seemingly Hais, which bristled with strange and exotic weaponry. The more Hammer thought about it, the more Blitz's plan made sense. It was going to be impossible for the Hais to resist, which meant this plan might have been custom made for just such an occasion.

He slapped Blitz on the shoulder, "Just so we're clear on this, if you get me killed, I'm gonna be pissed."

Blitz grinned, "Yeah, but what a way to go out, huh, boss man?"

Hammer grinned and motioned for them to go back. When they reached the control deck, they were met by Torque, Dusty and Tivex who reported nothing out of the ordinary since Hammer had ordered the search. Hammer sat back down in his chair and turned around to face the others and asked Torque directly, "Are you finally up to speed with the engines?"

Torque nodded, "Yeah, Cap, it just took a little longer than expected. Tivex knew a few tricks I hadn't thought of."

Hammer raised an eyebrow and looked at Tivex, "Really? Do tell."

"It was nothing special, Captain," answered Tivex, "I simply recalled some information Master Admiral Soren told me about this ship"

Hammer nodded, "Interesting. Anything else you remember that might help us?"

He watched as Tivex narrowed her eyes slightly back at him, "No, sir, not to the best of my recollection."

Hammer dropped his head lower, "Well, if something should happen to surface, I want to know about it."

Tivex simply nodded her understanding.

He took in a deep breath and let it out slowly, "Alright, we didn't find anything on this gray heap that is going to help us in the slightest so we're going to have to wing this mission as best we can. Our illustrious operations officer has come up with a rather interesting plan so I'm going to defer to his good judgement and let him explain what we're going to do."

Hammer nodded to Blitz who proceeded to lay out his plan for everyone. When he was finished Torque immediately turned to Hammer, "You can't be serious. You want me to do what?"

"You heard him, drain the fuel cells," answered Hammer.

Torque began laughing and ran a hand through his wild hair, "Cap, barring the fact that we have no clue which direction to be pointed in, you're asking me to jettison our only method of propulsion?"

Hammer nodded, "I'm not asking you, I'm ordering you to do it."

Torque's laughter subsided slightly, "You're serious?"

Hammer nodded again.

Torque stopped laughing but tried to keep the smile on his face, "This is nuts, sir. I mean, we have no idea how far the nearest outpost is."

"Actually, we do," said Hammer, "the first outpost is about ninety minutes past the border."

"Really? And may I ask how you figure that?" asked Torque.

Hammer just smiled, "Trust me, you can take my word for it."

He watched as Torque screwed up his face at the cryptic comment until it dawned on him what Hammer was talking about. The recognition was that Hammer and Dregs had passed the same outpost when they had gone into the Dominion unauthorized years ago. From his peripheral vision, Hammer could see Tivex staring at him and trying to figure out what was being said.

Torque's eyes widened, "Which means I need to get back down to the engines and vent the cells before we cross over."

Hammer nodded, "Exactly."

"May I ask why that needs to be done now?" asked Tivex.

"Because if we do it any closer their scanners might pick up the spent energy which gives us away," answered Blitz.

Tivex nodded, "I understand."

Hammer looked at Dusty, "When we cross over, make it look like we're supposed to be there."

Dusty nodded, "Not a problem, Cap, but I ain't too fluent in Hais."

Hammer winced. He had forgotten that the Hais could tell the difference between IEC technology and black market wares. He looked back to Torque, "How fast can you modify our translators?"

Torque's eyes bounced back and forth for a moment. An impish smile crossed onto his face, "I'll do you one better. There's some stuff down on the engine deck that I can make look like fenced goods. We have three hours till the border, I'll have it done in two."

Hammer nodded, "We need a main one for the Nightmare, too."

Torque wrinkled his nose, "Oomph, don't remind me where we are."

"We're also gonna need to get some disguises together," said Dregs, "or else we're gonna look pretty flaggin' obvious."

"And some restraints for Hammer," added Blitz.

Hammer turned to Blitz, "You're really enjoying this, aren't you?"

"Are you kidding me?" grinned Blitz, "Best. Day. Ever!"

"There's also somethin' ole shiny forgot about," said Dregs, "what about Tivex? Ain't never heard of an Akoni defector before."

Hammer watched Tivex scowl at Dregs, "Nor have I heard of a tactful Omarian."

Dregs smiled, baring his fangs, "Sorry, my pretty, is' the truth."

Tivex turned back to Hammer who merely shrugged, "He's right."

Tivex closed her eyes and shook her head, "Captain, you are aware that the Akoni do have our faults. While it remains true that there are no defectors, there is a small element among my people who do not follow IEC laws."

Hammer cocked his head, "I've never heard of that before."

"Me either," said Torque.

"Same here," said Blitz.

"It is not something to elaborate on," continued Tivex, "however, there are bad elements in every race, Captain."

"So, what? You'd pass yourself off as one of them?" asked Hammer.

Tivex nodded, "It would not surprise me if the Hais knew of the small contingent."

Hammer just blinked, "And you can pull this off?"

"I believe I have no other alternative with this plan."

"Oh, this, I've gotta see!" exclaimed Blitz.

Hammer leaned forward in his chair and put his elbows on his knees, "'Vex, I appreciate the fact that you're willing to go along with this but let's get this straight. You need to understand that what we're about to get ourselves into is very dangerous. You have to think on your feet and you have to react before you know you do."

Tivex then cocked her head to the opposite side that Hammer had before. She folded her hands in her lap with a look which caught Hammer off guard. It was almost as if whatever made her behave strangely at the Ninth Circle had passed. She spoke calmly again, "Captain, since I was reassigned to Team Seven, I have found it difficult to relate, really in the slightest, to many of the Teams unorthodox practices. I do not understand most of the mannerisms nor do I pretend to fall in with your ways of doing things. I realize that I am a newcomer to this form of service but that should not warrant me being ostracized from preforming whatever duties that I am assigned to the best of my abilities. I do not wish to become difficult but there are many things that you do not see about me that may prove bigger assets than you realize."

The words somehow hit Hammer in the chest like a bulldozer. From somewhere deep down inside his memory, Hammer heard Tivex's reasoning now as he had when they were younger. She had a point and a very valid one at that. She had once been like family and somewhere along the line he had taken that for granted. Still, there was the question of why she was acting so strangely. It nagged at Hammer but there wasn't time for that now.

Hammer looked down at the ground for moment and rubbed his hands together lightly, "How sure are you that you could pull this off?"

Tivex smiled slightly, "If given enough time, I believe I would be very convincing."

Hammer nodded. He looked at Blitz who widened his eyes as if he knew what Hammer was going to say. Blitz looked Tivex up and down and then looked at Hammer with his thumb up. Hammer looked at Dregs who looked back at him with utter contempt.

Dregs walked over to Tivex and began eyeing her top to bottom. He growled lightly, "Fine, but don't blame me if the pretty gets us all dead."

He looked back at Tivex, "Alright, Commander, you want your shot? It's yours."

"What do you mean?" she asked.

"We're going to play out this little charade, while we're at the outposts, you're the captain. Dregs takes over as your first mate and since I can see him drooling from here, Blitz is going to be in charge of me."

"Oh, slag yeah!" said Blitz enthusiastically.

Dregs spit on the floor, dropped his ears down and shook his head, "As if it ain't enough I have to answer to you."

Tivex just blinked, "Captain, you understand that I have no concept of what to do?"

"You'll have to pardon the phrase, 'Vex, but you're going to get a crash course in dirty and underhanded from Dregs," said Hammer, "listen to everything he says, do exactly as he tells you to and for the love of all things holy, follow his lead."

Tivex nodded in disbelief, "Aye, sir."

Hammer turned to Dregs, "Don't teach her anything from the Mynx."

Dregs looked back at Tivex and then to Hammer with a wicked, feral smile, "Oh, my captain now, I wouldn't dream of it."

"While we're on the stations, Dusty and Torque are going to be the cabin crew only, nothing fancy but I want Tivex to look as if she's got a good handle on building up a big crew. If I know the Hais, they'll respect a bigger show of force as opposed to three members."

"Aye, Cap," said Dusty.

"Aye, sir," echoed Torque.

Hammer nodded his approval, "While Tivex works with Dregs, Blitz and I are going to figure out how keep us hidden in there. Torque, get those translators up and working then dump the fuel. We're coming up on the three-hour mark so we need to get this done and do it now. Any questions?"

"Yeah," asked Torque, "you do realize that once we cross over, we're on our own right? No rescue this time, no going back and nothing gets between us and the Horizon"

Hammer nodded, "If it was easy they would've sent Star Team Five."

MASQUERADE

TIVEX LOOKED AT HERSELF IN THE MIRROR WITH DISBELIEF FOR THE SECOND TIME. THE reflection looking back at her seemed far stranger than what she was about do. She turned her head left and right trying to see some semblance of herself but was met by a stranger. She had spent two hours in the cargo bay with Dregs trying to learn what was to be the new aspect of herself. Special mannerisms, a new way of speaking as well as a variety of new ways to hold herself were just a few of his lessons. All of which proved to be more difficult for her than she originally thought. After she had grasped the basics of acting far below what her character was used to, Hammer and Blitz had joined them with what was going to pass for her new wardrobe. She had been apprehensive when she saw what she was going to be wearing. The outfit was a drastic obscenity to her nature but after Dregs pointed out an IEC uniform in the Dominion would most likely get her killed before she even spoke, she very reluctantly gave in.

As she looked at her new appearance, Tivex felt an exhilarating twinge of something very foreign to her. She was no stranger to knowing that females of any race held a certain power over their male counterparts. It was a power which she understood was capable of almost clouding male minds into having them do almost anything. Though this kind of power was very new to her, she cautioned herself not to fall victim to using it for the wrong reasons. Tivex even caught herself thinking of what she might be capable of under extremely different circumstances. What made the thoughts even more delicious was when she thought about the way Blitz and Dregs had looked at her when she had put the outfit on. Even more than that was when Hammer had been unable to look away from her.

Tivex had taken off her standard issue IEC uniform and replaced it with what Blitz had found for her. Apparently, he had found it in one of the crew quarters which had been left fairly untouched and believed the outfit would work flawlessly. She had argued that the clothes would not fit her properly but she was met with the reassurance that they would work exactly as the others were hoping for. She was able to squeeze into the black leather sleeveless top which was big enough for all four of her arms to fit through. When she had complained that she had difficulty breathing, Dregs had simply extended one of his claws and slashed the top between her breasts causing them to nearly spill out. The pants were equally as tight so she had tried to refuse them altogether. Blitz tossed the pants to Dregs who had done another number on those as well and now fit down below her waist, exposing her entire midsection. They now resembled the same outlandish pants Tivex had seen the prostitutes in The Hole wearing, no crotch for easy access. The only thing which concealed her feminine mystique from the rest of the galaxy now was a fabric belt that hung down just above her thighs.

Hammer ordered her to keep her hair free and to use something else Blitz had found in the same room as the clothes. Tivex had never used makeup and found it difficult at first to know what to do. Fortunately, or unfortunately depending on how she looked at it, she gradually figured out the right color tones to accentuate her features in a way she never had before. The end result had been what was now staring back at her from the mirror. Her long purple hair tumbled and cascaded over her shoulders in thick waves. Her bright, golden eyes were contrasted by the extremely dark eyeliner giving them an almost haunting look. She had used a lighter shade of purple on her lips which stood out against her gray skin but in a way that made them seem fuller, more alive somehow.

When she had finished with her new look, she had taken a deep breath and returned back to the cargo bay to give the new look a test run. She walked in the way Dregs had shown her and leaned seductively back onto one of the bulkheads. Tivex lowered her head, cocking it to one side and kept her eyes wide and fierce. She focused on the others as she spoke in low, drawing tones, "I'll bet none of you ever saw anything this sexy in your whole, pointless lives."

She knew the instant she spoke that the look had its desired effect. None of them could even blink for several seconds. Tivex felt their eyes scanning her, looking for any weakness. She kept her focus on Hammer noticing that he seemed to not be breathing. She also noticed that his cheeks began to turn a shade of red which was completely out of character for him. Dregs and Blitz began to circle her, eying her from top to bottom. Tivex heard Blitz's mechanical blue eye narrow at her, but from his added silence, she assumed she had pulled off the look.

Dregs was the first to speak. He looked back to Hammer, "Ashen stone, I'm good!"

Blitz walked back over with Hammer and asked, "Um, Dregs, what the slag did you do to her?"

Tivex thought about how Dregs had coached her. This was the attention she was going to be drawing and she had been told how to respond. It took only a split second for her to decide the appropriate comeback.

She pushed herself off the bulkhead and walked over to Hammer slowly. Hammer hadn't moved a muscle and she drew her forefinger down his chest as she leaned in close to him. She stuck out her bottom lip in a pouting fashion and said softly, "He made me bad."

Hammer just blinked and swallowed hard. He shrugged off the advance and looked over her shoulder at Dregs, "You took this a bit far, don't you think?"

"Oh, my captain now, she's perfect! I couldn't corrupt her as much as I wanted to but I'd be thinkin' I did me one damned fine job," said Dregs with a hearty smile, "the pretty might just pull this off now!"

Hammer returned his eyes to Tivex, "Right. Just tell me, when did you start using contractions?"

Tivex blinked and lost her character immediately. She looked back to Dregs and then to Hammer, "I did not realize I used one, Captain."

Hammer nodded slightly, "That's what I thought. You look the part 'Vex, but you need to keep in mind it's more than that. You'll have any Hais up in arms with the look but if you get a question you're not ready for, you have to keep it together."

Tivex nodded in understanding.

"And keep up with the vocabulary changes. I seriously doubt any of the not so nice Akoni speak with your dialect."

"Understood, Captain."

"And stone it all, stop calling me captain! Remember, out there, all I am to you is an easy payday."

She nodded again and felt her confidence return, "Anything else?"

She watched as Hammer's eyes widened again at knowing she was back in control. He grimaced, "Yeah, stop looking at me like that. You're scaring me."

Tivex saw the opportunity Hammer left open for her. She turned back to Dregs who nodded his approval. She dropped her voice down again and circled Hammer like a shark, "You think you're scared now? Wait till you see what I have in mind for you. Your price alone is worth more than your life."

Blitz roared with laughter. He slapped Hammer on the back, "Oh, boss man, I'm sorry but you have no idea how much fun this is gonna be!"

Hammer ordered Blitz to go with him back to the control deck but for Dregs and Tivex to remain behind and keep working out the subtleties she would need. Tivex noticed that when Hammer left the cargo bay, he had tried to subtly look back at her one more time. She knew that between her new image and from being able to get to him back on the landing pad, she was finally making headway.

Dregs and Tivex spent another hour going over the myriad of questions she most likely would be asked. Dregs kept up with a relentless barrage of criticisms and a tough way of enforcing his points. Every time she forgot an answer or blinked at the wrong time, Dregs would pull out his blaster and point it at her signaling that she had just gotten them all killed. He also made some final touches to her wardrobe by taking away her daggers and tossing them aside. He replaced them with two sword-like weapons he found along with some smaller blasters that she was to keep holstered unless they were absolutely needed.

For being one of the absolute worst instructors that she ever had, Tivex did have to admit the Dregs was thorough. She knew he had spent an exceptional portion of his life running with the lowlife scum, all of which had given him remarkable insight on situations like the one they were about to cross into.

When Hammer announced they were coming up on the border, Dregs gave Tivex one last look over, "Remember, pretty, if you get asked somethin' you don't know, make it seem like you don't care. Them grayed Hais are about the worst we got around and they ain't afraid to show or talk themselves up."

She looked at Dregs and softly smiled at him, "I must admit, Dregs, you would do remarkably well in special operations training."

Dregs huffed a laugh back at her, "Doubt it. You don't really think I'd give away all my best stuff to a bunch of rookie wannabes do you? 'Sides, I belong out here, the only thing you get pushin' a desk is soft."

Tivex brushed herself off from the roughhousing she and Dregs were finished with, "If it is all the same, please tell the captain I will be up momentarily? I would prefer a moment to gather myself together before the show begins."

Dregs grunted and nodded his head. He spun on his heels and walked out of the cargo bay. Tivex had also left the bay but returned to the quarters where she had applied the makeup.

She splashed some water on her face to cool down and now found herself staring back into the mirror. The look and act were one thing but the situation's reality was beginning to set in. She knew the Hais were a vastly powerful and proud race. They were also known to be some of the most underhanded and stealthy creatures in the universe. To cross them willingly was to invite your own demise and to fight them in combat was usually an exercise in futility. Dregs had told her of the oldest Hais saying, until the last breath. Tivex knew that meant that they would never shy away from conflict and they rather enjoyed combat of every kind.

Tivex also knew that they were obsessed with revenge on anyone or anything which had wronged them. The Hais could carry that same sense of vengeance through generations if necessary. While it was true that these fierce warriors had an almost admirable trait of never surrendering under any circumstance, their major downfall was their lust of accumulation. The more they had, the more they wanted, be it weapons, ships or especially females. Hais males were not choosy when it came to what race they wanted to mate with which now made Tivex a prime target, and even better distraction.

Tivex took a few more minutes for herself and mentally prepared for what was about to happen. She dried off her face and made a few last minute changes to her makeup. She left the quarters and returned to the control deck where the others were waiting for her.

She sat down in her chair and nodded to Hammer, "Apologies but a lady must look her best."

Hammer raised his eyebrow, "I'd hate to think of what you'd be like if this were permanent."

Dusty swung around in his chair and gaped at her, "Holy slag! Whew, y'all gonna take 'em by storm there, ma'am!"

Tivex smiled and brushed some hair behind her ear, "Let us hope so."

Dusty tipped his hat to her and spun back around. He looked down at his console and said, "Sixty seconds to the border, Cap."

"Copy," replied Hammer, "Torque?"

Tivex looked at Torque who flipped some switches, "Venting cells one and two now. Three should hold us for a while but if we run into anything out there other than outposts, we won't last long."

Hammer nodded but didn't turn around, "No time to worry about that now."

Tivex looked out the main view screen and saw nothing out of the ordinary. The border itself was just coordinates, there was no guard posts or patrol ships. There were, however, tracking beacons which would communicate directly with any ships computer and alert it that the border was about to be crossed. As the Beautiful Nightmare crossed the coordinates, she heard the beeping coming from Hammer's console. She watched as he cracked his neck to one side and motioned for Dusty to keep going.

She leaned over to Torque, "How can we pass so freely across the border when the Dominion is the direct adversary of the IEC?"

Torque leaned back in his chair, "Well, it's unusual but not unheard of for Hais to be in IEC space. Face it, it's not a perfect system and like you said, there's bad apples in every race." Torque pointed at Hammer and lowered his voice, "You know how much he hates the Hais for what they did to, well, you know? Yeah, that's nothing compared to what's going to happen if we manage to find Velkaso in there so believe me, we're going in whether they like it or not. As far as us just waltzing across the border, there's not a close enough outpost to know we're not who we say we are."

"Maybe a ship off course?" asked Tivex.

Torque nodded, "Either that or black market traders. The Dominion is big but most of their planets are real slag holes. I've heard about one of them, makes the Ninth Circle look like fun. We have the best stuff on our side so they sneak in more often than you'd think."

Tivex nodded slowly, "I was not aware such things still happened."

Torque grinned and kicked his feet up onto his console, "We, and I mean everyone in the IEC, have come a long way but we're nowhere as perfect as we pretend to be."

Tivex shifted back in her chair and saw that Hammer was like a statue in his seat. For a moment, she let herself try to place herself in his shoes. It was understandable why he was the way he was. She had technically never lost someone close enough to her as Dayna once had been to him. She had been close enough though, during the time Hammer was thought dead. When he returned, Tivex was given a sort of second chance although all of that seemed lackluster after the last few weeks. She thought about how he must have felt, and must still feel now. Having even the slightest bit of life return to normal only to have it torn away again. Tivex allowed herself to imagine the storm within Hammer, boundless rage twisting in the tornado of knowing it wasn't just the Hais waiting in the darkness of the Dominion. There was also Velkaso, the one creature she knew in her heart that if left to his own devices, Hammer would most certainly kill without remorse. She felt she was beginning to understand more about her old friend and knowing also that what little headway she had made would be lost somewhere across the border.

She watched as Hammer held steady in his chair. She imagined what he looked like from the front, his jaw set and unblinking eyes narrowed. Tivex knew instinctively Hammer was out for blood and there would be no stopping him until he had taken back what had been stolen from him. As much as she fought against it, she began to sympathize with Hammer. He had indeed been through hell and now found himself on the same doorstep which he seemed to be anchored. There was another battle coming, Tivex could feel it and for the first time found it extremely difficult not to side with him after all.

Time passed very quickly as they moved deeper into the Dominion Territory. A few Hais scout ships were seen but no one raised any alarms to worry about. Tivex had never seen Hammer so quiet before. He hadn't said more than two words to anyone since they crossed the border. She supposed it was his way of mentally steeling himself for what they were about to attempt or maybe it was his way of dealing with where they were. After all, not more than a few weeks ago, Team Seven had been sent out on a simple rescue and recovery mission. Now, they were rocketing full force into the belly of the beast. She had never wanted this assignment in the first place but now felt as the others must have as well and felt the nagging feeling in the back of her mind.

She looked around at the others and saw the determination in their eyes. Team Seven was not known for fear, they did not back down and they never showed weakness. There was something about them that drove them, calling out from their worst nightmares to seek out what no one wanted to see. They were the ones who were called when situations were too much to handle. Team Seven was more than just a Star Team, they were the only thing standing between the light and the dark, between disaster and triumph, between good and evil. And at the helm of their ship sat Hammer, the thundering heartbeat of the Team. The only man who could have possibly survived the Mynx and now ordered to go after his former master. Tivex had no doubt Hammer would keep his objective clear but she shuddered at what he might be willing to sacrifice to do so.

She was shaken from her mental state by Dregs who said, "Ten minutes to the outpost. We should be ready for 'em, my captain now."

Hammer merely nodded once and got up from his chair. For the first time since she was assigned to Team Seven, Tivex watched Hammer take his beloved black Star Team jacket off and fold it carefully. He walked back to the rear of the control deck and pulled the air vent grate off above him. With a touching dignity, Hammer gently placed the jacket out of sight and replaced the vent cover. He was wearing a tattered jumpsuit which looked similar to what the prisoners at the Ninth Gate were wearing. Blitz got out of his chair and rigged Hammer with the makeshift restraints Torque had built. True to form, Torque had fashioned the restraints with a trick release catch hidden where Hammer could get out of them in a moment if he had to.

Tivex watched as Hammer looked at Dregs somberly with a small grin, "Just like old times, huh?"

Dregs snarled back, "Keep your slag wired and don't do nothin' stupid."

"Just get it over with," replied Hammer.

Dregs nodded.

He stepped back and let Hammer roll his head back and forth a few times. Hammer rolled his shoulders and then looked back at Dregs with a nod. Dregs nodded back and lashed out at Hammer with blinding speed. Tivex watched Hammer take three quick punches to the face and two directly to his gut. Hammer stood for only a second before he collapsed on the ground heaving.

She jumped out of her chair and started over to Hammer, "DREGS!! What is the meaning of this?"

Blitz and Torque jumped in front of her and attempted to hold her back, "Tivex, it's okay!" shouted Torque.

Tivex brushed both off as if they weighed nothing, "I think not, Jeffrey!"

"'Vex, I'm alright," wretched Hammer, "Calm down."

Blitz grabbed one of Tivex's shoulders, "Ma'am, he can't go into an outpost and look like he's on a pleasure cruise. He has to look like we've been workin' on him."

Tivex knew by her reflection from Blitz's metal that her eyes were almost glowing with anger. She could also see she had doubled her breathing at the sight of Hammer being harmed. She twisted her head from Blitz to Hammer to Torque and finally to Dregs, "Savages! Is there any part of this plan that does not involve violence in one form or another?!"

"Not that I know of," said Torque.

"Yeah, it's a pretty standard order around here," replied Blitz.

Tivex turned to Dusty, "And I suppose you knew about this as well, Lieutenant?"

Dusty turned around and nodded, "Sorry, ma'am, but this ain't the firs' time one of us got knocked around some."

She shook her head in disbelief. She knelt down and put her hand under Hammer's chin and lifted it to face her own, "If you do not keep me informed of behavior like this, I promise you, I will find some method of leaving you on the first outpost that offers the most."

Hammer spit out some blood and grinned up at Tivex. He looked back at Dregs and said, "She's ready now."

Dregs nodded. He walked over and stuck his massive paw out to help Tivex up. Reluctantly, she took the help as he said, "Remember, pretty, villain. There be nothin' but monsters were we be goin'."

"Head's up, Cap, we're bein' hailed," called out Dusty.

Tivex looked at Hammer and tried to help him up but Hammer refused and shook his head, "It's your show now, 'Vex. Make us all look good."

She swallowed hard and stood back up. She walked up behind Dusty and put one of her hands on his shoulder, "Open the frequency."

Dusty nodded and flipped a switch. The translators Torque had put together took the place of their IEC wrist cuffs. They were worn in much the same fashion as any other in the Dominion, around the ear down and wrapping around the throat. He had also installed one for the ship which would seem less obvious. The speaker crackled to life with a voice which sounded broken and scattered, "This outpost Nexium. State business."

Tivex took a deep breath and answered, "Our business is none of yours. How much to refuel?"

The voice replied, "Cells?"

Tivex turned around to Torque who held up a finger. "One," she replied.

"Thousand," answered the voice.

"Then we'll trade," said Tivex sternly.

The voice laughed, "No trade for cell. You pay."

Tivex increased the anger in her voice, "You'd pass up what we have? Big mistake."

A moment went by before the voice called back, "What you have?"

"Refuel first, then we'll talk."

"Hahaha," laughed the voice, "big talk! Who you are?"

"The Beautiful Nightmare," answered Tivex.

The voice dropped its humor and stammered back, "D-D-Dock. Welcome."

The speaker went dead. Tivex turned around and looked at Hammer. He flashed her a thumbs up with a cockeyed smile. She looked at the others who all nodded their approval. She turned back around to the view screen and said to Dusty, "Obviously our predecessor frequented this Light forsaken place."

Dusty piloted the ship towards the blinking yellow lights below, "Welp, that's one thing that's gone right so far."

He brought the Nightmare down to the docking clamps and Tivex felt them engage. She motioned for Dregs and Blitz to grab Hammer and follow her. The sound of chains echoed behind her as she heard Hammer trying to keep up while shackled. The hatch slid open and two Hais guards were standing in front of her. They both blinked their eyes and looked to one another and them back to Tivex.

They smacked their lips together a few times barely able to take their eyes off her, "You not captain."

Tivex swished her hair back and tried to accentuate her breasts, "I am now."

The guards bowed their heads towards her and motioned for her to enter the outpost corridor. Tivex was met by some of the worst assaults on her senses she ever had. The outpost seemed like it was barely held together by the grease and grime caked in the corners and cracks. She was forced to take in the smell of long rotten food and spoiled alcohol as if she had known it her entire life. The outpost was by far and away one of the most rancid places she had ever set foot in and she was amazed her boot heels managed to not come loose from the trash she was walking through.

She did not dare to stop anywhere in the corridor as she asked, "Got anything to drink around here?"

The guard on her left was almost drooling, "Yes! Yes! Lots to drink! Come! Follow!"

Tivex let the guards lead the way so she could make sure Dregs was beside her.

Lowly, he growled, "Slam it down fast, pretty. It's gonna taste like hot, molten slag but if you don't, we're dead."

She looked at Blitz who was pulling Hammer along behind him like a dog, "Place reminds me of my first apartment, only cleaner."

Tivex raised her eyebrow and kept walking. The guards lead them into another area which wasn't quite as putrid as the corridor but it was far from sanitary. There were numerous other races crowded around tables, most of which Tivex had never seen before. All of them stopped talking as she walked by only to return to their excited hushed whispers moments later. The guards kicked a sleeping hulk of a creature out of its chair and motioned for Tivex and the others to sit down.

Tivex looked in disgust at the chair and turned to one of the guards, "Clean it."

The guard nodded excitedly and wiped the chair off with a cloth from his back pocket. Tivex smiled as sexually as she could and blew him a kiss. She motioned for Dregs to sit down but pointed for Blitz to remain standing with Hammer. The guards whistled over to what appeared to be a bartender who brought over a large bottle and glasses. One of the guards poured the drinks and passed them out. The other remained standing and positioned himself behind Tivex. Tivex took her drink and drained it down her throat as quickly as she had been instructed. Dregs was right, it was the foulest thing she had ever tasted.

She slammed the glass down onto the table and pointed to it, "It isn't going to fill itself."

The guard grinned wickedly and nodded to the one standing behind Tivex. The other one came back around and sat down with Tivex and Dregs.

They had another drink and she brushed some hair behind her ear, "So, boys, when do I get my fuel?"

"First, what happened to captain?" asked the first guard.

"She had a nice ship. I wanted it. It's mine now," smiled Tivex.

The second guard leaned in, "You Akoni. Never me see bad Akoni."

Tivex brushed her hand across the second guards face, "You should get out more, big boy."

The second guard looked as if he was going into spasms at Tivex's touch. He looked back to the first and sent his black tongue shooting out over his lower jaw. The first guard looked back at Tivex, "Tell about the trade."

Tivex pointed back to Hammer and motioned for the guards to lean in closer, "He's my trade."

"Bah! Got plenty human slaves!" said the guard.

Tivex smiled seductively, "You don't know who that is, do you?"

The second guard looked closely at Hammer, "Who is?"

"That's an IEC captain."

"Big deal," replied the first, "probably rookie anyway."

Tivex shook her head, "That's Dorran."

Both guards nearly dropped their glasses and hissed with excitement, "How much?"

Tivex looked at Hammer and then back to the guards, "Well now, that's the question isn't it? I need fuel cells, not money."

"Take! Take! All you want!" slobbered the second.

Tivex smiled again, "I could, but then that would leave me without a reason to stay around here a little longer."

Both guards turned to her with a look of desperate hope, "What you want?"

Tivex got up from the table and walked behind the guards. She knelt down between then so her breasts were eye level and pulled them in closer to her, "See boys, what I want is information. I have such a pretty little ship but I saw another bigger, stronger one that I want instead."

The guards were nearly drooling. "What look like?" asked the first.

"A modified Destroyer but with enough weapons to send anything in my way to the pit. Seen it?"

The second guard nodded excitedly, "Yes! Yes! Came here not long ago! Head for Cordila station!"

"Cordila station, huh?" asked Tivex in a drastically different girlish voice, "and which way is that?"

The first guard pulled out some paper and wrote the coordinates down for her. He licked his lips when she took the paper from him.

She smiled sweetly and asked, "Now why don't you boys go get my cells ready while I have another drink?"

The second looked longingly at her, "What about him?" and pointed to Hammer.

Tivex had anticipated this and pushed herself onto the guards lap. She wrapped her arms around his neck and said, "You can have him, or you could do the smarter thing."

"What that?" stammered the second.

"You can let me go find my ship and once it's mine I'll drop him right into your leader's hands. I tell them it was you who made sure they were the ones who got to dispose of him and you get showered with all the riches you'll ever want. Then, I'll come back here and we can christen my new ship like there's no tomorrow."

The second guard nearly passed out from the prospect of what Tivex was suggesting. His head nearly came clean off his shoulders from nodding so hard. Tivex got off his lap in order for him to grab the first guard to run off to refuel them. As the guards left, Tivex heard them arguing over which one of them was going to get the riches and the girl as they disappeared back down the corridor.

Tivex looked at Dregs and motioned for the four of them to also make their way back to the Beautiful Nightmare. As they were walking, Tivex looked around to make sure they weren't followed and asked Dregs, "Why did that guard stand behind me?"

Dregs huffed a laugh, "Because if you didn't drink or spit it out, he woulda slit your throat before you knew what happened. It's a dead giveaway that you've never tasted their booze before and that means you ain't who you say you is."

"But I have never tasted it," replied Tivex.

"Trust me," answered Dregs, "that's why I told you to get it down fast. Don't be surprised when it comes back up."

Tivex nodded and kept walking down the corridor. They reached the Nightmare and found it had been fully charged to her specifications. Judging from the coordinates the first guard had given her, there was a fair distance between the two and she hoped Torque hadn't vented out more than they needed him to.

The guards were waiting for them at the hatch, "You ready. Come back!"

Tivex switched instantly to villain mode. Even though her stomach was indeed beginning to churn and bubble, she kept a brave face as she kissed both guards on what passed for their cheeks, "Soon, boys."

They boarded up and closed the hatch behind them. As they walked back down the hallway to the control deck, Hammer turned to Blitz and said, "I can't believe she really drank that slag."

"It was not as if I had much choice," answered Tivex.

"I've got thirty to one she doesn't make it outta the dock," said Blitz.

Tivex turned to say something but all at once, she knew she was about to get sick. She merely looked at the others and bolted past them to get to the lavatory on the double. As she ran she could hear the others chastising her for having a weak stomach.

She returned to the control deck a good while later and slumped down into her chair. From the view screen, she knew they were far enough away from the first outpost that she could drop her act for a while.

The others turned and asked if she was okay. Tivex barely had the strength to reply, "Please tell me I do not have to go through that again."

"Sorry, 'Vex," said Hammer, "it's going to be leapfrog until we find him."

Tivex rubbed her stomach gently and leaned her head back to look at the ceiling, "In that case, I am going to need as much medicinal help as my digestive track can get." She heard the others, especially Dregs beginning to snigger and laugh at her. She pulled herself back up to the seated position and asked, "What is it now?"

Dregs could barely contain himself, "I may have forgotten to tell you somethin'. Akoni can't get used to Hais liquor. Somethin' 'bout allergic reactions or whatever. Your systems can't take it!"

"And you choose now of all times to tell me?" seethed Tivex.

Dregs nodded excitedly, "If I have to pass off bein' your first mate, pretty, you didn't really think I'd go along with that slag that easy, did you?"

Tivex noticed that besides Dregs, Hammer and Blitz were all looking at her with scrutiny. She couldn't be sure but she could have sworn they were again sizing her up for some reason. After the events on the outpost, Tivex felt as though she were exhausted and didn't want to deal with their antics further but she made a mental note to keep her eyes open. She couldn't put her finger on it but something seemed off about them more so than usual.

HIDE AND SEEK

TIVEX FELT HER BLOOD PUMPING THROUGH HER VEINS LIKE SHEER ACID AS SHE WATCHED HAMMER tighten his grip around the Hais guard's neck. The guard was trying to thrash his way out of the merciless onslaught but Hammer held his grip strong and steady. She watched as he arched his back, raising the guard a good six inches of the ground before he slammed the Hais down, rattling the guard with demonic intensity.

Hammer stood over the guard and whispered, "Try that again, you gray heap of slag, and it'll be the last thing you ever do."

The guard tried to wrap his fingers around Hammer's forearm but the second he lifted his arms, Dregs smacked them back down as he unsheathed his claws under the guard's neck. Dregs snarled and looked at Hammer, "Keep that thing quiet or we may as well be diggin' our own bloody graves!"

Hammer moved only his eyes to look at Dregs. His left arm was wrapped around the Hais' midsection and his right around his throat. Hammer was jamming one of his mock restraints into the Hais' vulnerable neck surface, "Exactly what do you think I'm trying to do?!"

Dregs twisted his head back and looked towards Tivex, "Any more of 'em?"

Tivex looked around the corner and shook her head, "Not that I can see."

Dregs looked back at Hammer and nodded.

Hammer whispered again to the Hais, "Now, you've got two choices. One, you move again and you're dead where you stand. Two, you tell me exactly where Velkaso is and I only consider icing you."

The Hais looked hopelessly left and right. The guard must have sensed there was no way out of his current predicament. He was covered from the front by Dregs, to the left by Blitz and from behind by Hammer.

The guard finally stopped struggling and managed to choke out, "He no here! I tell you that before!"

Dregs pushed his massive snout closer to the guard and sniffed. He withdrew and snarled at Hammer, "He's lyin'."

The Hais shook his head violently, "No! No here!"

Hammer looked at Tivex who was covering the door. He nodded to her to keep her ears and eyes open.

Tivex felt her senses heightened to a degree they never had been before. She could literally smell the fear perspiring from the guard as her pulse thundered in her ears for what seemed the thousandth time since the entered the Dominion. It had been desperately ill fate that she and the others had their cover blown. They had done the whole act again and again until Tivex believed they were never going to make any headway. When they had stopped at this station, the Hais guard from the first station just so happened to be there as well on a routine rotation. He recognized them immediately, although they hadn't seen him until he had almost given them the slip. The guard had run down a hallway and been met with a dead end courtesy of a door that was not operational. Tivex and the others had been on top of him in a matter of seconds and dragged the guard into an empty room. Blitz had been all for taking care of the guard permanently but had been overruled when Hammer suggested some creative interrogation.

Tivex tried to take a few deep breaths to keep her hands from shaking and nodded back to Hammer, "All clear."

Hammer refocused on the guard, "In that case, guess we're going for option one then. Goodbye." He pressed harder on the restraint and felt the Hais' knees begin to buckle.

The guard shrieked, "No! Wait! I tell! I tell!"

Tivex heard Dregs huff a muffled laugh, "Dominion material, huh? Doubt it."

Hammer hushed him and lightened his grip on the guard very slightly, "Talk fast."

The guard was barely able to squeak, "Put in two days ago. Has bargain for Dominion. Make invincible."

"Where is he?" asked Hammer through clenched teeth.

The guard shook his head, "Made meeting with sub generals at Rycos."

"We were just there, stony," said Blitz, "you're lyin' again."

"NO!" shrieked the guard again, "Sent back yesterday!"

"If that's true, then you've seen his ship," said Hammer, "you would've let him in here."

The guard nodded feverishly.

"What does his ship look like?"

"Like Nightmare but has more weapons. Can cut through ships!"

Hammer looked at Dregs who nodded his approval. He turned to Blitz who did also. He twisted his head back down to the guard, "Looks like you might live after all. And lucky you, you're going on a little trip."

"What?" croaked the guard.

"You don't really think I'm stupid enough to just leave you here, do you?" asked Hammer. "After all, you know who we are, I leave you here and we're as good as dead. You're coming with us so I can make sure you're not lying to me again. If I find out otherwise, believe me you filthy Dominion slag, you're not coming back."

"NO!" the guard yelled and tried to struggle again. Hammer held fast and looked at Dregs. The guard was knocked out cold and flipped over twice courtesy of the massive Omarian's punch. Hammer and Blitz scuttled over to Tivex who hadn't moved.

She looked back at them, "Nothing. Not a sound."

"Alright," said Hammer as he got back into his restraints, "Dregs, grab him and make sure he stays out. We need to move double time back to the Nightmare and get the slag out of here before anyone else figures out what's going on."

Dregs hefted the guard over his shoulder as if he was no more than a loaf of bread and nodded his readiness. Hammer gave the signal to Tivex who shook off the encounter as best she could and returned to her darker persona. Blitz kept a sharp eye out for anything or anyone following them and found they were in the clear.

They kept to the shadows as much as possible but there was no way to return to the Beautiful Nightmare without crossing through the common area. The trick was to make it look as if nothing was out of the ordinary but having an unconscious Hais being carried through by an Omarian was going to look bad any way Tivex could see it.

They stopped just short of the common area and Tivex turned around, "Dregs, follow my lead."

Dregs nodded, "Don't try nothin' stupid, pretty."

Tivex held her head up high and walked as nonchalantly as she could. The others followed her at a casual pace. Hammer made sure he kept his stride a more hobbled tone and made sure not to look up at anyone. They were footsteps from the corridor which lead to the Nightmare when Tivex heard what she had inevitably knew was coming.

The voice came from behind them, "Hey!"

Tivex stopped and turned around slowly, emphasizing her look of boredom and disdain, "What?"

"What think you're doing with him?" asked yet another Hais.

"What does it look like I'm doing?" replied Tivex, "I'm taking my prisoners to my ship."

The Hais blinked a few times and came closer, "Prisoners? No Hais ever prisoner!"

"This one is. He shorted me on a deal."

The Hais shook his head, "No matter, no prisoner. Especially to Akoni."

Tivex threw herself wholly into her role. She brushed a shock of hair off her shoulder and leaned down to the Hais, "You got a problem with Akoni?"

The Hais laughed, "IEC lapdogs. Put him down."

Tivex twisted her head back to Dregs and then back to the Hais, "Sorry, handsome, but a deal's a deal. He shorted me so I'm taking him with me till I get paid. You want me to leave him here, you're going to have to make me do it."

The Hais snarled, "No matter. No prisoner Hais. You put down or we have problem."

Tivex smiled at the guard and put both her right hands on his shoulder, "We already have a problem. I suggest you go about your business if you expect to see another dawn."

The guard moved his hand up to his coat and moved it so his sidearm was well in view, "Last chance, gray dog."

Tivex pouted her lips and then did something that even she would never have expected. Since the guard appeared to be right handed, she had purposefully stood more to his dominant side. Akoni were notoriously ambidextrous and Tivex held the guard far enough away so that she had drawn out one of her swords without him seeing it. The guard didn't know what was happening until it was too late. In the time it took him to threaten Tivex, she had cross drawn her sword and brought it up with blinding speed. The guard's right arm was severed at the shoulder and fell to the ground with a light thump. With her other left hand, Tivex grabbed his sidearm and threw it to Dregs.

The Hais slumped down onto the ground clutching at his shoulder stump. It heaved heavily and looked up at Tivex, "You dead, gray bitch."

"Not today," Tivex said as she smiled sweetly, "don't ever underestimate what you can't see. Now, I can kill you. Or let you hobble off before you bleed to death. The choice is yours but I wouldn't take too long."

The Hais lingered on the ground for only a moment longer before he crawled away. Tivex spun on her heel and lead the others back to the Nightmare. Dregs found some chain in the cargo bay and made sure their newest edition was secured in one of the other empty rooms for transport.

As soon as they were clear, Hammer slumped back into his chair and looked at Dusty, "Get us out of here, now."

"Where to, Cap?" asked Dusty.

"Back to Rycos."

Dusty whistled, "Musta been a heap of trouble in there."

"Why's that?"

Dusty pointed at Hammer, "Y'all got some spray on ya."

Hammer looked down at his jumpsuit and noticed that some flecks and streaks of blueish green blood decorated his front. He looked back at Dusty, "It's getting more and more dangerous the longer we're out here."

Dusty released the docking clamps and piloted the Nightmare away from yet another outpost. No one said much in the control deck for a while. Tivex was trying to wrap her mind around what she had just done. Granted that a significant number of things had changed ever since Kagen had reassigned her to Team Seven. She was all too new to this sort of everyday violence and none of it warranted her to be so aggressive. Tivex looked down at the multicolored blood that coated her hands and felt her stomach start to twinge again. What was happening to her? Her heart and soul were beginning to feel as cold and emotionless as the control deck's momentary bleeping computers.

It wasn't until Torque spoke up that Tivex was roused from her trance, "So, how was the food in there? Good? Personally, I think it'd be nice if just once one of you would ask the rest of us if we wanted any takeout, you know!" She saw Torque trying to give her a reassuring wink and grin.

She was about to reply when she found her throat begin to dry out. Tivex tried to swallow but found it impossible. Her heartbeat began to double as the shock of dismembering the Hais' arm set in deeper. Her hands were beginning to shake as she felt the walls begin to close in around her. As fast as she could, Tivex jumped out of her chair and ran out of the control deck. She ran down the main passage but found nothing more than the echoing of her footsteps off the walls. Tivex whipped around the corner into the cargo bay and tried with everything she could not to get sick again. Even though she tried to stop herself from doing so, she again emptied what little was in her stomach all over the floor. Tivex staggered over to the wall and felt her back slam hard against it. Her knees gave way and she sunk to the floor, burying her face in her hands. The tears felt like acid against her palms as she found herself unable to do anything more than let them flow out.

Tivex had no real estimation how much time had passed before she was able to stop crying. When she was able to lift her head again, she saw Hammer leaning against the wall opposite her. He looked her up and down and then came over to sit down beside her. He asked, "You okay?"

She dropped her eyes to the floor, "What have I become, Captain?"

Hammer drew in a deep breath and patted her arm, "You did what you had to, 'Vex. The Hais only respond to brutality and force. You know that."

Tivex tilted her head back to look up at the ceiling, "I understand that, Captain. You do not know how hard this is for me. The slope I am on is becoming more slippery with every foul act on those stations."

She heard Hammer smirk, "Yeah, that was out of character for you in real life, no doubt. What you have to remember is that you're only playing a part when we're on those stations. Without you doing this, we may as well just give up."

Tivex brought all four of her hands back up to her face and covered it once more, "Captain, I did not realize the ramifications of my actions until it was too late. The Hais may very well be our enemies but that is no excuse for treating one with such hostility."

Hammer shifted uneasily his fist involuntarily tightened, "That's up for interpretation. Personally, I could care less whether we ever left any of them alive."

Tivex dropped her arms down and let her gaze fall back to the floor, "I understand what you must feel but it is not the same for me."

Hammer tried to control his breathing. Tivex knew but didn't care what his justification was. He pulled out his flask and took a sip. After replacing the cap, he let out a long sigh. Hammer shook his head, "Tivex, you saw her. You saw what they did to her. If anyone else was sitting here, I'd tear into them with everything I've got but since it's you, I'll give you the short version. What we're up against out here is nothing short of walking right up to hell's front gate and kicking the door wide open. I get you're not comfortable with this whole thing but it's not any easier for any of us, myself included. Every time we set foot onto one of those pigs' stations, I'd give every credit I have to incinerate the bloody place twice."

Tivex drew in a deep breath. The time had somehow come for at least a fraction of the conversation she never thought possible. For the first time since childhood, she put her two left hands on his arm, "If there was anything I could have done for Dayna, I would have. I hope you know that."

"You already did. Blitz wouldn't be here if you hadn't acted so quickly."

"I was referring to-"

"I know who you were talking about."

"Then how is it that you can remain so stoic in situations like this?"

Hammer managed to smile to her gently, "I don't, I just make it look like I do. Every station we go to, I size every single one of them up and imagine how sweet it would be to unload a full clip on 'em."

Tivex smiled delicately back at him. The lines cut in his face over years of sacrifice seemed to deepen the moment. He looked as if the wall around him was beginning to fracture in more places than one. However promising this seemed to Tivex, she knew without a doubt that he would still need them up for the mission ahead. She replied, "That is borderline psychotic, Captain."

Hammer grinned, "Probably, but if you'd seen the slag I have, believe me, it makes your worst nightmare seem like a daydream."

"I just sliced off the arm of an unmatched opponent while endangering my fellow shipmates. And what makes it worse is that I did it without thought or provocation. He did not draw his weapon and yet I almost killed him," said Tivex, "does that not mean I now follow the same path you do?"

Hammer left her gaze and looked up at the ceiling. He laced his hands together behind his head and replied thoughtfully, "It doesn't mean anything like that. It just means you've got the same problem as the rest of the universe, a slag load of power and the ability to misuse it. 'Vex, whether you like it, understand it or want it, you're with Team Seven now. There's no deposit, no return and no going back. None of us are poster children for the IEC and every, single one of us is so slagged in the head it's really a miracle they haven't pulled the plug on us so far. The way we do things makes the Master Admirals cringe, none of us have the stability they want and yet somehow, they threw you into the middle of all of it. Welcome to our life, which as it happens, is yours now too."

Tivex turned her head back to the ceiling, "If I do not reflect my best character when it is needed most then I am no better than Velkaso, the Hais or any of the other colorful characters we've seen so far."

Hammer replied, "I admire that but in all honesty, there isn't a damned thing in the Dominion that's going to warrant your best, it's going to take the worst you got."

Tivex rolled her head back and was able to manage a small smile. A silvery tear rolled down her stony cheek, "Thank you for trying to cheer me up, Captain."

Hammer grinned at her, "Oh my, was that sarcasm in your voice I just heard?"

"It would seem you bring out the best in people," Tivex chided back.

Hammer huffed, "For what it's worth, next time, aim just a little to the left. He'd never have even felt it."

Tivex looked puzzled until it dawned on her what Hammer was talking about, "The Light save me from this assignment."

"Maybe," said Hammer as he rolled his head back with closed eyes, a content smile brewing on his face, "but the light always shows what you don't want to see."

"Such as?"

Hammer folded his hands on his chest, "Shadows, 'Vex, it always shows the shadows."

Tivex wiped the tear away, "You realize this is the first time we have been able to talk as we once did when we were young?"

The comment looked as if it hit Hammer in a way he hadn't expected. She was right, they had almost been inseparable when they were young but the years apart had driven a massive distance between them.

Hammer replied, "You're right. It's kind of nice."

Eighteen hours later, Hammer watched as the Rycos station returned into the view screen. It looked the way it had not more than four days prior and looked almost as appealing. He made sure Dusty kept the Beautiful Nightmare at a safe enough distance before entering into the communication range.

Hammer turned his chair around to face the others. He tented his fingers, "Before we do this, I want to make absolutely sure we've got the plan down solid."

Dusty pushed his hat back on his head, "Cap, we gone over it a hundred times already."

"And now we go over it a hundred and one," said Hammer lowly, "no mistakes."

"We move in, I scan the station and find Velkaso. As soon as we've got a good make on him, we dock, Blitz and I sneak over and get the Horizon out," answered Torque.

"What happens if you can't sneak onto his ship?" asked Hammer.

"Shadow games until he shows up," answered Blitz, "low and dirty."

Hammer nodded, "How do you get the Horizon out of there?"

"Any means necessary," replied Torque and Blitz together.

"Any trouble?" asked Hammer.

"Cut down anything in our way and don't wait for backup," answered Blitz.

Hammer leaned forward, "Both of you, listen to me very carefully. This part isn't a game. Since we can't risk Dregs or me getting recognized, you two are going in with Tivex. She calls the shots." Hammer craned his neck to look directly at Tivex, "And if you so much as smell something out of place?"

"Evacuate without hesitation," she answered.

Hammer nodded and rested his elbows on his knees, "I'm going to say this again for the last time, none of you know how dangerous he is. The Horizon is one thing but I'm not risking any of you, is that clear?"

"Aye, sir," echoed everyone.

Hammer shook his head and bellowed, "I SAID, IS THAT SLAGGING CLEAR?"

"AYE, SIR!" everyone shouted back.

Hammer leaned back and turned around, "Take us in."

Dusty gently throttled up the power and steered the Nightmare towards Rycos. Not more than a minute later the speakers again came to life, "Beautiful Nightmare? So soon? State business."

Tivex stood up and answered, "I've been lead to believe my primary contact for prisoner bounty returned to Rycos."

"Who tell you this?" responded the voice.

Tivex shot a look to Torque to see whether or not he'd scanned Velkaso's ship. Torque shook his head but kept working. Tivex returned her attention to the speaker, "One of your Dominion brothers."

"Who tell you this?"

"I don't know what his name is."

The voice chuckled, "Then you no luck! No dock without more information."

Tivex looked back at Torque a second time. Torque worked furiously and within a fraction of a second he flashed a thumbs up back to Tivex. She returned the chuckle and said, "Very well. Then I have no further need for him aboard my ship."

The voice faltered, "Wait...he with you?"

"That's correct."

"He left his post?!" screeched the voice.

"I wouldn't say he left it so much as I took him," giggled Tivex.

"We wait for you, dock six."

"Oh, I don't think so," commanded Tivex, "once I get paid, then you'll get your friend back. If you so much as come near me before that, my crew will dispose of him, most slowly."

"One hour," said the voice.

"Three," refuted Tivex.

"Two, no more."

"Done."

Tivex ended the transmission and nodded to Hammer. He turned back around and motioned for Dusty to dock. With an almost expertise now, Dusty found the dock and latched on in record time.

Before they opened the hatch, Hammer put his hand on Torque's shoulder and said, "Whatever you do, don't be a hero."

"Relax, Cap. I'm going in there with the walking wrecking machine and a four armed switchblade," winked Torque.

"I'm not joking, Torque. Anything happens, you run and run fast, get me?"

"Yes, mother," replied Torque with his own sneer of disdain.

Hammer shook his head and looked at Blitz lighting up another cigar, "Don't worry, Cap, I won't let him outta my sights."

Hammer nodded and slapped Blitz on the shoulder and took off down the hall with Dregs at his side. He had made absolutely sure Torque modified the communications system to send them back audio and visual feed on a high band frequency as not to alert the Hais that anything was being sent. They dove into the same room where their Hais prisoner had been given a heavy dose of sedative to keep him quiet.

Hammer looked at Dregs with angst, "We should be out there, not them."

Dregs shook his head, "No, my captain now. You, they might have been able to hide well enough but me, not a chance."

"What's the difference?"

Dregs tapped his huge paw on Hammer's head, "I get that but it ain't our time yet. Let the pawns do their stuff while the cavalry gets ready for the main event."

Torque wrinkled his nose at the smell that assaulted him the second the hatch was opened. He almost gagged twice before Tivex leaned down ever so slightly to him, "Keep your tongue pressed against the top of your mouth, it helps."

Torque nodded and did as she suggested. He found that his gag reflex was suppressed somewhat but there was still an aching nausea. He looked around at his surroundings and whispered to Blitz, "Are you kidding me? This is what you guys've been tromping through all this time?!"

Blitz sneered, "Yep. Good thing I don't have real lungs anymore."

Torque widened his eyes, "Consider yourself lucky."

Tivex shushed them both and lead the way down the rancid corridor until they reached the now familiar common area. Tivex lead them into the center of the area and looked at Blitz, "Do you see anything?"

Blitz shook his head, "No, but…" he put his hand up to his ear and said softly, "Cap, you readin' me?"

"Affirmative," crackled Hammer's voice.

"Cap, I'm gettin' a serious vibe from somewhere to our right. If I had to guess, I think somethin's calling out to me if you get my drift. What do you want us to do?"

"Stay as cool as you can. Make your way down to wherever you're getting the signal, slowly."

Blitz looked back up at Tivex and pointed to the right with his head. Tivex nodded and lead the others keeping her head on a swivel for any trouble. Torque kept his mission in the front of his mind but was unable to keep himself from almost gawking at what he was seeing. All around him were some of the most less than reputable creatures he had ever seen. To his left, he saw what must have been the biggest underground Helix manufacturing facilities anywhere. To his right were dozens of patrons all drinking something which smelled and looked like hydraulic fluid.

He was beside himself, "Wow, and I thought being greased up under the hood was dirty."

Blitz grinned, "Makes you appreciate your day job, huh?"

"What's that stuff they're drinking?"

"The same slag I have guzzled for a month," hissed Tivex, "now shut up and keep moving!"

Torque shot a look to her only to find she wasn't paying attention to anything but her surroundings. He raised an eyebrow and kept walking. They were getting nearer to another corridor when Tivex held up a hand for them to slow down. Torque watched as Blitz circled behind her and looked at what she was staring at. Diagonally to their left was a table encircled by a group of bar patrons numbering six altogether. They were huddled around it closely and talking in very hushed tones. Two were Hais, three Torque couldn't place but the other one was hidden from his view.

Torque watched as Tivex went rigid and looked at Blitz, "We've got company."

Blitz nodded, "Yeah, I see 'em. Those the same two from a few days ago?"

Tivex nodded, "The one on the far left was the one who I played up to."

Torque knew where this was headed. If the guards recognized her back on the station without owning up to her promises, things were about to get slagged. He said in a hushed tone, "Keep moving, they haven't seen us yet."

Blitz shook his head, "We can't. We can't get down that corridor without them seeing us."

Torque looked around and saw that some of the patrons had put down their glasses and were beginning to take notice of the strangers who were standing stock still in the middle of their home territory. "Slag!" he said, "Someone come up with something soon because we kinda stick out here."

Blitz looked at Tivex, "Your call, Commander."

Tivex looked down at the floor for a second before she returned her gaze back to the table, "The Light take it. I will handle them, you go for the ship. Wait until I have their attention and move out." Without waiting for a reply, she headed for the table.

Torque looked on in disbelief as the table erupted in foul, obnoxious behavior. He couldn't hear her, but Torque could see Tivex was already being pawed at by both Hais as she sat down on one of their laps.

Blitz grabbed Torque's arm and said, "Let's move, kid, they ain't gonna stay distracted for long."

Torque nodded, still unable to grasp what he was seeing and Blitz pulled him back towards the wall. As they reached the corridor, Torque shot a glance back towards the table in time to see one of the unknown creatures move out of the way and he caught the sight of something red, something very red, something that looked as if it were made of fire and blood. In the time it took him to register who it was he was staring at, things went drastically wrong.

As if the floodgates of both bad luck and bad karma themselves somehow managed to synch up, all hell broke loose. When the creature moved to the side, Torque managed to get a good look at none other than Velkaso himself. From his vantage point, Velkaso's back had been towards the bar so that he could easily just turn his head left to keep an eye on the corridor which lead down to his ship. Tivex had been trying to keep the attention on her but hadn't counted on her ability not working on Velkaso. When Blitz and Torque had approached the corridor, he hadn't even needed to move his head as he saw them long before Torque recognized him.

Velkaso bolted out of his chair and dove over the table towards Torque and Blitz. He was on top of Torque in a matter of milliseconds, drool slopping down his chin and pointing down the corridor, "Monsamet!"

Torque was momentarily saved as Velkaso was knocked off him in the blink of an eye by Blitz. Thankfully, Blitz outweighed Velkaso by a good two hundred or more, "RUN, KID!"

Torque scrambled to his feet and tried to run back into the common area but was met by two of the creatures who had been at the table and held fast. Torque tried to kick his way out of the hold but it was no use. The creatures held him fast as the third, along with the two Hais pulled Blitz off of Velkaso.

Velkaso held his jaw for a moment and looked at Blitz, grinning wildly, "*Velchavet. Karri Caan.*"

Blitz struggled against his captors but was also unable to move. He looked at Velkaso and spit at him, "I dunno what you just said, big boy, but let me down and we'll find out who's talkin' slag!"

Velkaso merely looked at him and laughed with an awful, chocked manner. He looked at the Hais and the other creatures and pointed to Blitz, "*Monbal.*"

The creatures nodded. Both reeled back and slammed their fists under Blitz's jawline. Torque watched in horror as Blitz rolled his head back and then straight down. Torque couldn't tell if Blitz was alive or dead but he began to fear the worst. Velkaso walked slowly up to Torque and grabbed his face. He pulled it down and stared into his eyes. He then took a clawed finger and ran it under Torque's throat down to his shirt. Velkaso hooked the chain around Torque's neck and pulled out something Torque had forgotten to take off, his dog tags.

Velkaso gazed down at the tags and then shifted his eyes up to Torque with a grin filled with as much malice and wickedness Torque had ever seen, "*Besamonmet ci dri?*"

Torque had no idea what to do or say. In the horror story he had head from his brother, he knew Velkaso would as likely to kill him where he stood if he said the wrong thing. He also knew, if he didn't say anything, he was most likely dead anyway. Only one thing came to his mind. Hammer had warned that if something like this happened, any one of them should immediately give up fighting and say his name.

Torque dropped his head in a bow and said, "Velkaso."

Torque heard Velkaso throw his head back in sadistic delight and screech with laughter as he thumped his chest, "*VELKASO*!!" He violently lurched Torque's head back up and moved in closer, "*IEC? Monhaess IEC!! Monbal*!!"

Torque saw one of the creatures bow his head towards Velkaso. It reeled back in the exact same way they had done to Blitz. Torque realized too late what 'monbal' meant as he saw the fist coming straight at him. His last conscious thought before the fist connected was that he hoped with everything he held dear that Tivex had somehow managed to get away. The punch jarred every sense Torque had and the stars swirled in his eyes. Just before he blacked out, Torque had the sickening feeling that just like everything else on this slagged mission, Tivex was probably right behind them.

VENGEANCE

TIVEX HAD NEVER SEEN HAMMER SO SILENT. IT WAS AS IF HE HAD BECOME CATATONIC DIRECTLY in front of her. From what she could see, his chest barely moved and he had yet to blink in almost five minutes. She looked towards Dregs to find him leaning forward in his chair, a look of fierce concentration on his face. She cast her gaze to Dusty who seemed almost afraid to so much as move in his seat. She swallowed hard and listened to the deafening silence thunder across the control deck. She felt her stomach twisting, crashing waves of nervousness through her entire body. She wanted to say something, anything, to try once again to explain what happened.

During the chaos, she had been knocked off guard when Velkaso darted from his seat. She hit the ground hard when the table was brought up just under her chin but not hard enough to have been knocked out. As she struggled to get back onto her feet to run to Blitz and Torque's aid, someone grabbed her and held on with a grip so strong something felt dislocated her chest which left her pretty much useless. Tivex had no idea what had happened to her swords during the fight but they were no longer in their scabbards and it was only been blind luck that she had been able to escape at all.

When she had finally been released, she found it almost impossible to breathe. She had slumped onto the floor clutching her right side with both arms as she scrambled to find her weapons. The problem was that the entire common area had come to life with an unholy bloodlust at hearing an IEC officer had penetrated their territory. The area erupted in a flurry of people running towards Velkaso and his minions while not paying her the slightest bit of attention. Seeing that there was nothing she could do to save the others, Tivex had crawled out of sight and slowly made her way back to the Beautiful Nightmare. Dusty was waiting for her at the hatch to make sure she wasn't followed using the other Hais they had taken prisoner as a shield. Dusty kicked the other Hais out into the corridor and struggled to help Tivex back into the ship.

As he helped her into the control deck, she found Hammer and Dregs waiting for them both. Hammer ordered Dusty to get the docking clamps loose and to get far enough away from the Rycos station before the entire Dominion armada was on top of them. They were now coasting freely in space and thus had not spoken a word since.

Tivex cleared her throat and said, "Captain, I-"

"If I were you, Commander," interrupted Dregs, "I'd keep my bloody mouth shut."

Tivex watched as Dregs drew out his claws in her direction. She looked back into his eyes and replied, "As you wish."

Dregs growled at her and looked back to Hammer, "We ain't got much time, my captain now."

Hammer didn't move but emanated a voice so dark, so devoid of mercy, it chilled Tivex to the bone, "Dusty, hail him."

"Uh, Cap-"

"I'm not asking, Dusty. Hail him. Now."

Tivex watched as Dusty turned back to his console and asked, "I don' know which is his, Cap."

Hammer got out of his chair and walked over to Dusty. Without so much as a passing fancy, Hammer pushed him out of his chair and slammed his fist into the communications button.

Hammer leaned close to the microphone, never releasing his jaw, "Velkaso, kasobushah."

Nothing happened for a moment. Tivex estimated that she could cut through the tension easily had she one of her swords. Dusty picked himself off the ground and shook his head at Hammer in frustration. Hammer appeared as if he couldn't care less as his eyes narrowed, waiting for a response. Finally, the speakers came to life with an awful, cringing, psychotic laugh. To Tivex, it sounded as if the voice was trying to laugh and scream at the same time while also peppering in some form of sadistic sadomasochism. She knew it was Velkaso. And somehow she knew, the eerie feeling of hate which was consuming both Dregs and Hammer was about to get much worse.

Velkaso stopped laughing and spoke clearly, "*Only few may speak my laugulage!*"

Hammer's grip tightened around the microphone so hard Tivex heard it snap. He spoke in a manner suggesting he was trying to control the rage inside but dangerously close to losing it, "Velkaso, you have something of mine."

"*Oh ho, I have much more than that!*" exclaimed Velkaso with glee.

Hammer cringed, "What do you want?"

"*First, you tell me who you really are, Nightmare. You tell Velkaso quickly and use truth or I gut your friends and send back to you...gradually.*"

"You already know who we are," hissed Hammer.

Velkaso laughed again, "*No. I know who the real captain was, you no her. You want me ask friends?*"

"Ah, bloody lead slag this," shouted Dregs as he thundered across the control deck next to Hammer and grabbed the microphone, "Velkaso! Monchavet jaduk velson kaari!"

Velkaso stopped laughing and changed his tone. It now dropped from a higher pitched register to a much lower, sinister octave. He drew out his words carefully, "*It cannot be...*"

"Like I always tole' you, 'master', someday I'd find you. I woulda burned down glory itself to hunt you down and RIP YOU TO PIECES!" roared Dregs.

Velkaso kept silent for a moment before saying, "*If you're there, it mean old monkaso there as well.*"

"It's payback time, 'master'," said Hammer in a tone which to Tivex suggested he was on the brink of starting Gray War two, "I've waited a long, long time for this."

Velkaso began to laugh again but much harder and faster, "*You? You think you have anything over Velkaso?! You no still know nothing! And what make it even better this time is what I have over you!*"

"Give them back and we might let you live," answered Hammer.

"*No, no, no, boys! You have nothing! I have your friends, I have better ship and I have Horizon! You can no win against me, boys, no one win against Velkaso!*"

Dregs shot a look over to Hammer with wide eyes. Hammer looked back at him in the same manner. Dregs rumbled lowly, "How do you of all slaggin' people know about the Horizon?"

Velkaso was almost unable to control his laughter, "*Always known where it was but smart enough to let someone else get it for me! Had I known it was you, monkaso, would've been too happy to follow your pathetic escape pod and would have INCINERATED IT!*"

Tivex felt the temperature rise at least five degrees from the heat spewing off Hammer and Dregs. Both looked as if malice coursed through them freely. It was a truly horrific sight to behold as they began to lose touch with their humanity, as it were.

Hammer was the first to speak, "Sounds to me like you're afraid to face us."

"*Face you? Face you?! You are nothing! You were nothing before and you nothing now! You have no chance!*" shrieked Velkaso.

"Prove it," hissed Dregs.

Although she had seen many things since her reassignment, Tivex had never seen anything like what was unfolding in front of her. Hammer and Dregs were actually trying to goad Velkaso into a fight of some sort. Whatever they meant to do, she desperately hoped they knew what they were doing.

Velkaso continued his laughter, "*Know this, before I watches you die beneath my feet, your friends beg for death before I do it slowly.*"

The floodgates of Hammer's rage burst apart suddenly. All vestiges of the boy Tivex had once known disappeared in an instant into the darkest shadows of hatred itself. His muscles tensed to the point that they corded under his skin. His jaw was set so tightly, Tivex feared he may crush his teeth into powder right then and there.

Hammer screamed into the microphone as his own treacherous laughter began to flow from him, "THEN COME FINISH IT! COME GET ME, YOU KUVVAAS WANNABE!!"

Tivex heard the screech from Velkaso as his ship appeared in the view screen in front of them. As he did, Hammer grabbed Dusty and threw him back into the pilot seat. Tivex could hardly keep up with the flurry of action as Dusty brought the Nightmare to full power and maneuvered their ship down and away from Velkaso's firing line. Hammer shoved Dregs into the command seat and shouted out something which Tivex couldn't understand. She had no idea what she should be doing but she knew well enough to stay out of whatever Hammer had in mind.

Dregs brought up every camera available and shown all the images on the view screen. Tivex watched as Velkaso overcompensated for where he thought the Nightmare was going to be and had to make a wide circle out and around to line up again. Dusty, having multiple battles under his belt pulled hard on the controls and vertically flipped the Nightmare over Velkaso to get behind him again.

Dusty looked at Hammer who merely shouted again, this time an order which Tivex had no problem understanding, "EVERYTHING YOU GOT, NOW!"

Dusty fired a barrage of laser shots directly at Velkaso's right thruster port. Tivex counted fifteen direct hits into the engine and saw it begin to spark and short out. Velkaso countered by applying his reverse thrusters causing his ship to slow down exponentially. Dusty saw the move and instinctively pulled up to avoid a collision but in doing so left the Nightmare open to any shots from below. Tivex heard the banging as Velkaso's top lasers tore into the Nightmare.

Dregs yelled out, "He's gonna try to tear us open from below!"

"The slag he is!" cursed Dusty.

As the Nightmare cleared over the top of Velkaso's ship, Dusty pulled a hard left yaw which caused Tivex to be thrown from her seat. He then dropped the nose down and fired again at where the control deck was located. He hit again and again on the left side of the main control deck outer assembly causing Velkaso's ship more damage than he had tried to deal out to them.

Velkaso's ship looked wounded but there was still more than enough fight left in it for Velkaso to fire his other thrusters as he positioned his ship for a frontal assault. There wasn't time for Dusty to move out of the kill zone as Velkaso lurched into the Beautiful Nightmare with a devastating blow to its nose. Tivex was knocked again across the control deck as she tried desperately to find something to hold on to. She picked herself off the ground and tried to get her bearings only to be grabbed by Hammer and pushed back to her console station.

He glared at her will hellfire in his eyes, "Damage report, NOW!"

Tivex tried to wrap her mind around what was happening but was only successful in simply nodding her head at Hammer. She quickly did a diagnostic and tried to convey her findings, "Damage to frontal nose guards! Nineteen percent and dropping! Hull breach in sector two and three!"

Hammer wrenched his neck over to Dusty, "Can we still attack?"

Dusty checked his console, "Weapons reading, eighty-five percent!"

"Then why the slag ain't you firing 'em?!" yelled Dregs.

Tivex looked at Dusty who suddenly became infected with the same blood rage as Hammer and Dregs and lowered his head down in a feral smile, "Good ashen question there, fluffy!" Dusty changed his weapon selection console to a much heavier artillery and pressed the trigger.

The control deck was rocked from side to side as armor piercing rounds began to fire. From the distance between the Nightmare and Velkaso, there wasn't enough distance to avoid the ammunition's blowback and Tivex feared that Dusty may have done more harm to them than he intended. Velkaso's ship was amazingly pushed back a good fifty feet from the onslaught and looked as if Dusty had torn apart their weapons controls.

As soon as they were free of Velkaso, Hammer turned back to Tivex, a look in his eyes that she could only describe as demonic, "You owe one to Torque and Blitz, 'Vex!"

"What? What do you-" she began.

Hammer grabbed under her arms and hoisted her up. Tivex had never known Hammer to have that kind of strength before. He put his finger to her lips, "Shh, get your zero suit on."

"What?!" she exclaimed.

Hammer smiled fiendishly, "I said, go put your slagging zero suit on and get ready!"

"Captain, I-"

"THAT'S AN ORDER, TIVEX!" thundered Hammer.

Tivex was now sure Hammer had lost all control but there was nothing else she could do to stop him. She rushed out of the control deck as fast as she could. In a special set of lockers installed behind the control deck were their backup zero suits. Master Admiral Soren had make sure Seretak fully understood that they were to be kept with the crew as if they were on any other IEC ship. Tivex could hear more screaming from the others as they fired relentlessly and she struggled to get her suit on. It was more than difficult as she was tossed from side to side by Dusty's erratic piloting skills.

She was just about to put her helmet on when Dregs came crashing through what was left of the control deck's doors. He looked at her for a moment and then winked at her with bared fangs. He ripped the door off his and Dusty's locker both and began to get his suit on as well, "Helluva party, eh, my pretty?"

Tivex just gawked at Dregs in disbelief, "Omarian, please, tell me what is going on?"

"Sweetness, right now ain't the time for formalities, it's just Dregs, okay?"

"Fine, Dregs, what is happening?"

"What's happening is we're gonna go get our boys back and we gonna do it *our* slaggin' way!"

"How? How are we to accomplish this?"

Tivex jumped as Dusty also dove through the door. Dregs tossed Dusty his suit. Dusty took off his hat and kissed it while tossing it over his shoulder, "Damn sorry that ain't goin' with us!"

Tivex was unable to do anything but stare at the others while they grinned from ear to ear.

She cast a look back to Dregs who merely shrugged, "How we're gonna do this is gonna be a real ride for ya, my pretty!"

Dusty was in other element altogether. He took Tivex's helmet from her and clicked it onto her neckpiece, "Don't wanna go outside without that, darlin'."

Tivex had enough. She grabbed both the others arms and said sternly, "I do not care which of you does it, but someone is about to explain to me what we are doing!"

"We're going over to Velkaso's ship and take care of him and whoever else gets in our way, permanently," said Hammer.

Tivex spun on her heels to face him. She hadn't even heard him sneak up behind her, let alone how he managed to already be in his zero suit. She looked him up and down and then glanced towards the control deck. All at once, it dawned on her.

She looked at Hammer again, "Am I to assume there is no one in control of this vessel?"

Hammer nodded.

"And we are going to pull off some other fantastic illusion in plain sight?"

Hammer nodded again.

Tivex widened her eyes, "And it is going to be overly dangerous with an extreme chance that none of us survives, correct?"

Hammer slapped her on the shoulder, "Think of it this way, it's either this or I leave you behind for losing my brother."

Tivex looked at Hammer, then to Dregs, then to Dusty. All of them were looking straight at her without mercy. There was nothing she could have done to prevent what happened on Rycos but it didn't matter to the men glaring at her now.

Dregs was first to step forward, "You're either with us, pretty, or we leave you here."

Dusty came next, "Sorry, Commander, but rank or not, family's family."

Hammer was last, "Your choice, 'Vex. Your suits got enough air to last a while but believe me, going out with us way would be a lot less painful."

Tivex looked around again at all of them. Inside, she somehow knew that this was the turning point that was inevitably going to happen. Through everything she had seen, Team Seven were the biggest bunch of outcasts and rejects that the IEC had. They didn't listen, they didn't follow directions and what was worst was they didn't care. The one and only endearing quality about them was how they stood together. Even though what happened to Blitz and Torque wasn't her fault, Hammer did put her in charge and they had been under her care. Two of her shipmates were now prisoner aboard Velkaso's ship when she could have just turned them around and found another plan.

In the time it took for her to realize this, a sudden and abrupt change began to well up inside her. Torque was her friend and she had let him down. Blitz had once nearly died in her arms and she had let him down as well. She had spent so much time with them since coming to

Team Seven, she couldn't believe she hadn't recognized her error before. A fire she had never known before lit instantly and burned inside her. It engulfed her in a fury that was as merciless as the others around her. If it meant her going into a very hostile situation with the others to free them, so be it. And if it cost her life to get them back, slag it.

Tivex looked all around her until she saw what she was looking for. She bent over and picked up a handful of ash left over from one of Velkaso's laser shots. She put two of her fingers into the ash and then drew a large number seven on her left shoulder.

She looked at Hammer and felt the words spill out of her although it seemed she was no longer in control of them, "I cannot guarantee I will know what to do."

Hammer scanned her eyes for a moment before the first echo of trust, the same one he once had as a boy glimmered for the briefest of seconds. That look was all she needed for validation as he said, "No sweat, 'Vex, none of us ever do!"

Dregs stepped in closer and slapped Tivex on the shoulder, "Stop worryin', pretty. Twenty to one says we slagged walkin' out the front door anyhows."

"And fifty more says we're dead the second they punch through," chimed in Dusty.

"Punch through?" asked Tivex.

Hammer stared down at his wrist controls at a small timer which was almost at zero, "Yeah. Get down, by the way."

"Excuse me?" asked Tivex.

It was a moot question. All four were tossed into the air a moment later as a screeching, metallic sound was heard in Tivex's headset. She looked down just in time to see a massive metal blade tearing through the floor beneath her. Tivex felt the gravity generator give out instantly as she pushed of the floor to avoid being sliced apart and somersaulted freely into the air. She watched as Dregs and Dusty did the same while Hammer seemed to stay put in midair. When Velkaso successfully penetrated the Beautiful Nightmare, the cutting edge of his ship was sufficiently wedged into the Nightmare's superstructure enough to prohibit him reversing his thrusters to free his own ship.

Dregs pushed off the ceiling and shot over to where Tivex had landed. He grabbed her by the back of her suit and said, "Time to get dirty!" With a massive surge of strength Dregs was able to push off the wall with Tivex in his arms as his head whipped around, "Move it, cowboy!"

Dusty wasted no time in following behind them towards Velkaso's ship. Hammer vaulted on top of the wreckage and positioned himself closest to where Tivex knew to be the nearest opening.

He adjusted something on his wrist and yelled out, "Clear!"

"Clear!" responded Dusty and Dregs.

Using the most devastating setting, Hammer raised both arms above his head and brought them down onto Velkaso's hull. The megawatt surged with intense lighting sparks as Hammer punched through the outer hull. So much was happening that Tivex was shocked she was able to comprehend what Hammer was about to do. Combining his rage, his strength and his megawatt Hammer was literally ripping a hole in the side of Velkaso's ship with his bare hands.

When enough had been pried away, Dregs pushed Hammer out of the way and dropped himself and Tivex into Velkaso's ship. Tivex hit the ground with a substantial thud as the other ships gravity generator was still working. Dusty dropped behind her carrying something in a bag followed by Hammer. Dusty immediately threw blasters to Dregs and Hammer while kicking Tivex's old daggers over towards her. Hammer pulled the hole closed as best he could and quickly sealed the opening. He turned to Dregs, chambered their weapons and went tearing off down the passage.

Dusty stayed behind with Tivex and double checked her suit. Tivex looked at Dusty with a look of genuine cluelessness. Dusty simply smiled at her, "Trust me, darlin', y'all gonna want as much air as you can save."

"They are not seriously planning on using live fire weapons in a zero gravity environment, are they?" she asked.

"Oh, they ain't plannin' nothin', darlin', they're countin' on it!"

"What about Torque and Blitz?"

"Blitz can handle no breathin' for a while," and Dusty patted his bag, "Ole Torque is already taken care of."

Tivex was about to say something else when Dusty pushed her to the ground and began firing his weapon at the two creatures that had materialized around the nearest corner. The two fell without any fight whatsoever and Dusty stuck out his arm to help Tivex up. She accepted as Dusty said, "Okay, now we find the boys."

"Velkaso could have them captive anywhere," Tivex replied.

Dusty nodded, "Yeah, but the one thing we got goin' for us is that this is still a Destroyer class, jus' like the Nightmare."

Tivex widened her eyes as she now began to understand fully what the others must have known from the beginning. There was only one way to get Torque and Blitz back. They had to get aboard Velkaso's ship which would be impossible if extreme measures weren't taken. When Hammer challenged Velkaso, it had never been about going head to head with him. Somehow, in that methodical mind of his, Hammer had the forethought to bring Velkaso in as close as he could so that the maniac would be enraged enough to try and ram his ship through the Nightmare.

What Velkaso didn't account for was that the Beautiful Nightmare was also a Destroyer class. Thusly, making it impossible to be sliced all the way through. Dusty's earlier maneuvers, erratic as they had been at first, now became more apparent to Tivex. What Dusty had done was taking out any chance of Velkaso being able to draw back after he had rammed them. The other huge advantage that Tivex and Dusty would have was that since they had spent so much time on the Nightmare, Velkaso's ship was laid out in much the same fashion. Hammer and Dregs would go do what they had to do while Tivex and Dusty found Torque and Blitz.

With Team Seven now aboard Velkaso's ship, Tivex understood what Hammer had been planning. They were going to find the others, eliminate Velkaso and take back the Horizon. It had all been nothing more than an elaborate ruse so Team Seven would be able to board Velkaso's ship without giving their hand away. It was an ingenious plan but it was also one of the most suicidal Tivex had ever heard of.

Dusty slapped her on the shoulder, "Knew you'd figure it out, darlin'!"

Tivex looked down the corridor, "Will they need help?"

"Doubt it. Let's get the boys and get the hell outta here. From what Hammer tole me time and again, I don't wanna get between him and Velkaso if I can help it."

Tivex and Dusty took off down the passage and began kicking in doors. Through her headset, Tivex could hear shouts and calls coming from all around her but was unable to pinpoint exactly what they were saying. Thankfully, Velkaso had a minimal crew with him and there were not many rooms they found occupied. Those that were found themselves taken out before they had any chance of defense. Tivex thankfully only had to dispatch two brutish creatures with her daggers, one in close range and another she had to work at considerably.

When the creature stopped twitching at her feet, Dusty ran over behind her and looked down at it, "Any sign of the boys?"

Tivex shook her head, "Is it not possible they may be with Velkaso himself?"

"Try two more doors down, hotness!" came the voice of Torque through the headset.

Tivex spun around and nearly knocked Dusty over. She reached the door and decimated it by using all four arms to punch it down. Inside, Blitz and Torque grinned widely at them both. Torque had a black eye and Blitz had a few new dents near his upper chest plate.

Blitz stood up and wiped some small debris off his shoulder, "What the slag took you so long?"

Dusty moved around Tivex and threw Blitz a blaster, "Stop whinin', princess, we're here now."

Blitz grabbed the blaster in midair and lifted his left eyebrow at Dusty. Dusty shrugged and tossed him something else. Blitz caught it and jammed the cigar in his mouth, "Alright, now I can party!"

Torque hopped off the bunk he was on and grinned widely at Tivex, "Next time, you think maybe I could get the drink and you get sucker punched?"

Tivex grabbed Torque with all four arms, "Jeffrey, I-"

Torque stopped her, "Slag it, let's just get out of here!" He looked at Dusty, "Big man planning what I think he is?"

Dusty nodded.

Torque grinned and motioned for the bag, "Can't seem to stay out of this thing this trip!"

When Torque was suited up, he flashed a thumbs up and Blitz said, "Now that we're all neat and pretty, how's about we go find our fearless leader and back 'im up?"

Everyone nodded and they ran back into the corridor towards the control deck. Along the way, the encountered what was left of Velkaso's crew. Tivex noted that only one other looked to be of the same race as Velkaso whereas the rest were a few Hais and the other creatures who had been in the Rycos common area. Everyone was all too happy to take care of anyone who got in their way with no quarter given.

They reached the control deck and Blitz pried the doors open, "Honey, we're home!"

What caught Tivex's eye first was the size of the room they just entered. The control deck was substantially modified to almost three times what Tivex had seen on any other ship. Huge banks of computer terminals lined the walls which all seemed as if they had been hacked apart and then rebuilt. A sort of throne sat in the center of the room built from whatever had been lying around at the time. Scattered at their feet laid the battered corpses of other races strewn about in various macabre poses. Tivex looked on in shock as she saw two of them were Akoni, their massive chests shattered open without so much as a struggle. And in the center of it all was Velkaso, laughing maniacally as he held his claws under the throat of another person, a human female struggling in vain against his uncompromising grip. Across from him crouched Hammer and Dregs, weapons trained towards him, unflinching determination in both their eyes.

Velkaso looked down at Hammer, *"Now, this is familiar, yes? Seems you still can't do anything right!"*

Hammer didn't even blink, "Don't think for a second I won't shoot through her to get to you."

"You no have what it takes to kill Velkaso! You lucky you hide behind gun!"

Dregs stood up and threw his weapon to the side. He extended his claws and sneered, "Looks like I ain't hidin'."

"I no want you, filthy traitor! I want monkaso boys!" Dregs took a step closer and Velkaso raised the woman up and inch into the air. She screamed in pain and terror as Velkaso said, *"Ah, ah, ah! Boys first!"*

In the excitement, either Velkaso didn't hear the rest of Team Seven come in or he didn't care. Blitz took a step forward, "Hey, gray for brains, why don't you try that slag with me?"

Velkaso threw his head back and laughed in triumph. He looked back at Hammer, *"You no teach friends nothing! How dare you try your pathetic attempt all over again? You really that stupid?!"*

Hammer turned towards the control deck's opening and dropped his weapon down, "BLITZ, BEHIND YOU!"

It was too late. Some of the corpses began to rise up from the ground and shake themselves off, seeming to reanimate as undead wraiths. The act took Tivex and the others by surprise, so much so they never saw the same happening behind them as well. In three heartbeats, Tivex and the others were surrounded by the rest of Velkaso's crew who had been told to act dead until they arrived. They were disarmed and led in front of Velkaso who was shaking with laughter. In her mind, Tivex figured out Hammer's plan to stop Velkaso but she never would have expected him capable of something like this. She had never been aware that such evil treachery existed and now it seemed that that very evil would be the death of them all.

She was thrown down to Velkaso's feet. She turned around to see the one that had disarmed her personally was another Akoni. She looked up at him, "Why, brother?"

The Akoni simply grinned, "Because I can, and I did."

Tivex felt her arms wrenched behind her and bound tightly as were the others. She felt Dregs slammed down behind her as he hissed at the other Akoni, "When I'm free, little man, please run and make it worth my time."

The only one not there was Hammer. She could only assume Velkaso had something truly awful planned for him. In every scenario she played in her mind over the years, this form of death had never, ever been one of them. She shut her eyes momentarily and whispered a silent prayer to the Light that her death be quick but she sincerely doubted it.

Velkaso finally stopped laughing. He lowered his head towards Hammer and said, *"You have nothing, boys! You always have nothing! You never learn and for that I swear you will suffer more than any other who dies before VELKASO!"*

Nothing happened. Hammer made no noise and if he had, Tivex doubted she would have been able to hear it over her own heartbeat.

Velkaso seemed to become angrier, *"You see? You no can even answer me!"* Tivex looked up to see him run his forked tongue across his vicious fangs as he looked down at her, *"Maybe her first?"*

Hammer still made no sound. There was a part of Tivex which began to wish whatever Velkaso was planning would just be over with. He dropped a leg back behind him and then shot it out as hard as he could into Dusty's chest. Tivex saw Dusty launched back at least ten feet and yell out in pain.

Velkaso turned back to Hammer, *"Nothing? Not so much as a whimper for me to stop? Very well!"*

Velkaso took the woman he was holding and picked her off the ground again. He raised her up far over his head and then began to bend her backwards. The woman screamed in agony but Velkaso didn't let up. After a moment, there was a sickening crunch as the woman's spine was broken and he threw her towards where Dusty had landed. She mewed for a moment longer before she fell silent and yet, Hammer did nor said anything.

Velkaso became enraged, "*DO YOU NOTHING, BOYS? PATHETIC, USELESS, GRAY COWARD!! HAVE I A MIND TO-*"

Tivex watched as Velkaso was knocked off his feet from something which moved faster than anything she had ever seen. Brilliant flashes of light began to fill the control deck as the blur beat into Velkaso remorselessly. Out of nowhere, Hammer had summoned the strengths to not only go after Velkaso, he was moving at a speed that Tivex thought impossible for humans.

As Velkaso shrieked in pain, Hammer screamed, "NOW, BLITZ!"

To Tivex' right, Blitz easily ripped out of his bonds and stood up. Some of the crew began to fire at him but the bolts bounced right off him. Blitz looked at the nearest crewman and blasted him dead center in the chest with his hidden blaster. Then, he switched from blaster to blade and cut the restraints off the rest. Without warning, Dregs raced up to the smaller crewmember who had tied him up and slashed with both paws into the crewman's throat. Dusty rolled over to Torque. Both picked up the nearest blasters and began firing at anything moving. Tivex ducted under the fire and pried her daggers out of the dead crewman's hand which had taken them from her and went to work at the crewman sneaking up behind Hammer. She cartwheeled and jammed one of her boots into the back of his neck, dropping him as if he were a loaf of bread onto the floor. Without thinking, she tumbled over twice and buried both daggers up to the hilt into his collarbone. The crewman screamed in agony before Tivex whipped around one more time and snapped his neck with her other leg.

She pulled out the daggers just as Blitz and Dregs got her under her arms and pulled her back up. "Nice moves, pretty," scoffed Dregs, "I think I might like you now!"

Tivex was about to say something when she noticed another two of Velkaso's lackeys coming up behind Blitz. She dropped down into a split and threw both daggers straight at their chests. Both fell limp to the ground and skidded to a halt in front of her.

Blitz turned around and then looked at Dregs, "Yep, I think I'm takin' her home to meet mamma after this!"

Tivex retrieved her daggers and was about to go help Hammer when Dregs stopped her, "No, pretty, that's for him, let him finish what needs be finished."

"What?!" exclaimed Tivex.

"Our job is to get the Horizon out of here," yelled Torque, "and we have about ten minutes to do it!"

Tivex looked back at Dregs who merely nodded, "Time to go."

Tivex widened her eyes, "Oh, no."

"Oh yeah, darlin'!" Dusty managed to spit out, "Time for some fireworks!"

Blitz leaned his head back to Torque, "You set?"

Torque jumped back over the railing and helped Dusty, "Nine minutes and thirty seconds from now and we either bail outta here or we're not gonna have to worry about any retirement parties!"

Tivex whipped her head around and pointed to the motionless body of the human woman, "What about her?"

Dusty shook his head, "Forget her, darlin', she never made it longer than a second or two when she hit me. Sadistic stone heart went an' punctured her lungs, never had a chance!"

Tivex made sure her daggers were handy as Blitz and Dregs began to fire as many rounds as they had into the control deck's hull. From the look in Torque's eye, she knew he had overloaded the main reactor as well as rerouting all the main star drive power into the central coiling. It was only a matter of time until Velkaso's ship blew itself apart. When Dregs and Blitz emptied their magazines, they grabbed the back of Tivex's suit and pulled her with them back out the control deck's destroyed doors. Tivex, facing backward, saw Dusty being helped by Torque. They were going to the Horizon and use it to blast free. Somehow there was a new sense beginning to form inside of Tivex, one that told her on instinct alone, here they went again.

SUCKER PUNCH

THANKFULLY, THE CARGO BAY WAS SITUATED IN THE SAME LOCATION AS ON THE BEAUTIFUL Nightmare so they had no trouble finding it. Dregs and Blitz took care of their entrance by basically bulldozing the doors off their hinges and sending them halfway across the bay. Dusty and Torque were covering them from the rear but there was little point. Whatever crew Velkaso had left, had been dispatched during the control deck fight and the ship was now more a graveyard than space vessel.

Some of the alarms still functioned however they did little more than sputter out a few shrill alerts. The cargo bay was the biggest mess Tivex had ever seen, various pieces of different classes of ships laid strewn about everywhere she looked. She saw the Horizon in the center of the bay looking as if Velkaso had tried multiple times to get it working and failed. There was no point and no time to idle about but she saw Torque stop, kneel down and pick up something from the ground.

Dusty ran up behind him, "What is it?"

Torque shook his head and threw whatever it was across the room with everything he had, "One of the vector casings off the Widow Maker!" He cast a despised look towards the bay's entrance and spit on the ground, "Cut my ship apart, will ya? Ooh, I wish I could do more to this heap than I did."

"I'll let you shoot whatever's left after we get the slag outta here!" yelled Blitz, "Move it, shorty, clock's tickin'!"

Torque nodded in disgust and ran over to the cargo bay's control terminals. He methodically began to type in command after command and shouted back to the others, "From here on out, get your helmets on and keep 'em there!"

Everyone did as they were told except for Tivex who looked towards the door, hoping to see Hammer, "What about-"

Dusty interrupted, "If he ain't here in the next three minutes, he's gonna try his ole' Tarzan trick."

Tivex looked at Dusty, "His what?"

"After he deals with Velkaso, he'll beat feet back here. If we're gone, he blows an air coil and rockets ta us with a tether line. He hooks on and we get as far away as we can," answered Dregs from over his shoulder.

Tivex just blinked as her mouth dried instantly, "You cannot possibly be serious?"

"It don't look like he's jokin', darlin'" grinned Dusty as he double checked her helmet settings.

The cargo bay was a blur of movement. Tivex wasn't sure exactly what she should be doing as the others ran around as if they had been overclocked. Torque was at the computer terminal, his fingers moving so fast Tivex couldn't keep up. Blitz and Dregs were moving debris out of the path the Horizon to enable it to be set out on the best possible clearance they could. Dusty was already inside the Horizon, disappearing towards the control deck without so much as a backwards glance.

Dregs and Blitz came flying back around towards her. Dregs pointed up to the Horizon, "Time to take our leave, pretty!"

Tivex turned back around in desperate hopes of seeing Hammer come crashing through the door at the last minute but there was no sign of him.

Torque ran up beside her and saw were she was looking. He shook his head, "I hate this part!"

"So do I," said Blitz authoritatively, "but it ain't like we got slag to say or do about it!"

"Less talk, more move," growled Dregs as he lifted Tivex off the ground and tossed her inside the Horizon.

Blitz and Torque landed right next to her as she rolled to get out of the way. Tivex picked herself off the ground and saw that Dregs was still on the ground outside. She looked down in disbelief as Dregs lowered himself down to the ground, almost onto all fours. He took in a great breath of air and then released it in a roar that literally made the ship below her quake. Apparently satisfied with what he had done, Dregs picked himself back up and vaulted into the Horizon to join the others.

Tivex looked to him to see what his display was all about but Dregs said nothing. He merely took off in the direction of the control deck to join Dusty. Torque and Blitz followed him leaving Tivex alone in the corridor. She looked back out and again saw no sign of Hammer. She was absolutely clueless on what was happening but it didn't take her long to figure out that she was needed in the control deck as well. She lowered her head and said a quick prayer to the Light for Hammer to somehow make it through safely and then took off to join the others.

Velkaso was still recovering from Hammer's last blow. He had been thrown across the entire length of the control deck and smashed into a repaired bank of terminals. His back had impacted so hard that the entire front casing had been torn from the terminal and landed beneath him.

Hammer watched Velkaso trying to shake off the punch but looking as if he were still dazed. Hammer looked with savage satisfaction from seeing his former master unsure of what to do next. The electricity was still surging through him, not from the megawatt but from the hatred burning inside him as if it had a mind of its own. Hammer knew that time was ticking away and he didn't have much of it left but he was having way too much fun to stop now. Mentally measuring where Velkaso would try to move to, Hammer sidestepped and slid over to where Velkaso was trying to pick himself up. Hammer grabbed the back of Velkaso's head and slammed it back into the terminal again.

Velkaso screeched in pain as Hammer picked him up off the ground and began to laugh, "Hahaha! Who's pathetic now, gray man, huh? Who's bloody laughing now?!"

Velkaso's eyes were almost rolling in their sockets, "You have still nothing...you no fight without help...useless boys..."

Hammer brought Velkaso down onto his bent knee as hard as he could and then rolled the demon off him. Hammer swung around and used the momentum to almost take flight into a fighter's crouch. He looked down at his fists and saw that some of the sparks had changed from bright blue to an almost dull green, the telltale sign the megawatt was almost out of power. Not hesitating for an instant, Hammer dove back at Velkaso and used the last of his power in a brutal double uppercut which sent Velkaso rolling back head over heels. His arms shot down and the megawatt fell off, leaving Hammer to use only what he had left, which was going to be far more than enough.

He leapt into the air and landed near Velkaso, eyes blazing, "You didn't really think I was going to make it easy, did you?"

Velkaso had barely stood up when Hammer landed. He lost his footing and stumbled back to the nearest railing. He clutched at his side and looked unable to stand fully up, "Boys use wretched sparks to hurt Velkaso? So predictable!"

Hammer saw Velkaso was hurt and that the time had come to end this. He cocked his head at Velkaso as if trying to decide where the kill shot should be aimed, "I've waited for this a long time, you evil, gray, monkaso, and I'm going to enjoy every slagging second."

"Monkaso? MONKASO?!" roared Velkaso, "HOW DARE YOU!"

With twice the aggressive speed Hammer had ever seen from him in the past, Velkaso lunged towards him with something in his hand. Hammer had only a split second to realize Velkaso had found some sharp debris from somewhere and was going to use it to run him through. Hammer dropped to the ground, feeling whatever it was swing right over his head and plowed his right fist into the place Velkaso had been holding earlier. Velkaso reacted by thundering his elbow into the side of Hammer's head, causing him to momentarily see swirling flashes of light dance in front of his eyes.

Hammer tried to move out of the way as Velkaso forced all his weight into a knee kick which connected right below Hammer's chin. Hammer felt himself knocked back at least five feet from where he had been as he fought with everything he had not to black out. He never saw it happen, but he felt Velkaso now land on him from somewhere and instinctively threw his hands up to counter Velkaso from burying whatever he was using into his chest.

Hammer rolled his head back and saw his original nightmare coming true all over again as Velkaso leaned in closer, *"No one defeats Velkaso, boys, NO ONE! You think you've won and yet again, I prove you have NOTHING! You friends may have destroyed my ship but I swear, boys, I WILL SEE YOU FIRST INTO OBLIVION!"*

Hammer felt the weight of Velkaso bearing down on him for all he was worth and struggled to find the right position with which to counter attack. There was little he could do from this angle but there was a lot Velkaso wasn't aware which was going to prove extremely useful in the next five minutes. Hammer felt a strength he had never known begin to coarse through him as a distant roar echoed down into the control deck.

"How the slag am I supposed to know?!" seethed Torque, "It might work, it might not!"

Dregs scowled at Torque, "Now might not be the best time to be second guessin' this plan, ratchet man. You get this wrong and we ain't gonna have to worry 'bout whether or not Hammer makes it."

Torque twisted his head back to Dregs, "You're not helping, furball."

Dregs sneered, "Never said I was."

Tivex watched as Torque was feverishly trying to get the main control panel operational again so that Blitz could take care of the rest. Velkaso and his crew had done a stellar job at ripping apart almost everything in the control deck but hadn't bothered to try to put anything back together again. The deck was even more a mess now than it had been back on that infernal island but now there was the added bonus of Velkaso's ship being rigged to blow in less than seven minutes. Even if they were able to get the Horizon working, Tivex had serious doubts whether or not they'd even be able to get safely far enough away from the ship.

She looked down at Torque, "Can I assist in any way?"

Torque smirked as he continued without looking at her, "If you wanna start praying, that might not be such a bad idea."

Tivex rolled her eyes, "How can you possibly be so obstinate at a time like this?"

Torque said nothing but continued at a pace which made Tivex wonder how he could work so fast. She turned to see Dusty leaning casually against a wall as if he hadn't a care in the world. Blitz was eyeing the circuitry that was hanging down from another one of the terminals. Tivex was truly beside herself as she wondered if any of these men were as scared as she was. If they were, they were amazingly good at hiding their emotions. She felt her heartbeat quicken and her hands began to shake as the realization began to sink in that there was really no way of out this. Either Torque was going to find a way to get the Horizon working or they were going down with the ship.

Panic began to get the better of her as she thought back to her medical lab. It had been so simple back then. Someone got sick or hurt, they came to see her. She took care of them and sent them on their way. She had only needed to go into space a handful of times for training or medical emergencies and she was all too happy to have let it stay that way. Now, here she was with the most unpredictable and most volatile Star Team in IEC history, trying to jump start a completely unknown starship while sitting inside of another ship which not conveniently was about to explode. Tivex fought hard to control her breathing and to keep herself focused but found it and impossible task.

Finally, Torque pushed himself out from under the terminal and shook his head at the others, "It's dead, completely dead. Whatever they did to this thing is way beyond what I can do with what I have around here."

"What are you saying?" said Tivex, more fear in her voice that she wanted.

Torque threw a broken piece of something or another onto the ground, "I'm sayin' we're not going anywhere."

Tivex felt the bottom of her stomach drop away and the sudden surge of adrenaline push through her. She was shaking so badly she was unable to hide it, "So now what?!"

Dregs stood beside Torque, "What about resetting the timer?"

Torque shook his head, "Nope. I mixed in an algorithm which changes itself every thirty seconds, even I can't turn it off."

"Welp, gents, and lady, it's been real," said Dusty, nodding his head towards the others, "I say we round up whatever we kin' and go find Hammer."

Tivex whipped her head around to Dusty and grabbed him by the shoulders, "Just give up?! Have you lost your mind?! Have you nothing to live for?!"

"Plenty, darlin', but ain't worth gettin' in a twist over. We all gotta go, right? So, let's go out strong!"

Tivex turned to Dregs for any sign of encouragement but found him only to puff out his chest at Dusty, "I'm with ya."

Torque cast a look behind him at the destroyed control deck, "Slag it, let's party."

"Honestly, I see why I stayed on as operations officer," said Blitz as he pushed through the others, "ain't one of ya got brains to think straight, I swear." Tivex turned on her heels and looked towards Blitz. He went over to the captain's chair and kicked it off its rivets. He pointed at the control terminal behind Torque and then tapped his head, "Cyber link me, remember?"

Torque slapped himself on the forehead and ran over to Blitz who crossed his arms. Torque looked him up and down and grinned, "Ship's blowing up, brother's off doing who knows what, and Tivex is flipping out. Sue me, I forgot!"

Blitz grinned back and slapped Torque on the back. In a matter of seconds, Torque rigged Blitz directly into the terminal. Almost immediately, Blitz's blue eye began to glow the same shade of blue as the rest of the terminals. The smile left his face as Blitz began to merge with the Horizon. Screen after screen began to illuminate the shimmering silver panels both overhead and around them. Tivex felt as if the entire weight of the universe was instantly lifted from her shoulders at seeing the Horizon somehow coming back to life, even after Velkaso had been at it. A few heartbeats later and the entire deck was alive again as though it had never gone offline.

Dregs sneered at Blitz, "Glad you remembered this!"

Blitz managed a half smile at Dregs, "You're buyin' the first round when we get outta here."

Tivex watched as Blitz motioned for Dusty to get ready to move the Horizon out of the cargo bay. Even though the Horizon was somewhat functional, she was nowhere near close enough to what was considered flight worthy. The new plan was to use the Horizon as a lifeboat and limp back into IEC territory as best they could. The one and only ace up their sleeves was that the Rycos station laid not more than eighteen hours from the border.

That was still another problem that Tivex still hadn't quite grasped as the Horizon was barely able to hold together as it was. She pushed the thought from her mind for at the present moment, she was satisfied her time had not yet come. Torque pressed something on his wrist control cuff and the cargo bay's main doors opened. From her headset, Tivex suddenly heard something. It was another kind of roar, very similar to what Dregs had done earlier but this one was different. It sounded more like some victorious battle cry but she wasn't sure what it was until Dregs' head shot directly up and looked back towards Velkaso's ship. For the first time since she had known him, Dregs looked happy, very happy. As if something inside of him was actually calm for once. She watched as a small, genuine smile began to cross his face, no fangs and no malicious intentions. Dregs let his head fall back and from her vantage point, she swore his ears were down in almost a regal pose.

Hammer turned his head up at Velkaso whose eyes were trained on his. Hammer felt his strength increasing tenfold as he pushed upwards on Velkaso's arms. Hammer had only a few more minutes before the ship around him would be torn apart. He felt Velkaso trying to push down with the debris with all his weight and in that split second, Hammer knew it was time.

For the first time in ages, Hammer allowed his mind to let go. He actually allowed his memories to come flooding back to the surface of his mind's eye. He allowed them to bubble and collide, allowed them to run rampant, allowed them their freedom. Even with Velkaso on top of him, Hammer felt a warm sensation beginning to flow down his arms and legs. They seemed stronger somehow, in a way he had never known before. He opened his mind further and momentarily blocked out Velkaso, seeing nothing but her face. The feeling grew stronger and Hammer felt as if his body were transformed into liquid titanium.

Finally, with the overwhelming sensation coming to a peak, he allowed his mind to take over completely and watched as Dayna's face disappeared into his own reflection. It was the younger version of himself, scared, weak and unable to act. Hammer felt his mouth curl and the fully open. The sound which reverberated from the darkest corner of his psyche could only be compared to the sound heard at the birth of the universe.

It was a guttural sound, untamed, feral but most of all, destructive, "ARGAHHHHHH!!"

With the strength of almost quadruple what he believed himself capable of, Hammer launched Velkaso into the air. Hammer shot up and roundhouse kicked into up to a fighter's stance. Velkaso came down and before he landed, Hammer smashed his fist into the back of Velkaso's head with a force so deadly and ferocious that he heard something snap before Velkaso landed on the ground before him. Not waiting for another opportunity, Hammer jumped over Velkaso and picked up the debris which had been aimed at him. Without mercy or forethought, Hammer kicked Velkaso over and plunged the debris directly into the demon's heart.

Velkaso shrieked, *"NO! NO YOU CAN KILL ME, BOYS! NO! I NO LET YOU!!"*

Velkaso kicked and writhed but Hammer never let up. His grip and footing were as deadlocked as his focus. Velkaso chocked out black blood all over his face as Hammer twisted the debris in his chest, clawing in rapid cessation at nothing and everything simultaneously. Hammer felt the smile on his face broaden as Velkaso began to lose strength, and felt his lips part as the demon's breathing became shallower and more sporadic. Finally, as if the symphony of pain and suffering came to its climax, Velkaso let out one last shriek of agony and moved no longer.

Hammer stood back up and put his foot on Velkaso's chest. He threw his head back, beat his chest and thundered his battle cry as loud as he could. At last, at long, glorious last, one vengeance was his, and his alone. As elating as it was to see Velkaso laid out in front of him, Hammer knew there was no more than minutes before the ship detonated. Just for good measure, Hammer kicked Velkaso in the head as hard as he could and then took off out of the control deck and back to the cargo bay.

If he was lucky enough, his Team would still be in the bay itself and he wouldn't have to attempt the tether maneuver. Hammer skidded to a halt in front of the cargo bay and made sure his helmet was ready to go. Once he opened the secondary hatch which has been automatically closed after the first ones had been destroyed, he knew the main doors would be open and thusly would have no air or gravity. Hammer made absolutely sure his boots were magnetized and slammed a fist into the door's control button. He saw and felt the massive rush of air moving towards the vacuum of space. Hammer stepped into the bay and saw the Horizon was already a good fifty feet outside the bay. So much for luck.

From the looks of things around him, it wasn't going to be hard to find something with which to attempt this trick again. The first time he had done it was back in basic training. This time he imagined it wouldn't be much different, no safety nets and no second chances. It was a very gutsy maneuver but it was the only one he had left.

He ran into the cargo bay and immediately began searching for anything resembling a tether cord. Parts of various ships decorated the floor and walls, obvious trophies from Velkaso's other conquests. Hammer thought about how many ships had fallen victim to that wretched being who laid dead in the control deck and wondered how in the universe Velkaso had always been able to escape capture. It made little difference now and there wasn't time to think about it anyway.

He looked up and saw the Horizon was still within distance for him to make the jump to board it but it wouldn't stay that way for much longer.

"I see him!" yelled Tivex.

The others rushed to the side where Tivex was standing. There were no openings large enough on this side of the Horizon to catch Hammer if he came barreling out of Velkaso's ship. The tear down the side only allowed Tivex a vantage point from where she was standing to look back towards Velkaso's ship. She pointed down to where Hammer was rushing around.

She turned to Dusty, "Can you reverse the thrust to get any closer?"

Dusty shook his head, "Sorry, darlin', the retro burners were damaged to begin with. I might be able to slow down some but it ain't gonna be much."

She looked down at Torque who shook his head. Tivex could see a great concern rising in Torque's eyes, "This thing was bad enough when we first saw it and me stripping it for parts didn't help."

Tivex bit her bottom lip and looked back to Hammer. She could see him scurrying about in an attempt to find something with enough reach to allow him his escape. The Horizon was beginning drift upwards and away from Velkaso's ship and she heard Dusty swear behind her, "Stone thing ain't respondin'. I got nothin' on vertical control."

Blitz, still linking with the Horizon, turned around. He pushed off the ground and floated back to an identical plate which mirrored the one he had managed to tap into the Horizon's power source the first time. He placed his hand down onto the plate and brought up the ships schematics, "Looks like we're venting too much on the landing thrusters below us, they're pushing us away too fast."

Torque joined Blitz and looked carefully at the ship's map. He leaned in closer to study them, "Yeah, and there's absolutely nothing we can do about it. The vent shaft to the stabilizers is shattered and even if it wasn't, I don't have anything to patch it with."

"What's that gonna do to our getaway?" asked Dusty.

"It's a slow vent, shouldn't throw us too far off coarse to get back to the border but it's gonna make it real hard for Hammer to get to us if he doesn't pick up the pace," answered Torque.

Tivex turned back and saw that Hammer looked as if he had finally found something useful and was already attaching it to one of the cargo bay's support columns. From the looks of it, Hammer was going to use a length of cable for a lifeline in case his aim was off. She watched as he double checked the column and bent down to tie the cable around his waist. He stopped and picked something off the floor as if something of unique interest had just appeared.

Tivex spoke but to no one in particular, "Now what is he doing?"

"Dunno," replied Dregs from her right, "but it's slowin' 'im down."

Tivex went to say something when she saw Hammer's head whip around to the cargo bay's main entrance door, drop the cable and head back the way he came. She pounded her fists into the railing and yelled, "NO! What is he doing?"

"You gotta be slaggin' kiddin' me!" responded Dregs almost at the same moment.

Tivex was unable to even blink when she saw what Hammer had gone back after. If there was any truth to what she had heard about the horrors that could happen in space, she was witnessing one right in front of her eyes.

The cable was as tight as Hammer could make it around the column. It wasn't the best he was hoping for but there was nothing else left with enough slack to allow him to reach the Horizon. The other problem was that there were only two oxygen coils left in the cargo bay with enough pressure to give him the extra boost he would need. He realized he was going to have one chance with this idea. If he came up short or overshot the Horizon altogether, there was no way Dusty would be able to swing around to come pick him up. From what he could see, the Horizon still had power but her hull looked as if a stiff breeze would blow what was left of her all over the Dominion Territory.

The last thing he would allow was to give in to any doubt that this plan would work. Once someone started to doubt their resolve, it was only a matter of time until they let their fear get the better of them and Hammer would not let that happen. The cable was tight around the column and he reached down to tie the other end to his waist. He cast a quick look at the countdown timer on one of the screens left on the wall. Four minutes to go, which left him one minute to tie up, one minute to fly over and two minutes to get anywhere but there. Hammer allowed himself a quick moment of sadistic reconciliation as he realized he always seemed to find himself on the business end of a ticking time bomb.

He grabbed the cable's end when something small floated past his boot. Normally, Hammer wouldn't have given it a second glance but something caught his attention from the corner of his eye. It was a hypodermic needle, with the plunger pushed all the way down. A very, very subtle greenish glow came from a few drops of liquid which were barely still attached to the needle itself. Hammer tilted his head slightly and wondered how a medical device such as this could have ended up anywhere near the cargo bay. As if on cue, he realized exactly how it could have been done.

Hammer dropped the cable and spun around to where the main entrance door was. There, leaning on the doorframe as if he had just come back from a night on the town was Velkaso, grinning as if he had just pulled off some fantastic illusion. He held a blaster in his right hand which looked to be modified to hold hull piercing rounds. In his left, he held another needle filled with the glowing green liquid which he jammed into his thigh and emptied completely.

In the second that it took for Hammer to realize who else was there, he also realized his mistake. He had been so consumed with his vengeance that he had completely forgotten Velkaso always kept a steady supply of original Helix with him as all times. When Velkaso had been clutching his side earlier, he must have masked the needle somehow. With enough Helix in his system, even his heart would have been able to heal after Hammer had tried to pierce it.

Velkaso wasted no time. He brought the blaster up to his shoulder and fired two explosive rounds at the Horizon. He then threw the blaster aside and lunged for Hammer, *"YOU GOES FIRST, BOYS!!"*

"GET DOWN!" shouted Dregs.

Tivex felt him grab ahold of her and throw her to the ground. She felt the wind knocked from her lungs as Dregs landed atop her. The others yelled out in their microphones but so much was happening Tivex lost all her bearings. One minute she was facing the ground, the next she was upside down and on the ceiling.

She tried to shake off the blast and regain her composure but she was having a hard time with no gravity, "What was that?" she yelled out.

"Concussive blast from the other ship!" shouted Dusty, "Dregs?"

Dregs floated back down to the floor and grabbed the railing for support, "ROWWWRR!" he growled, "He's still ALIVE?! How? HOW, DAMN YOU?!?"

"Who?" shouted Blitz.

"VELKASO!" thundered Dregs, "Why ain't he slaggin' DEAD YET?!"

Tivex desperately looked out the tear and saw Hammer indeed struggling once more with Velkaso. All words escaped her as she marveled at how that was even possible. From what she could see, Velkaso was in a zero suit of his own, apparently one with magnetic boots like Hammer's, and was facing off again on the doomed ship.

She was about to say something when there was another sound, this time from the Horizon. Tivex thought for a moment that the hull may have finally taken enough damage for it to buckle but the sound was coming from in front of them, not behind.

She heard Torque yell out, "What the slag is THAT?!"

Tivex whipped her head to the left and saw something happening to the front of the Horizon. A sort of compartment was opening up in front of them. The entire nose assembly was separating and as it split apart, something else rose up in its place. A massive, gyroscopic device slid upward and then locked itself into place. Three rings sat one inside one other all seemingly made up from the same material as the Horizon was. When it had fully locked into place, the smallest inner ring began to rotate, slowly at first and gradually picked up speed. As it became faster, the ring began to tilt outwards and then flipped itself vertically.

Torque pushed himself off the far wall and landed back where Blitz had been knocked to the ground. Torque helped him up and said with critical concern in his voice, "Talk to this thing and see what that is!"

Blitz placed his hand back on the pad and brought up schematics, maps and readouts with effortless speed. As he did, Tivex noticed his mechanical blue eye was now glowing with the same intensity as the equipment around them. Blitz turned and looked at Torque, "You see anything useful yet?"

Torque shook his head, "No, I don't want any of this! Get to engineering information and get it here quick!"

Blitz and Torque continued to work. Dusty got back to the controls and fiddled with them, "Dead stick! We're dead stick!"

Tivex turned to look back at Hammer but saw that the second middle ring of the gyroscope was now spinning the way the first had. Together, the rings were working in unison and another subtle glow began to emanate from their center. Tivex was not concerned with the spinning rings and went back to where Dregs was but didn't see him. She looked around the control deck praying he had not been stupid enough to bail out and try to help Hammer.

From the way that the Horizon was hit by Velkaso, it was now beginning to drift even farther away from his ship and was also now spinning very slowly in a three hundred and sixty-degree circle. Tivex could hear Dusty yelling at Torque to get the controls back online and Torque shouting back something about all the power was directed at whatever was spinning in front of them.

Suddenly, amidst the chaos, she heard Torque yell, "What the slag do you think I'm trying to do?! It's not like I have a…wait…what's wrong? Blitz, talk to me!!"

Tivex looked at what Torque was staring at. Blitz had become as still as a statue. His glowing eye was now seeming to somehow spin just like the gyroscope outside. His head dropped down slightly as he said in a hollow metallic voice, "Initiating final portal sequence."

"Huh?!" said Dusty as he swung around.

Blitz had yet to move a muscle. Torque floated over to him and waved his hand in front of Blitz's eyes, "Hey, tin man, don't short out on me now!"

Blitz only replied, "Destination targeted. Calculations nominal for prime directive one. Preparing to disengage final safety."

Dusty and Torque looked at each other in hopeless confusion. Dusty tried to shake Blitz out of his trance only to find him completely immobile. He shouted at Tivex, "Could use a lil' help over here, darlin'!"

Tivex was torn inside about what to do. She knew she could do nothing more than keep her eyes trained on Hammer, however, she knew exactly what he would want her to do. She was about to float over towards Blitz when something crashed down next to her. She looked in time to see Dregs perched precariously close to one of the openings.

Tivex threw her arm over to him, "NO!"

Dregs looked back at her, wild eyes glowing with the reflection below, "Ain't your fight, pretty."

"You cannot help him, Dregs! You cannot even reach him!"

"Reach him?" scowled Dregs, "You don't seriously think I'm that stupid."

"Would one of you two get the hell over here?!" shouted Torque.

Tivex just blinked at Dregs and looked over towards the others. The situation was getting worse by the second but if the Omarian was going to be obstinate about his revenge, there was nothing she could do to stop him now.

She shook her head and was about to again move over to help Blitz when Dregs grabbed her and pulled her down to the floor with him. He passed her something, "Here."

Tivex looked down and saw that it was one of the blasters from Velkaso's crew. Dregs must have taken it during their escape although she hadn't seen him do it. She held the blaster in her hands and looked back at him with a puzzled look on her face. He sneered back at her and revealed a second blaster in his other paw. Two? How the Omarian had managed to take one, let alone, two blasters without her even seeing them was a trait reserved for apparently former thieves.

Dregs nodded his head out the opening, "When we come around again, pretty, whatever you do, don' miss."

Tivex realized that she and Dregs were going to be Hammer's last chance at getting off that ship. The feeling in the pit of her stomach was all too clear that she was no marksman and that her hands were shaking too badly for a proper shot. She looked desperately at Dregs, "Dregs, Blitz needs-."

Dregs grabbed her neck and pulled her in close. She saw his helmet against hers, "He can handle himself! If you so much as says you're above doin' this, I'll kill you where you stand, Akoni! I don' care if you're a medic, a spy or whatever the gray you are! Right now, you 'n' me are the only chance my captain now has of goin' home. Stop actin' so afraid and at leas' pretend for a second you've got some guts in ya!"

Tivex heard more shouting but was unable to clearly make any of it out. She knew Blitz was in trouble, almost as much as Hammer. She felt the blaster in her hands and looked back up at Dregs. There was no room for mistakes with him and now she clearly saw there would be no mercy for her if she declined. There was a subtle feeling of acceptance on her part as she realized that for all he was worth, Dregs may have been the most loyal soldier she had ever seen before.

Tivex nodded at the hulking Omarian by her side and brought the blaster up to her shoulder. She took in a deep breath and tried to imagine how Hammer might've reacted if the situation was reversed, "I will not miss."

"You bloody better not, pretty."

Velkaso and Hammer were almost in range again and Tivex tried to keep herself steady. She could feel Dregs next to her but he was as motionless as the stars outside. She could feel the moment coming and a sort of exhilaration began to fill her without warning. For years, she had known about Hammer, about how he had been put through hell and feared for his life by the very being she was about to shoot. The sensation began to fill her as she thought about how Velkaso had taken Hammer away from his family and strangely, away from her. She was beginning to understand now how it was so easy for the others to follow Hammer the way they did. There was something about him that was unparalleled when it came to the unexpected and he was always willing to lay down his life for them. Yes, she thought, I can do this.

They were almost in range when the blast hit.

A brilliant blue, somewhat similar to the way sunlight pierced through a sapphire, appeared out of nowhere. It filled every inch of Tivex's vision and she was blinded by it. There was no sound other than that of her Team's shouting voices in her headset which began to sound very far off. Tivex felt the blaster ripped from her hands as the light engulfed her but for some reason she hadn't the strength to hold on to it anyway. She reached out for Dregs and found his arm groping out for her as well. They locked hands as the light grew brighter. Tivex couldn't see or hear Dregs but she could feel him holding onto her for everything he was worth. Tivex felt herself beginning to lose all her senses as the light reached a point where she could not even block it out with her eyes slammed shut. An overwhelming calmness crept into her, completely replacing the resolve she had forced into herself only moments before. It began to take her consciousness as the light had taken her senses. The light, she thought, somehow we were killed and I am being carried into the Light.

Tivex surrendered to her fate. She allowed herself to drift away into the warm, welcoming arms of nothiningness. Her last conscious thought was for her Team and she mentally uttered the highest Akoni prayer, may the others find their peace as well.

MISSING PIECE

THE WORLD AROUND HER SWAM WITH VISIONS SHE HAD NEVER DREAMT OF BEFORE. PICTURES which manifested themselves with an intensity Tivex could only describe as perfectly real yet always out of reach. She was looking down on a planet from somewhere she couldn't quite put her finger on. The planet was encircled with huge rings, both in vertical gold and horizontal silver. The planet looked as if it had never been lived on before, perfectly clear atmosphere under a pristine sun. Tivex felt as if the planet were almost calling for her, beckoning her to come closer but there was some kind of barrier which made that impossible. There was something about it which made her feel no fear, as if it was where she was always meant to be.

Tivex thought to herself that she could remember neither how she had arrived at this destination nor who had brought her here. As hard as she tried, she couldn't even remember more than five or ten minutes prior to seeing the planet. Actually, she thought, I do not remember anything before seeing this planet. She tried to look away but she found it impossible. Tivex found herself desperately yearning to get closer to the planet but she could get no closer.

She looked closer at the planet, seeing bright blue ribbons decorating parts of the surface. She tilted her head and tried to make out what they were. Rivers! She remembered, those must be rivers! But she had never seen water so blue. In fact, she had never seen anything so blue in her life. It was such a hypnotic blue that it caused her eyes to become dry from not blinking them. She tried to raise her hands to rub her eyes but her arms were not responding the way they always did before. Her eyes began to sting slightly but no so much that they were irritated. She tilted her head and stared into those blue rives, amazed that anything could be that brilliant. Surely, nothing she had ever seen before was that color.

Well, except for…for what?

Suddenly, Tivex began to feel the vision in front of her swirl slightly, as if her eyes had finally begun to blur. The planet was there, sure enough, but it was more difficult to see. Why had she remembered rivers in the first place? And why could she remember anything that could match that blue? Tivex felt an ever so slight concern begin to rise in her. She was having trouble remembering where she had seen that color before, as if it was of some massive importance.

Maybe she had become overcome somehow and needed to ask someone else's opinion. Perhaps, she thought, she should ask Dregs where they had seen this color before.

Wait, she thought.

Dregs…

Yes, she thought to herself, that's who would know. After all, he had been right next to her when-

Tivex's eyes bolted open as she woke up. She tried to sit up but something pushed her chest back down.

"Easy, pretty, easy." Dregs, still in his zero suit, looked over across from her and said, "She's alive."

She saw Dusty, also in his suit, swim into view and look down at her. She noticed his voice was not the happy go lucky tone as it usually was as it wavered a bit, "Gave us a scare, darlin'."

She felt Dusty's hand reach under her head to support it, although her body felt as if it had no weight of its own. Dusty took her upper left hand and held it reassuringly. She felt something slip into her lower right hand and lifted her head up enough to see Blitz.

His face was contorted in a manner which suggested he was in great pain, "We're all here, 'Vex."

"What happened?" croaked Tivex, becoming aware her body ached in ways she wasn't aware one could. She tried to look around and saw the mangled hull of the Horizon all around her. She had no concept of how much time had passed or what had just occurred. They had survived after all, if one were to call this pain surviving.

"We got the slag knocked outta us," answered Dusty, "you 'n' Dregs 'specially."

Tivex closed her eyes with a grimace, "Everything hurts."

"It wears off in a coupla minutes," said Dregs, "don't try ta force it."

It was all coming back to her now. The spinning gyroscope, the blinding, brilliant blue light, Velkaso, Hammer. Tivex's eyes blew open and she grabbed Dusty's collar, "VINCENT!"

She knew the second she looked into Dusty's eyes something was wrong. He tried to calm her, "He's, uh, he's…" he shot a desperate look over at Blitz.

Tivex wrenched her head over at Blitz, "Where is he?!"

Blitz tried to speak but then dropped his head down.

"He's gone," came an icy tone from somewhere behind Tivex.

She pushed the others off her and spun around. She saw a huddled shadow near where she and Dregs had been perched earlier. She floated over to the shadow and looked harder. Torque looked almost as bad as she felt. His face was ghostly pale, his eyes were bloodshot and he was shaking as if he were in the fit of some massive fever.

Tivex abandoned all her patience and she grabbed Torque hoisting him off the floor, "What do you mean, gone?"

Torque was as limp as she had ever seen someone. He stared blankly back at her as he pointed outside into space, "Never saw it coming."

Tivex, still holding Torque, twisted back to the others. None of them did so much as look at her. She looked back at Torque whose lips began to quiver. Tears began to spill down his cheeks as his head dropped back to the floor.

"No," said Tivex, "no, no, no, NO! I do not believe any of you! He is not gone! He is out there and you all have the audacity to tell me otherwise!"

Dregs pushed off the ground and floated to her slowly, arms raised to show he had no malcontent. He gently took Torque out of her arms and passed him over to the others. Dregs took Tivex's shoulder and turned her to look outside. He pointed out where he wanted her to look. Tivex followed his paw and saw something which made her blood freeze.

There was hardly anything left of Velkaso's ship. The entire front portion of his Destroyer class was sheared off as if it never had existed. A perfect concave circular cut stretched from top to bottom and through the entire width. All that remained was the aft portion where the thruster ports were and a fraction of the cargo bay's computer terminal station. There was no control deck, no engineering deck, no stabilizers, nothing at all except for empty space. Even most of what had been left from the Beautiful Nightmare after Velkaso's attack was sheared off in much the same way. Only a few segments of the control deck remained.

Tivex knew no explosion could have caused destruction like that and she turned to Dregs, "W-what did that?"

Dregs swallowed hard and dropped his head, unable to stomach the sight in front of them, "We did."

Tivex looked back at the remains. There were no words to describe what she was feeling. Rage, uncertainty and shock came to mind but none of them were strong enough. She tried to find the right words to say but she found it impossible to talk.

Someone floated up behind her and said, "It was an accident, darlin', honest. We didn' know 'bout that engine." She felt Dusty's hand on her shoulder, "One second we had 'im in our sights, next one come along and that thang fired up," he said nodding towards where the gyroscope had been.

Tivex felt her eyes welling up with tears. She didn't want to hear any of this. She wanted to turn around and see that arrogant smirk on Hammer's face that he always had. She felt her stomach begin to curdle as Dusty's words impacted her.

She turned and searched for Blitz. He was with Torque, holding the motionless figure in his arms. Blitz was barely able to get the words out, "We took that shot from Velkaso and I fell into that control plate. I don't know how it happened but when I did, the Horizon took over my system completely. Somehow, this ashen, gray piece of slag switched on!" He let go of Torque and punched as hard as he could into the control deck's terminal. The console suffered a massive dent which caused it to short out as Blitz tore off its cover plate and heaved it out into space, "I don't know how it happened and I can't access a damned thing in my memory core!" He turned back to Tivex with a look of sorrow she had only seen in him once before. He slumped onto the ground and tried to cover his face. He banged his head on the wall behind him, "It's all my fault…"

Tivex saw the bravest soldier she had ever known break down as if he and Torque were one in the same. She felt the wetness running down her cheeks as she felt out for Dusty. Dusty slid next to her without a word. She looked for any sign from Dregs but he merely shook his head.

Dregs flattened his ears down and seethed, "Only slaggin' human stupid enough to keep me around."

Tivex swallowed her tears back and asked, "Is there a chance?"

"What? That he coulda survived?" asked Dregs, shaking his head, "No way in hell."

"How can you be sure?"

"'Member what Soren said about this thing? Bein' able to jump without gates?"

Tivex nodded.

Dregs just motioned with his head outside, "Then it means we jus' sent Hammer into the great beyond without so much as a last drink." Dregs stared out into the stars, "Goin' through a jump gate without a ship? In nothin' more'n a cheap, second rate zero suit? And goin' through it with all that ship slag rigged to blow?" He shook his head, "Be like jumpin' naked into a dynamite whirlpool filled with razor blades."

"Hey!" said Dusty as he shoved Dregs against the hull, "You're not helpin'."

"I just tryin' to be honest," scowled Dregs, "not to mention the fact that when that portal opened up, there weren't no coordinates. Even if he coulda survived, we'd never find 'im."

Tivex heard every word Dregs said but the immense difficulty it was taking to absorb them was overwhelming. She turned her head and looked out at the wreckage again. As it twisted slowly in front of her, Tivex felt as she once had before when Hammer had been thought dead. Just as before, he had been taken from them by Velkaso, only this time she had been there too. She saw in all the horrific detail with her own eyes the very nightmare which had plagued him for most of his life. The more she tried to defy what Dregs said, the more the obviousness of the truth began to overtake her. From what she understood about jump gates, she knew how dangerous they were if the proper safety protocols were not taken.

Her heart seemed determined to break itself on her ribcage with the sorrow of being helpless against fate. She struggled against it but Tivex couldn't stop the memories beginning to flood her mind. Sounds of young Vincent laughing with her as she had tried to understand the concept of blowing out the candles of a birthday cake. The smirk he had given her when he finally beat her at chess and so on down a list which she now wished she never had. Almost instantaneously, those memories were replaced by the ones from the day she heard about the

Galileo. Those quickly gave way to how he had been when he was returned home after so long. After dealing with Velkaso personally, she couldn't and didn't want to image what he may have become if he had never been rescued. And now, now there was only some floating space junk to leave memorandum to the only human she could image being able to survive so many hardships. Hammer was dead and there was absolutely nothing she could do about it.

Tivex felt herself unable to do anything more than stare into the empty wasteland of space. No one said anything for a good while as they all floated in deafening silence. Tivex lost track of how much time passed as memory turned into emotion and emotion into memory. There was nothing else to be said or done now. She found herself becoming very receptive to the idea of just floating away too.

She was dragged back to reality when Dusty floated back next to her, "Darlin', I know now ain't the best time but we can't stay out here forever. Sooner or later, some Hais gonna come round this way and I suggest we get figure somethin' out before we gotta explain two slagged Destroyers."

Tivex turned to Dusty with an empty look in her eyes, "What do you suggest?"

Dusty had trouble even saying the words, "It's, uh, it's your call. With Hammer gone, you're the captain now."

It hadn't dawned on Tivex until that moment that because she was the first officer it also carried with it the responsibility of command in an event like this. She looked back at Dusty, "I am in no position to lead."

"That don't matter, pretty," breathed Dregs heavily, "none of us is right now."

Tivex looked and saw that both Blitz and Torque had finally steadied themselves but were completely traumatized. She looked out one more time at the wreckage and closed her eyes. Deep down, she knew that Hammer would not want the rest of his Team to wait around either and there was nothing more to be done.

Tivex looked back at Dusty, "How bad is the damage?"

Dusty shrugged, "If I had to guess, I'd say we'll still limp home and I do mean limp. We got enough power but them thrusters is banged up worse than before."

Tivex sniffled and nodded, "Then I suggest we leave while we still can. How far until the border?"

Dusty did some quick calculations in his head, "We made it a little ways back but nothin' close to what I'd say was a good distance. Still maybe, eighteen hours' best case scenario."

"How much oxygen do we all have left?"

"Barely enough if we left now."

Tivex nodded, "Make your preparations immediately."

Dusty nodded, "You got it, darlin'." He stopped and half smiled at her, "I mean, yes, ma'am."

Tivex, Dregs and Dusty helped Torque and Blitz get strapped into whatever they could throw together as chairs. When everyone was ready, Dusty powered up the remaining thrusters and Tivex felt the Horizon beginning to inch along back to the IEC border. If this was as fast as they were going to be able to go, getting back at all was going to be a miracle in itself. As the Horizon began to pick up a little speed, Tivex floated back and looked out at the wreckage one last time.

With a subtle wave and unable to suppress her feelings, Tivex said, "Goodbye, Vincent. May you finally find eternal rest in the Light. I will miss you more than you will ever know. Rest now, my dear friend, rest, and be at peace."

It was another close call getting back to the border. While there were no other ships in their flight path, Tivex and the others had run dangerously close to running out of oxygen. So close in fact that Tivex ordered Dusty to break radio silence and sent an SOS to Soren for immediate pickup. They barely made it across the border before their oxygen tanks were drained.

Soren and Tall'ani had been waiting for them with a ship that was usually used for deep space cargo runs. After being evaluated, Team Seven were issued into medical quarters while automatons were used to get the Horizon into hiding. As soon as the cargo bay doors were closed, they turned around and headed back to the Omarian bridge gate. Dregs and Dusty had helped Blitz and Torque into the medical bay where they were met by Silk, who had finally recovered from his injuries. Silk had not been told about what happened to Hammer but as soon as he saw his Team's faces, the excited smile faded from his, replaced with a look of extreme concern. Tivex watched as Dusty pulled Silk in closer and gave him the news. Silk tried to remain strong as best he could by slinging his arm around Torque to help him into bed, but Tivex saw him shaking.

Realizing the danger of finally having the Horizon secured and the absolute necessity to get it back to Earth as quickly as possible, Soren and Tall'ani had allowed Silk to come with them on the basis that Team Seven would need him. After everyone was squared away, Soren and Tall'ani lead Tivex to the mess deck and sat her down. Neither Soren nor Tall'ani pressured her into a full debrief, that would happen later back on Earth. After allowing her to regroup as best she could, Soren nodded to Tall'ani.

Tall'ani sat down across from Tivex and poured a hot beverage, passing it across the table. She saw the reaction on Tivex's face and said, "It's alright, Commander, it's not alcoholic."

Tivex managed the most basic half smile, "Thank you, ma'am."

Soren on the other hand pulled out his own flask and tipped it into another cup. He replaced the cap and sighed very heavily, "This isn't going to be easy."

Tall'ani nodded and motioned for him to pass the flask to her, "Understandable. I didn't know him outside of a few brief encounters but from what you've told me, his family is going to be devastated."

Tivex stared down at her cup without looking up, "The crew is no better."

Soren leaned back in his chair, "I've known Nick and Emma for a long time. Telling them he was gone once was hard enough. This is going to crush them."

Tall'ani took a sip from her cup, "Dorran was a soldier, Soren, and a Star Team captain at that. It's not like the life he chose was void of danger."

Soren swallowed his drink and set the cup down, "This operation was classified. Years back, Nick was a Marine so he knows what that means."

Tivex tilted her head up to Soren with an inquisitive look.

Soren looked back, "It means not only do I have to tell them their son was killed in action, I can't tell them how."

"Not even about Velkaso?" said Tivex quietly.

Soren shook his head, "That's the one thing I pray I can convince Jeffrey not to say without orders." answered Soren, "If they ever found out we intentionally sent him after Velkaso, I doubt the High Council would be too pleased about it."

Tall'ani swished the liquid in her cup around, "Apologies, Soren, but our military is trained from day one to follow orders. The how and why of any mission is irrelevant, regardless of danger. If his family comes from a military background, they should know that."

Soren turned to Tall'ani, "I understand what you're saying, Tall'ani, but you know better than I that every commanding officer is responsible for their underlings. The second we had proof of Velkaso was the second we should have pulled the plug on the mission."

Tall'ani folded her ears back, "The fact that it was Velkaso is still irrelevant! Dorran and that thief friend of his may have needed to be replaced on the mission but the fact remains I didn't hear Dorran even mention that he thought going himself would endanger the mission! He and Dregs had alternative motives and you knew that all along." Tall'ani turned back to her drink, "Apologies, but if anyone here believes I didn't have a hunch about this from the beginning you're sorely mistaken!"

"A hunch that got him killed," said Tivex quietly, "and quite possibly destroyed what little Team Seven had left going for it."

Tall'ani shook her head and narrowed her eyes, "Do you have any idea what could have happened if the Hais got their hands on the Horizon? Do you really have any concept?"

Tivex shook her head, "No, but there is little point of worrying about it now. It was in a state by itself when we found it. Torque stripped various parts from it to repair the Widow Maker and what is left of it can hardly be called useful." She looked up just in time to see Tall'ani glance at Soren. Soren returned her look with one of caution. Tivex couldn't quite make out what the look meant but it was the same one they had used after Silk was hurt after their escape from the island. Tivex felt her temper beginning to rise and looked from one to the other, "What? Am I wrong in my assumption?"

"That's not your concern, Commander." replied Soren sharply, "You may consider yourself on rack time until we reach Earth. Dismissed."

"Sir, I-"

"You have a Team that needs you right now, I suggest you see to them."

"But-"

"Did I stutter, Commander?" said Soren tilting his head and narrowing his eyes.

Tivex couldn't believe this but the problem was there was nothing else she could do. She stood up, "No, sir."

"Dismissed."

Tivex walked back to the doors. Before she pushed them open, she turned around to see if Tall'ani and Soren were watching her. They had gone back to being huddled together and using hushed voices. Tivex rolled her eyes and pushed through the doors. Outside, she tried to collect herself on what to say to the others. She turned to leave but nearly walked dead into Dregs who was leaning against the hull. Once again, she hadn't seen where he'd come from or how long he'd been there.

He fiddled with one of Tivex's old daggers as he looked down his snout at her, "So, what's the plan?"

"What plan?" she asked.

He motioned towards the mess hall with his head, "Them. What're they doin' with us?"

Tivex looked back at the doors and shook her head, "My guess is we go back to Earth. From there, I do not know."

Dregs huffed, "Oh, I thinks you might know more'n you're tellin' old Dregs, pretty."

Tivex looked back at him. Her Akoni patience had either stalled out momentarily or had failed altogether. She walked up to Dregs and pushed him against the wall. She leaned in close, "Listen to me very carefully, feline. I've had enough for one day. I'm going to go back to the medical bay and check on what's left of our Team. If you insist on taunting me further, believe me, I'd have no trouble meeting you in the cargo bay later."

She watched as Dregs looked down at her four hands forcibly holding him against the wall. He ran his eyes back up the length of her arms to meet hers. Dregs bared his teeth and smiled, "Well now, it's about time, Akoni."

"For what?" Tivex seethed.

"That you got yourself a lil spark left in ya. Good, was worried I'd lost ya back there. Glad to see I have my lil' protégé back."

She shook off the comment and felt her jaw clench, "Make sense."

Dregs managed to pull one of his paws free and slap her on the shoulder, "See, I gets to thinkin' why Soren and the lil kitty cat would only wanna talk to you before we go to Earth. Seems like they wanna know somethin' but no one supposed to talk before we're all together, standard dog 'n' pony show, ya know?"

Tivex shook her head.

Dregs looked over her shoulder to make sure they weren't being listened to and continued, "Standard operatin' procedure for Star Teams, us 'specially. No one gets debriefed alone so's if we slag the mission, ain't no one able to cover for no one else. Master Admirals all know that. So if they'd want you away from us now of all times tells me they got somethin' else up their sleeves they ain't tellin' us."

Tivex pulled back from Dregs slightly, "Are you saying there's still more to this?"

Dregs nodded and motioned for them to start heading back. Tivex released her grip and they walked back to the medical bay, "All that aside, even I know there's a dead giveaway to tell if you gots somethin' on your mind."

"Such as?"

Dregs smirked, "You just used more contractions. You don't know it yet but when you stop tryin' ta be miss perfect, you come down a few levels. If you woulda come outta there, actin' like you usually do, ya know, all kept together, then I woulda thought somethin' was up. If I came at ya with both barrels and you didn't do nothin' about it, trust me, I woulda dropped you before you knew what was happenin'."

Tivex continued walking, "A test?"

"Yeah. Ya done real good in the Dominion but I didn't trust you, up til two minutes ago."

"Then why are you so concerned with what Soren and Tall'ani wanted?"

Dregs cast a look behind them, "Cause my captain now just died tryin' to save our sorry hides. I seen that boy go down to hell, spit in the devil's face, come back, and then book a return flight back in. He just kep' comin'. No matter what that gray, ashen slag did to him, he jus' kep' comin'. Never seen nothin' like 'im and I sure as slag ain't gonna sit by and let him go out for nothin'."

Tivex looked at Dregs, a look of feral hunting on his face, "For now, all we can do is allow events to unfold. Until we know what the larger picture is, there is little point in making more of a scene than we should."

Dregs growled, "You should know I hate waitin'."

Tivex stopped him and put her hands on his arm, "Dregs, until we are told otherwise, I am still the acting captain for Star Team Seven. Now is not the time for rash or harsh action. Please, do not make me order something you do not wish to hear."

Dregs looked down at her hands and then to her. He flattened his ears again and looked hard into her eyes. With as much resistance as he could muster, Dregs put up a finger, "One. I'll give ya this one, pretty, but patience ain't my strong point."

Tivex managed again a half smile, "We will work on proper titles later."

Dregs scowled at her, "Don't push it."

For a moment, Tivex swore she saw the faintest glimmer in Dregs' eyes. It was the same one she had seen him have with Hammer. A much smaller, and drastically different version of it of course, but she was beginning to learn how to handle this crew along with her new place in it. She hated from the very bowels of her soul that it had taken Vincent's death to solidify her into more of a leader, but for now, it was all she had to go on.

They walked back in silence to the medical bay to be with the others. Between them and Earth stood another week long journey and anything else that could happen along the way. Tivex looked around at her crew, bruised, battered and mentally drained as anyone she had ever seen pass under her stethoscope. That was a thought in and of itself. She was now back in a medical setting and she would trade it all to be back in her chair in the Widow Maker's control deck.

With him…

A clear, pristine day shown its warmth down onto the shuttle docks. As she watched the others file down the ramp onto the ground, Tivex turned around to take one last look at the cargo ship that had brought them home. She had no idea what the next step was going to be but she knew whatever it was would reveal itself in due time. How strange, she thought, I have known this planet my entire life and yet how alien it feels to be back.

She followed suit and collected her bag, slinging it over her shoulder and feeling the weight of it substantially less than that of the memories she also carried. They seemed determined to pull her down to the ground with every step she took down the ramp and she psychosomatically felt her legs far stiffer than they actually were. Tivex was so lost in thought that she stumbled at the foot of the ramp and nearly fell into Dregs.

He caught her and gruffed a laugh, "Easy, pretty. Takes a while to get your footing."

Tivex managed a small smile at him, "You almost seemed chivalrous."

Dregs narrowed his eyes at her and growled softly, "Keep it up and next time I step to the side."

Tivex was beginning to understand the way Dregs worked although she knew she would never have the bond with him as Hammer did.

Team Seven was to return to IEC headquarters for a full debrief with Soren, Tall'ani and the other Master Admirals. Tivex was unsure if Kagen, Jaleer or Kosos would attend but it made little difference to her. Being paraded in front of a superior officer panel was one thing, but Soren and Tall'ani had left on a separate shuttle before their cargo ship had docked with the Earth space station. Their cold shoulder mannerisms were becoming increasingly irritating to Tivex. What made it even worse was the inevitable fight that was going to happen whether she wanted it to or not. She watched closely as Torque and Blitz walked with Dregs. She couldn't hear what they were saying but she knew the conversation anyway.

During the trip home, Tivex had awoken to find both Torque and Blitz's beds both empty. She got up to look for them but they were not in the medical deck. Tivex walked down a few of the cargo ship's corridors but found nothing. She turned to go back but heard something clanging from the cargo bay.

Oh no, she thought.

Once she heard that sound she immediately knew where they were.

Tivex had entered the cargo bay and saw the Horizon. The sight of it sickened her to no end. She shook her head and walked to the original tear she and Torque had found back on the island. Tivex hoisted herself into the ship and walked towards the control deck. There she found Torque rigging Blitz to the control terminal.

"Do you mind telling me what the slag you two are doing?" she asked.

Torque spit the screwdriver he had between his teeth onto the ground and answered, "What's it look like?"

"It looks to me that you two are disobeying direct orders to stay away from this ship," replied Tivex.

"Sorry, 'Vex, I didn't hear any orders," said Blitz.

"Yeah, me either," added Torque.

Tivex bit her lip and looked at the ground, "Why does everyone on this Team disregard authority?"

Torque shrugged, "Because it's fun?"

"No," answered Tivex, "it's because you think the rules don't apply to you." She had abandoned her Akoni verbiage and resigned herself to stop thinking about it anymore. So much had changed that she couldn't care less about propriety anymore.

"Rules don't apply when the orders are slagged," said Blitz, puffing out a plume of smoke from the corner of his mouth, "besides, ain't no one gotta know about it."

"That's the problem, you know and I know."

"Yeah, but we ain't gonna say nothin'," said Blitz.

Torque went back to work, "Right now, Tivex, I could care less about what the brass wants. All I care about is trying to figure out what the hell happened out there. Hammer deserves that much."

Tivex couldn't bring herself to look at him but nodded in silent agreement. The only thing that had brought Torque back from the brink of hysteria was when he had been pulled into a room by Dregs who didn't come back out for over an hour. Tivex didn't know what had been said, but when he came back, Torque had a look of resolve in his eyes. Blitz, on the other hand, had been all too happy to regain his composure after Torque had whispered something to him. Again, Tivex didn't know what but she assumed it had given him a spark of his old glory back. Since then, Team Seven began the slow and arduous healing process but in a most unexpected way.

Tivex was now the captain, which meant for better or worse, she was now in charge of them. Being in charge was a relative term. She knew she could no more control them than she could fly, but there was an unspoken effect beginning to happen. Tivex found the more she stopped trying to criticize them, the more flexible they became with her. There was no getting respect on Team Seven, that was something which had to be earned. And it didn't come cheap either.

Tivex looked back at the others, "What are you trying to do?"

"Good question, I have no idea," said Torque, "I'm trying to access Blitz's memory core but for some reason, I can't get into it."

"Really?"

"Yeah, really," replied Blitz disdainfully, "he's been wrenching on me for over an hour and ain't got jack to show for it."

"Maybe if I wasn't inhaling half of that slag awful cigar smoke every ten seconds, I'd be able to figure this out!" said Torque as he smacked Blitz in the head.

Blitz blew a kiss to Torque, "Whatever makes you sleep at night, princess!"

Tivex was astounded to see small vestiges of her friends coming back. She walked up and looked down at what Torque was doing. She tilted her head to one side and said, "If I may?"

Torque shrugged.

Tivex took one of Torque's instruments, the one which looked like a small tuning fork and pressed it against one of Blitz's terminals, "Can you access anything yet?"

Blitz sat silent for a moment before shaking his head, "Nothin'."

Tivex nodded and looked again, "Did you see this?" she asked Torque.

"See what?"

"His memory port. What happened to it?"

"Whoa, wait a minute," said Torque.

"Hey! Both of ya! This is my head here," Blitz said, "you mind telling me what you're looking at?"

"Yeah," replied Torque, "since when did you get an upgrade?"

"Upgrade? What're you talking about?"

"Your memory port," said Tivex, "why are there two?"

"What?!" exclaimed Blitz, "That's impossible!"

"Got that right," added Torque.

Tivex knelt down to look into Blitz's eyes, "Yes, I know that. I was there when you were put back together, remember?"

Blitz scowled at her, "Yeah, that I do but how are there two now?"

Tivex looked at Torque. Torque looked around him and said, "The Horizon. It did something to you."

"Like what?!"

"I don't know but it got to you ever since…"

"The shard," finished Blitz.

"Yep."

"So what do we do about it?" asked Blitz with concern.

"If it were up to me, nothing," answered Tivex, "leave well enough alone for now."

"And yet, I still didn't hear you say that," said Torque as he jammed a power cable into the second port. As soon as he did, Tivex knew the truth.

In the instant the cable clicked home everything changed. The Horizon had almost come alive again as Blitz once again became one with the ship. Had it not been for their tinkering, things might have gone down a completely different path than they were about to.

Tivex watched as the others made their way from the docks up to IEC headquarters. She felt quite certain that what was about to happen was most likely going to end with Team Seven being sent directly back to the Ninth Circle. This time, however, they were not going back on a stopover.

They walked up to the main entrance and were cleared. Tivex tried to keep her breathing as normal as she could but she found that her nervousness was due more in part to her anger with IEC than it was fear. She could feel her pulse quicken as she went over the plan again. In all her life, she never imagined she would be doing something like this. She felt now what the others must have felt on a more than daily basis.

Team Seven walked into the entrance and up to the elevator bank. As they waited for their car, Dregs looked at the others and sneered, "Anyone not ready?"

Silk peeked out over his mirrored sunglasses, "You gotta be kidding me, I was born for this slag!"

"Same here," grinned Dusty.

"Elevator's slow," said Torque, "I'd offer to fix it for them but I'm pretty sure it's a moot point now." He grinned beatifically from behind his wild hair.

"What about you?" said Dregs in Tivex's direction.

She merely looked back at him with grim determination on her face, "Do I look like I'm running?"

Dregs snarled his approval as the elevator car finally arrived. They entered and Blitz punched in the number for the main meeting room. When they arrived, they walked up to the secretary on duty.

She looked at them puzzled, "Oh! Star Team Seven, you're not due in for another half hour."

"Yeah," sneered Dregs, "we know. We wanted a word with the boss beforehand."

"I'm sorry but Master Admiral Soren is unavailable at the moment. You'll have to wait until after the inquest."

"Tell him it's an emergency," replied Tivex.

The secretary looked at her, "I'm sorry, Captain, but that's impossible right now."

"Oh this is already boring the slag outta me," said Blitz as he pushed passed her and marched down to Soren's office. The secretary tried to go after him but found herself captured by Dusty and Silk and pushed into another room. When they got to the office, Blitz looked back at Tivex. She nodded and Blitz grinned widely.

Without another moment's hesitation, Blitz kicked in Soren's door and Team Seven flooded in. Tivex saw Master Admiral Soren was on a video call and jumped nearly three feet off his chair when they stormed in. Soren went to end the call but Dregs jumped on top of his desk and knocked the screen across the room.

"WHAT IS THE MEANING OF THIS?" thundered Soren.

Dregs, still on top of the desk, pushed his massive foot into Soren's chest, "Right now, you have two options. One, I ice your sorry hide right now. Two, you start talking, lyin' son of a Gray Man!"

Tivex watched as Soren, wide eyed and half scared from the invasion tried to regain his composure, "I will have you in chains for this, traitor!"

"Don't make me laugh, sir," said Blitz, "you lied to all of us. You sent us out there without even telling us what the Horizon was capable of! You sent us after Velkaso, knowing what would happen! You knew everything!"

"W-what?" stammered Soren.

"We heard him, sir," hissed Torque.

"Heard? Heard who?"

"Hammer, Admiral," said Tivex from Dreg's left, "he's alive."

Soren looked from person to person, "That's impossible."

"Really?" said Blitz, "Somethin' tells me you're lyin' about that too. He's alive, sir, and you know where."

Soren looked around the room at Team Seven. Tivex saw him searching for any possible way out of talking but found himself surrounded. Tivex could feel the tension in the room, she let it fill her, strengthen her, fortify her resolve, "And now you're going to tell us where to find him."

Soren smacked his lips together a few times, "How did you contact him?"

"Contact nothin'. There wasn't more 'n' one word," growled Dregs, "but it was him…and you know it."

"We hotwired the Horizon, sir," said Torque, "through Blitz. It took some doing but it seems there were a few things you might have told us before you sent us out there and let us believe my brother was dead!"

"Jeffrey-" Soren started.

Dregs pressed down harder on Soren, "Give it up, Admiral! All we wanna know right now is where our slaggin' captain is."

Tivex watched Soren again look around but found no way out and no choice whatsoever. Dusty and Silk moved on either side of Soren and sat down on his desk on both sides of Dregs. Torque and Blitz moved to their sides and stood, arms crossed and vengeance in their eyes.

Tivex tilted her head at Soren, "Whatever happens to us, understand this. We've made special precautionary measures inside the Horizon. Maybe you'll find them, maybe you won't. In either case, you've got two minutes to start talking before I send the signal and that ship is made brutally public, to everyone."

Soren looked up at her and shook his head, "I didn't want any of this."

"We don't care, sir. I'd start talking, Dregs looks a little itchy," taunted Torque.

Soren dropped his eyes first and then his head. He took a deep breath and dropped his arms down onto the desk. He loosened his collar and Tivex saw he knew there was no point in hiding anymore. Soren wet his lips and swallowed hard, "You do realize, after me telling you this, you'll be hunted down by the High Council and charged with treason?"

"I'm shakin'," hissed Dregs with bared fangs.

Soren nodded, "In that case, you're right. I lied to all of you because I had to. Not because it's classified but because there was no other choice. You're also right, Hammer is alive but it's not so much as where, but when. Tell me, what do you all know about the Gray War?"